The Mystic Chronicles
Book 3

The war between Heaven and
Earth ends where the soul begins.

The Mystic Chronicles

Paths of Providence

BY ERHROLE NAVARRO

PATHS OF PROVIDENCE.
Book Three of the Mystic Chronicles Series

Copyright © 2026 by Erhrole Navarro.
Cover art by Luisa Galstyan.

This book is a work of fiction. Names, characters, places, and incidents either are the product of the author's imagination or are used fictitiously. Any resemblance to actual persons, living or dead, events, or locales is entirely coincidental.

First Edition.
Self Published in the United States.
San Diego, California. Visit us online at erhrole.com or www.mysticchronicles.com

Library of Congress Control Number: 2025923629
Hardcover ISBN: 979-8-9905744-6-5
Paperback ISBN: 979-8-9905744-9-6
Ebook ISBN: 979-8-9905744-7-2

John 13:34

*"I give you a new commandment, that you love one another. Just as I have
loved you, you also should love one another."*

~

*In loving memory of Ethan Matthew Navarro
November 20, 2002 to October 27, 2023*

PROLOGUE

The old stories teach that when the boundaries of the world begin to stir, fate does not whisper—it remembers. And the echoes of what was once forgotten rise again through those chosen to bear them.

Last year, the Durant family learned this truth firsthand. What began as a search for answers became a descent into ancient mysteries older than any relic they guarded. As Maya and Myst Durant unlocked memories from a life centuries past, the veil between realms thinned, revealing dangers that had slept beneath history's dust. Temples awakened. Symbols glowed with buried purpose. And a compass—silent for generations—turned with a will of its own, pointing them toward truths long hidden.

Together with Elan and Kaira and the reborn Knights of St. Michael, the twins confronted the threat that shadowed their steps. Dante Malvagio's rage, twisted by Verendana's influence, nearly brought ruin upon the world. But through courage, sacrifice, and the sacred relics reclaimed—Jupiter's Bolt, Neptune's Tears, and the forgotten artifacts guarding the balance of realms—the family prevailed. Dante fell. Verendana vanished. Yet something deeper remained unsettled.

Victory did not restore peace. It only opened another door.

In the aftermath, Nykronus—teacher, guardian, and one of the few who understood the nature of the realms—disappeared without a trace. His final warning spoke of ancient gateways weakening, of forces gathering strength in places where shadows hold memory. And as the seasons shift, his fears prove true: cries from sacred sites reach across continents, visions seize Maya's dreams with increasing intensity, and Myst feels the tug of something older than magic guiding his path.

The relics hum again. The compass glows in Elan's hand, not with direction, but with urgency. And the subtle fractures between worlds—once invisible—now shine like cracks in cosmic glass.

The Durant-Mazza family has always been protectors of the old ways, defenders of what binds heaven, earth, and the unseen. But the forces stirring now reach beyond any threat they've faced. What was uncovered in the battles of the previous summer was only the beginning.

Ancient powers are moving.

Forgotten warnings are returning.

And the paths ahead—once straight—now twist toward a convergence written across centuries.

Destiny has begun its call again.

And this time, the price of answering may reshape all realms.

PART ONE

"The truth is not always the same as the majority decision."
— **St. John Paul II**

CHAPTER

ONE

Lazarus embarked on the narrow crystalline path, boots finding purchase on the translucent surface. Jagged edges caught ethereal light, casting prismatic patterns across his face. The path wound between massive stones that drifted through Aethoria's purple-tinged atmosphere, their lazy circles hypnotic in their grace.

Tendrils of luminescent mist coiled around the floating rocks, their ghostly fingers reaching out before dissipating into nothingness. The stones ranged from small boulders to island-sized masses, their surfaces etched with ancient runes that pulsed with a faint blue glow.

A section of the crystal path had crumbled away, leaving a dangerous gap. Lazarus raised his hand, and the shadows beneath the floating rocks responded to his will. They condensed into solid ribbons of darkness that wove together, forming a bridge across the chasm. His footsteps echoed with quiet confidence as he crossed the shadow construct.

The air hummed with an otherworldly resonance, a vibration that thrummed through Lazarus's bones and set his teeth on edge. Shafts of light pierced through gaps between the floating rocks, bringing the sharp, metallic taste of raw magic and the chill whisper of ancient power. They created ever-shifting patterns that danced across the crystalline path. Something that might have been wind whispered ancient secrets in languages long forgotten.

"Home sweet home," Lazarus murmured, navigating a particularly treacherous bend without breaking stride. His fingers traced familiar patterns in the air, directing shadows to clear debris from his path. He'd walked these ways countless times, and each floating rock was a landmark in his mental map of this realm.

The path widened as it curved around a massive floating boulder. Nestled between two converging light beams, a crystalline archway emerged from the mist. Its surface caught the ethereal light, refracting it into thousands of tiny rainbows scattered across its faceted surface.

Lazarus passed through the archway, and his breath caught at the sight before him. The cavern stretched upward into impossible heights, its walls forming a natural cathedral that defied earthly architecture. Massive columns of translucent stone twisted toward a ceiling lost in shadows and mist, their faceted surfaces fracturing every stray light beam into rainbow cascades.

Ancient runes carved deep into the walls pulsed with steady azure light, their script flowing like liquid metal across the crystalline surfaces. The symbols moved and shifted, rearranging in endless patterns that spoke of forgotten knowledge.

Shelves of pure crystal hung suspended in the air, defying gravity as they rotated in slow, deliberate orbits around the chamber's heart. Each shelf held texts of various sizes - some bound in leather that had long since cracked with age—others made of materials that shimmered and changed as he looked at them.

Light filtered through the crystalline structure, breaking into countless rainbow fragments that danced across the chamber floor. The effect created an ever-shifting kaleidoscope, painting the air itself with colors that had no names in any mortal tongue.

Despite having visited this place countless times, Lazarus felt his usual mask of indifference slip. His eyes widened as he took in the play of light and shadow, the dance of knowledge suspended in the air. A small smile tugged at the corner of his mouth - the first genuine expression to cross his face in longer than he cared to remember.

In the center of the chamber, a pedestal of pure crystal rose from the floor. Unlike the other crystals in the room, this one remained clear as glass, unmarked by rune or inscription. Lazarus moved toward it, his footsteps echoing in the vast space. The floating shelves parted before him, creating a path to the heart of the library.

Lazarus traced his fingers across the faded parchment he'd discovered in an ancient tomb. The map's edges crumbled at his touch. However, the intricate diagrams remained clear—three interlocking circles drawn in ink that still gleamed after centuries—Earth, Purgatory, and Aethoria, bound together by lines of power he'd spent months decoding.

Beyond the map, the tomb walls held a madman's legacy—equations and symbols that spoke of realm boundaries. Each marking Lazarus had painstakingly transferred to his journals until translation filled volumes with forbidden knowledge.

He'd found the breakthrough in a hidden chamber beneath the tomb's floor: a ritual circle etched in crystal, designed to test the barriers between worlds. These barriers, it was believed, were the cause of the imbalance in the realms. He'd activated the ritual circle with his blood, watching as shimmering energy walls materialized around him. The barriers between realms became visible—paper-thin in some places, impenetrable in others.

The texts spoke of a vast library, a knowledge repository that existed between spaces. This library, it was believed, held the key to restoring balance to the realms. References appeared in fragments across different ruins, each piece adding to the puzzle. Lazarus collected them all, plotting locations on his ever-growing map of Aethoria.

He'd prepared methodically, gathering crystals that resonated with the same frequency as the barrier walls. Each one had to be cut precisely, aligned with mathematical perfection. The calculations alone took months, but Lazarus worked without rest. Sleep became an afterthought, food a distraction from his purpose.

He'd finally plotted the library's location in his workshop, surrounded by charts and artifacts. The crystalline paths leading to it wound through impossible spaces, crossing boundaries that should have been absolute. But the math was perfect, and the theories were sound.

Lazarus packed his supplies with practiced efficiency - crystals, maps, and the journals containing his research. His hands moved with certainty born of countless hours of preparation. The last journal had barely settled into his pack when crimson light erupted behind him, casting his shadow across the crystalline floor. The air crackled with energy as Verendana stepped through, her dark robes billowing around her despite the still air.

"The barriers grow thinner." Verendana's fingers tightened around her crystal shard until her knuckles whitened. Her voice carried ancient power but couldn't quite mask her trembling excitement. "Just as you predicted."

Lazarus turned from the pedestal, his expression neutral. "The calculations were accurate. Three cycles of the Blood Moon and the walls between realms will be at their weakest."

"After all these years of preparation." Verendana's fingers traced the edge of a floating shelf. "Remember when you first found me in that monastery? A blind girl tending to ancient texts she couldn't even read."

"You had already memorized every word through touch alone. Your dedication impressed me."

"And you gave me sight." Her eyes, now a striking amber, met his. "More than that - you showed me the truth. The real meaning behind Valentine's teachings."

Lazarus nodded. "The prophecy speaks of balance restored. They assumed it meant maintaining the barriers."

"They were wrong." Verendana's lip curled. "The true balance lies in breaking them completely. Letting the realms merge as they were always meant to."

"The Three Marias grow restless." Lazarus moved closer, his voice dropping. "They sense our work."

"Let them. Their power wanes with each passing cycle. Soon, they'll be unable to maintain the separation they created."

A sharp, distant sound cut through their conversation - a rhythmic tik-tik-tik that seemed to come from everywhere and nowhere.

Verendana's head snapped up. "The guardians."

"They're earlier than expected." Lazarus's hands moved through practiced motions, gathering shadows around them. "The Tiktik never venture this deep into Aethoria."

The sound grew fainter, though both knew this meant the creatures drew closer. Verendana's fingers curled around a crystal shard at her throat, its surface gleaming with stored power.

Lazarus pulled an ancient scroll from one of the floating shelves, its surface shimmering with opalescent script that shifted beneath his touch. He unrolled it carefully on the crystal pedestal, revealing text written in a spiral pattern that seemed to move inward toward the center.

"The prophecy speaks of three seals," he traced the spiraling text with his finger. "When the Marias' power wanes, the barriers fracture. Earth bleeds into purgatory, purgatory into Aethoria, until all walls collapse."

Verendana leaned closer, her amber eyes scanning the shifting text. "But here - this passage about the Blood Moon ritual. If we harness enough power during the convergence..."

"We could trigger the collapse early." Lazarus's voice carried an edge of excitement. "The text describes a ritual requiring three sacrifices, one at each seal point. The blood must be willingly given."

"The consequences?" Verendana's fingers ghosted over the scroll's surface.

"Total merger of all realms. The dead would walk among the living. Spirits and mortals existing in the same space." Lazarus's eyes gleamed. "Perfect balance."

Verendana drew back, her expression troubled. "The death toll would be catastrophic."

"A necessary price for enlightenment." Lazarus rolled the scroll closed. "You're not having doubts?"

Before Verendana could respond, the tik-tik-tik sound intensified. Dark shapes materialized from the shadows - bird-like creatures with glowing red eyes and elongated beaks. Their wings spread impossibly wide, blocking the crystal chamber's exits.

The Tiktik spirits circled overhead, their calls growing fainter despite moving closer. These ancient guardians, known for leading their victims astray, had served the Marias since the realms were first separated.

"They're trying to confuse us," Lazarus said, gathering shadows around his hands. "Don't trust your ears."

The first Tiktik dove, its razor-sharp beak aimed at Verendana's throat.

Lazarus tracked the Tiktik's movement through the shadows it cast rather than its misleading sounds. The creature's form flickered between solid and ethereal—one moment, it was a massive bird with obsidian feathers; the next, it was a wraith-like shape of pure darkness.

He pulled shadows from the corners of the chamber, weaving them into razor-sharp tendrils that sliced through the air. The Tiktik dodged with impossible speed, but Verendana was ready. Crystal shards erupted from her hands, catching the light and multiplying it into blinding beams that forced the spirit to solidify.

Ancient words tore from Verendana's throat—each syllable a hammer blow that sent the wall runes pulsing with frightening intensity. The chamber's crystalline surfaces responded, sending rainbow-fractured light in controlled bursts that caged the second *Tiktik*.

"The binding circle!" Lazarus called out, his voice cutting through the disorienting tik-tik-tik echoes.

Understanding flashed in Verendana's eyes. She danced between the floating shelves, her movements precise as she herded the trapped Tiktik toward the chamber's center. Lazarus did the same with his ensnared target, using his shadow constructs to guide it.

The third Tiktik swooped down, its beak extending to an impossible length. Lazarus caught the attack with a wall of shadow. At the same time, Verendana's crystals refracted light through it, causing the creature to screech in pain.

Together, they forced all three Tiktiks into the pedestal's area. Verendana's crystals and Lazarus's shadows wove together, forming a complex pattern of dark and light. The runes on the chamber walls flared bright azure, responding to their combined power.

The Tiktik's forms began to dissolve, their essence drawn into the binding circle etched beneath the crystal pedestal. Their misleading calls faded to whispers, then silence, as they were sealed away in crystalline prisons no larger than a fist.

Lazarus brushed crystalline dust from an ancient text, its pages nearly translucent in Aethoria's ethereal light. A loose page slipped free, covered in diagrams he'd never seen. His heart quickened as he recognized St. Michael's personal seal in the corner.

The page detailed five distinct realms - heaven and hell at opposite poles, with earth suspended between them. But what caught his attention were the two barrier realms - purgatory and Aethoria - depicted as protective shells preventing direct contact between the major domains.

"This changes everything." His fingers traced the intricate lines connecting the realms. "St. Michael wasn't maintaining the barriers - he was weakening them."

Verendana moved closer, her amber eyes scanning the text. "The Order's true purpose..."

"Was to prepare for their collapse." Lazarus's voice carried quiet intensity. "Each generation of knights further eroded the walls between realms. The Three Marias weren't guardians - they were wardens, trying to prevent the inevitable."

The chamber's crystals pulsed with deeper blues as Verendana processed this revelation. "Then our work..."

"Continues what St. Michael started centuries ago." Lazarus carefully folded the page. "The Order lost its way, forgot its original purpose. They became so focused on maintaining barriers that they missed the signs."

Verendana's fingers curled around her crystal shard. "The Blood Moon ritual - it's not just about breaking seals. It's completing a process that's been in motion since the beginning."

"Precisely." Lazarus tucked the page into his coat. "We're not destroying the natural order. We're restoring it to what it should have been all along."

Above them, the crystalline cathedral's runes shifted, ancient power responding to their discovery. The light filtering through the walls took on a crimson tinge as if the very realm acknowledged the weight of their revelation.

"The first seal point," Verendana said. "It has to be where it all began."

Lazarus nodded, shadows gathering around him like a cloak. "Mount Arayat. Maria Sinukuan's domain."

CHAPTER
TWO

Maya jerked upright, sheets tangled around her legs like binding chains. Sweat plastered her dark hair to her neck and forehead, her heart hammering against her ribs. The bedroom's shadows stretched long and deep, cast by moonlight filtering through half-drawn curtains.

Her hands shook as she pressed them against her temples, the vision still burning behind her eyes. She'd seen it—worlds bleeding into each other like watercolors in the rain. The barrier between realms had grown thin as tissue paper, torn in places where ancient powers pushed through.

Crystal spires pierced the sky of a modern city, their ethereal light mixing with neon signs and streetlamps. Floating islands drifted between skyscrapers while cars navigated roads that twisted impossible geometries. People walked past angels with burning wings, their phones capturing videos of demons haggling at coffee shops.

The image shifted in her mind—a great cathedral made of light and shadow, its architecture defying earthly physics. Within its halls, she'd glimpsed figures in ancient armor studying texts that predated time itself. Their weapons gleamed with power meant to guard the walls between worlds, yet something felt wrong about their purpose.

Maya kicked free of the sheets, cold air hitting her skin. The vision had shown her Mount Arayat split open like a cracked egg, spilling golden light into the sky. Maria Sinukuan's domain transformed into a nexus point where Aethoria bled through, its ethereal landscape merging with Philippine soil in the Palawan Jungle.

The room spun as another flash hit her - rivers of luminescent energy cutting through city streets, trees sprouting crystal fruits, and people discovering they could breathe magic-like air. Reality itself buckled and reformed, creating something new from the pieces of broken barriers.

Her fingers clutched the medallion at her throat, its metal warm against her palm. She vividly remembered the night her Grandma Gianna and Lola Rose gave her the pendant that once belonged to her great-great-grandmother Isabella Durant as it grew warmer with each passing thought. Isabella had called it the Nexus Heart.

The artifact pulsed once, twice, as if responding to her vision. She'd seen this coming, seen the merging of realms that others called apocalypse but felt more like evolution.

Maya's eyes burned, literal light seeping from beneath her lids. The medallion's pulse synchronized with her racing heartbeat, each beat sending energy waves through her room. Books lifted from her desk, pages fluttering like startled birds. Her hair floated around her face, caught in an invisible current.

The vision dragged her back under. Streets twisted into Möbius strips as reality folded in on itself. She watched a businessman check his watch while floating three feet off the ground, unaware of his situation. A group of teenagers walked through the wall of a convenience store, their bodies phasing through solid matter as if it were smoke.

In the heart of the city, a temple from Aethoria materialized - its spires crafted from crystallized time, with windows that showed glimpses of different eras simultaneously. Through one pane, she saw ancient warriors training. Through another, robots from a possible future scanned data streams made of pure light.

The medallion grew hotter. Objects in her room spun faster - pens, papers, her phone - caught in the aftermath of what she witnessed. A crack appeared in her mirror, but instead of breaking, it revealed a sliver of Aethoria's landscape behind the glass. Golden deer with starlight in their antlers grazed on fields of luminescent grass.

Mount Arayat split wider in her mind's eye. Maria Sinukuan stood at its peak, her form shifting between woman and deer, between flesh and pure energy. The mountain's core leaked golden light that rewrote the laws of physics wherever it touched. Trees grew upside down, their roots drinking starlight. Water flowed upstream, carrying fish that swam through the air as easily as through liquid.

Maya's eyes snapped open, now glowing like twin moons. Her room had become a zero-gravity chaos of floating objects, each one trailing threads of golden energy. Through her window, she saw the first signs of change touching the real world - a shimmer in the air like heat waves, but instead of distorting reality, it was revealing what lay beneath it.

A soft thump drew Maya's attention as Asha landed on her bed. The cat's black and orange fur rippled with an inner glow. Her feline eyes reflected the golden light still trailing from the floating objects.

"You saw it too." Maya's voice cracked. The medallion's heat pulsed against her skin.

Asha padded closer, her paws leaving luminescent prints on the sheets. Each step steadied the chaos in the room, objects drifting back to their places like leaves settling after a wind. The cat acted as an anchor, drawing Maya back from the edge of overwhelming vision.

"The barriers weren't meant to last forever." Asha's voice carried the weight of ancient knowledge. "What you see isn't destruction - it's transformation. Like a butterfly breaking free of its chrysalis."

Maya ran her fingers through Asha's fur, drawing comfort from the familiar texture even as energy sparked between them. "Maria Sinukuan knows. She's preparing for it."

"The Three Marias have guarded the boundaries since before time had shape." Asha pressed her head against Maya's hand. "But even they understand that change must come. The question isn't how to stop it, but how to guide it."

The cat's warmth spread up Maya's arm, calming the tremors in her muscles. Outside her window, clouds gathered with unnatural speed, their edges limned with traces of gold. Lightning flickered within their depths, but no thunder followed - as if the storm held its breath.

"Look." Asha's tail curved toward the window.

The gathering storm painted the night sky in shades of violet and deep blue, its silence more powerful than any thunder could be. Lightning branched between clouds like golden veins, illuminating their shapes from within. Rain began to fall, each drop catching and holding light like tiny stars descending to Earth.

Maya watched the furious display, feeling its power mirror the changes she'd witnessed in her vision. The storm's silence pressed against her windows, heavy with promise and possibility.

Dawn painted the estate grounds in watercolor hues. Maya stretched her muscles on the frost-covered grass, her breath forming clouds in the crisp morning air. The medallion's weight pressed against her chest, a constant reminder of the vision she had last night.

Nykronus stood at the edge of the training circle, his dark robes absorbing the early light. "Focus on the space between breaths. Power flows through those gaps."

Maya closed her eyes, letting her awareness expand. The medallion warmed against her skin as she found the rhythm Nykronus described - the pause between inhale and exhale where possibility lived.

"Now, reach for it."

She extended her hand toward a fallen leaf. Golden light traced her fingers like liquid sunshine, and the leaf rose from the ground. It spun in lazy circles, dancing on invisible currents of energy.

"Good. Add another."

A second leaf joined the first, then a third. Maya felt the connections between them like silk threads in her mind. The leaves wove patterns in the air, their movements growing more complex with each passing moment.

"Your control has improved." Nykronus circled her, his footsteps silent on the grass. "But control isn't enough. You must understand the nature of what you command."

The leaves burst into a golden flame that consumed nothing, transforming into pure light that Maya shaped into spheres. They orbited her hand like tiny planets, each pulsing with its own heartbeat of power.

"The barrier between worlds isn't just weakening - it's evolving. Those able to channel these changes must learn to guide them." Nykronus gestured, and the spheres of light expanded, revealing glimpses of other places within their depths. Ancient forests, crystal cities, paths that wound between stars.

Maya held the visions steady, sweat beading on her forehead. The medallion's heat spread through her chest, down her arms, feeding power into the floating orbs. Each showed a different facet of reality, a window into possibilities that existed beyond regular sight.

Maya's arms trembled as she held the spheres of light steady. The power coursing through her veins felt different - wilder, more challenging to contain. Sweat dripped down her neck despite the morning chill.

"Your energy signature has changed." Nykronus stepped closer, his dark eyes narrowed. "The Nexus Heart's influence grows stronger."

She gritted her teeth, trying to maintain the delicate balance. The spheres wobbled in their orbits, their surfaces rippling like disturbed pools. Images within them blurred and shifted—crystal spires melting into ancient forests, star paths twisting into impossible geometries.

"I can handle it." Maya shifted her stance, attempting a simple repositioning of the spheres. The movement should have been basic and practiced hundreds of times before.

The medallion flared against her chest. Power surged through her arms like lightning, transforming the controlled spheres into explosive bursts of energy. Golden light erupted outward, shattering her carefully constructed defenses. The force knocked her backward, sending her stumbling across frost-covered grass.

Nykronus raised a hand, containing the wild energy before it could spread further. His expression darkened as he studied the dissipating traces of power. "This is beyond normal progression. The Nexus Heart is responding to something."

Maya pushed herself up, her hands still crackling with residual energy. The simple exercise had never backfired like that before. Her skin buzzed with excess power, making it hard to focus.

Asha appeared at her side, the cat's fur standing on end. Her golden eyes were fixed on the estate's main path. "Rose and Francisco are coming. They're almost at the training grounds."

"We need to contain this quickly." Nykronus gestured, and the remaining traces of wild energy vanished. "Your Lola can't see you like this."

Maya forced her breathing to steady, pushing down the power still surging through her system. The medallion's heat faded slowly, but she could feel it waiting, like a storm gathering strength.

Maya slumped into her chair at the long mahogany dining table, the morning's training session still burning through her muscles. Sunlight streamed through tall windows, catching the steam rising from pancakes and fresh coffee platters.

Her father, Elan, stood at the head of the table, his military bearing softened by the "Kiss the Cook" apron he refused to take off. Years of Marine service had left silver threading his dark hair. Still, his movements remained precise as he passed around a plate of crispy bacon.

Beside him, Maya's mother, Kaira, arranged fresh flowers in a crystal vase, her architect's eye making each stem fall perfectly into place. Her long black hair was tied back, revealing the gentle curves of her face that Maya had inherited.

Lola Rose sat beside her new husband, Francisco, and their hands were linked to the table. Despite being in her sixties, Rose's skin glowed with vitality, and her curly black hair showed barely a trace of gray. Francisco beamed at her as he reached for the coffee pot.

Looking like a younger version of Maya's father, Uncle Jhan was engaged in a deep conversation with Grandma Gianna Mazza. His animated gestures contrasted with Gianna's composed demeanor as she sipped her tea, the silver crosses on her necklace catching the morning light.

Across the table, Myst caught Maya's eye. Her twin brother's brow furrowed as he studied her face, noting the shadows under her eyes and the slight tremor in her hands as she reached for a glass of orange juice. He tilted his head in silent question, but Maya shook her head slightly. This wasn't the time or place to discuss what had happened during training.

"Maya, you're looking pale." Myst's voice cut through the breakfast chatter. "Rough night?"

Kaira's hand stilled over the flower arrangement, her dark eyes fixing on Maya's face. The shadows under her daughter's eyes triggered an old, familiar ache in her chest. She set down the flowers and moved to Maya's side, pressing her hand against her forehead.

"You're burning up." Kaira's fingers traced the chain of Maya's medallion. "And this - it's hot to the touch."

Elan cleared his throat, sliding another stack of pancakes onto Maya's plate. "Nothing, some breakfast won't fix. Remember how you used to make these for me, Mom? With banana slices and chocolate chips?"

"Ay nako, you and your sweet tooth." Rose shook her head, but her eyes crinkled with affection.

Kaira wasn't so easily distracted. She pulled Maya's chair closer, studying her daughter's trembling hands. "When did this start? Have you been pushing yourself too hard with your studies?"

"I'm fine, Mom." Maya reached for her juice, but Kaira steadied her hand when some nearly spilled.

"Let me make you some ginger tea." Kaira started to rise, but Maya caught her wrist.

"Really, I just need food." Maya forced a smile that didn't reach her eyes.

Elan stepped in, his movements deliberately casual as he topped off everyone's coffee. "Speaking of food, who's ready for the story about the time Jhan tried to cook Thanksgiving dinner?"

"Oh no." Jhan groaned, but his eyes lit with genuine amusement. "Not the turkey incident."

"Yes, the turkey incident." Elan launched into the tale, his voice just a touch too loud, his gestures a fraction too animated. His eyes darted to Maya between sentences, noting every tremor, every forced smile.

Kaira remained perched beside Maya, one hand resting protectively on her shoulder. She let Elan's story wash over the table, drawing attention away from their daughter. Still, her fingers never stopped their gentle, worried circles on Maya's back.

Maya pushed her pancakes around the plate, barely tasting the food. The medallion's heat pulsed against her chest in rhythm with her heartbeat, making it hard to focus on the conversation flowing around her. Her fork scraped against the ceramic as her hand trembled.

A water glass three seats down slid an inch to the left. Maya blinked, unsure if she'd imagined it. But then the flower vase shifted, roses tilting at an odd angle. The movement caught Myst's attention, his eyes narrowing as he tracked the subtle disturbances.

Grandma Gianna's teacup rattled in its saucer. The liquid inside rippled, creating concentric circles that spread outward in all directions. Maya gripped the table's edge, trying to steady herself, but the power coursing through her veins refused to settle.

The silverware began to vibrate, producing a soft metallic hum that threaded beneath the ongoing conversation. Forks and knives inched across the tablecloth as if drawn by invisible magnets. A spoon lifted half an inch off the table before clattering back down.

Elan's voice faltered mid-story as his coffee cup slid away from his hand. He grabbed it before it could topple, dark liquid sloshing dangerously close to the rim. His eyes met Maya's across the table, concern etched in the lines around his mouth.

The chandelier above them swayed, though no breeze stirred the air. Crystal pendants clinked together in an eerie melody. Maya's breathing quickened as she fought to contain the pressure under her skin.

A butter knife launched off the table, embedding point-first in the wall behind Francisco's head. Rose yelped, jerking away from the sound. Before anyone could react, every glass on the table exploded simultaneously, showering the family with crystalline shards and splashing drinks across the pristine tablecloth.

Maya walked down Market Street, the medallion's residual heat a constant presence against her chest. San Francisco's familiar landscape had undergone a transformation overnight. Golden threads of energy wound through the air like spider silk, visible only when sunlight struck them at the right angle. They stretched between buildings, connected street signs, and wove through crowds of oblivious pedestrians.

A businessman crossed her path, his briefcase trailing wisps of green light that spoke of ambition and greed. A street musician's guitar leaked purple notes that twisted into visible sound waves, carrying fragments of emotion to everyone who passed. Maya's heightened senses picked up each signature, each unique frequency that normal people couldn't perceive.

The city's pulse beat beneath her feet. Through cracks in the sidewalk, she glimpsed ley lines glowing like molten gold, their ancient paths carving channels of power beneath San Francisco's streets. They converged at unexpected points—a forgotten fountain, an old brass door handle, and a weathered cornerstone that predated the 1906 earthquake.

Cable cars rumbled past, their tracks humming with accumulated decades of mechanical energy that had transformed into something more. The famous hills were alive with unseen currents, each slope and valley channeling forces as old as the Earth.

A group of pigeons took flight, their wings leaving trails of silver light in the air. Maya watched the ethereal traces fade, understanding now why they always gathered at certain intersections. The birds were drawn to pools of power that collected like invisible ponds.

Near Union Square, she passed a fortune teller's shop. The neon "PALM READINGS" sign flickered with genuine prophetic energy. However, she doubts that the reader inside can see the true threads of destiny wrapped around their door frame like vines. The threads pulsed with deep blue light, reaching out to snag passing auras, testing for potential.

Maya realized that the city had always held magic. But now she saw how it flowed and gathered, how it transformed mundane moments into something extraordinary. Each piece of gum stuck to the sidewalk held memories. Every window reflected more than just light. San Francisco wasn't just a city - it was a living tapestry of overlapping energies, each layer telling its own story.

Maya paused at the corner of Powell and Market as dark clouds rolled in from the bay. The weather shifted unnaturally, transforming the sunny morning into twilight within minutes. Around her, pedestrians stopped to stare at the sky, phones raised to capture the phenomenon.

The clouds twisted into spiral patterns she'd never seen before, their centers glowing with that same golden energy she'd been seeing all morning. The wind whipped through the streets, carrying the smell of ozone and something older, like the scent of ancient stone.

"Look at that!" A woman pointed at a patch of clouds that formed a perfect hexagon, its edges sharp as knife cuts.

"It's not supposed to rain today," a man in a business suit muttered, frowning at his weather app.

Lightning flickered between clouds but produced no thunder. Instead, it left after-images that hung in the air like neon signs, pulsing with colors that shouldn't exist in nature. Maya watched patterns emerge in the static - symbols and letters from forgotten languages.

A group of tourists huddled under the awning of a coffee shop, recording the display on their phones. "This can't be real," one of them said. "It looks like some kind of special effect."

The wind picked up, sending newspapers spinning in tight circles that defied gravity. They rose in perfect spirals, forming columns toward the strange clouds. People backed away from the phenomenon, their expressions shifting from curiosity to concern.

"Mom, the pigeons are glowing!" A child's voice cut through the growing murmurs. Maya turned to see a young girl pointing at a flock of birds perched on a nearby building. Their feathers shimmered with silver light - the same energy trails Maya had noticed earlier, but now visible to everyone.

The medallion burned against her chest as more civilians stopped to witness the inexplicable events unfolding around them. Car alarms began blaring in a synchronized pattern. Traffic lights cycled through their colors in impossible sequences. The very air seemed to vibrate with building pressure.

Maya pressed her hand against a building's stone facade, feeling vibrations pulse through her palm. The barrier between worlds had grown as thin as tissue paper. Through gaps no wider than a breath, she caught glimpses of other places - crystal spires piercing violet skies, forests of silver-barked trees, paths that wound between stars.

The medallion's heat spread across her chest as more rifts appeared. They flickered at the edges of her vision like heat mirages, each one offering a window into another realm. A businessman walked through one without noticing, his suit jacket briefly shimmering with other-worldly light.

The sounds of traffic faded, replaced by whispers in languages never spoken on Earth. The air grew thick with possibility, heavy with multiple realities pressing against each other. Maya's heightened senses detected the strain of natural laws struggling to maintain their separation.

A child's chalk drawing on the sidewalk began to move, stick figures dancing across concrete before vanishing into cracks between dimensions. Leaves fell upward from trees, drawn toward rifts that hung invisibly in the air. The city's normal rhythm fragmented as multiple timestreams bled together.

The ground beneath her feet shifted—not an earthquake—something more profound, more fundamental. Reality itself groaned under the pressure of colliding worlds. Maya stumbled as waves of dizziness washed over her. The medallion flared hot enough to burn, its power responding to the dimensional disturbance.

Through the haze, she saw other realms superimposed over San Francisco's streets. Ancient ruins overlaid modern buildings. Trees grew through sidewalks, their branches reaching into impossible spaces. The sky fractured into a kaleidoscope of different atmospheres, each visible through widening cracks in the fabric of space.

A massive tremor rocked the city - not physical, but metaphysical. Maya fell to her knees as reality buckled. The medallion's power surged through her body, trying to stabilize the weakening barriers, but the force was too great. Around her, the world began to tear apart at the seams.

Maya lunged forward as a bus-sized rift tore open above Market Street, spewing forth crystalline creatures that resembled twisted versions of earth animals. Their razor-sharp limbs clicked against the pavement as they scuttled toward screaming civilians.

The medallion's power coursed through her veins as she thrust both hands upward. Golden energy erupted from her palms, forming a barrier between the creatures and a group of tourists, who were frozen in terror. The shield hummed with ancient power, sending ripples through the air, causing smartphones to malfunction and car alarms to wail.

"Get inside! Now!" She pushed back against a crystal-horned beast that slammed into her barrier. Sweat beaded on her forehead as she maintained the shield while herding people toward nearby buildings.

A security guard stared open-mouthed as Maya deflected another creature with a blast of pure force. "What the hell are you?"

"Someone trying to help." Maya's arms trembled with effort. The medallion burned against her skin as she drew more power, weaving it into nets of golden light that caught and contained the otherworldly beings.

Phones recorded her every move as she worked. Social media would explode with footage of the girl throwing golden energy around downtown San Francisco. But she couldn't worry about that now - lives were at stake.

Maya's hands traced complex patterns in the air, remembering movements Nykronus had drilled into her that morning. The rift's edges began to seal, reality knitting back together under her guidance. The creatures shrieked in alien voices as they were pulled back through the closing tear.

"Did you see that?" A teenager's voice carried over the crowd. "She's like some kind of superhero!"

"Those weren't special effects," another witness muttered. "That was real magic."

Maya's legs buckled as the last of the rift sealed. The medallion's heat faded to a dull warmth, leaving her drained but satisfied. Around her, dozens of phones captured her every move as she steadied herself against a lamp post.

Police sirens wailed in the distance. Maya knew she should leave before they arrived, but exhaustion made her movements sluggish. The crowd pressed closer, their questions overlapping:

"Who are you?"

"What were those things?"

"How did you do that?"

Maya pushed through the growing crowd, scanning for anyone still in danger. The medallion's warmth guided her movements as she wove between gawking onlookers and fleeing civilians. Her newfound senses picked up traces of otherworldly energy lingering in the air— dangerous pockets that could spark more rifts.

A child's cry pierced through the chaos. Maya spun toward the sound, catching sight of a young girl trapped beneath a fallen newsstand. Crystal shards from the creatures' passage had created a cage of razor-sharp spikes around her.

"Hold still!" Maya knelt beside the structure, studying how energy flowed through the crystalline formation. The patterns reminded her of Nykronus's lessons about force distribution. She pressed her palm against the nearest spike, channeling power through the point of contact.

The crystal responded to her touch, its molecular structure shifting as she manipulated the energy binding it together. Hairline fractures spread through the formation, following the paths she directed with her mind. The spikes crumbled into harmless dust, clearing a path to the trapped child.

Maya helped the girl crawl free, checking her for injuries. "Are you okay? Where are your parents?"

"Sarah!" A woman pushed through the crowd, tears streaming down her face. "Oh god, Sarah!"

Mother and daughter collided in a desperate, yet tender, embrace. Maya stepped back, already scanning for other threats. Her heightened awareness picked up distortions in the air - aftershocks from the dimensional tear that could spawn more dangers.

She moved methodically through the area, using her powers to neutralize unstable energy pockets before they could manifest. Each intervention drained more of her strength, but she refused to stop while people remained at risk. The medallion's heat pulsed in time with her efforts, supporting her actions while warning her not to push too far.

A ripple of gasps drew her attention to a storefront where reality had grown thin. Through the wavering air, tentacles of shadow probed for weakness. Maya reached deep into her reserves, drawing forth golden light that she shaped into a barrier. The shadows recoiled from her power, retreating back through the dimensional weak point.

Maya's arms shook as she maintained the barrier against the shadow tentacles. The medallion's power thrummed through her, raw and overwhelming. She needed precision, not just brute force.

Asha appeared beside her, the cat's fur rippling with orange energy. "Focus on the edges. Like threading a needle, not swinging a hammer."

Maya nodded, adjusting her stance. She narrowed the barrier, concentrating the same power into a smaller area. The golden light intensified, burning brighter but with more control. The shadows hissed as they retreated.

"Three more weak points detected," Asha's tail swished as she tracked the disturbances. "Two blocks south, one in the alley behind us. I'll guide civilians away from those areas."

The cat darted through the crowd, her glowing form drawing the attention of the people. Wherever Asha ran, people followed instinctively, clearing vulnerable zones before rifts could form.

Maya moved between the weak points, each barrier requiring less energy as she refined her technique. The medallion's heat steadied to a manageable warmth. She wove smaller, stronger seals that closed the dimensional tears with surgical precision.

"Police helicopter incoming," Asha called out as she herded a group away from a forming rift. "News vans approaching from the east."

Camera flashes sparked around them as people recorded the glowing cat and the girl wielding golden light. Maya heard reporters shouting questions, their microphones thrust forward like spears.

"Who are you?"

"What's happening to our city?"

"Is this connected to the strange weather?"

Maya kept working, sealing the final weak point as media crews pushed through the crowd. She'd have to disappear soon, but not before ensuring everyone's safety. The role of the Guardian came first - publicity could wait.

Maya's muscles ached as she sealed the last dimensional tear. The golden energy faded from her hands, leaving behind exhaustion that seemed to seep into her bones. Camera flashes continued to spark around her like lightning bugs in the twilight.

Asha wound between her legs, fur still rippling with orange light. "Time to go. You've done what was needed here."

Sirens wailed closer. Red and blue lights painted the buildings as police cars blocked off the streets. Maya spotted news vans threading through the emergency vehicles and camera crews spilling onto the sidewalks.

She pressed her hand against the medallion, drawing on its remaining warmth. The artifact responded with a pulse of energy - not enough for more barriers, but sufficient for what she needed next.

Golden light wrapped around her like a cocoon. Maya felt her feet leave the ground as the power lifted her above the crowd. Gasps and shouts followed her ascent.

"Look! Up there!"

"Someone get a clear shot!"

"Don't let her get away!"

Asha leaped impossibly high, landing on Maya's shoulder as they rose above the chaos. Together, they drifted toward the rooftops, leaving a scene of confusion and wonder. Phones tracked their departure until the gathering storm's darkness swallowed them whole.

The medallion's power set them down gently on a distant roof. Maya's legs buckled as the last of the golden light faded. She leaned against a ventilation unit, breathing hard.

"Well," Asha settled beside her, tail swishing. "That's certainly one way to announce our presence to the world."

The Durant family gathered around Lola Rose's expansive dining table, plates heaped with steaming Filipino cuisine. Maya picked at her chicken adobo while the adults buzzed with worried conversation about the day's events.

"It's all over social media." Reagan placed her phone in the center of the table, showing shaky footage of golden barriers and crystalline creatures. "They're calling her the Guardian of San Francisco."

Reagan sat at the far end of the table. She scrolled through her phone while Austin leaned beside her, his Polo shirt crisp against his dark skin.

"Look at the energy signature," Austin said, pointing at the screen. His Marine background colored his analysis. "Nothing like this in our classified briefings."

Reagan squeezed his hand beneath the table, their engagement ring glinting. "We need to contain this. SFPD is flooded with calls."

As Elan's oldest friends—Reagan since high school, Austin from their Marine days —they had supported her through much. But this situation dwarfed their usual challenges.

"Maya. My baby." Kaira reached across the table, squeezing Maya's hand. "You could have been hurt."

"She handled herself well." Elan's voice carried a hint of pride beneath his concern. "But we need to be more careful. The whole city saw what happened."

Lola Rose made the Sign of the Cross. "First, the twins travel through time; now this. What's next?"

"The Order needs to step in." Austin leaned forward. "We can help protect her identity and control the narrative."

Myst spoke around a mouthful of rice. "She was amazing, though. Did you see how she saved that little girl?"

"That's not the point." Kristinn set down her fork. "What if someone recognizes her? What if they come after her?"

"Or after all of us." Jhan gestured with his spoon. "We need a plan."

Grandma Mazza's weathered hands smoothed the tablecloth. "The Nexus Heart chooses to share it's power with her for a reason. We must trust in that."

"Trust won't stop the media circus." Francisco shook his head. "Or the government agencies that'll want to investigate."

"The powers are getting stronger." Maya's quiet words cut through the chatter. "I can feel it. Today wasn't just random - something's changing."

Silence fell over the table as they absorbed her words. The silverware clinked, and the ceiling fan's hum filled the pause.

Reagan broke the tension. "Whatever's coming, we face it together. That's what family does."

"Together," the others echoed, though worry still creased their brows.

Maya pushed back from the table, her chair scraping against the tile floor. "I couldn't just watch those creatures hurt people. My trip to Aethoria helped me unlock these powers for a reason."

"Powers we barely understand," Elan's jaw tightened. "You need training, protection-"

"I had training. Nykronus showed me how to control it." Maya's hand pressed against the medallion, its warmth pulsing in response. "And Asha was there to guide me."

The glowing cat materialized on the table, orange light rippling through her fur. "She's not wrong. Maya handled the situation with remarkable control."

"That's not the point." Kaira reached for Maya's hand, but Maya pulled away. "Baby, there are people out there who will want to use you, study you-"

"So I should hide? Pretend this isn't happening?" Maya stood, frustration building in her chest. "The barriers between worlds are breaking down. I can feel it. Today was just the beginning."

Reagan's radio, from the Order of St. Michael's headquarters, crackled with chatter about mysterious lights downtown. She switched it off with a sharp click. "We need to be smart about this. Set up protocols, establish safe houses-"

"I'm not some witness protection case." Maya paced the dining room, the medallion's heat spreading across her chest. "I'm a Guardian. A Knight. That means standing between people and danger, not hiding in safe houses."

The room fell silent as ancient power rippled through the air. Maya's vision blurred at the edges, reality growing thin. The medallion's warmth intensified the warning of another vision approaching. She gripped the back of her chair as the familiar sensation of being pulled elsewhere began to build.

"Maya?" Kaira half-rose from her seat, concern etched on her face.

"It's happening again." Maya's voice sounded distant to her own ears as the vision took hold. "Another message coming through..."

Maya's world tilted sideways as the vision seized her. The dining room dissolved into swirling darkness, replaced by ancient stone walls covered in Latin text that writhed like living things. Through the gloom, a figure emerged - tall and imposing, with thick dark waves of hair falling past his shoulders and eyes that held the weight of centuries.

The medallion burned against her chest as Lazarus stepped forward, his movements fluid and purposeful. His fingers traced the glowing text on the wall, each word pulsing with an eerie light. Maya recognized fragments from the sacred text she'd discovered in Chapter 1, but here, they formed new patterns, revealing darker meanings.

"The mirror shows two faces," Lazarus's voice echoed unnaturally. "One of salvation, one of judgment."

Behind him, shadows coalesced into shapes - armies gathering, portals opening between worlds, reality fracturing along ancient fault lines. The vision shifted, showing Lazarus standing before a massive obsidian mirror, its surface rippling like black water.

Maya's body convulsed as the vision's grip tightened. Distantly, she felt herself collapse, caught by strong arms before she hit the floor. The medallion's heat became almost unbearable.

"Hold her steady!" Elan's voice cut through the haze of the vision. His hands cradled her head as she thrashed.

Myst pressed close to his twin, his own power reaching out to stabilize her. "She's burning up. The Medallion-"

"Don't touch it!" Maya managed through gritted teeth as the vision began to fade. The last image seared into her mind: Lazarus stepping through the mirror, trailing tendrils of darkness that reached hungrily toward our world.

Reality snapped back into focus. Maya was on the dining room floor, surrounded by the worried faces of her family. Her father's arms supported her while Myst knelt beside them, his hand clasped tightly in hers.

"I saw him," she gasped, struggling to sit up. "Lazarus. He's found something—a mirror and ancient texts. He's going to tear everything apart."

CHAPTER

THREE

Benevento shimmered in the July heat of 1962, its ancient stones baking under an unforgiving Italian sun. Nykronus adjusted his fitted leather jacket - perhaps too warm for the weather. Still, he couldn't shed his signature look even in this era. His boots clicked against the cobblestones as he made his way through narrow streets where Fiats and Alfa Romeos squeezed past market stalls.

The Order's headquarters rose before him, a Renaissance palazzo that masked its true nature behind weathered marble and climbing vines. Modern security cameras blinked red among carved cherubs. At the same time, while spell-traces glimmered in the afternoon light - invisible to mortal eyes but clear as day to his trained sight.

He paused at the heavy wooden doors, their bronze handles worn smooth by the hands of centuries. His fingers brushed the pendant hidden beneath his shirt, its familiar weight doing little to calm his nerves. This assignment marked a turning point - his first solo mission for the Order of St. Michael.

A guard booth stood to one side, incongruous against the historic facade. The guard inside wore bell-bottom slacks and a polyester shirt, but his eyes held the sharp awareness of a trained operative.

"Papers?" The guard's Italian carried a Roman accent.

Nykronus handed over his credentials, watching as they were checked against both modern records and an ancient tome bound in leather and silver.

The doors swung open with a groan of ancient hinges. The entrance hall stretched before him, its marble floor inlaid with protective sigils that pulsed faintly in response to his presence. Modern fluorescent lights clashed with oil paintings of stern-faced priests and warriors from centuries past.

A small group waited at the far end - three figures in contemporary clothes that couldn't quite hide their otherworldly bearing. The woman in the center wore a flowing paisley dress, but her posture conveyed a sense of battlefield command. Her companions flanked her like honor guards; their relaxed stances belied alert eyes.

Nykronus straightened his jacket and strode forward to meet his welcome committee, each step echoing in the vast space.

Down the grand hallway, a younger Professor Xicato burst through a side door, papers spilling from his arms. His wire-rimmed glasses sat crooked on his nose, and chalk dust peppered his tweed jacket.

"Ah, you must be the specialist they sent." The professor juggled his stack of documents, a fountain pen clattering to the floor. "Though I expected someone more..." His eyes darted over Nykronus's leather jacket and boots.

Nykronus bent to retrieve the pen, its gold nib catching the light, "Academic?"

"Precisely." Xicato snatched the pen back, tucking it into his breast pocket. "I've spent twenty years studying the artifacts in question. What could a..." He waved his hand vaguely at Nykronus's attire, "...person of your background contribute?"

"Knowledge takes many forms, Professor." Nykronus kept his voice level, though amusement tugged at his lips. The professor's skepticism was nothing new - he'd faced it across centuries.

"Yes, well." Xicato shuffled his papers, creating a small blizzard of loose notes. "The texts are this way. Though I must insist that you wear gloves. These documents are irreplaceable."

They walked down a corridor lined with glass cases. Xicato rattled off dates and provenances, his earlier disdain forgotten in his enthusiasm. His steps quickened as they approached a heavy oak door marked "Special Collections."

"The binding alone dates to the fourth century," Xicato said, fumbling with a ring of keys. "The parchment shows evidence of palimpsest - text written over earlier writing. Fascinating really, the way-"

"The way they used sacred texts to hide forbidden knowledge." Nykronus finished.

Xicato's keys froze mid-turn. "How did you...?"

"As I said, Professor. Knowledge takes many forms."

The professor's mouth opened and closed like a fish out of water. For the first time, he looked at Nykronus with something approaching respect.

Nykronus followed Xicato through a maze of corridors, each turn revealing another layer of the Order's complex. Modern offices gave way to medieval stonework, fluorescent lights replaced by gas lamps that cast dancing shadows on the walls.

"Your research on the Mithraic cults caught our attention," Xicato said, pausing before a display case filled with ancient weapons. "Particularly your analysis of their ritual practices."

"The connections between their ceremonies and certain unexplained events were... compelling." Nykronus kept his tone neutral, though his fingers itched to touch the ceremonial dagger behind the glass - he recognized it from a battle centuries ago.

Xicato led him down a spiral staircase, the temperature dropping with each step. "We've assembled quite a collection here. Artifacts, texts, relics from every major civilization." His hand trembled slightly as he gestured to another room. "Though some items are too sensitive for general viewing."

The professor's pace quickened past a heavy iron door marked with warning symbols. Nykronus caught a whiff of incense and something else - a metallic scent that raised the hairs on his neck.

"The main archives contain over ten thousand volumes." Xicato's voice echoed off the stone walls. "Everything from parish records to..." He cleared his throat. "Well, more specialized materials."

They passed a reading room where researchers bent over ancient tomes, their modern clothes at odds with the medieval furnishings. One woman looked up sharply as they passed, her eyes following them with too much interest.

Xicato's hand strayed to his jacket pocket, where he touched something hidden there. "The library's this way. Though I should warn you - some of our older texts can be... temperamental."

The corridor opened into a vast chamber lined with towering bookshelves. Bronze ladders curved along rails, providing access to the highest levels where leather-bound volumes sat thick with dust. At the center stood a massive oak table, its surface carved with protective symbols that pulsed faintly in the dim light.

A young woman emerged from between the towering shelves, her dark hair pulled back in a practical bun. Silver pins shaped like ancient Roman keys held wayward strands in place. Her movements were precise as she shelved a massive tome bound in cracked leather.

Nykronus's breath caught. Even from across the room, power radiated from her like heat from summer stones. Not the raw force wielded by warriors, but something more profound - the quiet strength of knowledge preserved through ages.

"Ah, Miss Mazza." Professor Xicato gestured her over. "Our newest researcher needs orientation to the restricted section."

Gianna Mazza crossed the room, her sensible shoes silent on the stone floor. Her white blouse and knee-length skirt were simple but elegant, though smudges of dust and ink stained her fingers. A pendant hung at her throat - a silver wheel marked with symbols Nykronus hadn't seen since Constantinople fell.

"Welcome to our little corner of history." Her voice carried hints of both Italy and America, warm as aged wine. She extended her hand, and when Nykronus clasped it, a spark jumped between them. Her eyes widened slightly.

"You've felt it too, then?" Nykronus kept his voice low. "The way these books whisper?"

A smile tugged at her lips. "Most people think I'm strange when I mention that." She pulled a key ring from her pocket, the metal singing faintly. "The restricted section is this way, if you're ready to hear what they have to say."

She led him past rows of books, some chained to their shelves, others floating slightly above worn wood. Her fingers trailed along spines marked with gilt letters and mysterious symbols, greeting each volume like an old friend.

"The texts respond to her," Xicato murmured. "I've never seen anything like it. Books that burn others' hands open at her touch. Scripts that blur for most readers become clear under her gaze."

Nykronus watched as Gianna unlocked an iron-bound chest, ancient parchments rising at her approach like flowers turning toward the sun. Her movements were those of a dancer, graceful and sure, as she guided the fragile pages to a reading stand.

Nykronus watched as Gianna's fingers danced across the ancient texts, translating passages from languages that had been dead for millennia. Her knowledge wasn't just academic - she understood the deeper meanings, the hidden connections between seemingly unre-lated texts.

"This reference here," she pointed to a line of Greek text, "connects to a Coptic prophecy about the three mountains. Most scholars miss it because they focus on the literal translation."

"The Three Marias." Nykronus leaned closer, his shoulder brushing hers as he studied the text. "Filipino mountain guardians disguised as Christian saints."

Her eyes lit up. "You know of them? Most Western scholars dismiss those prophecies as folk tales."

"The best prophecies hide in plain sight." He traced a symbol in the margin - three interlocking circles. "Like this one about a child born centuries after her conception."

Gianna pulled another volume from the shelf, its pages crackling with age. "That reminds me of something..." She flipped through the brittle pages with practiced care until she found what she sought. "Here - a Byzantine text about time-touched souls."

Their heads bent together over the manuscripts, trading insights about prophecies from different cultures that echoed the same themes.

Hours slipped by as they discovered shared patterns in texts from Rome to Manila.

"Wait." Gianna paused at a page filled with intricate diagrams. "Look at this." She pointed to a drawing of a woman holding what appeared to be a modern compass, but the manuscript dated to the 9th century. Below it, the Latin text spoke of a traveler unbound by the chains of time.

"The ink's different here," Nykronus noted how the writing shifted from brown to deep black midway through the passage. "Like someone added to the prophecy centuries after it was first recorded."

"Or..." Gianna's fingers traced the words, "like someone went back to write it."

Gianna spread another ancient text across the oak table, its pages crackling beneath her careful touch. Nykronus stood at her right shoulder while Professor Xicato peered through his wire-rimmed glasses from her left. The library's gas lamps cast dancing shadows across weathered parchment and faded ink.

"The syntax here is unusual," Professor Xicato tapped a line of text. "It doesn't match classical Latin."

"Because it's not classical." Nykronus leaned closer. "This is vulgar Latin, the common tongue. See how the word order shifts?"

Gianna nodded, her silver hair pins catching the lamplight. "Like someone trying to transcribe spoken words rather than formal writing." Her fingers traced the letters. "And look at these marks in the margins - they're not scholarly annotations."

"Navigation coordinates?" Professor Xicato squinted at the tiny numbers.

"Celestial measurements." Nykronus pulled down an astronomical treatise from a nearby shelf. "They match star positions from the early medieval period."

Gianna compared the two texts side by side. "The same coordinates appear in both, but written centuries apart." She reached for another volume, this one bound in cracked leather. "And here again, in a Byzantine merchant's log."

The three researchers fell into a rhythm, passing books back and forth across the table. Gianna's practical knowledge of ancient languages complemented the professor's academic expertise, while Nykronus filled in the gaps with insights that spanned centuries.

"These references to the Three Marias keep appearing." Professor Xicato spread out his notes. "But the context changes. Sometimes they're mountain spirits, sometimes Christian saints."

"Or perhaps they're both." Gianna opened a worn journal, its pages filled with sketches of Philippine landscapes. "The old ways often hide behind new faces."

Nykronus traced a series of interconnected symbols that bordered the journal's pages. "The same patterns appear in Roman temple carvings. And here-" he pulled another text from the pile, "-in early Church documents."

Gianna's breath caught as she turned another page. Among the dense Latin text, a particular passage stood out - the ink darker, fresher than the surrounding words. She beckoned Nykronus closer.

"Durant." The names jumped from the page in that stark black ink. "This can't be right. This is a modern surname in a fifth-century text."

Nykronus peered at the passage. The words seemed to shift under his gaze, rearranging themselves like pieces of a puzzle. "The prophecy speaks of bloodlines converging - joining of East and West."

Together they began to translate, their different skills complementing each other. Gianna's fingers traced each word, her knowledge of medieval Latin dialects bringing clarity to obscure phrases. When she stumbled over a particular term, Nykronus supplied meanings from even older tongues.

"This section describes a woman born out of time," Gianna translated, her voice steady despite the impossible words. "A child of two worlds, conceived in one century but born in another."

"And here," Nykronus pointed to a complex series of astronomical symbols. "These aren't just star charts. They're time markers - specific configurations that only align once every thousand years."

Professor Xicato shuffled through his notes, comparing dates and positions. "The next alignment matches calculations I've been working on. It's due within our lifetime."

Gianna moved to a passage heavy with Greek marginalia. Her lips moved silently as she decoded the ancient script. "There's more. It mentions something about three mountains and their guardians." She switched smoothly to translating a section of Aramaic text that wound around the page borders. "The Marias are mentioned again, but the context is different - more immediate."

Nykronus added his own insights, filling in gaps where time had erased words or meanings had shifted. Between them, the prophecy took shape—a complex web of bloodlines, celestial events, and sacred places spanning continents and centuries.

Gianna's heart raced as each translation revealed new connections. Her fingers trembled slightly as she traced the ancient text, the familiar Latin letters seeming to pulse with hidden meaning. The prophecy wasn't just a collection of disconnected predictions - it was a map, a guide written across centuries.

"Look at this." She pointed to a series of interlocking symbols. "The same pattern appears in texts from Rome, Byzantium, and the Philippines. But they're not just decorative."

Nykronus leaned closer, his presence steady at her shoulder. "They're coordinates. Each intersection marks a point of power."

Professor Xicato spread his star charts across the table, overlaying them with the ancient diagrams. "The alignments match perfectly. But there's something else..."

Gianna's breath caught as she decoded another passage. The words seemed to leap from the page, their meaning crystal clear despite the archaic language. Her hands shook as she gripped the edge of the table.

"It's not just about the Three Marias or the Durant bloodline." Her voice dropped to a whisper. "The prophecy speaks of a guardian - someone meant to protect something far more valuable than mountains or artifacts."

She turned the page, revealing a detailed illustration she'd somehow missed before. The image showed a woman holding what appeared to be a modern compass, but the manuscript dated centuries before such instruments existed. Below it, in that stark black ink that seemed fresher than the surrounding text, was a name she knew all too well.

"Mazza." Gianna's finger traced the letters. "My family name. Written in a text that's over a thousand years old."

"This is preposterous." Professor Xicato paced between the towering shelves. "We can't base research decisions on prophecies and family names. The academic implications alone-"

"The academic world isn't prepared for these truths." Nykronus spread his hands over the ancient texts. "These coordinates, the astronomical alignments - they point to something bigger than scholarly papers."

Gianna watched them from her seat at the oak table, her mind racing. The familiar weight of her silver pendant pressed against her throat as she considered both perspectives. "Perhaps there's a middle ground."

"Middle ground?" Xicato's voice cracked. "There's protocol, procedure. We can't just chase mystical connections across continents based on a few coincidences."

"Coincidences?" Nykronus traced the fresh black ink that spelled out 'Durant.' "The same symbols appear in texts separated by centuries and oceans. The astronomical calculations align perfectly with modern star charts."

"Which is exactly why we need proper documentation, peer review-"

"While forces beyond your understanding move into position?" Nykronus's eyes flashed. "The alignments won't wait for academic approval."

Gianna stood, her chair scraping against stone. "Both approaches have merit." She lifted the text with her family name. "Professor, you taught me the importance of rigorous research. But Nykronus is right - there's an urgency here that traditional methods won't address."

"What do you suggest?" Xicato slumped against a bookshelf.

"We document everything." Gianna pulled a fresh notebook from her bag. "But we also follow these leads. The coordinates give us concrete locations to investigate. We can maintain academic standards while acknowledging the... unusual aspects of our findings."

Nykronus nodded slowly. "A balanced approach. Though time may not be our ally."

"Two weeks." Gianna looked between them. "Give me two weeks to cross-reference these texts with the library's full collection. Then we'll have a clearer picture of where to focus our investigation."

"One week," Nykronus countered.

"Ten days," she offered. "Any faster and we risk missing crucial connections."

Professor Xicato straightened his glasses. "I'll arrange access to the restricted archives. But everything gets documented. Everything."

The evening air wrapped around them like silk as they walked through Benevento's cobblestone streets. Gas lamps cast pools of golden light, their flames dancing in the gentle breeze. Gianna pulled her shawl tighter around her shoulders.

"My grandmother used to tell stories about the old ways." She traced her fingers over the silver pendant at her throat. "How certain families were chosen to protect sacred knowledge."

"Did you believe her?" Nykronus matched her pace, close enough that their shoulders brushed.

"I thought they were just tales. Until I started working at the library." Her lips curved. "The books... they spoke to me. Like they knew me."

"Some souls carry ancient echoes." His voice dropped lower. "I recognized it in you the moment we met."

They paused at a stone fountain, its waters catching starlight. Gianna dipped her fingers in the cool spray. "And you? Where did your journey begin?"

"Centuries ago, it seems." His eyes held shadows deeper than the night. "I've walked many paths, seen empires rise and fall. But never found anyone who understood until now."

Heat bloomed in Gianna's cheeks. She turned to face him, drawn by the weight of unspoken things between them. "Do you believe it's fate? These ancient prophecies pointing us together?"

"I believe in choices." He lifted his hand, brushing a strand of hair from her face. "Even when destiny deals the cards, we choose how to play them."

His touch lingered on her cheek. Gianna's heart thundered against her ribs as she tilted her face toward his. The space between them was charged with electricity, years of solitude dissolving in a single breath.

A church bell tolled in the distance, startling a flock of pigeons into flight. They sprang apart as wings filled the air, the moment shattered by beating feathers and echoing chimes.

Gianna's hands trembled as she spread the genealogy charts across her dining room table. The morning sun streamed through lace curtains, illuminating centuries of carefully documented bloodlines. Nykronus stood behind her, his presence steady as she traced the connections.

"The Durant line intersects with the guardians of Mount Arayat." Her finger followed a branch that stretched back to pre-colonial Philippines. "And here - the Mazza family ties directly to the Order of St. Michael."

"East meets West." Nykronus pulled out a chair and sat beside her. "The prophecy speaks of a union that bridges worlds."

"Maya Durant." Gianna circled the name in red ink. "Born in the ninth century but conceived in our time. The dates match perfectly with the astronomical alignments."

"A child out of time." His voice carried weight. "The convergence of sacred bloodlines creates a guardian more powerful than any before."

Gianna sank into her chair, the magnitude of the discovery settling over her like a heavy cloak. "This means everything we thought we knew about causality, about time itself..."

"It is more complex than we imagined." Nykronus spread his hands on the table. "The past influences the future, but the future also shapes the past."

"We can't let this knowledge fall into the wrong hands." Gianna gathered the papers with swift, decisive movements. "The implications - if someone tried to prevent this union..."

"Or exploit it." Nykronus's jaw tightened. "There are those who would use such power for their own ends."

Gianna moved to her grandfather's old roll-top desk, pulling out a false bottom to reveal a hidden compartment. "These records need to be protected, preserved for the right moment." She placed the documents inside, along with their translations and notes.

"We become guardians ourselves." Nykronus helped her secure the compartment. "Keeping watch until the time is right."

"Until the bloodlines converge." Gianna closed the desk with firm resolve. "We protect this knowledge with our lives."

Gianna paced the length of her study, her fingers twisting the silver pendant. The morning light caught dust motes dancing in the air as her mind raced through possibilities. Could it be Marco, her younger brother in Milan? Or Isabella, her cousin, who worked as a nurse in Rome?

"What if I'm meant to meet a Durant?" She stopped at the window, watching sparrows flit between branches. "Or maybe it's meant for someone else in the family - one of the children yet to be born?"

"You're getting ahead of yourself." Nykronus's voice carried a gentle warning. "These prophecies, these ancient texts - they're guidelines, not mandates."

"But the alignments, the timing-"

"They are fascinating historical records." He moved to stand beside her. "But you can't live your life waiting for destiny to unfold. That's no different than those fairy tales your grandmother told you as a child."

Gianna's shoulders tensed. "This is different. We have proof-"

"We have fragments of stories, written by people trying to make sense of forces beyond their understanding." Nykronus touched her shoulder. "Don't let these ancient words become a cage. Live your life, make your choices. If the prophecies are true, they'll unfold in their own time."

She released her grip on the pendant, letting out a long breath. "You're right. I can't spend every day wondering if each new person I meet might be a Durant."

Gianna unfolded a weathered parchment, its edges crumbling despite her careful touch. The ancient text spoke of a darkness that would rise when the Three Marias' powers aligned—a force that threatened to tear apart the very fabric of time itself.

"This changes everything." Professor Xicato adjusted his glasses. "If what the prophecy says is true, we're not just preserving history. We're preparing for a battle."

"Not us." Nykronus traced the celestial coordinates. "Our descendants. The timing places this threat centuries from now."

Gianna's fingers brushed over the stark black ink of the Durant name. "Then we need to ensure they're ready. Create a system to pass down what we've learned."

"I can establish a secure archive within the university." Xicato pulled out his notebook. "Hidden, but accessible to those who know where to look."

"And I'll document everything we've discovered." Gianna glanced at the growing pile of translations. "Create a guide for future generations."

Nykronus placed his hand over hers. "I'll remain watchful through the years, guiding those who need to understand."

The weight of his words hung in the air. Gianna met his gaze, understanding flowing between them. His promise to stay and watch over what they'd discovered carried a deeper meaning.

"You won't be alone in this vigil." She turned her hand to intertwine their fingers.

"No," he agreed softly. "Not anymore."

Professor Xicato cleared his throat and gathered his papers. "I'll begin the arrangements at the university. We'll meet again next week to coordinate our efforts."

After he left, Gianna and Nykronus stood in comfortable silence, still connected by their joined hands. The prophecy lay open before them, its final lines stark against the aged parchment:

"When the mountains weep and stars align, the child born of time's wound shall face the shadow that devours light. In her blood flows the power of three worlds - only she can mend what was broken or shatter all that remains."

CHAPTER

FOUR

The monitoring screens at St. Michael's San Francisco command center flickered with infrared signatures. Ancient runes pulsed along the edges of modern LCD displays, merging centuries-old magic with cutting-edge technology. Kaira's fingers danced across the haptic interface, adjusting thermal overlays of the ritual site in Muir Woods.

"Multiple heat signatures converging on the stone circle." She zoomed in on the topographical display. "The ley line readings are off the charts."

Reagan leaned over the command table, her police captain's badge catching the blue glow of the monitors. "I've got tactical teams on standby. Where do you need them?"

"Here and here." Kaira marked two points on the 3D terrain map. "The old ward stones will give them cover. But these aren't ordinary cultists - they're using some kind of tech-augmented ritual focus."

The ancient symbols etched into the command center's walls hummed with increasing intensity. A warning klaxon blared as red lights strobed across the operations floor.

"Containment field breach at the perimeter." Reagan grabbed her tactical gear. "They've broken through the outer defensive ring."

Kaira's hands flew over the controls, activating the site's dormant protection spells. Modern security cameras merged their feeds with mystical sensors, painting a complete picture of the incursion. Dark figures moved with inhuman speed, carrying devices that pulsed with corrupted magical energy.

"Malefic Assembly." Kaira's voice hardened. "They've evolved. These aren't the crude ritualists we faced before."

"Teams Alpha through Delta, move to intercept." Reagan barked orders into her comm unit. "Full spectrum containment protocols. Watch for techno-magical hybridization."

The command center's main screen showed tactical teams taking position around the ritual site. Ancient stone monoliths stood in stark contrast to the operators' advanced combat gear. Spelled ammunition clicked into reinforced magazines as operators charged their blessed combat rifles.

"Confirmation on target identification." A tech analyst called out. "Malefic Assembly signatures match database records. They're using modified focusing crystals, ma'am. Unlike anything we've seen before."

Kaira and Reagan shared a look. The Order's age-old battle had entered a new phase, where the line between technology and magic grew increasingly blurred.

Erikson Ghostcloak strode through the armory's reinforced doors, his tactical vest already loaded with blessed magazines. The Order's insignia gleamed on his shoulder patch as he grabbed an M4 carbine from the weapon wall, muttering ancient Norse protection runes passed down through generations of his family.

Stanley Wyatt's Australian drawl crackled over the comms. "Got eyes on the eastern perimeter. These bastards brought some nasty toys."

"Copy that." Erikson checked his rifle's enchanted optics. "Zoe, status on the sonic disruptors?"

"Frequencies calibrated." Zoe's voice carried over the tactical net from her position in the mobile command post. "My EDM setup's ready to shake their ritual patterns apart."

Maya Durant moved with fluid grace through the prep area, helping teams load specialized ammunition. Blessed silver rounds clinked against magazines while her mother, Kaira, coordinated with Reagan's tactical elements.

"Remember, people - these aren't standard cultists." Erikson addressed the assembled strike teams. "They've merged arcane focuses with modern tech. Watch your sectors and trust your enhanced gear."

The Order's deployment bay hummed with activity. Operators checked spell-enhanced body armor and synchronized their augmented reality displays with the command center's mystical sensors. Ancient symbols glowed along modern rifle barrels as protection wards activated.

"Tactical overlay online." A tech specialist calibrated the neural network linking their forces. "Magical signatures integrating with thermal imaging."

Stanley's feed showed him adjusting his cowboy hat before securing his night vision goggles. "Got movement at the tree line. Multiple targets carrying some kind of crystalline devices."

"Teams One through Four, move to primary positions." Erikson outlined attack vectors on the tactical display. "Zoe's sonic array will disrupt their ritual while we-"

The command center's doors burst open. A figure in archaic Templar armor strode in, chainmail clinking beneath futuristic tactical gear. Ancient runes blazed along his sword blade, which hummed in harmony with the rifle slung across his back.

The armored figure staggered, his sword clattering against the command center's floor. Blood trickled from beneath his pauldron, staining the ancient chainmail. His face—the same face depicted in countless paintings and statues throughout history—contorted in a look of confusion.

Erikson caught him before he hit the ground. The warrior's armor felt impossibly light, crafted from materials that seemed impossible to exist. Ancient runes pulsed along the metalwork, technologies beyond modern understanding integrated seamlessly into the classical design.

"Where..." The warrior's voice carried power even in its weakness. "What is this place?"

Kaira's hands trembled as she approached. Every detail matched the Order's historical records—the distinctive profile, the legendary armor, even the specific pattern of his beard. This was no impostor.

"You're safe." Reagan helped Erikson lower him into a chair. "You're among friends."

His eyes darted around the command center, taking in the mixture of modern technology and ancient mystical defenses with growing bewilderment. "I don't... I can't remember..."

Stanley removed his cowboy hat as he dropped to one knee. "It's really him. Saint Michael himself."

The warrior winced, touching his temple. "That name... I know it, but..." Blood dripped from a gash above his eye.

The command center's warning systems screamed to life. Multiple breach alerts flashed across the tactical displays.

"Perimeter defenses failing!" A tech shouted from his station. "Malefic forces advancing on all sides!"

The warrior's head snapped up, combat instincts overriding his confusion. His hand found his sword's grip even as he struggled to stand.

"Sir, you're injured." Erikson steadied him. "Let us handle-"

"No." His voice carried the weight of centuries. "I may not remember who I am, but I remember how to fight."

The tactical displays showed that enemy forces were converging on their position. Whatever had brought Saint Michael to them, there was no time to process it.

Erikson crouched behind a fallen redwood, his enchanted rifle trained on the tree line. Night vision amplified the ambient light, painting the forest in shades of green. The first Malefic cultist burst from the undergrowth—but something was different. Crystalline implants pulsed beneath their skin, forming networks of artificial veins that carried corrupted magical energy.

"Contact front!" He squeezed the trigger. Blessed rounds sparked against a shimmering energy shield.

A massive shape lumbered through the trees behind the cultists.

The Bungisngis towered over its handlers, its single eye gleaming with an unnatural red light. Metallic components had been grafted onto its gray flesh, turning the already formidable creature into something worse.

"They've augmented the giant!" Stanley's voice crackled over comms. His position erupted in automatic fire.

The Bungisngis' laugh boomed through the forest, but there was nothing natural about it. The sound carried harmonic frequencies that made Erikson's enhanced combat systems crackle with interference. His heads-up display flickered and died.

Cultists advanced in coordinated patterns, their crystalline implants synchronizing with each other. Energy fields merged and overlapped, creating corridors of protection through the Order's firing lanes. The giant smashed through ancient ward stones, its augmented strength shattering protective barriers that had stood for centuries.

"They're using the Bungisngis as a focus!" Zoe's voice cut through the static. "The implants are channeling their power, amplifying their shields."

The giant's eye fired a beam of concentrated energy, slicing through the canopy. Trees crashed down around Erikson's position. He rolled clear, coming up firing. His blessed rounds pinged off the cultists' layered defenses.

"Fall back to secondary positions!" Reagan coordinated the tactical retreat. "Standard ammunition is ineffective against their shields."

The Bungisngis roared again, its technologically enhanced voice scrambling communications. Cultists moved with inhuman speed, their augmentations pushing them beyond normal limits. Crystal formations sprouted from their bodies, growing and adapting to the Order's attacks.

Erikson had never seen anything like it - the perfect merger of ancient monster and modern technology, turning an already deadly force into something that defied conventional response. The Malefic Assembly had evolved, and the Order's traditional tactics were no longer effective.

The warrior moved with fluid grace, despite his injuries, as muscle memory took over where conscious thought failed. His sword flashed in deadly arcs, cutting through the cultists' energy shields as if they were paper. Each strike carried centuries of combat experience, even if the memories themselves remained locked away.

Reagan coordinated with her tactical teams through hand signals as their comms crackled with interference. She directed suppressing fire while Zoe's sonic array targeted weak points in the cultists' defenses. Stanley's position shifted to higher ground, his blessed rounds finding gaps in the merged energy fields.

A temporal distortion rippled through the air. Elan materialized at the edge of the battlefield, Austin and Myst flanking him. They emerged from swirling mists, weapons already drawn and ready for combat.

"Mom, we got your signal!" Myst rushed to join Maya's position near the command post.

"Those implants," Austin scanned the battlefield through his rifle's scope. "They're channeling raw power from the giant."

Elan felt *Winterstar* pulse at his hip, the ancient blade vibrating with increasing intensity. The sword resonated with the warrior's presence, drawing energy from some unseen source. Raw power coursed through the weapon's hilt, spreading up Elan's arm in waves of cold fire.

The warrior - Saint Michael - paused mid-strike, his own blade humming in harmony with *Winterstar*. Their eyes met across the battle-field, recognition flickering in the saint's confused gaze. The two swords pulsed in sync, their combined energy making the air crack with potential.

"Elan," Reagan called out, "the swords - they're connecting somehow!"

The power building between the blades grew stronger, *Winterstar*'s crystal core blazing with white light. Elan could barely maintain his grip as the sword drew more energy from Saint Michael's presence. Ancient magic swirled around them both, responding to some deeper resonance neither fully understood.

Maya's skin prickled with an unnatural chill. The air around the ritual site felt wrong—like static before a lightning strike. She pressed her hand against one of the ancient ward stones, its surface cold despite the summer heat.

"Something's not right." Her fingers traced the worn runes on the stone. The usual background hum of protective magic had changed pitch, becoming discordant. "These wards are being corrupted from within."

She reached out with her inherited sensitivity to temporal energies, a gift bestowed upon her by her distant past of birth. The magical currents flowing through the ground had shifted, twisting into unfamiliar patterns.

"Mom!" Maya called to Kaira over the tactical net. "The ley lines - they're being redirected."

Before anyone could respond, dark shapes emerged from the treeline. But these weren't the tech-augmented cultists they'd been fighting. These figures moved with a liquid grace that defied human limitation. Their forms rippled and shifted, caught between human and animal aspects.

"Aswang!" Stanley's voice carried over the chaos. "They've got bloody aswang with them!"

Behind the shape-shifters came another group - robed figures moving with practiced precision. Their hands wove complex patterns in the air, ancient Filipino symbols blazing in their wake. But these weren't the traditional healers and spiritual guides Maya had read about in the Order's archives. These babaylan radiated corrupted power, their once-sacred abilities twisted to dark purpose.

The aswang's bestial forms crashed against the Order's defensive line. Blessed bullets tore through their shifting flesh, but the wounds sealed almost instantly. The corrupted babaylan's spells shattered protective wards that had stood for centuries, their violated knowledge turning ancient defenses against their makers.

The combined assault overwhelmed the perimeter. Maya watched in horror as the last ward stone cracked, its protective runes going dark. The site's final defensive barrier collapsed in a shower of mystical sparks.

They were through.

Stanley twirled the twin axes, their enchanted blades humming with ancient power. Norse runes blazed along the hafts as he waded into the mass of cultists, his cowboy hat somehow staying firmly in place despite the chaos. The axes sang through the air, cleaving through corrupted shields and augmented flesh with equal ease.

Zoe's fingers danced across her electric lute's strings, her voice rising above the battlefield's din. The instrument's modified pickups channeled both electricity and magic, each chord rippling with temporal force:

"Time slows like honey in the dark,

Your steps falter, miss their mark,

In this moment between breath and bone,

You dance to rhythms not your own..."

The song's power manifested as visible waves of energy, catching cultists in its temporal wake. Their movements became sluggish, crystal implants flickering as they struggled against the magical inter-ference.

Maya drew Moonbow's string back, the weapon's silver surface gleaming with internal light. She didn't need to look to know Myst had positioned himself exactly where she needed him. The twins moved in perfect synchronization, years of training amplified by their temporal connection.

The arrow blazed from Moonbow's string just as Myst rolled forward, drawing enemy fire. Maya's shot threaded through the gap he created, striking a corrupted babaylan in the chest. The arrow erupted in a burst of moonlight, disrupting the dark spellweaver's ritual.

"Shift left," Myst called out, already moving. Maya pivoted smoothly, another arrow materializing on Moonbow's string. Her brother's blade flashed, keeping the aswang at bay while she lined up her next shot.

The twins flowed around each other like water, Maya's arrows providing covering fire. At the same time, Myst's close-quarters combat kept enemies from closing in. Moonbow sang in her hands, each shot finding its mark with uncanny precision. The weapon's power grew stronger as she embraced its connection to Artemis, silver light trailing in the wake of every arrow.

A shimmering portal materialized at the edge of the battlefield, crackling with arcane energy. Nykronus stepped through, his dark robes billowing in an unseen wind. Asha prowled at his heels, her orange and black fur beginning to pulse with an inner light.

Maya watched as the ancient mage raised his hands, speaking words that made reality itself shudder. Lightning arced between his fingers, but not regular electricity - this energy seemed to bend and twist through multiple dimensions, leaving afterimages burned into the air.

Asha's form blurred as she darted between cultists, her glowing fur leaving trails of light that solidified into barriers of force. Where she passed, the corrupted babaylan's spells unraveled, their dark magic dissipating against her radiance.

Nykronus wove complex patterns with his staff, each gesture unleashing waves of power that transformed cultists into living statues. Their crystal implants crackled and sparked, overwhelmed by magic far older than their technological adaptations.

"Circle of binding!" Nykronus's voice boomed across the battlefield. Asha responded instantly, racing around a group of aswang in a tight spiral. Her glowing fur traced a perfect circle, and Nykronus slammed his staff into the ground. The circle erupted into a pillar of golden light, trapping the shape-shifters in mid-transformation.

Maya's next arrow flew through one of Asha's light trails, the projectile absorbing the cat's power. It struck an augmented cultist and exploded in a burst of orange and black energy, shorting out their crystalline enhancements.

Asha leaped onto the Bungisngis's shoulder, her small form now blazing like a miniature sun. The giant's cybernetic implants sparked and smoked where her light touched them. Nykronus seized the opportunity, his hands weaving a complex counter-spell that targeted the creature's magical vulnerabilities.

The cat's fur pulsed in time with Nykronus's incantation, each wave of light stripping away layers of technological corruption from the ancient monster. Together, they worked to separate the giant's natural form from its artificial augmentations, their combined power cutting through the Malefic Assembly's dark innovations.

The warrior staggered against a fallen tree, his breathing labored. Despite his injuries, power radiated from him in waves—raw, untamed energy that made the air crackle. Behind him, ethereal shapes flickered in and out of existence, like television static trying to form a picture.

Maya caught glimpses of massive wings stretching outward, their ghostly outline spanning twenty feet or more. But they wouldn't fully manifest, dissolving into motes of light before reforming again. The warrior's face contorted in frustration as he tried to control the power surging through him.

"I should know how..." His fingers tightened on his sword hilt. "The knowledge is there, just out of reach."

Another pulse of energy rippled outward. This time, the wings solidified for a brief moment - crystalline feathers of pure light catching the moonlight. Their brilliance illuminated the entire battlefield, causing the cultists to shield their eyes from the light. But just as quickly, they fragmented back into dancing particles.

The warrior growled in frustration. Each attempt to manifest his proper form sent spasms of pain across his features. The wings continued their strobe-like appearance - flashing into existence for split seconds before dissolving again. Sometimes only one wing would form, or they would appear as mere outlines of divine light.

"Your body remembers, even if your mind doesn't," Nykronus called out. "Don't force it. Let the power flow naturally."

The warrior nodded, relaxing his rigid posture slightly. The wings stabilized somewhat, though they remained translucent and flickering. Their light pulsed in rhythm with his heartbeat, growing stronger when he moved to defend his allies and fading when he tried to consciously control them.

Even in this diminished state, his presence affected the battlefield. Where the spectral wings passed, cultists' augmentations malfunctioned. The corrupted babaylan's spells unraveled. The aswang retreated from his flickering radiance, their shapeshifting powers disrupted by proximity to his divine energy.

Reagan signaled to Austin with practiced efficiency, their years of tactical training evident in every movement. She took up position behind a fallen column while Austin circled left, his rifle covering the eastern approach. No words needed - they'd run this pattern countless times in preparation for moments like this.

Austin caught Maya's eye and tapped his shoulder twice. She nocked an arrow, understanding instantly. The move they'd perfected during late-night training sessions in the backyard came naturally now. Austin dropped to one knee, providing a stable shooting platform while Maya used his shoulder to steady her aim. Moonbow's silver light illuminated their synchronized movements.

Myst slid into position beside them, his blade ready. The twins moved like mirror images, Maya's arrows creating openings that Myst exploited with precise strikes. They'd developed this rhythm since childhood, spending hours coordinating their attacks until they could anticipate each other's moves without needing to speak.

Kaira's voice cut through the chaos with familiar authority. "Pattern Delta!"

The family shifted seamlessly. Reagan and Austin split wide, creating a crossfire zone. Maya elevated her position while Myst dropped low, establishing layered fields of fire. They'd drilled these formations in their backyard, using garden furniture as cover and tennis balls as projectiles. Now those playful practice sessions paid deadly dividends.

Elan moved to the center of their formation, *Winterstar* blazing in his grip. His presence completed their defensive circle—a position they'd refined over years of Sunday afternoon "training picnics," where combat drills mixed with family meals. Each member knew their role, understood their spacing, and could read subtle shifts in stance that telegraphed the next move.

The family unit flowed like water, years of practice evident in every coordinated strike. Maya's arrows created openings that Myst exploited. Reagan and Austin's covering fire allowed Kaira to maneuver. Elan's sword work complemented them all, filling gaps and strengthening weak points. They weren't just fighting as individuals - they were moving as a single organism, their bonds forged through countless hours of preparation.

Maya watched the last ward stone crack, its protective runes sputtering like dying embers. The corrupted babaylan's dark magic seeped into the ground, tainting the ancient ley lines that powered the site's defenses. Each pulse of their twisted power sent tremors through the earth, weakening barriers that had stood for centuries.

The Bungisngis slammed its fists into the ground, cybernetic enhancements amplifying its already formidable strength. Fissures spread outward from the impact points, cutting through the remaining protective circles like knife wounds. Dark energy bubbled up through the cracks, corroding the sacred symbols etched into the stone.

"The outer ring is compromised!" Reagan's voice carried over the chaos. She fired another burst at an approaching aswang, but the creature's liquid form simply flowed around the blessed bullets.

Moonbow pulsed in Maya's hands as she targeted another corrupted babaylan. The arrow struck true, disrupting their ritual, but the damage was already done. Their dark magic had taken root in the site's foundations, spreading like poison through its mystical infrastructure.

The air grew thick with conflicting energies—the pure power of the ancient wards battling against the Assembly's corrupted forces. Sparks of golden light clashed with tendrils of oily darkness. The site's defenses fought back, but they were being overwhelmed by the sheer volume of tainted power being channeled against them.

Maya felt the shift in her bones as another ward fell. The protective dome that had shielded the site flickered and partially collapsed, leaving gaps in its magical coverage. Through these breaches poured more cultists, their crystal implants glowing with stolen power.

The sacred ground beneath their feet began to change. Where the corruption spread, the grass withered and died. Ancient stones cracked and blackened. The very air became harder to breathe as the site's natural defenses were twisted and perverted by the Assembly's dark influence.

Stanley's axes cut through another wave of cultists, but for every one that fell, two more pushed through the failing barriers. The site's remaining wards flared weakly, struggling against the tide of corruption that threatened to overwhelm them completely.

The warrior St. Michael's muscles tensed as another wave of cultists approached. Though his memories remained fragmented, his body knew exactly what to do. His sword arm moved with fluid precision, his sword cutting through the air in practiced arcs that spoke of centuries of combat experience.

Three cultists attacked simultaneously. He parried the first strike without conscious thought, his blade finding gaps in their augmented armor that he shouldn't have known existed. His footwork shifted seamlessly into patterns learned long ago, each step placing him exactly where he needed to be.

"This stance..." He blocked an overhead strike while pivoting to dodge another. The movements felt as natural as breathing, muscle memory carrying him through complex defensive formations that his mind couldn't quite remember learning.

A corrupted babaylan hurled a sphere of dark energy at him. His free hand rose automatically, fingers tracing a sigil in the air. Golden light erupted from the gesture, completely dissolving the attack. The display of divine power surprised him as much as his opponents.

"How did I..." He stared at his hand for a split second before instinct took over again. His sword moved in a complex pattern, leaving trails of holy light that coalesced into burning symbols. The nearest cultists stumbled backward, their crystal implants crackling and smoking at the mere proximity to his divine energy.

More symbols appeared around him, each one perfectly formed despite his conscious mind not recognizing them. They hung in the air like burning brands, responding to subtle shifts in his stance. When he stepped forward, they moved with him, creating a mobile zone of divine protection that disrupted both technological and magical attacks.

His body remembered what his mind had forgotten - the weight of wings he couldn't fully manifest, the precise application of divine power, the ancient forms of combat that had once been as familiar as his own name. Each movement unlocked another fragment of muscle memory, his physical form recognizing its true nature even as his thoughts struggled to catch up.

Maya watched as the warrior moved with impossible grace, each strike precise and devastating. Members of the Order of St. Michael emerged from their defensive positions, their faces showing recognition. An elderly priest crossed himself, tears streaming down his weathered cheeks. A younger nun gripped her rosary so tight her knuckles went white.

"It's true," the priest whispered. "The stories passed down..."

The warrior's movements triggered something profound in Maya's mind. Images flashed through her consciousness - ancient battles, divine wings spread across medieval skies, a sword blazing with holy fire. The memories weren't hers, yet they felt intimately familiar, as if she'd witnessed them firsthand.

Another flash - she saw the warrior as he once was, radiant and terrible in his divine aspect. The image overlapped with his current form, revealing what was missing and what had been lost. His struggles to manifest his true power made sense now; he was fighting against centuries of dormant muscle memory.

The Order members moved in practiced formation around him, their modern tactical gear contrasting with the ancient symbols emblazoned on their armor. They knew these movements, had trained for this moment through generations of sacred preparation.

The corrupted babaylan's defenses crumbled under the combined assault. Their dark magic couldn't stand against divine power wielded with such precision. The aswang retreated, their shapeshifting abilities disrupted by the warrior's presence.

Victory came at a terrible price. The sacred site lay in ruins, its ancient wards shattered beyond repair. Half the Order members who'd participated in the defense lay wounded or worse. The ground itself was scorched black where corrupted magic had taken root, the damage perhaps permanent.

Maya watched as Austin helped Reagan limp away from the battlefield, her leg badly injured. Myst clutched his side where an aswang's claws had found their mark. Even in triumph, the cost of their stand weighed heavily on them.

Maya surveyed the devastation alongside Nykronus. The ancient ritual site, once humming with sacred energy, now lay silent and dead.

Blackened stone crumbled beneath her feet as she picked her way through the debris. Where holy symbols had been carved into the ground, only twisted scars remained.

"The ley lines are corrupted," Nykronus said, kneeling to touch the scorched earth. "The Assembly's dark magic has poisoned them to their very core. It will take decades, perhaps centuries, for this ground to heal - if it ever does."

Reagan held up a shattered ward stone, its protective runes now dark and lifeless. "We lost three centuries of accumulated power. The barriers that kept this place hidden, the ancient spells woven into its foundations - all gone." Her voice cracked. "The Order has maintained this site since the Crusades. Now there's nothing left to maintain."

Asha prowled the perimeter, her fur still glowing faintly. Where she stepped, tiny sparks of pure energy tried to take root, only to wither in the corrupted soil. The cat's ears lay flat against her head, sensing the wrongness that now permeated the sacred ground.

The warrior stood apart from the others, his translucent wings still flickering in and out of existence. His face showed a mix of anger and deep sorrow as he took in the destruction. Though his memories remained fragmented, the weight of this loss pressed against his soul.

"I should have remembered sooner," he said, gripping his sword hilt. "If I'd accessed my full power earlier..." The wings flared briefly before fading again, his frustration evident in every line of his body.

Nykronus approached him carefully. "The fact that you remembered at all is remarkable. Your divine essence has been dormant for centuries. That you managed to manifest even this much of your true form likely saved many lives today."

The warrior's response was cut short by a pulse of energy from his sword. Golden light rippled along the blade, responding to his turbulent emotions. The weapon recognized its true wielder, even if he couldn't fully remember his own nature.

Nykronus stepped closer to examine the blade at the warrior's side. His eyes widened with recognition.

"Elan, your sword - Stellata d'Inferno. And its twin..." He gestured to where Heavenshard lay wrapped in cloth near Michael's pack. "Lama di Eternità."

Elan's hand drifted to Winterstar's hilt. The moment his fingers touched the cold metal, energy surged through him. Images flashed through his mind - the swords being forged simultaneously, one from a fallen star's burning core, the other from a fragment of heaven itself. He saw them wielded together by divine hands, cutting through darkness with perfectly balanced strikes of judgment and mercy.

"They're connected," Elan said. "Two halves of the same whole."

Stanley nodded eagerly. "I studied these in the Order's armory archives. Stellata brings winter's judgment, burning cold enough to freeze hell itself. While Lama di Eternità guides with truth's light, healing what its sister blade destroys. Together, they're meant to maintain balance - one to punish, one to restore."

The warrior looked between them, frustration evident on his face. "I don't understand any of this. These weapons, this place..." He gestured at his flickering wings. "Even my own form eludes me. How did I get here? What am I meant to do?"

"The swords know," Stanley said. "They were forged for a single righteous wielder - someone who could balance divine wrath with divine grace. The legends say wielding them separately risks shattering reality itself."

"The memories will return," Nykronus assured him. "Your essence recognizes these blades, even if your mind does not yet remember."

Reagan spread satellite photos across the makeshift command center they'd set up in the Durant Estate's living room. Red circles marked attack sites spanning three continents - each targeting locations of mystical significance.

"The pattern's unmistakable," Kaira traced lines between the locations. "Every strike occurred during a lunar phase transition. They're not just hitting random targets - they're following ancient ley line confluences."

"The Assembly's gotten bold," Reagan pulled up incident reports on her tablet. "Police departments worldwide reported the same MO - corrupted babaylan leading the attacks, backed by augmented cultists and aswang strike teams."

Maya studied the photos while Asha prowled between them, her tail twitching. The cat's fur glowed brighter near specific marked locations, confirming their supernatural significance.

"They're gathering power," Myst said, pointing to energy readings from the sites. "Each corrupted location feeds dark energy into their network. The more sites they take, the stronger they become."

The family gathered around the dining table, sharing worried looks. Austin pulled up additional intelligence from Order sources on his laptop while Stanley examined ancient texts for historical precedents.

"If they corrupt enough sacred sites," Elan gripped Winterstar's hilt, drawing comfort from its cold certainty, "they could permanently damage the world's magical infrastructure."

"Worse," Kaira's voice was grim. "They're not just destroying - they're converting. Each corrupted site becomes a beacon for dark forces. A foothold for whatever they're trying to bring into our world."

Reagan's phone buzzed; her face paled as she read the message. "Order intelligence just identified their next targets." She pulled up a map showing three locations pulsing with warning indicators. "They're planning simultaneous attacks on the winter solstice - one in the Philippines, one in Ireland, and one right here in California."

"The Philippines site," Kaira leaned forward, "that's where the Three Marias converge. If they corrupt that nexus point..."

"And the Irish location is an ancient Order sanctuary," Stanley added. "Houses artifacts we can't afford to lose."

"The California target," Reagan zoomed in on the map, "is Mount Shasta. One of the strongest natural wells of pure energy on the West Coast."

Maya traced the lines between attack sites on the map, her finger hovering over each point where the Assembly had struck. Something about the pattern nagged at her consciousness - not just the timing with lunar phases, but the specific locations themselves.

Asha jumped onto the table, her paw landing directly on Mount Shasta's marker. The cat's fur glowed brighter, and Maya felt a surge of recognition. These weren't random sacred sites - they formed a larger geometric pattern, like a complex circuit board etched across the Earth's surface.

"Look," Maya pointed to where three ley lines intersected. "Each corrupted location serves as an amplifier for the others. They're not just gathering power - they're building a network. The dark energy flows between sites, growing stronger with each new connection."

Across the table, Elan's hands tightened on Winterstar's hilt. The sword pulsed with cold light, responding to some fragment of memory stirring in his mind. Images flashed through his thoughts - similar patterns carved into ancient stone, divine wings spread across star-filled skies, battles fought at nexus points of power.

"I've seen this before," he said, his voice distant. "Not these exact locations, but the strategy. During the first war..." He trailed off, frustration crossing his face as the memory slipped away.

Nykronus watched Elan closely as the warrior's eyes glazed over, his grip tightening on Winterstar's hilt. The sword pulsed with an icy blue light that seemed to reach across the room toward where Heavenshard lay wrapped in cloth. A golden glow answered from beneath the fabric, creating a bridge of luminescence between the two blades.

"The swords," Nykronus stepped forward, his voice barely above a whisper. "They're communicating."

Elan's breath caught as images flooded his mind. He saw Michael - not as he appeared now, but radiant and terrible in his full divine glory. The archangel wielded both blades in perfect harmony, Winterstar's judgment balanced by Heavenshard's mercy. The vision shifted, showing battles fought across centuries, the swords passing from wielder to wielder, always seeking to be reunited.

"The blades remember," Nykronus placed a hand on Elan's shoulder, steadying him as the visions continued. "Michael's presence has awakened something in them - and in you. These aren't just memories of the past. The swords are showing you possibilities, paths that might yet be taken."

The golden light from Heavenshard intensified, meeting Winterstar's cold radiance in a swirling dance of energy. Each pulse brought new fragments of understanding—glimpses of ancient knowledge encoded in the very essence of the divine weapons.

"Your connection to Michael runs deeper than we realized," Nykronus observed as the light show began to fade. "The swords recognized it before any of us did. They're trying to tell us something about who you really are."

Maya watched her father struggle with the fragments of his true nature. Each recovered memory seemed to physically pain him, like pieces of a broken mirror cutting as they tried to reassemble themselves. The wings flickered at his back, more suggestion than substance, unable to fully manifest while his identity remained fractured.

"The Three Marias site," Maya said, drawing attention back to the map. "It's not just a convergence point - it's a keystone. If they corrupt that location, it could cascade through the entire network they've built. The other sites would amplify the corruption exponentially."

Elan nodded, another fragment clicking into place. "The sanctuaries were placed at these points for a reason. They don't just protect - they maintain balance. Corrupt one, and the others become vulnerable."

Elan studied the pattern of attack sites marked on the map. His military training kicked in, enabling him to recognize the methodical nature of the Assembly's strikes. These weren't random targets of opportunity - this was a coordinated campaign.

"They're isolating each sanctuary," he traced the lines between corrupted locations. "Cutting off support routes, surrounding key positions. This is siege warfare on a global scale."

Kaira leaned over his shoulder, her architectural background lending a fresh perspective. "The sacred sites form a natural defensive network. By taking these specific points, they're not just gathering power - they're dismantling our ability to respond."

"We need to split up," Reagan pulled up personnel rosters on her tablet. "The Order doesn't have enough trained teams to defend all three locations simultaneously."

Maya placed Asha on the table, watching as the cat walked deliberately between the marked targets. The feline's fur glowed brighter near certain intersections, confirming their supernatural significance.

"The Philippines team needs someone who understands the Three Marias," Kaira said. "I should lead that group."

Elan's jaw tightened at the suggestion of separation, but he nodded.

"Stanley and I will take Mount Shasta. The Order's strongest presence is here - we'll need that backup when they strike."

"Ireland," Reagan checked her phone, "Austin's already coordinating with the Order chapter there. We can have a team on the ground within-"

A sharp crack interrupted her planning. Asha's fur stood on end, every hair blazing with warning light. The cat let out a yowl that made their ears ring.

Elan felt Winterstar pulse at his hip, the sword's cold energy responding to some unseen threat. Across the room, Heavenshard's golden glow pierced through its wrappings.

The map on the table began to smoke where Asha's paw made contact with it. New lines of power appeared, burning themselves into the paper - connections they hadn't seen before, revealing a pattern far more complex and dangerous than they'd imagined.

"That's impossible," Kaira breathed, staring at the emerging design. "These ley lines... they're not just connecting the sanctuaries. They're forming a-"

Another crack split the air. The map burst into flames.

Maya stared at the burning pattern emerging on the map, her heart pounding. The lines weren't just connecting - they formed a massive pentagram spanning across continents. But this wasn't a simple five-pointed star. Additional lines crisscrossed between the points, creating an intricate web of dark energy channels.

"It's a summoning circle," Nykronus moved closer, his face grim. "The corrupted sites aren't just power sources - they're anchor points for something far worse."

Asha's fur blazed brighter as more details burned themselves into the map. More miniature pentagrams nested within the larger pattern, each one positioned at a nexus of corrupted ley lines. The cat's tail lashed back and forth as she traced the emerging design with her paw.

"The Three Marias site," Kaira said, her finger hovering over the central point in the Philippines. "It's not just a keystone - it's the focal point for the entire array. These other locations..." She traced the lines connecting to Mount Shasta and Ireland. "They're like amplifiers, channeling power toward the center."

Maya watched as the last lines seared themselves into the paper, completing the terrible geometry of the Assembly's actual plan. The nested pentagrams pulsed with a sickly light, each one a potential gateway for whatever horror they intended to summon.

"They're not trying to corrupt the sanctuaries," Elan's hand gripped Winterstar's hilt as understanding dawned. "They're turning our own defensive network into a weapon. Each sacred site they corrupt becomes part of their summoning array."

The map crumbled to ash, but the image was burned into their minds—a vast web of dark energy, ready to channel untold power into a single, devastating ritual.

CHAPTER

FIVE

Elan's study smelled of leather and old parchment. Moonlight filtered through the bay windows, casting long shadows across the mahogany desk where ancient texts lay open. The soft glow caught the edges of mounted weapons that lined the walls - each one with its own history, its own battle scars.

Michael stood before a glass case containing a weathered gladius. A halo shifted between solid and translucent above his head as he examined the Roman short sword. The blade's copper-green patina spoke of centuries buried beneath sacred ground.

"This belonged to Marcus Aurelius." Michael's voice carried the weight of memory. His armored hand phased through the glass. "He wielded it at the Battle of Carnuntum."

Elan looked up from the texts spread across his desk. "The Emperor himself?"

"One of his Praetorian Guard. A member of our Order, though we bore a different name then." Michael moved to study a Celtic war axe mounted nearby. "Each weapon here has touched our fight against the darkness. Some failed. Others prevailed."

The archangel's golden armor caught the moonlight, creating

patterns that danced across the walls of the study. His wings remained folded close, yet their presence filled the room with an other-worldly energy that made the air crack with potential.

"You've guided them all?" Elan asked.

"I choose those who are ready to bear the burden." Michael turned to face him. "Just as I chose you."

The warrior-angel's gaze held centuries of battles won and lost, of champions risen and fallen. His face carried both the serene beauty of heaven and the stern resolve of a general who had led countless armies.

"The weapons are but tools," Michael gestured to the collection. "It is the wielder's heart that determines the outcome. You understand this better than most, Elan Durant."

"Where is Maya?" Michael's gaze swept the study, noting the absence of Elan's daughter.

"With Nykronus." Elan checked his watch. "Reagan and Kaira are there too. They're meeting at Reagan's place to work out our next moves."

Michael's wings rustled. "The ancient one has much knowledge to share, but his methods may not be enough."

"That's why I sent Kaira and Reagan with them." Elan strapped on his shoulder holster. "You know they run the Order's operations on the West Coast."

Myst perched on the window seat, his notebook balanced on one knee. The conversation between his father and the archangel fascinated him, but something nagged at his thoughts. He sketched quick notes, connecting lines between theories that had formed since meeting Michael.

The archangel's amnesia didn't align with biblical accounts. Every text Myst had studied portrayed Michael as all-knowing, eternal. Yet here he stood, gaps in his celestial memory as evident as the scars on his armor.

"Excuse me," Myst cleared his throat. The sound came out smaller than intended. Both his father and Michael turned to face him.

Michael's piercing gaze made Myst's skin prickle. The archangel's presence filled the room with an electric charge that made focusing difficult. "You have questions."

"Your memory loss." Myst flipped through his notes. "The texts mention you leading armies since the beginning of time. But you don't remember parts of your past. That suggests something happened. Something powerful enough to affect an archangel."

Michael's wings shifted, catching moonlight like polished bronze.

"The timing coincides with the rise of certain pagan cults." Myst's voice grew stronger as he laid out his theory. "Specifically, ones that practiced ritual magic aimed at usurping divine power."

"An interesting hypothesis." Michael's tone revealed nothing.

Myst fumbled with his pen. "There are accounts of artifacts capable of binding celestial beings. If someone had found one-"

"You believe I was trapped?" Michael's expression remained unreadable.

"Or transformed. The texts aren't clear on whether archangels can be..." Myst trailed off, suddenly aware of how presumptuous he sounded.

The silence stretched between them, broken only by the soft rustle of Michael's wings. Elan watched the exchange with careful attention, his hand resting near the hilt of his sword.

"Your mind serves you well," Michael said at last. "But some mysteries are better left unexplored."

Myst nodded, dropping his gaze back to his notebook. The weight of unasked questions hung in the air like a cloud of smoke.

Elan studied Michael's guarded expression. The archangel's response to Myst's theory confirmed his own suspicions about the nature of the memory loss. He'd seen similar patterns in veterans recovering from trauma - the careful way they navigated around specific topics, the strategic gaps in their recollections.

"There might be ways to recover those memories," Elan said. "The Order must have records, rituals perhaps-"

"The traditional methods have failed." Michael's wings shifted, casting fractured shadows across the floor. "Prayer, meditation, even direct communion with the divine. The memories remain locked away."

"What about less traditional approaches?" Elan leaned forward in his chair. "The Order has access to artifacts, sacred relics that might-"

"Too dangerous." Michael's armor clinked as he paced the study. "Many who sought such power were corrupted by it. I will not risk unleashing something worse in pursuit of memories that may be better left forgotten."

Elan understood the weight behind those words. Some doors, once opened, couldn't be closed again. Yet the tactical part of his mind couldn't ignore the strategic disadvantage of an amnesiac archangel leading their fight.

"Then we start small," Elan said. "Focus on recent memories first, establish a timeline. Work our way back methodically."

Michael paused by the weapons case. "You suggest a soldier's approach."

"It served me well in the Corps. Break down the impossible into manageable pieces."

The archangel's expression softened slightly. "Perhaps you're right. But first, you both need training. The enemy grows stronger while we debate the past."

Myst looked up from his notebook. "Training? With you?"

"The Order's traditional methods, combined with what I remember of heaven's warfare." Michael's wings spread slightly, filling the study with their metallic gleam. "We begin tonight."

Elan nodded, recognizing the shift in Michael's stance from contemplative to commanding. The discussion of memories would wait - for now, they needed to prepare for whatever darkness approached. His marine training kicked in, already calculating what equipment they'd need.

"Oorah," Elan said, rising from his chair.

The training room beneath Elan's house hummed with ancient power. Runes carved into the stone walls glowed with a soft amber light, creating a sacred circle where heaven's warfare could be safely practiced. Myst's fingers traced the familiar symbols: protection, containment, and strength.

Michael stood in the center, his armor catching the runic light. His wings remained folded tightly against his back, yet their presence added to the crackling energy that filled the space.

"Watch closely." The archangel's movements flowed like liquid metal. His blade carved geometric patterns through the air - circles within circles, lines intersecting at precise angles. Each form seemed to bend reality around it, leaving traces of golden light in its wake.

Elan mirrored the movements with his own sword, his years of martial training allowing him to adapt to the celestial forms with ease. His blade sang through the air, not quite matching Michael's perfect geometry but coming close.

Myst hung back, notebook forgotten in his hands as he studied the patterns. Something about the forms nagged at his mind - they reminded him of the diagrams in ancient texts, the sacred geometry used in ritual magic. But these weren't just shapes drawn on paper. These were living mathematics, equations written in motion and light.

"The angles matter," Michael demonstrated a complex sequence that seemed to fold space around his blade. "Each degree corresponds to a divine principle. Forty-five for justice, ninety for truth, thirty for mercy."

Myst's eyes widened as he recognized the pattern. The forms weren't just combat moves - they were prayers written in motion, each sequence a complete verse in the language of heaven. He watched his father execute a combination, seeing how the angles built upon each other like words forming sentences.

"The sword is secondary," Michael corrected Elan's grip. "The true weapon is the sacred geometry you create. Your blade simply traces the patterns that already exist in creation."

Myst scribbled quick notes, mapping out the relationships between angles and divine attributes. The mathematical precision of heaven's warfare fascinated him. Each movement was both art and science, beauty and devastating power wrapped in pure mathematics.

Elan's muscles burned as he executed another sequence. The movements felt familiar—not just from his Marine training, but from something more profound and older. His body remembered patterns his mind had forgotten, like echoes from another life.

"These forms," Elan paused mid-stance. "They're similar to Roman gladiatorial techniques."

Michael nodded. "The Order preserved many combat arts through the centuries. Some were passed down through military traditions."

As Elan shifted into the following sequence, Winterstar hummed in his hands. The blade's surface rippled like water, catching starlight and responding to Michael's presence. It's a usual cold bite warmed, becoming almost eager in its movements.

"Your sword recognizes heaven's authority," Michael stepped closer, examining the blade. "It was forged in sacred fire, tempered with divine purpose. She likes you; you are truly bonded."

Winterstar's surface shimmered brighter, its metal singing a note that made the runic circles pulse with increased intensity. The weapon seemed to lean toward Michael of its own accord, drawn to his celestial energy.

Michael reached out, his armored hand hovering above the blade. The moment his fingers neared Winterstar's surface, a spark jumped between them. The archangel jerked back, his wings flaring wide as his eyes grew distant.

"The forging..." Michael's voice carried a hint of recognition. "I remember flames that burned with winter's chill. A star that fell..." He pressed his hand to his temple, ancient memories struggling to break through.

"What else?" Elan kept Winterstar steady, watching as Michael's face contorted with the effort of remembering.

"Snow falling in Rome. The smith worked through the night while I..." Michael's voice faltered. His wings trembled, shedding motes of golden light. "The metal came from..."

The memory slipped away like water through his fingers. Michael lowered his hand, his expression returning to its usual stern composure. But something had changed - a crack in the wall that sealed away his past.

The clash of blades echoed through the training room. Elan lunged forward, Winterstar cutting through the air in a perfect forty-five-degree arc. Michael parried with Heavenshard, their weapons meeting in a shower of divine sparks.

The moment their swords connected, Michael staggered back. His eyes went wide, wings spreading involuntarily as images flooded his mind.

Rain poured over the Tiber River; lightning illuminated the massive bulk of Hadrian's Mausoleum. Angels perched on its parapets, their wings spread against storm-dark skies. Below, Roman legionaries fought shoulder-to-shoulder with celestial warriors, their blades slick with demon blood.

A Roman general stood at the fortress gates, sword raised high as creatures of shadow pressed against the Roman lines. Michael saw himself there, golden armor blazing like a second sun as he led a charge against the darkness.

"The siege," Michael gasped, dropping to one knee. His wings trembled, shedding particles of light that danced through the air. "Hadrian's tomb... we defended it."

The battlefield stretched before his mind's eye - a hellscape of mud and blood and holy fire. Lightning struck in impossible patterns, drawing sacred geometries across the sky. Demons shrieked as they fell, their bodies dissolving into ash. Angels wielded flaming swords alongside mortal steel, while priests chanted prayers that made the very air shimmer with power.

Water from the Tiber rose in great walls, blessed by divine command to crash down upon the enemy ranks. The Earth split, and the heavens roared as all elements joined the battle. The very stones of Rome seemed to pulse with sacred energy, responding to the clash between celestial and infernal forces.

Elan lowered Winterstar, watching as Michael pressed both hands to his temples. The archangel's armor rang with a sound like distant bells, his form flickering between solid and ethereal as the memory took hold.

"I remember," Michael's voice cracked with the weight of centuries. "We fought to protect something hidden beneath the mausoleum. A relic of tremendous power..."

Myst's hand trembled as he sketched the geometric patterns. His vision blurred, notebook falling from nerveless fingers as ancient memories crashed through his mind like a tidal wave.

Stone walls rose around him - not the training room's familiar confines, but the torch-lit corridors of a Roman villa. The scent of olive oil and incense filled his nostrils. His small hands traced similar patterns on papyrus while an old man in a toga nodded approvingly.

"The angles must be precise, young one," the teacher's voice echoed across centuries. "These are not mere drawings - they are keys to divine power."

Myst gasped, stumbling back against the training room wall. The memory felt real, lived-in, complete with sensations and emotions he'd never experienced. Yet they were his memories, from another life, another time.

"Dad," Myst's voice cracked. "I remember studying these forms. In Rome. Before..."

Elan crossed the room in three quick strides, steadying his son with a firm grip on his shoulder. The tactical part of his mind clicked pieces into place: Michael's fractured memories, Myst's sudden recall, and the geometric forms that seemed to bridge heaven and earth. This wasn't a coincidence.

"The patterns you're drawing," Elan picked up Myst's fallen notebook. "They match the forms Michael's teaching exactly."

"Because I learned them before." Myst's eyes were distant, seeing across time. "In my first life. We were preparing for something... something big."

Michael's wings rustled as he approached. "The siege I remembered. These forms were part of Rome's defense."

Elan studied the diagrams in Myst's notebook, comparing them to the glowing patterns Michael had traced in the air. The precision, the mathematical relationships between angles - it was all there, preserved across centuries in his son's muscle memory.

"We need to know more." Elan's Marine background kicked in, assessing tactical advantages. "If Myst remembers studying these forms, there might be records, scrolls, something preserved from that time."

"The Vatican archives," Myst whispered, ancient knowledge surfacing. "My teacher... he stored his most important texts there."

Elan held his phone up so everyone could see Theodora, one of the Order's oldest members, on the screen. She was calling from Benevento headquarters. The historian's face looked tired, but her eyes sparkled with excitement as she sorted through ancient papers at her desk from the Vatican Archives.

"I found something remarkable," Theodora adjusted her glasses, "Records of Saint Michael's last known apparition before his appearance in San Francisco. It was in Tlaxcala, Mexico, in 1631."

Michael's brow furrowed as he tried to grasp at memories that weren't there. His wings shifted restlessly, casting moving shadows across the training room walls.

"The records say he appeared to a young indigenous man named Diego Lázaro," Theodora continued, holding up a yellowed document. "He revealed the location of a spring with healing properties. The site became the Shrine of San Miguel del Milagro."

"I don't remember this," Michael said, his voice tight with frustration.

Elan observed the archangel's reaction. Each revelation seemed to pain him, like pressing on a wound that hadn't fully healed.

"The shrine still stands," Theodora added. "Pilgrims visit it to this day."

Myst closed his notebook with a decisive snap. "We should go there. If it was Michael's last known location, there might be clues about what happened to his memories."

"Agreed," Elan nodded, his tactical mind already plotting logistics. "If something happened there that affected Michael's memory, we might find traces of it."

Tlaxcala, Mexico

The old church in Tlaxcala stood against the Mexican sky, its weathered stone walls holding centuries of prayers. Elan's boots crunched on the gravel path as he approached the site of Saint Michael's last known apparition. The air felt different here - charged with an ancient power that made Winterstar hum at his side.

Myst trailed behind him, notebook in hand, documenting the subtle changes in atmosphere. His fingers traced the air, following invisible lines of force that seemed to converge on the church.

"There," Michael pointed to a worn stone archway partially hidden by climbing vines. Ancient symbols carved into the stone pulsed with a faint golden light as they approached. "The entrance to the sanctuary."

Beyond the arch, rough-hewn steps descended into darkness. As they moved deeper underground, the walls began to glow with a soft amber radiance. Geometric patterns similar to those they'd practiced emerged from beneath centuries of dust—sacred mathematics etched in stone.

The stairway opened into a vast circular chamber. At its center, a spring bubbled up through carved channels in the floor, its waters catching and reflecting light in impossible ways. The entire room was inscribed with overlapping circles and triangles, creating a complex mandala of protective geometry.

"The wards are still active," Michael's wings brushed against symbols that flared at his touch. "These patterns... they're the same ones we used in Rome."

Elan felt the power thrumming through the stone beneath his feet. The protection spells woven into the sanctuary's very foundation remained strong, undimmed by time. Each line and angle contributed to an intricate defense that even centuries couldn't erode.

Water from the spring trickled through channels that followed the geometric patterns, creating a living circuit of blessed power. The liquid seemed to glow from within, carrying the same divine energy that made Winterstar sing.

"The spring Diego Lázaro found," Myst knelt beside one of the channels, his fingers hovering above the luminescent water. "But this chamber predates his vision. Someone built this sanctuary long before Saint Michael appeared to him."

Elan's flashlight beam caught dark stains on the stone walls. Not rust or water damage - these marks bore the distinct pattern of ancient battle. Scorch marks from holy fire scarred the ceiling in geometric patterns, while deep gouges in the floor spoke of weapons far more powerful than mere steel.

"Someone tried to breach this sanctuary," he said, running his fingers along a particularly deep slash in the wall. The stone still hummed with residual energy, making his skin tingle.

Myst examined the damaged sections, comparing them to his notes. "These burns match the defensive patterns we practiced. Someone activated the wards - violently."

They reached a heavy stone door covered in celestial script. Michael placed his hand on the surface, but nothing happened. His wings drooped slightly.

"The locks have been changed," he said. "My authority alone isn't enough anymore."

Elan unsheathed Winterstar while Myst pulled out his notebook. The blade's cold light illuminated more geometric patterns carved around the doorframe.

"Dad, here," Myst pointed to specific symbols. "We need to trace these forms simultaneously. It's like a combination lock, but with sacred geometry."

Elan positioned himself on one side of the door while Myst took the other. Following his son's directions, Elan used Winterstar to trace precise angles in the air. Myst mirrored his movements, creating complementary patterns that made the carved symbols pulse with increasing brightness.

The door's surface began to glow as father and son worked in perfect synchronization, their movements flowing like a choreographed dance. Each completed form built upon the last, weaving a complex web of divine energy.

With a sound like distant bells, the massive door swung inward. Beyond lay a circular chamber untouched by time. At its center stood an altar of pure white stone, and upon it rested something wrapped in cloth that shimmered with its own inner light.

Elan approached the altar, Winterstar's glow intensifying with each step. The shimmering cloth seemed to pulse in response, like a living thing sensing their presence. His fingers tingled as he reached for the fabric, some instinct telling him this was what they'd been searching for.

The cloth fell away to reveal an intricate construct of light and geometry floating above the stone. Golden lines traced complex patterns in the air, forming a three-dimensional seal that rotated slowly. Each facet caught the light differently, refracting it into impossible colors. At its core, a dense cluster of symbols pulsed with barely contained power.

Michael staggered back, his wings flaring wide. Recognition blazed across his face as the seal's light played across his armor. His hands trembled as he reached toward it, then pulled back sharply as if burned.

"This is..." Michael's voice cracked. "This is what took my memories. I remember standing here, agreeing to..." He pressed his hands to his temples, fighting against the seal's power. "The Order needed me to forget something. Something vital."

The construct spun faster as Michael spoke, its patterns shifting and realigning like a celestial combination lock. Each rotation revealed new layers of complexity - barriers designed to contain not just memories, but entire chunks of reality.

"It's not just a seal," Michael said through gritted teeth. "It's a key. My memories were locked away to protect..." His words cut off as another wave of resistance from the construct washed over him. The seal flared brighter, actively fighting his attempts to remember.

Elan watched as Michael's form flickered between solid and ethereal, the archangel's very essence struggling against bonds he himself had apparently accepted centuries ago. The construct's light cast strange shadows through Michael's wings, highlighting the tension in every line of his body as he fought against his own forgotten choices.

Myst's fingers traced the geometric patterns in the air, mirroring the seal's rotation. His movements held a practiced grace that went beyond his current lifetime. The complex mathematics flowed through him with the ease of muscle memory—knowledge carried across centuries.

"These configurations," Myst's voice held a mix of wonder and certainty. "I designed them. Or rather, I helped design them. I think..."

Elan watched his son work, noting how the seal's light seemed to bend toward Myst's gestures. The construct responded to his presence, its rotations slowing slightly as if recognizing a familiar touch.

Michael moved closer to Myst, his wings casting prismatic

shadows through the seal's glow. "The Order must have needed some-thing hidden-something so important that even I agreed to forget it."

"Look at these variance patterns," Myst pointed to shifting lines within the construct. "They're meant to adapt, to strengthen over time rather than decay. Whatever this seal protects, it was meant to stay hidden for centuries."

A flash of movement caught Elan's attention. Maya stood in the doorway, her dark hair stirring in an unfelt breeze. She stepped into the chamber, drawn by the seal's pulsing light.

"I felt it calling," she said, moving to stand beside her brother. "Like a song I used to know."

The construct's rotation shifted again as Maya approached, its patterns realigning in response to her presence. The twins stood on either side of the seal, their combined energy making the chamber's ancient wards hum with renewed power.

Maya's fingertips traced the geometric patterns, her touch causing ripples of light to spread through the construct. The seal's rotation accelerated, golden lines blurring into streams of radiance that wrapped around her arms like luminous ribbons.

The construct pulsed, its light shifting from gold to a deep violet. Energy crackled between Maya and the seal, arcs of power that made her hair float in an electric dance. The chamber's ancient wards flared in response, their patterns igniting with matching violet fire.

Images burst through Maya's mind - torchlit corridors, the scratch of quill on parchment, voices chanting in Latin. She saw herself in Roman robes, working alongside Myst to inscribe complex formulae. Their younger hands moved in perfect synchronization, weaving protective magic into scrolls while Michael watched over them.

Michael collapsed to his knees, his wings flaring wide as the seal's power surged. Golden armor cracked and reformed, light bleeding from the seams as memories fought against their bonds. His form flick-ered between solid and ethereal, threatening to tear apart.

"Maya, stop!" Elan lunged forward, Winterstar singing through the air as he cut through the energy streams connecting his daughter to the seal. Myst grabbed Maya's shoulders, pulling her back as the construct's light intensified to blinding levels.

The seal shuddered, its perfect geometry fracturing along one edge. A sound like breaking glass filled the chamber as a single facet of the construct shattered, releasing a burst of contained memory. The remaining patterns spun wildly, trying to maintain their integrity as ancient power leaked into the air.

Michael staggered to his feet, his wings settling as the initial shock subsided. He moved closer to the fractured seal, studying the intricate patterns with newfound recognition.

"These formations..." Michael traced the air where Myst's hands had been. "I know this work. Your signature is unmistakable, even across centuries."

Elan watched his son absorb this revelation, Winterstar still humming with residual energy at his side.

"So Myst helped create the seal that took your memories?" Elan kept his voice steady, though his mind raced with implications.

"Not just helped," Michael said. "The mathematical precision, the adaptive properties - these are hallmarks of his work. The Order must have needed his expertise for something this complex."

Maya brushed fragments of golden light from her sleeves. "But why would they need both of us? The seal responded to our combined presence."

"Twin powers," Myst opened his notebook, sketching rapidly. "One to build, one to bind. The Romans understood the power of duality."

Elan's phone buzzed. He answered to find Rose on the line, her voice crackling through Elan's phone, breaking their contemplation. "The archives show increased demonic activity around known seal locations. Whatever you've disturbed has caught attention."

"We need those texts from the Vatican," Elan said. "If Myst's original notes survived, they might tell us what the Order was trying to protect."

A low rumble shook dust from the chamber ceiling. The sanctuary's wards flared briefly, ancient defenses responding to an unseen threat.

"The patterns are shifting," Myst pointed to the walls where geometric lines writhed like living things. "Something's testing the boundaries."

"These sanctuaries," Michael's eyes widened with sudden understanding. "They're not just holy places - they're part of a larger network. A defensive grid spanning continents."

The remaining fragments of the seal pulsed in agreement, its light synchronizing with the sanctuary's awakening wards.

Michael stumbled back, his wings flaring with sudden intensity as memories crashed through the fractured seal. His eyes blazed with divine fire as centuries of locked knowledge flooded back.

"The children," he gasped. "They weren't just students. Myst was my apprentice, crafting seals to contain forces beyond mortal comprehension. The mathematics, the sacred geometry - he developed them all."

Elan watched his son's face as understanding dawned on it. Myst's hands trembled as he touched the geometric patterns etched into his notebook, recognizing his own work across the centuries.

"I remember the library," Michael continued, his voice gaining strength. "Myst would work through the night, designing ever more complex barriers while Maya..." He turned to her. "You were the key. Your presence activated the seals, gave them their power."

Maya touched the fractured construct, violet energy crackling between her fingers. "That's why it responded to us both."

Rose's voice cut through the phone again. "There's more. The Vatican archives reveal a pattern: each seal location corresponds to a major point of demonic incursion. Whatever you contained, it was meant to stay hidden forever."

The sanctuary trembled again, this time with greater force. The wards pulsed with increasing urgency as geometric patterns shifted across the walls like living mathematics.

"The grid is destabilizing," Michael's wings spread defensively. "Breaking this seal has weakened the others. We need to reach the Vatican archives before-"

A deep crack split the chamber floor, cutting through ancient protective circles. Dark energy seeped through the break, corroding the sacred geometry.

Elan raised Winterstar as shadows gathered in the corners. "How long until whatever's contained breaks free?"

"Not long," Michael drew his sword. "The seals were connected. Break one..."

"And they all start to fail," Myst finished, recognition burning in his eyes as more ancient knowledge surfaced.

The crack widened, releasing a whisper of something that made the air itself recoil. Through the growing breach, they glimpsed movement - something vast and dark stirring from ancient bonds.

CHAPTER
SIX

The memory hit Myst like a physical blow, dropping him to his knees in the sanctuary. The present world dissolved, replaced by the searing heat of a Roman summer, in the 9th century, and the clash of steel against otherworldly bone.

Blood trickled down his arm as he backed against a crumbling column. The marble still bore traces of gilt paint, a testament to Rome's fading glory. His leather armor, reinforced with bronze plates bearing sacred geometries, deflected a demon's claws. The creature's twisted form writhed against the evening sky, its multiple limbs testing his defenses.

Fires burned across the seven hills, painting the Palatine in shades of amber and crimson. The air crackled with unnatural energy as reality itself buckled under the weight of the demonic invasion.

"Hold the line!" Mars's voice carried across the forum, his wings blazing with divine light as he rallied the remaining defenders. Roman legionaries fought alongside members of the Order, their discipline maintaining formation even against supernatural horrors.

Myst's fingers traced patterns in the air, mathematical principles taking physical form as barriers of pure energy. The symbols he'd spent years perfecting now meant the difference between survival and annihilation.

Maya's presence resonated through their twin bond as she channeled power into the defensive grid. Her violet energy merged with his calculations, strengthening the walls between worlds. Together, they'd developed this system of protection, but never at this scale.

A centurion stumbled past, his shield bearing fresh claw marks. "The eastern quarter is lost. They're pushing toward the Temple of Venus."

Myst's heart clenched. The temple housed one of the primary seal anchors, part of the network they'd spent years creating. If it fell...

He pushed off from the column, geometric formulas already forming in his mind. The price of major magic always came due, but with Rome itself at stake, what choice did they have?

The demon lunged again, its twisted form defying the laws of nature. Myst met its attack with a blade inscribed with equations of banishment, each strike calculated to disrupt its physical form.

The demon's essence scattered as Myst's blade struck true, but three more materialized in its place. Behind them, Verendana's laughter rang across the forum as she directed waves of corrupted Manes against the defenders. The ancestral spirits, twisted from their protective nature into weapons of destruction, tore through the ranks of legionaries.

Mars materialized in a burst of crimson light, his spear cutting swaths through the demon hordes. "The pact is broken. The gods stand with Rome!"

Minerva appeared at his side, her aegis shield blazing. Vesta's sacred flame formed a barrier around a group of wounded soldiers while Jupiter's thunderbolts lit up the night sky. The gods had come to honor the pax deorum—the divine agreement that had protected Rome for centuries.

But even their divine power seemed insufficient against the tide of darkness. Warin slipped between shadows, his assassin's blade finding gaps in celestial armor. Each strike corrupted what it touched, turning divine ichor black.

Lucifer rose above the battlefield, his fallen glory casting a shadow that dimmed even heavenly light. Wings of darkness spread across the sky as corrupted Lares - once household guardians - turned against their former charges. The genius loci of Rome itself wavered, the spirit of the eternal city buckling under the assault.

Lemures - angry ghosts of the unavenged dead - swirled in hungry packs, seeking victims among the living. Their hollow screams drove men mad, turning brother against brother in fits of supernatural terror.

"The seals are failing!" Maya's voice carried across their bond as another anchor point collapsed. Mathematical certainty crumbled in the face of chaos.

Mars rallied his forces for another charge, but exhaustion showed in every movement. Divine and mortal blood mingled on the cobblestones as more defenders fell. The Order's lines contracted, giving ground step by precious step.

Myst's calculations revealed the brutal truth - they were losing. Each failed equation, each broken seal, brought them closer to defeat. The very foundations of Rome groaned under the assault as reality frayed at the edges.

Through the chaos, Myst spotted his sister Maya engaged with a pack of demons near the Temple of Mars. Her blade sang through the air, each strike precise and deadly. The fighting style their mother, Kaira, had taught them merged with ancient Roman techniques, creating a fatal dance.

Maya's violet energy pulsed with each strike, mathematical formulas swirling around her like a protective cocoon. A demon lunged, its claws raking empty air as she pivoted away. Her counterstrike separated its head from its shoulders, the creature dissolving into ash.

"The eastern seal!" Maya's voice carried across their bond. "We need to stabilize it!"

Myst fought his way toward her, his own blade cutting through corrupted spirits. The twins moved in perfect synchronization, covering each other's blind spots as they advanced. Years of training, both past and future, had forged them into a seamless unit.

Blood dripped from a gash in Maya's arm, but she showed no sign of slowing. Her face held the same determined expression he'd seen countless times during their training sessions in San Francisco. Those peaceful moments now felt like another lifetime.

As Myst dispatched another demon, memories of his fallen comrades crashed through his mind. Isolde's songs had once filled their halls with hope. Wulfstan's steadfast presence had anchored them through countless battles. His parents, Kaira and Elan, had sacrificed everything to prepare them for this moment. And Nykronus - their mentor had guided them through the mysteries of time itself.

The realization hit him harder than any demon's blows. This wasn't just about defending Rome. The corrupted Manes, the twisted Lares - this same darkness would threaten their own time. Every seal they lost here weakened the barriers between worlds, creating vulnerabilities that would echo through centuries.

His fallen friends had known this truth. They had died protecting not just Rome, but the future itself. As another wave of demons approached, Myst raised his blade. He wouldn't let their sacrifices be in vain.

Myst staggered as a new vision tore through his consciousness, one different from the battle raging around him. The geometric patterns of his defensive magic twisted, forming a window into somewhere-somewhere else.

Towering structures of glass and steel reached toward the sky, their heights dwarfing even the most significant monuments of Rome. Metal carriages lay abandoned in wide stone streets. The vision focused on a massive red bridge spanning a vast bay, its framework partly collapsed as winged horrors perched upon its towers.

His stomach lurched as he witnessed demons he'd never seen before, their forms more horrific than anything in the current battle. They rampaged through the strange city, tearing through walls as if they were parchment. Corrupted Manes flowed like dark rivers between the buildings, their ancestral protection perverted into pure malevolence.

The streets ran red with blood; bodies lay scattered across decorated walkways. Strange glowing symbols that reminded him of captured lightning flickered and died in the buildings' walls. The air itself seemed to burn, carrying the stench of sulfur and decay.

A figure that could only be Verendana stood atop one of the glass towers, her power magnified beyond anything he currently faced. She directed waves of demons with casual gestures, her laugh echoing across centuries. The corrupted power of St. Valentine's curse had grown, feeding on centuries of darkness.

Myst watched helplessly as a temple-like building with a domed roof collapsed, its white stones stained crimson. People in strange clothing fled in terror as lemures swooped down from above. Their screams carried the same note of despair he heard in Rome, proving that human fear transcended time itself.

The vision shifted to a harbor where ships of metal and glass burned. Beyond them, an island fortress stood besieged by creatures that dwelled in the depths. The water itself seemed alive with malevolent purpose, pulling victims into its dark embrace.

The vision faded, leaving Myst back in the heat of battle. He parried a demon's strike while processing what he'd witnessed. The same patterns repeated - Rome's fall, San Francisco's destruction. History cycling through periods of darkness and light, each revolution growing more intense.

Maya's blade flashed beside him as she cut down another corrupted Mane. "They're pushing us back!"

Mars hurled his spear through a cluster of demons, the weapon trailing divine fire. But for each creature he destroyed, two more emerged from the shadows. Even the gods struggled against the tide of darkness.

Minerva's shield deflected a blast of corrupted energy. "The barriers between worlds grow thinner. We cannot hold them forever."

The truth hit Myst like a physical blow. They weren't just fighting for Rome - they fought for every city that would follow. Each demon they failed to stop here would grow stronger across centuries. Each corrupted spirit would spread its taint through time itself.

The defensive formations they'd practiced, the seals they'd crafted - none of it was enough. They needed something more potent than mathematics and ancient magic. Something that could transcend time itself.

Maya caught his eye across the battlefield, and he felt her agreement through their bond. Their current path led only to defeat..

"We need help," Myst called out as he fought his way toward his sister. "Someone who understands both times, both battles."

Maya nodded, her blade singing through another demon. "Michael. He's fought these battles before."

Myst's mind raced through possibilities. The Archangel had guided humanity since its earliest days. If anyone knew how to break this cycle of destruction, it would be him.

"We find him," Myst said, determination hardening his voice. "Whatever it takes."

Maya touched his arm, violet energy flowing between them. "Together, for now, we retreat."

They turned toward the Caelian Hill where Michael was last seen, their blades ready. Finding an Archangel in the chaos of battle wouldn't be easy, but they had no choice. Time itself hung in the balance.

~

Caelin Hill Sanctuary

Myst navigated through the darkened halls of the sanctuary, his footsteps echoing off ancient stone. Marble columns rose into shadows above, their carved surfaces telling stories of battles long past. Flickering oil lamps cast dancing shadows across frescoes depicting angels and demons locked in eternal combat.

The air grew heavier as he descended deeper into the heart of the sanctuary. Geometric patterns etched into the floor formed protective circles, their mathematical precision a comfort to his analytical mind. Each step triggered calculations of trajectory and force - old habits that had kept him alive through countless battles.

The central chamber opened before him, its domed ceiling lost in darkness. Tall windows filtered moonlight through colored glass, painting the floor in shades of blue and gold. At the chamber's heart stood a simple altar, unadorned except for a single burning candle.

Michael's presence filled the space before Myst saw him. Divine energy rippled through the air, making the protective geometries glow with reflected power. The Archangel materialized beside the altar, his wings folded against his back. Unlike the ornate depictions in the frescoes above, Michael appeared as a warrior in battle-worn armor. His sword hung at his side, its edge gleaming with other-worldly light.

"You seek answers about what is to come in the future." Michael's voice carried the weight of millennia.

"I saw a vision of a futuristic city in flames." Myst approached the altar, his own blade sheathed in respect. "I think it was San Francisco, in the future, where my parents are from. The same patterns we face here in Rome, but on a larger scale. The corrupted Manes, Verendana's power - it all grows stronger across time."

"The darkness adapts." Michael traced a pattern in the air, creating an image of the future city. "What you fight here will echo through centuries. Each victory or defeat shapes what is to come."

"Then help us break this cycle. There must be a way to stop it before it reaches that point."

Michael's gaze held ancient wisdom and profound sadness. "The future is not set, but neither is it easily changed. Your presence here, your knowledge of both times, creates possibilities that did not exist before."

Michael's form shimmered as he moved around the altar, his armor catching the candlelight. Myst watched the Archangel's deliberate movements, noting how even simple gestures carried divine weight.

"Verendana's corruption of the Manes strikes at the heart of Rome's spiritual defenses," Michael said. "The dead should protect their descendants, not prey upon them. By twisting these ancient bonds, she weakens the barriers between worlds."

Myst's fingers traced one of the geometric patterns on the floor. "The mathematical formulas we use - they're not enough anymore."

"No. Numbers alone cannot counter what she has unleashed." Michael placed his hand on the altar, causing the candle's flame to flare. "The Manes must be restored to their proper role. Their corruption spreads through time itself, weakening the natural order in every age."

"How do we restore them?" Maya asked.

"There are ancient rites, forgotten by most. They require sacrifice—not of blood, but of connection. Those who share bonds across time can serve as anchors, helping realign the spiritual forces that Verendana has distorted."

Myst turned towards his sister Maya and thought of their parents, Kaira and Elan. "You mean reincarnated souls?"

"Yes. Each life creates patterns that echo through time. Those who have lived multiple lives understand these connections instinctively. Their memories, though often hidden, contain the keys to restoration."

Myst's hand tightened around the hilt of his blade as Michael's words hung in the air. The candlelight cast strange shadows across the Archangel's face, making his divine features seem almost human for a moment.

"The dagger Verendana used," Myst said. "The same one Nykronus used on our parents. That's what started all this, isn't it?"

Maya stepped closer to the altar. "St. Valentine's curse flowed through that blade."

"The beginning of a terrible magic." Michael traced a symbol in the air, and an image of the dagger appeared - its curved blade dark with ancient power. "Such weapons demand a price. The magic of reincarnation, of souls traveling through time, creates ripples that cannot be easily contained."

"Our parents knew the cost," Maya whispered. "They chose to bear it anyway."

"The price of wielding such power is steep." Michael's armor clinked softly as he moved. "Each soul that passes through time leaves a tear in the natural order. These tears must be mended, or darkness seeps through."

"And Verendana found a way to exploit those tears," Myst said. "She's using them to corrupt the Manes."

"Yes. The dagger was forged with forbidden knowledge—the ability to sever souls from their natural cycle of death and rebirth. When used by St. Valentine, it created the first breach. Every soul touched by its power since then has widened that breach."

Maya's fingers brushed against her own blade. "So what's the real cost of reincarnation?"

"Each soul that returns must eventually pay its debt to death," Michael said. "The natural order demands balance. Those who cheat death create instability in the fabric of reality itself. This instability attracts darker forces, like moths to flame."

Myst's chest tightened as the weight of Michael's words settled over him. The faces of his fallen comrades flashed through his mind - Isolde's gentle smile, Wulfstan's steadfast courage, countless others who had given everything for their cause. He couldn't let their souls fall into darkness.

"There must be a way to protect the souls of the innocent," Myst said. "Our fellow Knights. My parents. To give their sacrifices meaning. We need to put a stop to this instability."

Michael's wings shifted, casting strange shadows across the chamber floor. "You understand what you're asking? The price would be steep."

"I do. I'll pay it." Myst stepped forward, his voice firm. "Their souls deserve peace. And the future needs a fighting chance."

"You would take their burden upon yourself?" Michael's divine gaze pierced through him. "Anchor their souls to the natural cycle, protect them from corruption?"

"Yes." Myst felt Maya's concern through their bond but pressed on. "What are your terms?"

Michael placed his hand on the altar. "I can use my divine power to shield their souls, guide them safely through time. But you must serve as the anchor. Your own soul would be bound to this duty, unable to reincarnate until balance is restored."

"How long?"

"Centuries, perhaps more. You would exist between worlds, neither fully living nor dead, until each protected soul completes its natural cycle."

Myst thought of his parents, of the future they came from. Of San Francisco in flames. His jaw set with determination. "I accept."

"You understand there's no going back? Once done, this cannot be undone."

"I understand." Myst met Michael's gaze without flinching. "Do it."

Myst gathered the ritual components with trembling hands. Ancient texts lay scattered across the sanctuary floor, their pages marked with complex geometrical patterns that seemed to shift in the candlelight. Maya helped him arrange crystaline bowls in a precise formation, each filled with sacred water from seven different springs.

"You don't have to do this," Maya whispered, her voice breaking. She placed a bowl of frankincense at the center of the pattern.

Myst continued drawing chalk lines between the vessels, checking his calculations against Michael's instructions. "We both know I do. Someone has to anchor their souls."

"Then let me help carry the burden." Maya grabbed his arm, her fingers digging into his sleeve.

"No. Please." Myst's hand shook as he placed the final bowl. "Let me have this."

Maya pulled him into a fierce embrace, her tears soaking into his shoulder. For a moment, they were children again, huddled together during thunderstorms in their Benevento home. The memory felt sharp enough to cut.

"I'll find you," she promised. "Whatever it takes, however long it takes. I'll find a way to bring you back."

Myst pressed his forehead against hers, their twin bond humming with shared grief and love. "Just keep the world safe. That's all I need."

They separated slowly, both knowing these were their final moments together. Maya helped him arrange the sacred herbs - rosemary for remembrance, sage for cleansing, lavender for peace. Each ingredient had been blessed by Michael himself, infused with divine power.

Myst removed his sword belt, laying his blade beside the ritual circle. The geometric patterns he'd drawn pulsed with soft light, responding to the building energy in the chamber. He took one last look at his sister, committing every detail of her face to memory.

"I finally understand all of mom's lectures about anything and everything," he said with a weak smile. "I wish I could tell Dad... tell him I'm proud to be his son."

The weight of Myst's choice pressed down on him like physical chains. His fingers traced the ritual circle one final time, checking each line and angle. The geometric precision that had always brought him comfort now felt like a prison of his own making. But when he thought of his parents, of all the souls touched by Valentine's curse, the burden became bearable.

Michael stepped forward, his divine presence filling the chamber with ethereal light. The Archangel's armor gleamed with an inner radiance that made the sacred waters in the bowls ripple. His wings unfurled, casting shadows that danced across the sanctuary walls.

"This sacrifice will echo through time," Michael said, his voice carrying the weight of centuries. "You will become a guardian of souls, protecting them from corruption as they complete their natural cycles."

Myst knelt at the circle's edge, his knees pressing against the cold stone. "I understand."

Michael drew his sword, its blade blazing with holy fire. He touched the flat of the blade to Myst's right shoulder, then his left. Divine energy coursed through Myst's body, making his muscles seize.

"By my authority as Heaven's warrior," Michael intoned, "I bind you to this sacred duty. Your soul will stand as anchor and shield until balance is restored."

The Archangel began to circle Myst, his footsteps leaving trails of light that merged with the ritual patterns. Each bowl of sacred water began to glow as Michael passed, their contents rising into the air in delicate streams.

Maya watched from beyond the circle, tears streaming down her face. Through their bond, Myst felt her grief and love wash over him. He held onto that connection like a lifeline as Michael raised his sword overhead.

"Begin," Michael commanded.

Myst took a deep breath and started reciting the ancient words, his voice steady despite his racing heart. The ritual circle flared to life, geometric patterns burning with divine fire. Above him, Michael's wings spread wide, casting a protective shadow as the ceremony began.

Divine fire traced the edges of the ritual circle as Michael began the sealing ceremony. Myst knelt at its center, his body rigid with determination. The geometric patterns he'd drawn pulsed with otherworldly energy, each line precise and purposeful.

Michael's sword, Heavenshard, touched the ground, sending ripples of power through the sanctuary floor. "Speak the words," he commanded.

Myst's voice cracked as he recited the ancient Latin phrases. Each syllable felt like lead on his tongue, heavy with binding power. The sacred waters rose from their bowls, forming a spinning circle of light around him.

Pain lanced through his chest as Michael's blade drew an arc through the air. The Archangel's wings cast shifting shadows across the ritual space, their divine presence making the very air crackle with electricity.

"Your memories will be sealed," Michael said, his voice echoing with celestial authority. "The knowledge of both times, both lives, locked away until balance is restored."

Myst gasped as invisible bonds wrapped around his soul. He felt Maya's presence through their twin bond, which was growing distant, like a star fading at dawn. Tears streaked down his face as decades of memories - battles fought, loves lost, families torn apart - began slipping away.

Michael's armor blazed with holy fire as he completed the final seal. The ritual circle erupted in blinding light, geometric patterns burning themselves into reality itself. Myst screamed as divine energy coursed through him, transforming his very essence.

When the light faded, Myst slumped forward. His eyes were vacant, memories of his family, his sister, his mission - all locked behind Michael's celestial barriers. He would walk through time as a guardian, but the price was everything that made him who he was.

Maya rushed to catch him as he fell, but her hands passed through his form. Her brother was already becoming something else - neither entirely spirit nor flesh, bound to his eternal duty.

"It is done," Michael declared, lowering his sword. The ritual circle dimmed, its purpose fulfilled. Myst's sacrifice was complete, his soul transformed into an anchor for others. The price of protection had been paid in full.

The divine energy pulsed through Michael's form, his armor crackling with celestial power. His memories began to fragment - faces blurring, names fading, centuries of service splintering like shards of glass. He gripped Heavenshard tighter, using the blade's familiar weight to anchor himself against the tide of forgetting.

"The price must be paid by all," Michael's voice resonated through the chamber. "Even I cannot escape the balance."

Maya watched as the Archangel's wings started dissolving into pure light. His features softened, becoming less divine and more human with each passing moment. The geometric patterns beneath his feet flared in response, their mathematical precision containing the raw power of his transformation.

"Remember," Michael struggled to form the words, "there is always hope. Each ending..." He gasped as another wave of memory loss hit him. "Each ending carries the seed of a new beginning."

The ritual circle pulsed with increasing intensity. Michael's armor began to crack, divine light spilling through the fissures. His sword, Heavenshard, hummed with otherworldly resonance as its master's essence prepared for rebirth.

"In the next life," Michael's voice grew distant, "seek the truth. The patterns... they remain..." His form began to blur as divine energy was barely contained within his rapidly failing physical form.

Maya shielded her eyes as Michael's transformation reached its peak. The Archangel's body erupted into pure light, his essence fragmenting into countless brilliant streams of light. These ribbons of divine power shot in all directions, piercing through the sanctuary walls as easily as arrows through mist, each carrying a piece of Heaven's warrior into the world.

The chamber fell silent, geometric patterns still smoldering on the floor. Where Michael had stood, only a single feather remained, slowly dissolving into starlight.

PART TWO

"To love is to will the good of the other."
— St. Thomas Aquinas

CHAPTER

SEVEN

Newgrange, Brú na Bóinne, Ireland

Moonlight spilled across the ancient stones of Newgrange as Maya traced the perimeter, her tactical gear a stark contrast against the weathered megalithic art. The Order's latest sensor arrays hummed softly, their blue LEDs reflecting off the carved spirals—modern technology meshing with five-thousand-year-old wards.

Asha padded beside her, the cat's black and orange fur starting to glow subtly. Her paws made no sound on the damp grass.

"Something's different tonight." Maya adjusted her night vision goggles, switching between spectrum modes. The Order's command center had upgraded its gear with enchanted components that could detect magical signatures.

The protective wards shimmered like heat waves, their ancient power amplified by the quantum processors buried beneath the soil. Maya's hand brushed the grip of her sidearm - loaded with blessed ammunition that could harm both physical and ethereal threats.

A ripple of wrongness passed through the air. The wards flickered, their steady blue light corrupting to a sickly purple. Asha's fur brightened, orange patches now blazing like embers.

"Maya." The cat's voice was tense. "The energy patterns are shifting. Like at Glastonbury."

The mention triggered a flash in Maya's mind - St. Michael standing before her, sword blazing, his wings casting shadows across ancient stones. The memory felt both distant and immediate, like a photograph slowly developing.

She tapped her tactical comm, connecting to the Order's mobile command post, which was parked discreetly behind the visitor center. "Control, this is Durant. We have a ward disruption on the eastern approach. Asha confirms energy corruption similar to previous sites."

The Nexus Heart at her throat pulsed once, its warning clear. Maya drew her weapon and activated its magical enhancements, causing runes etched along the barrel to glow with a soft blue light. The weight felt reassuring in her grip as she scanned the perimeter.

"Multiple breaches forming." Asha's tail lashed back and forth. "They're trying to overwhelm the wards systematically."

Maya tracked the failing defensive lines through her enhanced vision. Purple corruption spread like cracks in glass, following the carved spirals that had protected this site for millennia. Her training kicked in as she identified the pattern - whoever was attacking knew the ward architecture intimately.

"Control, we need reinforcements. Pattern suggests insider knowledge." She kept her voice steady despite the implications. A traitor in the Order meant all their sacred sites were vulnerable.

The comm crackled with interference. Through the static, she caught fragments: "...signals blocked...backup teams...ten minutes..."

A low hum built in the air, making her teeth ache. The spiral carvings began to glow with an inner light, but not the usual sacred blue. This was wrong - sickly and pulsing.

"Maya, move!" Asha launched herself at Maya's legs, knocking her sideways as a bolt of purple energy crackled through the space where she'd stood. The stone where it struck blackened and crumbled.

Rolling to her feet, Maya spotted dark figures materializing through the corrupted wards. Their robes seemed to absorb the moonlight, leaving only shadow where faces should be. The Order's intel had warned about these cultists, but seeing them firsthand sent ice through her veins.

"The eastern ward junction is failing." Asha's fur blazed brighter, casting orange light across the ancient stones. "If it falls, the whole network goes down."

Maya checked her ammunition and tightened her grip. "Then we hold that junction." She moved toward the threatened section, keeping to the shadows while marking targets. The cultists hadn't spotted her yet, as they were focused on their ritual.

Behind her, Asha's pawsteps were silent on the dew-covered grass. "Just like Glastonbury?"

"Just like Glastonbury." Maya thumbed off her weapon's safety. "Except this time, we know what we're dealing with."

~

San Francisco, California

Reagan Mazza's fingers flew across the holographic interface as alerts flashed across the command center's main display. The quantum-enhanced systems processed data from sacred sites worldwide, their status indicators shifting from stable blue to warning amber.

"Teams Alpha through Delta, maintain perimeter positions." She adjusted her headset, keeping her voice steady despite the cascade of warnings. "Echo team, redirect to support Durant at the eastern junction."

The command center hummed with activity, its servers processing terabytes of data from the Order's global sensor network. Ancient wards, enhanced by modern technology, reported their status through crystalline displays that lined the walls. Reagan had overseen the installation of these systems, merging centuries-old protection spells with quantum computing.

"Ma'am, we're losing contact with the Newgrange teams." A technician's voice cut through the controlled chaos. "Something's interfering with communications."

Reagan switched her main display to the Irish site's feed. The tactical overlay showed Maya's position, but the signal kept cutting in and out. Interference patterns matched those from the Glastonbury incident - magical disruption targeting their enhanced equipment.

"Route backup power to the communication arrays." She pulled up the site's ward architecture, noting the spreading corruption. "And get me a direct line to the Vatican. We need authorization for Protocol Seven."

Screens flickered as satellite feeds tracked multiple anomalies converging on sacred sites across Europe. The Order's AI flagged patterns in the data - coordinated attacks, all following the same playbook. Reagan recognized the signatures from her years of analyzing magical threats.

"All teams, be advised - hostiles are using enhanced disruption techniques." She marked key defensive positions on the tactical display. "Switch to backup frequencies and maintain distance from compromised wards."

The command center's ward crystals pulsed with increasing intensity, responding to the rising magical interference. Reagan checked the chronometer - seven minutes until reinforcements could reach Maya's position. She'd have to help her friend hold out until then.

The quantum processors beneath Newgrange whined as power surged through the enhanced wards. Maya watched the holographic overlay through her tactical display, ancient runes now augmented with streaming data. The Order had spent decades perfecting this fusion of old and new - crystalline matrices channeling magical energies through silicon pathways.

Her wrist computer beeped, detecting the first anomalous energy signature. The reading pulsed across her display in angry red—a corruption pattern she'd seen before. The cultists were using a techno-magical hybrid, turning the Order's own innovations against them.

"Energy spike at thirty degrees." Asha's fur rippled with orange light as she tracked the disturbance. "They're probing the ward matrix."

Maya switched her goggles to the thaumic spectrum. The wards appeared as interlaced lines of force. Still, dark spots were forming where the enemy's corruption ate through the defensive matrix. Her enhanced ammunition hummed in response to the rising magical energies.

The cultists' chanting grew louder, their voices emitting harmonic frequencies that caused the quantum sensors to scramble. Maya's tactical display flickered as interference patterns rolled across the screen. The ward's power crystals pulsed erratically, their carefully calibrated frequencies disrupted by the sonic attack.

A massive surge of energy rocked the ancient stones. Maya's sensors screamed warnings as multiple ward sections failed simultaneously. Through the chaos of alerts and flashing displays, she saw the eastern junction's protective barrier shatter like glass, leaving a gaping hole in Newgrange's defenses.

"Major breach detected!" Asha's voice cut through the cacophony of alarms. "They've compromised the primary ward structure!"

Through the ward breach, reality twisted like a torn canvas. The dimensional tear sparked with corrupt energies, its edges crackling with purple lightning that left afterimages in Maya's enhanced vision. Her sensors overloaded, screens filling with error messages as they tried to process the impossible readings.

A figure stepped through the rift. Tall, with dark waves of hair falling to his shoulders, he moved with an unnaturally fluid grace. His skin held a healthy glow despite the corruption surrounding him, though faint scars traced patterns across his exposed forearms. Maya's tactical display struggled to get a lock on him, the targeting reticle jumping erratically.

The cultists flanking him were nothing like the shadows she'd faced before. Where once they'd worn simple robes, now their forms were encased in crystalline armor that pulsed with the same purple energy as the rift. Techno-magical components were grafted directly into their bodies - quantum processors merged with flesh, ward crystals protruding from joints and spines. Their faces were hidden behind masks that seemed to absorb light, but Maya caught glimpses of glowing circuitry beneath.

"The Order's defenses grow more sophisticated." The tall man's voice carried a subtle rasp, yet held warmth that seemed at odds with the corruption surrounding him. "But they still cling to their old ways, their ancient stones and forgotten words."

The cultists moved with inhuman precision, their enhanced bodies allowing them to flow through space like liquid shadow. The crystals embedded in their armor resonated with the corrupted wards, creating feedback loops that further destabilized the site's defenses.

Asha's fur blazed brighter as she tracked their movements. "Maya, their energy signatures are completely wrong. They've found a way to invert the ward matrices."

The tall man turned, brown eyes scanning the shadows where Maya crouched. A slight smile played across his features, bringing momentary youth to his timeless face. "I can sense you there, child of two times. Come, let us speak of what's to come."

Maya's fingers tightened on her weapon as the tall man's words cut through the chaos. Something in his voice tugged at her, a familiar resonance that made her want to step from the shadows. Her tactical display flickered with warnings as she shifted position.

"He's trying to draw you out." Asha pressed against Maya's leg, the cat's fur pulsing with urgent orange light. "Don't engage. The ward structure is completely compromised."

The tall man took another step forward, his movements liquid grace despite the corruption swirling around him. "Your silence speaks volumes. The Order taught you well - but they haven't told you everything, have they?"

Maya's throat tightened. Questions burned in her mind, demanding answers. How did he know about her dual nature? What truths lie hidden in the Order's archives? Her boot scraped against stone as she started to rise.

Asha's claws dug into her tactical pants. "Maya, no. This is exactly what they want. The eastern approach is still clear - we need to fall back to the secondary position."

The cat's words cut through the hypnotic pull of the man's presence. Maya forced herself to check her tactical display. The corruption was spreading faster now, purple energy eating through the remaining wards like acid through paper. Their window of escape was shrinking.

Maya began a careful backwards retreat, keeping her weapon

trained on the tall man. At the same time, Asha guided her through the shadows. The cultists' crystal armor hummed with increasing intensity, resonating with the corrupted wards.

"The truth will find you eventually," the man called after her. "It's in your blood, after all."

Maya bit back the questions rising in her throat. Asha was right - engaging would only play into their hands. She focused on her footing as they picked their way through the ancient stones, putting distance between themselves and the ward breach.

Maya's tactical display flickered as she tracked the enhanced cultists. Their crystal implants pulsed with corrupt energy, sending cascading waves of interference across her sensors. The quantum processors in her gear struggled to compensate, throwing error messages across her HUD.

"Order teams, engage!" The command crackled through her comm as Echo squad burst from concealed positions. Their blessed ammunition sparked against the cultists' crystalline armor, leaving scorch marks but no severe damage.

The tall man raised his hand. Purple energy coalesced around his fingers, merging with streams of data that flowed through the crystals embedded in his arm. Maya's enhanced vision caught the impossible merger of magic and technology - ancient power flowing through quantum pathways.

A blast of corrupted force knocked three Order agents off their feet. Their protective wards shattered, overwhelmed by the hybrid attack. The cultists moved with mechanical precision, crystal joints whirring as they closed in on the fallen agents.

Maya squeezed off two shots. Her enhanced rounds pierced one cultist's armor, shattering a power crystal. Dark energy sprayed from the wound, but the creature didn't slow. Its mask turned toward her position, sensors probing the darkness.

"Their implants are tied directly into the ley lines." Asha's fur rippled with orange light as she analyzed the energy patterns. "They're drawing power from the site itself."

The tall man gestured again. This time, the quantum matrices beneath Newgrange responded to his call. Sacred blue light corrupted to purple as he seized control of the Order's own defensive systems. Warning klaxons blared as the site's enhanced wards turned against their creators.

Maya dove behind a stone as automated defense turrets swiveled toward Order positions. Their blessed ammunition, now tainted by dark energy, chewed through cover. Echo squad scattered, their tactical formations breaking under the assault.

The cultists pressed their advantage, moving in perfect synchronization. Crystal implants hummed at frequencies that made Maya's teeth ache. Their enhanced bodies flowed like liquid shadow, closing the distance with inhuman speed.

Through her tactical display, Maya watched more rifts tear open around the site's perimeter. Dark energy poured from the breaches, corrupting everything it touched. The quantum sensors went crazy, unable to process the impossible readings as technology and magic merged in ways that defied reality.

A flash of divine light pierced the chaos as St. Michael materialized on the battlefield, his wings casting massive shadows across the ancient stones of Newgrange. The archangel's armor gleamed with celestial fire, his sword blazing like a star gone nova.

Elan and Myst emerged from dimensional rifts on either side, their enhanced weapons already tracking targets. Maya's heart leaped at the sight of her father and twin brother - the Durant family reunited in combat once again.

The familiar way Elan moved triggered a cascade of memories in Maya's mind: training sessions in the Order's facilities, her father teaching her and Myst to coordinate their attacks. The muscle memory remained even as the fragments of her past struggled to align.

"Formation Delta!" Elan's command cut through the chaos. Maya's body responded automatically, muscle memory taking over as she shifted position. Myst mirrored her movement on the opposite flank, just as they had practiced countless times.

St. Michael engaged the tall man directly, their clash sending shockwaves of power across the battlefield. The archangel's sword met streams of corrupted energy in explosive bursts that lit up the night.

Maya's hand moved to her back, fingers wrapping around Moonbow's grip. The ancient weapon hummed with power as she drew it, its silver surface catching the light of combat. The bow seemed to sing as she nocked an arrow, its magic resonating with her own.

Myst's enhanced rounds provided cover fire as Maya took aim. The twins moved in perfect sync, their coordination honed by years of fighting together.

The clash of celestial steel against corrupted energy sent ripples through time itself. As Michael's sword met the tall man's power, memories cascaded through the archangel's consciousness. Each strike triggers echoes of battles fought across millennia.

A parry deflected purple lightning, and Michael saw Rome burning. Nero's forces had wielded similar corruption, their dark rituals threatening to tear reality apart. The smell of smoke and incense mixed with screams as Christians fled through the catacombs beneath the eternal city.

Another exchange, blades of light against shadow. The battlefield shifted to Orleans, where Joan had stood against impossible odds. Michael had guided her sword arm then, just as he now guided his own. The girl's unwavering faith had burned brighter than any corruption.

A blast of power forced Michael back a step. Constantinople fell in his mind's eye - not to the Ottomans, but to darker forces that history had forgotten. The city's great walls had held against mortal armies, only to crack under assault from beings that twisted both magic and metal to their will.

The tall man pressed forward, his attacks carrying frequencies that set the quantum matrices screaming. Michael's wings flared as he recognized the pattern - the same harmonic corruption that had threatened the sacred site they fought on. Then as now, the enemy sought to merge ancient power with modern technology.

Each clash of power against power brought fresh remembrance. The trenches of Verdun, where desperate prayers had drawn him to defend against mustard gas given horrible life by occult science. The hidden battles of the Cold War, fought with weapons that merged nuclear fire with forbidden knowledge.

The memories crashed through Michael's consciousness like

waves against stone. Yet he remained anchored in the present, his divine nature allowing him to process past and present simultaneously. The enemy's tactics might evolve, but their corruption remained familiar—a darkness he had faced in countless forms across the ages.

The cultists' crystal armor deflected conventional weapons, but Moonbow's arrows carried divine power. Maya's first shot pierced a cultist's enhanced plating, shattering the corrupt crystals embedded in its chest. The creature fell, its hybrid systems failed as sacred energy coursed through its form.

Elan advanced methodically, his marine training evident in every precise movement. He called out targets, directing his children's fire with practiced efficiency. The Durant family flowed across the battlefield like a single organism, each member anticipating the others' moves.

Through her tactical display, Maya watched in horror as new rifts tore open across the battlefield. These weren't the clean quantum portals used by the Order - these tears in reality leaked corruption like infected wounds. Her sensors struggled to categorize the beings that emerged.

Aswang prowled through on all fours, their traditional shapeshifting abilities enhanced by crystalline implants that let them shift forms with mechanical precision. Their eyes glowed with purple light as targeting systems merged with supernatural hunting instincts.

Ancient babaylan shamans stepped forth, their sacred healing powers twisted by dark technology. Where they once channeled nature's energy, now they directed streams of corrupted data through quantum matrices grafted to their flesh. Their chants carried digital undertones that made Maya's enhanced audio filters crackle.

A massive bungisngis crashed through, its single eye replaced by a glowing purple lens. Cybernetic enhancements amplified its legendary strength, while its infamous laughter now carried frequencies that disrupted the Order's communication systems.

But it was the corrupted Manes that chilled Maya to her core. The ancestral spirits had been forcibly merged with quantum processors, their ethereal forms given terrible substance through crystal and circuitry. They drifted through the battlefield like digital ghosts, their once-protective nature perverted into something predatory.

Even the diwata had not been spared. The nature spirits emerged with their beautiful forms encased in corrupt crystal, their connection to the natural world replaced by hybrid techno-magical bonds that let them manipulate both data and reality.

"Switching to pattern delta-seven!" Reagan's voice cut through the interference. Order teams responded instantly, their tactics adapting to the new threat. Enhanced ammunition was adjusted to match the frequency of the hybrid entities. At the same time, blessed weapons were quickly recalibrated to channel both sacred and electronic countermeasures.

Maya watched the Order's defensive lines reform through her tactical display. Years of training kicked in as teams adjusted their formations to account for the enemies' impossible abilities. Quantum processors hummed as they analyzed attack patterns, feeding tactical data to the agents even as they engaged in combat.

Maya shifted positions as Elan directed another coordinated assault. The Durant family's practiced movements flowed like a deadly dance - Myst providing suppressing fire. At the same time, Maya's arrows found weak points in the corrupted armor. Elan's enhanced rounds kept the hybrid creatures at bay, buying precious seconds for his children to reposition.

"Cross pattern, mark three!" Elan's command sent Maya and Myst diving in opposite directions as a corrupted babaylan unleashed a blast of techno-magical energy where they'd stood moments before. The twins rolled to their feet in perfect sync, their weapons already tracking new targets.

But for every enemy they dropped, two more emerged from the rifts. The corrupted Manes phased through solid cover, their quantum-enhanced forms ignoring physical barriers. Enhanced Aswang bounded across the battlefield with impossible speed, their crystal implants gleaming as they shifted between forms.

Maya's tactical display filled with more red dots than she could track. Her fingers moved automatically to nock another arrow. Still, doubt crept in as she watched the horde of hybrid creatures advance.

Even with St. Michael engaging the tall man, even with the Order's teams adapting their tactics, they were being pushed back step by step.

A piercing laugh cut through the chaos - not the disrupting frequencies of the cyber-bungisngis, but something far more ancient and cruel. The sound made Maya's enhanced audio filters screech with feedback.

Through the most significant rift stepped a woman whose beauty had been twisted by corruption. Her dark hair writhed like living shadows, and her eyes blazed with purple fire. Crystal formations grew from her shoulders like broken wings, pulsing with the same corrupt energy that powered the hybrid creatures.

"Verendana." Asha's fur bristled, and the orange light flared bright enough to cast shadows. "The Order's records didn't show she had this level of enhancement."

Elan gave a determined look, "Something isn't right. She rarely makes an appearance and has always operated in the background."

The woman raised her hands, and the quantum matrices beneath their feet responded to her call. Sacred ground turned traitor as ancient stones merged with modern technology, transforming Newgrange into something that should not exist.

Maya drew an arrow onto Moonbow as Verendana strode forward, her crystal-enhanced form distorting the sensors. The woman's beauty held a corrupted quality that made Maya's skin crawl.

"Give me back my son." Verendana's voice carried harmonics that set Maya's teeth on edge. "Return Dante to me, and perhaps I'll grant you a swift death."

Maya's hand tightened on Moonbow as confusion swept through her. "Your son? Dante Malvagio...he belongs in the deepest and darkest prison where his influence can't touch another soul."

"The medallion you wear." Verendana's eyes fixed on Maya's chest, where the ancient relic hung. "It holds more power than you could possibly understand. Power enough to trap a soul between worlds."

The medallion grew warm against Maya's skin as understanding dawned. Michael's sudden appearance, along with the strange energy readings, connected everything.

"The Order has protected that artifact for centuries." Lazarus materialized beside Verendana, his presence carrying the weight of ancient tragedy. "They never understood its true purpose. Never knew it could serve as a prison for beings like us."

St. Michael's voice rang out across the battlefield. "You perverted its sacred power, tried to use it to bridge worlds that should remain separate."

"And once we free my brother," Lazarus smiled, the expression holding no warmth, "once Dante is released from your primitive trap, there will be no force in heaven or earth that can stop us. Technology and magic, sacred and profane - all barriers will fall."

The medallion pulsed against Maya's chest as if responding to their words. Through her tactical display, she watched energy patterns shift and swirl around the ancient artifact, frequencies that defied both scientific and magical analysis.

Verendana raised her crystal-enhanced hand. "Last chance, child. Give me back my son, or watch everything you love burn."

Maya's heart pounded as the medallion's warmth spread through her chest. Energy coursed through her veins, different from the enhanced abilities she'd trained with. This power felt ancient, pure—a birthright she hadn't known she possessed.

Light bloomed from her core, spreading outward in waves of silver-blue radiance. The corrupted energy from Verendana's attacks splashed harmlessly against the barrier that formed around Maya and her family. Elan's eyes widened as the protective field enveloped him, while Myst reached out to touch the shimmering wall with wonder.

"The Guardian's gift." Asha's fur rippled with orange light. "Your mother's bloodline carries more than just enhanced abilities."

Maya's mind reeled at the revelation. Her scattered memories struggled to align - training sessions with the Order, combat drills with Nykronus, her parents, and brother. But beneath it all lay something more profound, a legacy passed down through generations.

"Your mother knew." Elan's voice cracked. "She tried to tell me before she disappeared, tried to explain why they would come for you both. Before I went back in time to find you."

Verendana's laughter held bitter recognition. "Of course. The

Durant twins - born of a Guardian's blood. With Mazza's blood. No wonder my son's prison has held for so long."

The medallion pulsed faster against Maya's chest as understanding crashed through her. Every mission, every enhancement, every fragment of her fractured past - it all served to prepare her for this moment. She and Myst weren't just Order agents, nor were they children of Durant or Mazza. They were the latest in a line of Guardians stretching back centuries.

Power surged through Maya's body, making her gasp. The barrier around them flared brighter as ancient energy merged with her enhanced abilities. Her tactical display went crazy, unable to process the readings as Guardian power interfaced with quantum systems in ways that shouldn't be possible.

The medallion blazed like a miniature sun, its light throwing stark shadows across the battlefield. Maya felt Myst's matching surge through their twin bond as their shared heritage awakened fully. Their combined power sent ripples through reality itself, making the corrupted rifts waver and distort.

Images of Aethoria—the realm where she had ventured to unlock her true potential and destiny, flashed before her eyes.

The twin swords hummed with increasing intensity as St. Michael and Elan brought them together. Heavenshard's pristine glow merged with Winterstar's fierce radiance, their combined light casting strange shadows across the battlefield. Maya watched her father's movements through her tactical display, tracking the energy signatures as the ancient weapons resonated in harmony.

Elan and St. Michael swept the blades in a crossing arc, releasing a wave of pure force that cut through the corrupted creatures' ranks. Where Winterstar's edge brought divine judgment, Heavenshard's light offered redemption - corrupted flesh and crystal alike sublimated into cleansing flame.

The swords' fusion created attacks unlike anything in the Order's combat databases. Maya's enhanced vision caught fragments of quantum equations dissolving as sacred geometries took their place. Each strike rewrote local physics; the blades' combined power rendered the hybrid entities' defensive protocols ineffective.

A corrupted Aswang leaped for Elan's flank, its crystal implants flaring with purple fire. Without breaking stride, he brought the crossed blades up in a fluid motion. The creature hit the resulting energy field and simply ceased to exist, its hybrid form unmade by the swords' unified purpose.

Through their bond, Maya felt Myst's wonder at their father's display. The Durant twins had trained with enhanced weapons their entire lives, but this was something else entirely. Heavenshard and Winterstar moved like extensions of Elan's will, their ancient power responding to his marine discipline and unwavering focus.

More corrupted entities pressed forward, their hybrid forms twisting reality around them. Elan and St. Michael met their charge with methodical precision, the fused blades singing through the air. Where Winterstar's edge severed quantum matrices, Heavenshard's light purified the wounded space-time. Together, the swords maintained reality's proper shape even as the battle threatened to tear it apart.

The weapons' resonance grew stronger with each strike, their individual powers amplifying rather than competing with one another. Through her tactical display, Maya watched the energy patterns spiral outward in mandala-like formations. Sacred and profane, order and chaos - the ancient blades maintained perfect balance as they restored proper harmony to the battlefield.

Maya watched Zoe take position on a raised section of corrupted ground. The ancient bard's bleach-blond hair whipped in the energy currents as she pulled a sleek electric lute from her back. Ancient runes glowed along its modernized frame, merging old magic with cutting-edge sound technology.

Zoe's voice cut through the chaos, her rock ballad carrying harmonics that made Maya's enhanced systems resonate. The sound waves pulsed with both acoustic and digital power, each note precisely calibrated to boost neural and physical performance.

"Through darkness deep and light divine,

Stand strong, warriors, hold the line,

Ancient power with modern might,

Rise up, heroes, win this fight!"

Maya felt a surge of strength through her muscles as Zoe's enhanced battle song took effect. Her movements became faster, more fluid. The Order's tactical systems integrated seamlessly with the sonic boost, updating targeting solutions to account for their increased capabilities.

Across the battlefield, Austin directed a swarm of blessed drones, their sensors picking out weak points in the corrupted entities' defenses. Stanley and Erikson moved in perfect sync, centuries of shared combat experience evident in their coordinated attacks. Smoke grenades filled the air with sanctified particles that disrupted the hybrid creatures' targeting systems.

"Shifting to pattern omega-three!" Austin's command sent the drones into a new formation as Stanley launched a volley of stun grenades. The explosions released both electromagnetic and spiritual energy, temporarily shorting out the corrupted crystals embedded in their enemies' flesh.

Erikson's movements blurred as Zoe's song reached a crescendo. He darted through the smoke screen, enhanced grenades finding their marks with deadly precision. Each explosion created a localized field that compelled the hybrid entities to maintain a single form, thereby preventing their unnatural transformations.

Maya tracked it all through her display, watching as ancient magic and modern warfare merged into something entirely new. Zoe's voice soared above the chaos, her battle song weaving protection and power into every note.

St. Michael moved with divine grace, each strike of Heavenshard creating ripples of sacred energy that pushed back the corruption. His combat style transcended mere physical movement - reality itself seemed to bend around him as he fought. Where his blade touched corrupted flesh or crystal, purifying light burned away the taint.

The archangel's wings spread wide, casting golden shadows across the battlefield. His sword techniques flowed like liquid light, centuries of martial knowledge distilled into a perfect economy of motion. No movement was wasted, no strike without purpose.

But even St. Michael's divine prowess couldn't stem the tide forever. The Order's defensive lines buckled under the relentless assault. Enhanced agents fell back step by step as corrupted entities pressed forward. Their blessed ammunition ran low; the hybrid creatures seemed endless.

Reagan coordinated emergency protocols through static-filled channels. "Section three compromised! Fall back to secondary positions!" Her voice carried the strain of watching their carefully planned defenses crumble.

Maya watched through her tactical display as red dots overwhelmed blue ones across the battlefield. The Order's enhanced agents fought with desperate skill, but their positions were being overrun. Sacred wards flickered and failed as corrupted energy ate through their foundations.

Verendana's forces pushed harder, sensing victory was within reach. Her crystal-enhanced followers struck with increasing confidence, their hybrid abilities overwhelming even blessed weaponry. The corrupted Manes phased through walls while cyber-enhanced Aswang bounded over barricades.

The moment stretched taut like a bowstring about to snap. Maya felt it in her bones - they approached a critical turning point where all their plans would either succeed or shatter. The medallion burned against her chest, responding to the mounting tension.

Cracks appeared in the ancient stones beneath their feet as reality strained under the opposing forces. The Order's remaining defensive positions began to crumble, their enhanced barriers failing under the onslaught of corrupted power. Sacred ground turned traitor as Verendana's influence spread, transforming their carefully prepared battleground into hostile territory.

Maya watched in horror as the last defensive ward collapsed under Verendana's assault. The corrupted energy spread like poison through the sacred ground, turning ancient stones into crystalline formations that pulsed with sickly purple light.

"We can't hold!" Reagan's voice crackled through the tactical channel as another section fell. Enhanced agents scrambled backward, their blessed ammunition spent against the endless tide of hybrid creatures.

St. Michael staggered; Heavenshard's pristine glow flickered as corruption seeped into the very foundations of their sanctuary. His wings drooped, golden feathers dimming as the sacred energy that sustained them was twisted and corrupted.

The archangel's eyes went wide, his face frozen in an expression of sudden recognition. Through her tactical display, Maya caught a surge of energy emanating from his divine form - not the usual sacred wavelengths, but something deeper. A memory, ancient and powerful, burning through quantum matrices and enhanced sensors alike.

"The network." St. Michael's voice carried both wonder and urgency. "How could I have forgotten? The sanctuaries were never meant to stand alone."

Maya's enhanced vision caught fragments of data streaming from the archangel's awakened memory - images of interconnected holy sites, sacred geometries linking ancient grounds across continents and centuries. Each sanctuary was a node in a vast web of power, designed to support and strengthen the others.

"The corruption spreads too fast," Elan called out, Winterstar's edge barely holding back a wave of hybrid entities. "Even if there are other sanctuaries, we can't reach them in time."

"We don't need to reach them." St. Michael raised Heavenshard, its light pulsing in time with the medallion against Maya's chest. "They were always connected. We just needed to remember how."

The archangel's revelation cascaded through Maya's tactical systems, ancient knowledge merging with modern analysis. Every sacred site they'd fought to protect, every holy ground they'd defended - they were all part of something larger. A network of power and protection that spanned the globe, waiting to be reactivated.

Maya's heart sank as she watched another squad of Order forces fall back. The corrupted entities surged forward, their crystal-enhanced forms twisting reality around them. Enhanced agents dragged wounded comrades behind crumbling barricades while blessed drones provided covering fire.

"Section five is lost!" Reagan's voice crackled through the comm. "All units, fall back to emergency positions!"

Elan swung Winterstar in a desperate arc, buying precious seconds for retreating agents. The sword's edge cut through corrupted flesh and crystal alike, but for every hybrid creature that fell, two more took its place.

Through the chaos, Maya caught a familiar energy signature on her enhanced display. Her breath caught as the reading resolved into a clear signal - one she hadn't seen since that fateful day in San Francisco.

A figure materialized at the edge of the battlefield, power rolling off her in waves that made Maya's sensors fluctuate wildly. Kaira Mazza stood tall among the retreating forces, her enhanced abilities radiating an authority that made even the corrupted entities pause.

"Mother," Maya whispered, the word carrying through their tactical channel.

Kaira's eyes found Maya across the battlefield, decades of strategic experience evident in her measured gaze. The Order general's enhanced systems interfaced smoothly with their remaining defenses, analyzing weak points and calculating possibilities.

But even as hope flickered through their ranks at Kaira's arrival, Maya saw the truth in her mother's expression. The corruption had spread too far, too fast. Sacred ground turned against them with increasing speed, ancient stones warping into crystal formations that pulsed with sickly light.

St. Michael's wings drooped further as another ward collapsed, golden feathers dimming in the growing darkness. Elan's enhanced strength began to falter, Winterstar's strikes coming slower against the endless tide. Their carefully planned defenses, meant to hold back Verendana's forces, crumbled one by one.

Maya watched through her tactical display as more red dots overwhelmed blue ones. The Order's positions collapsed in a cascading failure, their blessed ammunition depleted against an enemy that seemed limitless. Even with Kaira's arrival, they were losing ground faster than they could adapt.

CHAPTER

EIGHT

Vatican Archives, Rome, Italy 1962 A.D.

The leather-bound tome crackled as Gianna opened it, dust motes dancing in the early morning light that filtered through the Vatican Archives' high windows. Her fingers traced the intricate script - was it Aramaic? No, something older. The characters shifted beneath her touch, ancient meanings rising to the surface of her mind like bubbles in clear water.

At twenty-three, she'd already mastered twelve languages, but this was different. The text spoke to her in ways that transcended mere translation. The words held weight, presence, as if the forgotten tongue refused to stay buried in history.

Gianna adjusted her wire-rimmed glasses and pulled the book closer. The archives spread around her in towering shelves, manuscripts and scrolls carefully preserved behind climate-controlled glass. Her small desk sat wedged between two massive cases, a stack of texts waiting for her attention.

"Another one?" Cardinal Luciani's footsteps echoed across the marble floor. "That's the third pre-Biblical text you've decoded this week."

"This one's different." Gianna didn't look up from the page. "The syntax suggests it predates the Dead Sea Scrolls, but there are references to events that happened centuries later."

The Cardinal peered over her shoulder, his brow furrowing. "I see only random markings."

"It's as clear as Italian to me." Her pencil flew across her notepad, transcribing passages that seemed to write themselves through her hand. "Look at this section - it's describing ritual practices that weren't documented until the early Christian church, but the language structure is all wrong for that period."

She reached for another text, comparing passages with practiced ease. Languages flowed through her mind like music - ancient Hebrew harmonizing with Latin, Greek counterpoints weaving through forgotten dialects that had no modern names.

The Cardinal watched her work, his expression unreadable. Gianna barely noticed, lost in the rhythm of translation. Other linguistic scholars spent years mastering a single dead language. For her, they simply unfolded, each one a key unlocking doors to understanding humanity's oldest secrets.

Heavy doors groaned open, breaking Gianna's concentration. Two figures strode through the archive's entrance - one tall and distinguished in flowing robes, the other compact and muscular in modern dress. Nykronus and Xicato. Their unexpected presence sent a chill down her spine.

"We need your expertise." Nykronus swept toward her desk, his dark eyes fixed on the text before her. Ancient scrolls rustled beneath his arms.

Cardinal Luciani stepped back, crossing himself. "The archives are restricted-"

"Vatican clearance." Xicato flashed a gold-sealed document. "Direct from the Holy Office."

Nykronus spread the scrolls across Gianna's desk, covering her current work. The parchment bore marks of extreme age, edges crumbling despite careful preservation. "These were discovered beneath the foundations of Santa Maria Maggiore during renovation work."

Gianna's hands hovered over the delicate surface. The script flowed in elegant curves, similar to the text she'd been studying but with subtle differences. "This dialect... It's like nothing I've seen before."

"Look here." Nykronus pointed to a specific passage. "The recurring pattern."

The words shifted in Gianna's vision, rearranging themselves into familiar forms. "It's talking about three mountains... three guardians." Her finger traced the lines. "Something about a convergence."

"A prophecy?" Cardinal Luciani leaned closer.

"More like a warning." Gianna pulled her notebook closer, transcribing the strange symbols. As she wrote, other marks on the parchment caught her attention - tiny glyphs hidden between the main text, almost invisible unless you knew where to look. They pulsed with a faint luminescence that seemed to respond to her touch.

"These markings..." She touched one gently. The symbol flared beneath her finger, leaving an afterimage burned into her vision. "They're not just decorative."

Gianna's hand moved across the page as if guided by an unseen force, the ancient symbols flowing through her like a river of forgotten knowledge. The text spoke of three mountains, each guarded by a powerful female entity. Her breath caught as the translation crystallized in her mind.

"The Three Marias," she whispered, the words escaping before she could stop them.

Nykronus's hand brushed against hers as he reached for the parchment. The brief contact sent an unexpected spark through her fingers. "You recognize these references?"

"Filipino folklore." She shifted in her chair, aware of his proximity. "But this text predates Spanish colonization by centuries. It shouldn't exist."

His dark eyes met hers, and she noticed flecks of gold in their depths she hadn't seen before. "Sometimes the oldest truths hide in plain sight."

Gianna forced her attention back to the manuscript. The symbols danced beneath her fingertips, their meaning unfolding with increasing urgency. "This section describes a ritual involving all three guardians - Maria Makiling, Maria Cacao, and Maria Sinukuan."

"The convergence." Nykronus leaned closer, his shoulder brushing against hers. The scent of old books and something else - mountain air, perhaps - surrounded him. "What else?"

Her pencil paused over a particularly complex passage. The characters seemed to resist translation, twisting away from conventional meaning. Nykronus's hand covered hers, steadying her grip on the pencil. The warmth of his touch sent another jolt through her system.

"Trust your instincts," he murmured. "You see more than just words on that page."

She swallowed hard, trying to ignore how his presence affected her focus. The text gradually yielded its secrets, revealing details about sacred sites and celestial alignments. Each revelation drew Nykronus closer, his scholarly interest evident in the intensity of his gaze.

Cardinal Luciani cleared his throat from somewhere behind them. Gianna startled, suddenly aware of how close she and Nykronus had drawn together over the manuscript.

Gianna's fingers traced the intricate diagrams at the scroll's edge, revealing a complex series of interconnected spheres. The symbols shifted, forming new patterns that sparked recognition in her mind.

"These aren't just decorative borders." She pointed to the central sphere. "Look - Earth sits at the center, but these other realms..." Her voice trailed off as the full implications hit her.

"Aethoria." Nykronus's finger traced the upper sphere. "The sacred counterweight to purgatory."

"A cosmic balance." Gianna's heart raced as the ancient text began to reveal its secrets. "Aethoria guards the gates of heaven as purgatory guards against hell. Earth exists between them, protected by both."

Xicato paced behind them, his boots clicking against the marble floor. "The balance is shifting." He pulled a worn leather journal from his coat. "Reports are coming in from holy sites across Asia. The barriers between realms are thinning."

"The Three Marias maintain those barriers." Gianna's translation flowed faster now, urgency driving her pen across the page. "Their mountains aren't just sacred sites - they're anchor points."

Xicato's face darkened. "Then we have a serious problem." He spread photographs across the desk - satellite images of Mount Makiling, Mount Lantoy, and Mount Arayat. Each showed strange atmospheric disturbances, swirling patterns visible even from space.

"The prophecy speaks of this." Gianna's finger stopped at a passage near the bottom of the scroll. The characters blazed with an inner light as she read them aloud. "When the three peaks weep golden tears, when the sun walks backward through the twelve houses, the veils between worlds will tear like silk in a storm."

"And the timing?" Nykronus asked.

Gianna checked the astronomical references in the text, her blood running cold. "The reverse solar progression begins within our lifetime."

Cardinal Luciani pulled a brass key from his robes and moved to a section of the wall that appeared solid. His fingers found an invisible seam, and a panel swung open to reveal a narrow passage.

"You mentioned bloodlines, and I did some digging. The name Durant sounded familiar. Well, the Durant texts are kept separate." He gestured for Gianna to follow. "Few know of their existence."

The hidden chamber beyond held a single shelf of leather-bound volumes, their spines unmarked. Gianna's hand moved of its own accord, selecting a book as if it called to her. The cover bore no title, just a symbol she recognized from her research.

"These records trace back to ancient Rome." Nykronus's voice was soft in the confined space.

Gianna opened the book. Unlike the earlier texts that required careful translation, these words spoke directly to her mind. Images flooded her consciousness - women in different eras, each bearing the same mark. They stood before councils, decoded messages, spoke in tongues that had never been written down.

"The text mentions my surname," she whispered.

Her fingers traced a family tree that sprawled across multiple pages. Names jumped out at her - some she recognized from her grandmother's stories, others were completely unknown. But each entry resonated with a familiar energy.

"The Mazza women served as bridges." Cardinal Luciani pulled another volume from the shelf. "Between cultures, between times, between worlds."

Gianna turned a page and gasped. A detailed sketch showed a woman who could have been her mirror image, dressed in Roman clothing. The date beneath read 838 AD. The woman held a scroll covered in symbols identical to those Gianna had just translated.

"Your ancestors understood languages that existed before written history." Nykronus touched the page gently. "They preserved knowledge that would have otherwise been lost."

The books seemed to pulse with energy under Gianna's hands. Each page revealed new connections and a deeper understanding of her family's role in preserving humanity's oldest secrets.

Gianna's fingers trembled as she closed the text. The weight of her family's legacy pressed against her chest, making it hard to breathe in the cramped chamber.

"The Mazza women weren't just translators." Nykronus pulled another volume from the shelf. "They were guardians of balance between realms. Your grandmother's work with the Vatican wasn't a coincidence - she continued a tradition spanning two millennia."

"The Three Marias maintained physical boundaries." He traced the symbol on the book's cover. "Your bloodline preserved the knowledge of how those boundaries functioned. Without both, the walls between worlds would have crumbled ages ago."

Cardinal Luciani nodded. "That's why the Church protected your family through the centuries. The Inquisition, witch hunts, political upheavals - we kept your ancestors safe because they kept us all safe."

Gianna studied the cardinal's face, searching for any hint of deception. His eyes met hers with steady conviction. The same conviction she'd seen in her grandmother's gaze when sharing family stories that had seemed like fairy tales.

"You knew my grandmother." It wasn't a question.

"She was one of the finest scholars I ever worked with." Cardinal Luciani's expression softened. "She spoke of you often, said you showed even greater potential than she had."

"Why didn't she tell me any of this?"

"Protection, perhaps." Cardinal Luciani placed a weathered hand on her shoulder. "Or preparation. Some truths can only be understood when we're ready to receive them."

Xicato emerged from the shadows, a leather case in his hands. "Speaking of truth - there's something else you need to see." He unzipped the case and removed a manuscript wrapped in silk.

The fabric fell away to reveal gilt-edged pages bound in ancient leather. Gianna recognized the seal pressed into the cover—the mark of Saint John the Divine.

"Is that..." Her voice caught.

"The original Revelation," Nykronus confirmed. "Written in a language only someone with your natural gift can fully comprehend."

The manuscript's pages rustled beneath Gianna's fingers, and the air in the cramped chamber grew thick with static electricity. The words on the ancient pages began to blur, shifting like smoke across her vision.

A cool breeze swept through the windowless room, extinguishing the electric lights. In the sudden darkness, three points of golden light materialized before her. The lights expanded, taking feminine forms that radiated power and grace.

Maria Makiling stepped forward first, her form shimmering like sunlight through leaves. Her hair moved in an unfelt wind, crowned with flowers that bloomed and withered in endless cycles.

"The veils grow thin," Makiling's voice echoed in Gianna's mind rather than her ears. "Our mountains weep."

Maria Cacao emerged next, her presence rich and dark as the earth itself. Golden ships sailed through the air around her head like a crown of ancient memories.

"The barriers weaken," Cacao's words tasted of bitter chocolate and sweet fruit. "Our powers fade."

Maria Sinukuan materialized last, fierce and regal. The air around her crackled with barely contained energy, and at her feet, precious metals bloomed like wildflowers.

"Dark forces gather," Sinukuan's voice rang like steel on stone. "They seek to break the ancient bonds, to tear open the gates between worlds."

The three Marias moved in perfect synchronization, their combined light casting strange shadows on the archive walls. Their voices merged into one:

"Your blood carries the key and will be unlocked by the daughter of a Durant. The knowledge preserved by your line must not fall into shadow's hands. Forces older than time itself stir from their slumber, and they hunger for what lies beyond the veil."

Gianna's skin tingled as their power washed over her. The air grew heavy with the scent of mountain flowers, cacao beans, and metal fresh from the forge.

"The prophecy speaks true," they intoned. "When the sun walks backward, when our mountains weep golden tears, the choice will fall to you. The price of failure is beyond measuring."

The three Marias vanished, leaving Gianna swaying on her feet. Nykronus caught her before she stumbled, his arm steady around her waist. The warmth of his touch anchored her as the room spun.

"Easy." His voice rumbled close to her ear. "Their presence can overwhelm even the most prepared minds."

Gianna leaned into his support, her heart racing from more than just the supernatural encounter. The scent of mountain air and ancient books enveloped her, familiar yet mysterious like Nykronus himself.

"You knew this would happen." She turned to face him, still within the circle of his arm. "That's why you brought me here."

"I suspected." His dark eyes held hers, flecks of gold dancing in their depths. "But I didn't expect them to manifest so strongly. Your connection to the ancient powers runs deeper than I imagined."

His free hand brushed a strand of hair from her face, the gesture both protective and intimate. Static electricity crackled between them, an echo of the Marias' power or something else entirely.

"How long have you watched over my family?"

"Centuries." His thumb traced the line of her jaw. "Though none have affected me quite like you."

The admission hung in the air between them, heavy with unspoken meaning. Gianna felt the truth of it resonate through her bones, an understanding that transcended mere words. Whatever force had drawn them together reached far beyond duty or coincidence.

"The Mazza bloodline," she whispered. "You've been protecting it all this time."

"The bloodline." His voice softened. "And now, you."

In that moment, surrounded by ancient texts and lingering traces of supernatural power, Gianna recognized the connection between them for what it was - something both ancient and new, powerful and fragile. His role as protector had evolved into something far more complex, just as her own role extended beyond mere translator.

The candles cast dancing shadows across the ancient texts as Gianna rubbed her tired eyes. Stacks of manuscripts surrounded her and Nykronus at the heavy oak table, their pages yellow with age. The scent of old leather and parchment mingled with the beeswax candles.

"Look at this." She slid a text toward him, their fingers brushing as he took it. The contact sent warmth spreading up her arm. "These symbols match the ones from the Durant records."

Nykronus leaned closer, his shoulder pressing against hers. "Soul-binding rituals. The ancients believed certain bloodlines carried inherent connections to supernatural forces."

His proximity made it hard for her to focus on the intricate diagrams. The candlelight caught the silver at his temples, softening his features. She found herself studying the curve of his jaw instead of the text.

"Here." His voice dropped lower as he pointed to a passage. "The binding wasn't just about power - it was about protection. A guardian's soul could be bound to their charge, creating an unbreakable link."

"Like you and my family?" The words slipped out before she could stop them.

His dark eyes met hers, gold flecks dancing in their depths. "The binding evolves with each generation. Adapts. Grows stronger."

"And with me?" Her heart pounded against her ribs.

"With you..." His hand covered hers on the manuscript. "It's different. More intense than I've ever experienced."

The candles flickered, casting intimate shadows across their faces. Time seemed to slow as he traced her knuckles with his thumb. The archives faded away until only this moment existed - his touch, his nearness, the weight of centuries of connection between them.

"The texts speak of rare instances," he murmured, "when the binding transcends its original purpose. When protection becomes..." He trailed off, leaving the word unspoken between them.

Gianna turned her hand beneath his, threading their fingers together. Ancient magic hummed beneath her skin where they touched, a resonance that felt both familiar and thrilling.

Gianna pulled away from Nykronus, her mind snapping back to their urgent situation. "The Malefic Assembly has eyes everywhere. If they learn about the Durant texts-"

"They already suspect." Cardinal Luciani paced the length of the archive. "Verendana's agents have been probing Vatican defenses for weeks."

Xicato spread blueprints across the table, covering the ancient manuscripts. "I've been thinking about reinforcing the ley line network around critical sites." His finger traced glowing patterns that pulsed beneath the surface of the paper. "There is energy that flows through these convergence points. We can create a barrier that masks magical signatures *with magical* signatures."

"But will it be enough?" Gianna studied the intricate web of lines. "The Assembly has centuries of accumulated knowledge, and they're always one step behind us."

"That's why I've designed a second layer," Xicato revealed, showing another diagram. "Sacred geometry combined with 20th-century tech-nology. Motion sensors tied to blessed silver threads, electromagnetic fields tuned to specific frequencies that disrupt dark magic."

Nykronus examined the plans. "Clever. The old ways and the new, working in harmony."

Gianna returned to the Durant text, scanning passages she'd previ-ously overlooked. The characters shifted under her gaze, revealing hidden meanings. She gasped as understanding bloomed.

"The binding rituals - they're not just about protection." Her fingers traced the ancient symbols. "They're keys. Each Mazza woman carried a piece of a larger cipher, passed down through generations."

The others gathered around as she decoded the text. "Look here - when aligned with the astronomical charts, these passages form a complete sequence. A way to strengthen the barriers between realms."

Cardinal Luciani leaned forward. "Can you translate it?"

"Yes." Gianna's hand moved across the page, transcribing symbols that seemed to flow directly from her consciousness to the paper. "But we'll need something from each of the Three Marias' mountains. Elements that carry their essence."

Gianna traced the ancient symbols, her fingers trembling. The weight of generations of knowledge pressed against her chest. Across the table, Nykronus sorted through stacks of manuscripts, his movements precise and measured.

"We can't keep this contained forever." She looked up from the text. "Other scholars might piece it together, especially with the astronomical alignments approaching."

"Knowledge shared is knowledge vulnerable." Nykronus paused his sorting, dark eyes meeting hers. "The Assembly has infiltrated universities, museums, even some church archives."

Cardinal Luciani cleared his throat. "I propose we create a secure archive. Multiple locations, each holding partial information. Like a puzzle with pieces scattered across continents."

"The Vatican vaults could house the astronomical charts." Professor Xicato spread blueprints across the table. "My contacts in Asia could protect the ritual components."

Gianna shook her head. "Splitting the knowledge makes it harder to access in an emergency. What if we need to reference multiple texts quickly?"

"She's right." Nykronus moved to stand behind her chair, his presence warm against her back. "We need a balance between security and accessibility."

His hand brushed her shoulder as he leaned forward to examine the texts. The touch sent electricity racing down her spine. When she glanced up, his face was inches from hers.

"What about creating copies?" Her voice came out softer than intended. "Encrypted versions only someone with Mazza blood could decode?"

"That could work." His breath stirred her hair. "Your natural ability to read the texts could become the key itself."

Cardinal Luciani and Xicato bent over the blueprints, discussing vault specifications. Gianna found herself hyper-aware of Nykronus's continued proximity, the subtle shift as he rested his hand on the back of her chair.

She turned another page, but the symbols blurred before her eyes. His scent surrounded her - the smell of ancient books and mountain air. When their fingers brushed over a particular passage, neither pulled away.

"We should start with the most critical texts," she murmured, not looking up. His thumb traced small circles on her shoulder.

"I'll help you translate." His voice rumbled low near her ear. "Whatever you need."

The promise in those words extended far beyond mere translation, and Gianna's heart raced at the implications.

Gianna pulled back from Nykronus, creating space between them. "We can't do this. What if I'm meant to be with a Durant? The prophecies, the bloodlines-"

"What if you are?" Nykronus's voice remained steady. "Or what if it's your sister? Your cousin? A descendant generations from now?"

She wrapped her arms around herself, trying to steady her racing thoughts. The weight of centuries pressed down on her shoulders - every choice, every action rippling through time like stones cast in still water.

"I can't ignore the responsibility. My family's legacy-"

"Is part of who you are, not all you are." Nykronus stepped closer, but didn't touch her. "You can't live your present paralyzed by possibilities, letting ancient prophecies dictate your heart."

Gianna's fingers traced the edge of the Durant manuscript. "The stakes are too high. If we make the wrong choice-"

"There are no wrong choices, only different paths." His words carried the wisdom of centuries. "The prophecies speak of what might be, not what must be. They're guidelines, not chains."

She looked up at him, seeing the truth in his eyes. The same determination that had driven him to protect her family for generations now focused solely on her.

"I'm scared," she admitted. "Not just of making the wrong choice, but of making any choice at all."

"Then let's start with one decision at a time." He gestured to the texts spread before them. "We secure these records first. Create the encrypted copies. Then..."

"Then we see what happens?"

"One day at a time." He held out his hand.

Gianna took it, feeling the familiar spark of connection. "We should use a combination of old and new methods to seal the information. Something that bridges past and present."

"Like us," he said softly.

She squeezed his hand, allowing herself to embrace the possibility of a future not bound by ancient prophecies. "Like us."

Gianna's fingers traced the intricate patterns she'd drawn across multiple pages. Ancient symbols merged with modern cryptographic sequences, creating layers of protection that could only be unlocked by someone with her bloodline. Beside her, Nykronus arranged biblical texts in precise formations.

"Revelations 12:1," she murmured, copying the verse into her cipher. "The woman clothed with the sun." The words shifted under her pen, transforming into complex patterns that matched the energy signatures of the Three Marias.

Nykronus placed his hand over hers as she completed another sequence. "Each layer strengthens the whole. Like threads in a tapestry."

The touch sent warmth spreading up her arm. Their eyes met, and Gianna saw centuries of dedication reflected in his gaze. This wasn't just about protecting knowledge anymore - it was about protecting their shared future.

Cardinal Luciani approached with a silver vessel containing blessed oil. "The final seal requires both of your essences."

Gianna pressed her thumb into the oil, then pressed it to the central page. Nykronus did the same, their prints overlapping. The paper hummed with power as ancient words of protection flowed from Gianna's lips.

"By mountain, sea, and sacred ground," she chanted in the old tongue. "By earth's bounty and heaven's crown."

The Three Marias' power coursed through her veins as she spoke, their essence merging with the protective spells. Each word formed another layer of security, another barrier against those who would misuse this knowledge.

Nykronus's voice joined hers, their words weaving together like the very fabric of reality. The manuscripts glowed briefly before settling into ordinary-looking papers - their true nature hidden beneath layers of magic and mathematics.

"It's done," Gianna exhaled, feeling the weight of responsibility settle more comfortably on her shoulders. The knowledge was secure, protected by both ancient magic and modern ingenuity.

Nykronus gathered the encoded papers, his movements careful and reverent. "We've created something unprecedented - a bridge between worlds, between times."

"Between us," Gianna added softly, and his smile told her he understood precisely what she meant.

Gianna pressed her palm against the final manuscript, feeling the ancient power thrum beneath her skin. Beside her, Nykronus placed his hand over hers, their combined energy sealing the texts with layers of protection both magical and mundane.

"The realm convergence information is the most dangerous." She traced the intricate patterns that detailed how worlds could bleed together. "If the Assembly ever discovered these points of weakness..."

"They won't." Nykronus's thumb brushed across her knuckles. "What we've created here goes beyond traditional wards. Your bloodline, my guardianship - they've evolved into something new."

She turned to face him, still within the circle of his arms. The archives faded away, leaving only this moment to remain - his dark eyes fixed on hers, centuries of dedication transformed into something determined.

"We'll need to monitor the seals," she said. "Work together to maintain them."

"Together." He drew her closer. "No more watching from the shadows. No more denying what's between us."

Gianna's hand found his chest, feeling his heartbeat strong and steady beneath her palm. "The Mazza legacy..."

"It is stronger with both of us protecting it." He touched her cheek. "Guardian and ward, past and present, bound by choice as much as duty."

The final text pulsed with completed magic as their lips met. Gianna felt the power settle into place.

CHAPTER
NINE

Dawn painted the monastery courtyard in shades of amber and gold. Maya rolled the medallion between her palms, its surface warm against her skin. The familiar weight grounded her as she centered herself for morning practice.

Asha perched on the ancient stone wall, her black and orange fur catching the early light. Her luminescent eyes tracked Maya's movements with feline intensity.

Maya lifted the medallion, channeling energy through its crystalline core. The power flowed stronger than before, raising goosebumps along her arms. Blue-white light spiraled outward, forming intricate patterns in the air.

"This is different." Maya's fingers trembled as she tried to direct the surge. The energy resisted her control, pushing against her will like a wild horse straining at the reins.

Asha's tail twitched. Her whiskers bristled with static electricity.

The light show drew attention from early risers heading to morning prayer. A monk paused mid-step, prayer beads slipping from slack fingers. Two novices pressed their faces against a window, pointing and whispering.

Maya's heart raced. Sweat beaded on her forehead as she fought to contain the expanding web of energy. The medallion pulsed, its glow intensifying to a level beyond anything she'd experienced.

"No, no, no." She gritted her teeth. The power surge built like a wave, crackling through the air. Static made her hair stand on end.

Asha leaped down from her perch, circling Maya's feet with an urgent meow.

The energy reached critical mass. Light exploded outward in a brilliant flash, knocking Maya backward. The medallion burned hot against her chest as raw power coursed through her body.

Maya staggered to her feet, ears ringing from the power surge. Her phone buzzed in her pocket - another news alert. She pulled it out, hands still shaking.

The screen lit up with footage from yesterday's incident downtown. There she was, medallion blazing as she redirected the runaway truck before it plowed into the crowd. The clip had gone viral overnight.

"GUARDIAN ANGEL OR VIGILANTE?" scrolled across the bottom of the screen. Social media hashtags flooded the comments: #TheGuardian, #MiracleWoman, and #WhoIsShe.

"Your control's improving." Asha stretched languidly. "But your landing needs work."

Maya scrolled through the reactions. Shaky phone videos showed her interventions from different angles. Witnesses described the mysterious woman who appeared in flashes of blue light, preventing disasters and vanishing just as quickly.

Her phone rang. Mom's face appeared on screen.

"Have you seen the news?" Kaira's voice carried a mix of pride and worry. "Your father's monitoring the coverage from the command center. The energy signatures are drawing attention."

"I know." Maya rubbed her temples. "But I couldn't let those people die."

"We're not saying you should have." The background hum of computers and tactical displays filtered through the speaker. "But we need to be strategic. The wrong kind of attention could compromise everything."

A new alert popped up - amateur footage of blue energy crackling around a collapsing building support. The Guardian materializing to evacuate trapped workers.

"The realm boundaries are thinning," Asha observed. "Your powers are responding to the shift."

Maya watched the footage loop again. The raw energy that had just knocked her down in practice looked controlled and precise on screen. But she remembered the strain, the feeling of barely containing it.

"We need to accelerate your training." Kaira's tactical mind clicked into gear. "If the boundaries continue weakening, you'll need perfect control."

Maya pocketed her phone with a heavy sigh. The Order had protected humanity for centuries, yet no one knew their sacrifices. Her recent headlines felt almost like stealing credit from countless hidden heroes who came before.

"The world deserves to know who keeps them safe." She traced the ancient symbols carved into the monastery wall. "All those lives saved, battles won, evil thwarted - and history remembers none of it."

"Secrecy protects both the Order and those we guard." Asha wound between Maya's feet. "The Malefic Assembly would exploit any weakness, any exposed thread."

Inside the command center, screens displayed global monitoring feeds. Senior members huddled around the tactical table, faces grim. Maya recognized her mother's voice rising above the murmurs.

"The situation is deteriorating." Kaira gestured to energy signature maps. "First the boundary disruptions, then Maya's powers amplifying, now Saint Michael himself manifesting? The pattern suggests major metaphysical instability."

"Our enemies will capitalize on this chaos." Erikson jabbed at incident markers spreading across the display. "We're spread too thin containing the publicity from The Guardian sightings. If the Assembly launches a coordinated strike-"

"They already are." Reagan burst through the door, tablet extended. "Breaking news from Vatican City - St. Peter's Basilica has been attacked. Multiple casualties. Security footage shows Assembly operatives extracting something from the Vatican Grottoes."

The room erupted in controlled chaos. Alerts blared from monitoring stations. Maya's medallion hummed against her chest, responding to the surge of tension.

Her phone buzzed with the public news alert: "TERRORIST ATTACK AT VATICAN - HISTORIC RELIGIOUS ARTIFACTS STOLEN - MULTIPLE DEAD."

Maya's head snapped back as a vision hit her with the force of a physical blow. The command center dissolved around her, replaced by cascading streams of data and electromagnetic waves visible as ribbons of light crisscrossing the sky.

She saw cell towers piercing the veil between worlds like needles through fabric. Satellites orbited overhead, their signals creating a web that pressed against the boundaries of reality. Social media feeds manifested as rivers of glowing information, billions of concurrent connections straining the natural order.

Her consciousness expanded outward, taking in the full scope of modern technology's impact on the metaphysical plane. Wireless signals penetrated ancient wards. Digital networks created new pathways between dimensions that were never meant to connect.

The vision shifted to Aethoria. The realm's crystalline structures pulsed with unstable energy, their normal ethereal glow disrupted by interference patterns. Where technology concentrated in the physical world, corresponding areas of the spiritual plane showed signs of decay.

Maya watched in horror as a new tower activated in downtown San Francisco. Its waves rippled through multiple dimensions, weakening the barriers between worlds. A crack formed in the fabric of reality itself, leaking raw power into the physical plane.

Her medallion burned against her skin, resonating with the disturbed energies. Through its connection, she sensed the growing imbalance between technology and ancient magic. Humanity's digital evolution had accelerated beyond the natural order's ability to adapt.

The vision released her suddenly. Maya stumbled, catching herself against the command center wall. Her chest heaved as she processed what she'd witnessed.

"The digital age." She pressed her palm against her medallion, still hot from the supernatural download. "It's not just changing our world - it's destabilizing the boundaries between all realms."

Asha's fur stood on end, crackling with residual energy. "The ancient magics were never meant to coexist with such pervasive technology. The natural balance is failing."

Maya slumped into a command center chair, her head still spinning from the vision. Asha leaped onto the tactical table, her paws landing between holographic markers of dimensional disturbances.

"Think about what happens when word gets out." Asha's tail swished through a projection of energy signatures.

Zoe placed her hand on Maya's shoulder. "Silicon Valley billionaires, tech corporations, governments - they'll all race to breach the barriers first. Just like they carved up Earth's resources."

Maya's stomach turned as the implications hit home. "They'd try to colonize Aethoria."

"Exploit its power. Mine its crystals. Build server farms in the ethereal planes." Asha's luminescent eyes narrowed. "The same greed that polluted the oceans and razed the rainforests would devastate realms humans were never meant to touch."

The Vatican attack footage played on nearby screens. Maya recognized the Assembly's signature energy weapons, but something was different. The magical signatures showed traces of technological augmentation.

"They're already trying." Maya pointed to the hybrid energy patterns. "The Assembly's combining ancient artifacts with modern tech. That's why my powers are amplifying - they're forcing connections between worlds that should stay separate."

Asha's fur bristled. "The natural order maintained balance for millennia. But humanity's digital web is creating cracks faster than the barriers can heal."

Maya's medallion pulsed as another alert lit up the command center. A tech company's quantum computing experiment had triggered supernatural phenomena in three cities simultaneously.

Her eyes widened as the pieces clicked into place. "That's why the Order stayed hidden all these centuries. It wasn't just about protecting humanity from supernatural threats..."

"It was protecting the other realms from humanity," Asha finished.

Maya shot to her feet. "The Assembly's Vatican attack - they didn't just steal artifacts. They're going to leak proof of other realms to the public. Start a corporate arms race to breach the boundaries."

Benevento, Italy

Stanley's boots echoed against the stone steps as he descended into the Order's weapons vault beneath the monastery. Ancient torches flickered to life, responding to his presence with a soft blue glow. The familiar scent of oil, metal, and old magic filled his nostrils.

He paused at the security scanner, placing his palm against the crystalline panel. Modern technology merged with ancient wards - an elegant solution for protecting centuries of accumulated weapons and artifacts.

The heavy doors swung open. Row upon row of weapons lined the vault walls - swords that had tasted demon blood, spears forged in holy fire, axes blessed by forgotten saints. Each piece carried its own history, its own power.

His attention snapped to the far corner. A faint humming filled the air, growing stronger with each step. The display cases housing the most dangerous weapons vibrated, their contents resonating with unseen energy.

"What in blazes?" Stanley approached a trembling sword rack. Saint George's blade pulsed with inner light, its golden hilt warm to the touch. Next to it, William the Conqueror's mace sparked with electrical discharge.

The sacred weapons had never behaved in this manner before. Stanley moved deeper into the vault, checking each section. Everywhere he looked, ancient armaments stirred as if waking from a long sleep.

Joan of Arc's banner rippled without wind. Sampson's jawbone crackled with barely contained lightning. Even the simple wooden staff of Saint Patrick thrummed with power.

Stanley's combat instincts screamed danger. He pulled out his phone, snapping pictures of the phenomenon. The images showed halos of energy surrounding each weapon, growing stronger by the minute.

"Reagan, you need to see this." He sent the photos to the California command center. "Every blessed blade and holy relic in the vault just powered up. Like they're preparing for war."

The combined energy of the weapons raised the temperature in the vault. Sweat beaded on Stanley's forehead as he documented the unprecedented event. His hand instinctively gripped the hilt of his own sword. This blade had served him faithfully across centuries of reincarnations.

Stanley pulled out a handheld scanner, sweeping it across the vibrating weapons. The digital readout spiked, numbers climbing beyond normal parameters. Energy signatures he'd never encountered before pulsed through the ancient steel and blessed wood.

"These readings don't make sense." He adjusted the scanner's settings, double-checking the calibration. The device's screen flickered as it struggled to process the data. "It's like they're drawing power from multiple realms simultaneously."

He pressed his palm against the nearest display case. The glass hummed beneath his touch, resonating with the weapons inside. Through his connection to the Order's ancient magics, he sensed the shift in dimensional boundaries. The barriers between worlds had grown thin, allowing power to leak through in unprecedented ways.

"Command, the vault's defenses are adapting." Stanley watched as crystalline formations spread across the walls, the Order's protective wards evolving to contain the growing energy. "The ancient security systems are reconfiguring themselves."

He moved through the vault, documenting the changes that had occurred. Centuries-old weapon racks rearranged themselves, grouping artifacts by their energy signatures. Blessed blades aligned with sacred spears, forming geometric patterns that channeled and stabilized the surging power.

The vault's temperature continued rising. Stanley wiped sweat from his brow as he activated emergency cooling systems. Modern climate control merged with magical frost wards, fighting to keep the supercharged weapons from overheating.

A sharp crack echoed through the chamber. Stanley spun toward the sound. Raphael's staff - one of the vault's most powerful relics - had broken free of its containment field. The staff floated upright, golden light rippling along its length. Other weapons followed suit, rising from their displays as if called to attention.

The arsenal of blessed armaments hung suspended in the air, points aligned toward an unseen threat. Their combined power filled the vault with blinding radiance. Stanley's own sword pulled at its sheath, responding to the activation of its ancient companions.

The command center's monitors cast a harsh blue glow across Kaira's face as she studied the incoming reports. Red alert markers multiplied across the global map - Paris, Tokyo, São Paulo, Sydney. The Assembly struck with coordinated precision, targeting sacred sites and technological hubs simultaneously.

"They're not just stealing artifacts." Elan traced the pattern of attacks. "Each target connects to both ancient power sources and modern infrastructure."

Kaira pulled up satellite imagery of the Vatican attack. "Look at the energy signatures. They've modified their weapons with quantum processors. The combination is allowing them to breach dimensional barriers."

The tactical display showed waves of disruption spreading outward from each strike point. Ancient wards flickered and failed as technology-enhanced magic tore through their defenses.

"We need to deploy strike teams." Elan accessed the Order's personnel roster. "Hit them before they can complete whatever ritual they're planning."

"Our forces are spread thin." Kaira highlighted active response units. "Half our teams are containing supernatural outbreaks caused by the weakening barriers. The rest are protecting key sites from follow-up attacks."

Elan's jaw tightened as another alert flashed across the screen. "London's under attack. They've breached the Tower's defenses."

"That's not possible." Kaira zoomed in on the security feeds. "Those wards have held for centuries."

"Not against this." Elan enhanced the footage. Assembly operatives wielded staffs crackling with hybrid energy - ancient wood wrapped in circuitry and quantum processors. "They're using our own artifacts against us, supercharged with bleeding-edge tech."

Kaira's fingers flew across the console, coordinating the Order's response. "We need to adapt our tactics. Traditional containment won't work if they keep forcing connections between realms."

"The boundaries between worlds are collapsing." Elan studied the energy readings. "Each attack accelerates the decay. If we don't stop them soon..."

"Then every nightmare, demon, and dark god humanity's ever feared will come pouring through the cracks." Kaira pulled up the Order's emergency protocols. "And that's assuming the physical world can handle the strain of multiple realities colliding."

Maya traced the attack patterns displayed across the command center screens. Something about their placement nagged at her consciousness. The Assembly wasn't just targeting random sites - they were following an ancient geometric pattern she'd seen in the Order's archives.

"Look." She connected the points on the map. "The attacks form a ritual circle. Each site corresponds to a nexus of technological and spiritual power."

Across the room, Myst pored over combat footage from Vatican City. He paused on frames showing the Assembly's hybrid weapons, analyzing their construction. Years of tactical training merged with his innate understanding of both modern tech and ancient magic.

"We can counter their weapons." He pulled up schematics on his tablet. "If we reconfigure our own artifacts with quantum shielding, we can disrupt their ability to breach the barriers. The Order's blessing ceremonies already create a compatible energy matrix."

"That could work." Kaira studied his proposed modifications. "But we'd need time to implement the changes across our arsenal."

"Then we split our forces." Elan marked defensive positions on the tactical map. "One team adapts our weapons and protects key sites.

The other tracks down the Assembly and stops whatever ritual they're planning."

Maya nodded. "I'll lead the strike team. My powers are stronger now - I can sense their dimensional tampering."

"I'll coordinate weapon modifications," Myst said. "Erikson and Zoe can help implement the hybrid defenses."

"Reagan and I will run tactical support from here." Kaira assigned remaining personnel to critical locations. "Elan, take a team to reinforce the London containment zone. That's likely their next major target."

"I'll get Nykronus and Stanley to meet me in London. I'm proud of you all. Stay safe, I'll see you soon." Elan looked around the room with love and admiration.

The assignments fell into place with practiced efficiency. Strike teams gathered their gear while support units began retrofitting the Order's ancient arsenal. Maya felt the weight of responsibility settle across her shoulders as she prepared to lead her first major offensive.

Myst's fingers flew across the holographic interface as he recalibrated the quantum processors. Around him, the Order's tech lab hummed with activity. Ancient weapons lay arranged on workbenches, their blessed steel gleaming under LED lights.

"Pass me the neural interface," he called to one of his engineers. The device looked like a simple circuit board, but Myst sensed the magical currents flowing through its crystalline components.

He carefully attached the processor to a consecrated sword. The blade's surface rippled as modern technology merged with centuries-old enchantments. Digital readouts confirmed a stable connection - the quantum systems weren't fighting against the weapon's inherent magic.

"Energy signature holding steady," reported Sarah, one of his top specialists. "The blessing ceremonies created perfect quantum entanglement points."

Myst nodded, studying the hybrid weapon's performance metrics. The Order's ancient rituals had unknowingly prepared their arsenal for this technological evolution. Each blessed blade contained patterns that matched the principles of quantum computing.

"Start mass production." He transferred the successful configuration to the lab's fabrication units. "Priority goes to front-line response teams."

The lab's 3D printers whirred to life, laying down microscopic circuits infused with blessed materials. Nearby, engineers attached the completed components to weapons pulled from the Order's vaults. Each successful integration brought them closer to countering the Assembly's dimensional attacks.

Myst moved between workstations, checking progress and making adjustments. His tactical training enabled him to identify potential weaknesses in the hybrid designs. The tech had to enhance the weapons' existing powers without compromising their supernatural effectiveness.

"Sir, first batch is ready for field testing."

Myst picked up a modified combat staff. The ancient wood felt warm against his palm as built-in sensors analyzed his biometric data. Streams of code scrolled across the embedded display, translating magical energy readings into tactical data.

He activated the weapon's combat systems. Blessed energy merged seamlessly with quantum calculations, creating an entirely new form of power. The staff's effectiveness against dimensional breaches would be significantly higher than that of traditional methods.

Erikson crouched behind a fallen pillar, analyzing the Assembly's attack patterns. Their hybrid weapons created dimensional rifts, but the effects weren't instant. He noticed a brief power surge before each breach—a potential weakness.

"Target the processors, not the artifacts," he radioed to his strike team. "Three-second window between activation and breach."

His modified blade hummed with quantum-enhanced power. The Assembly troops advanced, their weapons crackling with corrupted energy. Erikson waited for the telltale surge, then struck. His blade severed the quantum circuits before they could fully power up. The ancient staff in his opponent's hands went dark.

"Confirmed kill on the hybrid tech," he reported. "The blessed components still work without the processors. Strip their upgrades, and they lose the dimensional advantage."

Back at the command center, Myst's tablet lit up with an incoming call from Reagan.

"London team's implementing the new combat protocols," Reagan's voice came through clear despite the background chaos. "Erikson's technique is working. We're seeing seventy percent reduction in successful breaches."

"Good." Myst pulled up the global tactical display. "How's Mom holding up?"

"I'm fine, sweetie." Kaira joined the call from her station. "Coordinating with Vatican security to protect the remaining artifacts. Your weapon modifications are making a huge difference."

"The Assembly didn't expect us to adapt so quickly," Reagan added. "They're falling back to defensive positions around their ritual sites."

Myst studied the energy readings from his sister's location. "Maya's team should be reaching the Paris nexus point soon. If we can disrupt their ritual circle..."

"We'll cut off their access to the quantum-magic interface," Kaira finished. "Keep those weapons coming, Myst. We need every advantage we can get."

Myst calibrated another set of quantum processors, his movements precise and confident. The modified weapons performed better than he'd anticipated - each integration strengthening their defenses against the Assembly's attacks.

"You've really come into your own," Zoe said, approaching his workbench. Her blonde hair was tied back, and her hands were covered in conductive gel from working on the neural interfaces.

Myst glanced up from his work. "Just doing what needs to be done."

"No, it's more than that." Zoe picked up one of the completed weapons, admiring the seamless blend of technology and blessed steel. "Look at you - leading the tech division, innovating hybrid defenses Elan would be proud of."

A warm feeling spread through Myst's chest at the mention of his father. "You think so?"

"I know so. He has that same quiet strength, the ability to see solutions others missed." She set down the weapon. "The way you adapted the blessing ceremonies for quantum enhancement? Pure Durant thinking."

The lab's monitors flashed with incoming data. Their modified weapons had successfully repelled another Assembly attack in Rome. The dimensional barriers held firm, reinforced by Myst's hybrid defenses.

"London team reporting in," Sarah called out. "Zero breaches in the last hour. The new configurations are holding."

Myst allowed himself a small smile. His father had taught him to trust his instincts, to blend modern innovation with ancient wisdom. Those lessons were now helping to turn the tide.

"Command center confirms Assembly forces are retreating worldwide," Zoe read from her tablet. "Their hybrid weapons can't compete with our adaptations."

The lab erupted in cheers. Myst felt the weight of uncertainty lift from his shoulders. They'd done it - found a way to protect the boundaries between worlds while preserving the Order's sacred arsenal.

Maya stared at her hands in disbelief as ripples of energy coursed through her fingers. The air around her shimmered like heat waves rising from hot pavement. A familiar tingle ran up her spine - the exact sensation she'd felt during the Assembly's dimensional attacks.

Asha sat nearby, her black and orange fur glowing with an inner light. The cat's emerald eyes tracked Maya's movements with ancient wisdom.

"Focus on the space between spaces," Asha's voice echoed in Maya's mind. "Reality isn't fixed - it flows like water. You can learn to direct that flow."

Maya reached out, feeling the subtle boundaries between dimensions. The air thickened around her hand, becoming almost solid. She pushed gently, watching reality bend and flex under her touch.

"Good. Now imagine a door." Asha padded closer, her paws

leaving luminescent prints. "Not a physical door - a threshold between here and elsewhere."

Maya closed her eyes, concentrating on that image. The air split open before her, revealing glimpses of other places - sun-drenched meadows, crystalline cities, starlit voids. Her heart raced at the possibilities.

"Careful." Asha's tail brushed Maya's leg. "Don't open the door yet. First, learn to feel its edges."

Maya traced the boundary with her fingertips. The dimensional tear responded to her touch, contracting and expanding like a living thing. She sensed the complex patterns holding reality together - delicate lattices of energy that could be rewoven with proper training.

"The Assembly forces connections." Asha circled the shimmering portal. "You must learn to guide them naturally. Let the boundaries part willingly."

Maya relaxed her grip on the dimensional energies. The tear sealed itself smoothly, leaving only a faint ripple in the air. She felt drained but exhilarated by this newfound ability.

"You're a Boundary Walker." Asha sat back on her haunches. "One who can step between worlds without breaking them. With practice, you'll learn to navigate the spaces in between."

Maya's vision shifted as she concentrated, the world taking on new depths. Ghostly lines crisscrossed the air around her - some thick as rope, others delicate as spider silk. Each thread marked where one reality brushed against another, forming an intricate tapestry of dimensional boundaries.

"The lines are getting clearer," she whispered to Asha. The cat's form seemed to exist in multiple places at once, overlapping with versions of herself from adjacent realities.

"You're seeing the true nature of your role," Asha replied. "Guardians don't just protect physical spaces - they maintain the integrity of these boundaries."

A warm presence washed over Maya. Three distinct energies, each carrying the essence of mountain peaks and ancient wisdom. She recognized them from her studies - the Three Marias of Philippine lore.

Their power felt familiar, like a long-forgotten memory that had finally surfaced.

"They were Guardians too," Asha explained. "Maria Makiling, Maria Cacao, Maria Sinukuan - each tended the boundaries between the mortal world and the realm of spirits. Their mountains were more than just territory - they were anchor points for reality itself."

Understanding bloomed in Maya's mind. The Assembly's attacks weren't just damaging physical locations - they were unraveling the very framework that kept different dimensions separate. She felt the Three Marias' knowledge flow into her, generations of Guardian wisdom crystallizing into instinct.

Maya raised her hands, watching energy spiral between her fingers. The dimensional threads responded to her will, weaving themselves into stronger patterns. Power surged through her body as she embraced her heritage, the combined strength of countless Guardians flowing through her bloodline.

The boundaries around her pulsed with new vitality as she touched them, healing weaknesses she hadn't even noticed before. She wasn't just seeing the dimensional fabric anymore - she was becoming one with it, a living extension of reality's fundamental architecture.

Maya's medallion burned against her chest, its surface blazing with an intensity she'd never felt before. The ancient metal pulsed in rhythm with the dimensional disturbances, which made her skin crawl. She pressed her hand against it, feeling waves of energy cascade through her fingers.

"Something's wrong." She burst into the Order's command center where her family had gathered. "The boundaries - they're all vibrating at once."

Elan and Kaira looked up from their tactical displays. Myst set down the hybrid weapon he'd been calibrating. The urgency in Maya's voice drew them closer.

"Show us," Kaira said.

Maya closed her eyes, extending her awareness outward. The dimensional threads that usually flowed like gentle streams now thrashed violently, their patterns chaotic and strained. She projected what she sensed onto the command center's holographic display.

"Damn," Elan breathed. The visualization showed reality itself buckling under immense pressure.

Asha materialized beside Maya, her fur crackling with ethereal energy. "The convergence we feared is approaching. All dimensions are being drawn together, like moths to a flame."

"How long?" Myst asked, studying the energy patterns.

"Days, perhaps." Asha's tail lashed anxiously. "The Assembly's attacks weakened key anchor points. Now something far older is taking advantage."

The medallion flared again, forcing Maya to grip the edge of the console. Images flooded her mind - ancient beings stirring from dimensional pockets, barriers dissolving like sugar in rain, reality folding in on itself.

"We need to gather the other Guardians," Kaira said. "Call in everyone."

"It won't be enough," Asha warned. "This convergence is beyond anything in recorded history. The Three Marias themselves would struggle against such force."

The command center's sensors began wailing as dimensional breaches appeared worldwide. Not the controlled tears the Assembly had created - these were raw wounds in reality itself.

Maya's medallion pulsed one final time, its surface etched with new symbols that glowed with warning light. The message was clear - their world stood on the brink of fundamental change, and all their knowledge and power might not be enough to stop it.

CHAPTER
TEN

Ancient symbols carved into marble walls cast dancing shadows as holographic scanners swept across their surface. Myst adjusted the calibration on his tablet, watching as each sacred pattern was digitally mapped and analyzed.

St. Michael stood in the center of the chamber, his presence filling the space with an otherworldly radiance. His armor gleamed despite the dim lighting, each plate etched with patterns that matched those on the walls.

"These seals were placed here during the First Crusade," Michael said, running his hand along a particularly complex geometric design. "Your modern instruments may help us understand their true purpose."

Myst nodded, studying the three-dimensional rendering taking shape on his screen. "The patterns form a mathematical sequence - but it's unlike anything I've seen before. The ratios seem to shift depending on how you view them."

"Sacred geometry operates on multiple levels of reality simultaneously." Michael moved to another section of the wall. "What appears as simple decoration to mortal eyes often contains deeper truths."

The scanner beeped as it detected a new pattern hidden beneath centuries of wear. Myst enhanced the image, revealing an intricate series of interlocking circles and triangles.

"There - that's the ritual configuration we need." Michael's wings shifted slightly as he examined the digital reconstruction. "The preparation must follow these exact proportions."

Myst began marking points on the chamber floor with luminescent chalk, carefully measuring the distances between each node. The scanner projected guidelines to ensure perfect alignment with the ancient templates.

"The physical layout is only part of it," Michael cautioned. "Each seal must be activated in precise sequence." He demonstrated by touching one of the marks, causing it to flare with divine energy.

Myst attempted to replicate the gesture at the next point, but the energy flickered and died. "The resonance isn't stable," he observed, adjusting his calculations.

"Your human nature makes it more challenging," Michael explained. "But your bloodline carries enough divine essence to make it possible. Try again."

Myst closed his eyes, letting the mathematical patterns flow through his mind. The sacred geometry felt familiar somehow, like a half-remembered dream trying to surface. He placed his hand on the next seal point, focusing on the precise angles and ratios encoded in the ancient symbols.

This time, a faint blue glow emanated from his fingertips. The light traced the chalk lines, forming luminescent connections between the nodes. His tablet screen flickered as the energy patterns interfered with its sensors.

"The memories are there," Michael's voice seemed to come from a great distance. "Let them guide you."

Images flashed through Myst's consciousness - fragments of other times, other places where these same patterns had manifested. His hand moved instinctively to the next point, and the glow intensified. The chamber's stone walls seemed to pulse with an inner light as each seal activated.

His tablet's holographic display warped and stretched, the digital renderings merging with the actual light patterns now dancing across the chamber. Ancient and modern, physical and virtual, past and present - all bleeding together in ways his instruments couldn't properly process.

The geometric web grew more complex with each activated node. Myst felt power building in the array, resonating with something ingrained in his DNA. His fingers traced the following sequence without conscious thought, following paths laid down centuries before his birth.

A high-pitched whine filled the air as his devices struggled to handle the energy surge. The tablet's screen distorted further, numbers and symbols scrolling past faster than he could track. The sacred patterns on the walls began to shine with their own inner fire.

Suddenly, a massive power spike surged through the array. Every electronic device in the chamber went dark with a sharp crack. The geometric light patterns vanished, plunging them into total darkness.

Seconds later, emergency lights sputtered back to life. Myst's tablet rebooted, its screen showing cascading error messages. The chalk lines on the floor still glowed faintly, holding the template of what had been activated.

Myst blinked away the afterimages as his vision adjusted. The tablet in his hands crackled with residual energy, its screen flickering between ancient symbols and modern diagnostics.

"The seals responded to your blood memory," Michael said. His armor had taken on an iridescent sheen, reflecting patterns that weren't physically present in the chamber. "The combination of your technology and the old ways has awakened something."

The chalk lines pulsed with a steady rhythm now, like a heartbeat flowing through the geometric array. Myst's scanning program had managed to capture partial data before the surge. He swiped through the readings, correlating them with the ancient texts stored in his database.

"These energy signatures match descriptions from the Vatican archives." He projected a holographic overlay onto the chamber walls, highlighting where the patterns aligned. "But the resonance is amplified beyond anything they recorded."

Michael placed his hand on one of the central nodes. Divine light rippled outward, interacting with the digital projection in ways that defied physics. "Your instruments give us precision the old masters could only dream of. But it's your inheritance that makes the connection possible."

The words triggered something in Myst's mind. The chamber seemed to fade around him as memories not his own surfaced...

He saw these same walls centuries ago, when the stone was fresh-cut and the symbols newly carved. Templars knelt in a circle, their armor gleaming in torchlight as they conducted the original ritual. Michael stood among them, guiding their movements as they traced the sacred patterns.

The vision shifted. He watched through another's eyes as hidden meanings were encoded into the geometric forms. Each line and angle is carefully calculated to channel divine energy in specific ways. The mathematics were both familiar and alien - principles his modern training recognized but couldn't fully explain.

The flashback faded as quickly as it had come, leaving Myst gasping. His tablet had recorded a spike in neural activity, but couldn't interpret the data. The chalk lines at his feet glowed brighter, responding to his heightened awareness.

"The first memory returns," Michael observed. "Your ancestors helped create these seals. Their knowledge flows in your blood. We were observers existing outside of this plane of existence."

The chamber walls rippled like water, and Myst's vision split. He saw himself and Michael standing amid the geometric patterns while simultaneously watching robed figures perform an ancient ritual in the same space. The two scenes overlapped, past and present occupying the same reality.

In this doubled awareness, he noticed ethereal versions of himself and Michael hovering above both scenes—translucent observers existing on a plane entirely separate from their own. The chalk lines he'd drawn matched perfectly with trails of energy left by the ancient ceremony.

Knowledge surfaced in his mind, sharp and clear. He remembered standing in this chamber centuries ago, helping Michael prepare the seals that would protect the convergence of realms. The mathematics hadn't just been symbols - they were a language that spoke directly to the fabric of reality.

The robed figures moved in precise patterns, their chants weaving through the geometry. Each step activated another node in the array, building a lattice of divine energy that bridged dimensions. Myst watched his past self guide them through the sequence, Michael's presence anchoring the ritual.

His modern tablet chirped, detecting energy signatures that exactly matched the ancient ceremony. The digital readouts aligned perfectly with the calculations he remembered. Numbers and symbols that had seemed mysterious moments ago now made perfect sense.

Understanding crashed through him like a wave. The ritual hadn't just been about protecting the physical chamber - it had created a template that could be replicated and adapted. His modern technology wasn't just recording the past; it was providing a framework to enhance and improve the original workings.

"The patterns," Myst breathed, watching the overlapping realities pulse in sync. "They're not just mathematical formulas - they're a bridge between times and realms."

The chalk lines flared bright blue as the knowledge was fully integrated. Past and present merged for a moment as the same divine energy flowed through both iterations of the ritual. In his double vision, Myst saw his ethereal self nod in approval as the pieces finally fell into place.

The chamber dissolved around Myst as the memory pulled him deeper into the past. Stone walls transformed into pristine marble columns, and the musty air filled with incense and candlelight.

He inhabited his ancient self now - younger, dressed in the robes of a scholar-priest. Scrolls covered in complex equations and diagrams littered the workspace before him. His hands moved with practiced efficiency, calculating ratios and plotting geometric patterns that ordinary mathematics couldn't describe.

"Your work progresses well." Nykronus materialized from the shadows, his dark robes seeming to absorb the candlelight. Despite his youthful appearance, his eyes held the wisdom of centuries.

Ancient Myst's fingers traced a particularly complex series of interlocking circles. "The divine proportions reveal themselves in unexpected ways. Each calculation opens new possibilities."

"You see patterns others miss." Nykronus examined the scrolls. "Your gift for sacred geometry surpasses even the elder priests."

The mathematical formulas danced in Ancient Myst's mind - not just symbols on parchment, but living expressions of universal truth. He understood now why these memories had been sealed away. The knowledge was too vast, too powerful for a single lifetime to contain.

"The ratios aren't just measurements," Ancient Myst explained, sketching a new diagram. "They're doorways between realms. Each intersection creates a resonance that-"

"That bridges dimensions," Nykronus finished. "Yes. Your insights will help forge the foundations of what's to come."

Ancient Myst's hand moved across the parchment, geometric patterns flowing from his quill with supernatural precision. The mathematics felt as natural as breathing - complex calculations that would take modern computers hours to process manifested instantly in his mind.

Nykronus watched the equations take shape, a slight smile playing at the corners of his lips. "Your gift was no accident, young one. The patterns chose you as much as you chose them."

Ancient Myst's quill danced across the parchment, leaving trails of calculations in its wake. The mathematics flowed through him like music - each formula a note in a grand symphony of universal truth. His mind processed complex theorems that had confounded scholars for generations, seeing solutions with crystal clarity.

"Remarkable," Nykronus murmured, examining a scroll filled with intricate geometric patterns. "These calculations - they perfectly describe the resonance between physical and divine realms. Even our most learned priests couldn't map these relationships."

Ancient Myst barely heard him, lost in the pure mathematical poetry unfolding before him. His quill traced new patterns—circles within circles, triangles that shifted between dimensions. These ratios captured the very rhythm of creation. The calculations came faster now, spilling onto the parchment in an elegant dance of numbers and symbols.

The geometric design began to shimmer as he worked, faint traces of blue light outlining each perfect curve and angle. Ancient Myst paused, watching as divine energy flowed through his calculations, illuminating hidden connections he somehow knew would be there.

Nykronus drew in a sharp breath. "Those patterns - that light. This is St. Michael's divine mathematics. Knowledge kept secret since the foundation of creation itself." His dark eyes fixed on Ancient Myst with newfound intensity. "No mortal mind should be able to comprehend these formulas, let alone reproduce them with such precision."

Myst finally had a wave of understanding crash through him as he watched himself in the flashback. The familiar feel of the calculations, the way the knowledge seemed to flow from some deep well of memory - it wasn't just natural talent or divine blessing. These were lessons he had learned before, studying directly under St. Michael's guidance in a previous life. The mathematics felt like coming home because he was remembering, not learning.

"I was a big part of all of this," Myst whispered, watching the glowing patterns pulse in harmony with his heartbeat. "Before this life. I was already working toward all of this centuries later. Wild..."

The memory shifted, and Myst found himself standing in a vast chamber beneath the Vatican. Ancient maps covered the walls, connected by glowing lines of sacred geometry that pulsed with divine energy. His past self moved between the displays, adjusting calculations and fine-tuning the resonance patterns.

"The network must span the entire known world," St. Michael said, his armor reflecting the blue light of the geometric web. "Each node reinforces the others, creating a lattice of protection."

Myst watched through his past self's eyes as his hands traced new connections on the maps. The mathematics flowed naturally, each calculation expanding the sacred pattern. Lines of power connected sacred sites across continents - churches, monasteries, and ancient temples converted to Christian use.

The Order's seal took shape at each intersection—a complex geometric pattern that appeared deceptively simple to the untrained eye. But Myst recognized the divine ratios encoded in every line and curve. The seal wasn't just a symbol - it was a mathematical formula that tapped into the fundamental forces of creation.

"I designed this," Myst whispered, the knowledge crystallizing in his mind. "The Order's seal - I created it to anchor the protection network."

In his memory, his past self sketched the final iterations of the seal, infusing each line with sacred geometry. The pattern seemed to breathe as divine energy flowed through it, creating a resonance that rippled across the network of ley lines.

St. Michael nodded in approval as the seal's power manifested. "Your gift for divine mathematics made this possible. The network will stand for centuries, guarding against forces that would threaten the balance."

The maps pulsed with blue fire as the network activated fully for the first time. Myst felt the energy surge through the geometric patterns, connecting sacred sites across thousands of miles. Each seal reinforced the others, creating a web of protection that transcended physical space.

The mathematical principles behind it all clicked into place in Myst's mind—not just remembered, but understood at a fundamental level. He saw how the sacred geometry created harmonic frequencies that resonated with divine power, how each calculation contributed to the greater whole.

The implications hit Myst with crystal clarity. The ancient protection grid wasn't just a historical artifact - it was a living system that could be enhanced with modern technology. His tablet's scanning program had already mapped portions of the network, detecting energy signatures at known sacred sites worldwide.

"The seals aren't just passive barriers," Myst said, pulling up a holographic map overlaid with geometric patterns. "They're nodes in a worldwide web of divine mathematics."

Michael nodded. "The original network was revolutionary for its time. But your ancestors knew technology would advance."

Myst's fingers flew across the tablet, correlating ancient calculations with modern data. The protection pattern revealed itself in perfect mathematical harmony—a blend of sacred geometry and quantum mechanics that transcended conventional physics. Each seal point acted as both receiver and transmitter, creating a self-reinforcing field of divine energy.

The chalk lines at his feet pulsed brighter as he input the final calculations. His tablet interfaced seamlessly with the ancient system, digital precision enhancing the sacred mathematics. The geometric patterns began to shimmer with renewed power.

"System initializing," Myst announced, watching energy levels spike across the network. "Modern processors handling the calculations, original divine framework providing the power."

Blue light rippled through the chamber as the upgrade took hold. The holographic display showed seal points activating across the globe, each node pulsing in perfect synchronization. Ancient and modern, digital and divine, merged into something entirely new.

The chamber walls vibrated with contained power as the system reached full activation. Myst's tablet screen flared bright enough to cast shadows, its processors barely keeping up with the surge of data. The chalk lines blazed like blue fire, geometric patterns lifting off the floor to form three-dimensional shapes in the air.

A wave of energy pulsed outward through the network, each seal point amplifying and redirecting the power. The protection grid hummed with newfound strength, its capabilities expanded far beyond what the original builders had imagined possible.

The geometric patterns cast shifting shadows across Myst's face as Nykronus stepped into the circle. The ancient being's dark robes seemed to absorb the pulsing blue light, creating an otherworldly contrast against the illuminated chamber walls.

"What you remember is no accident," Nykronus said. "Your soul's journey was... different from the others."

Myst's tablet continued recording energy signatures as Nykronus traced one of the geometric lines with his foot. The pattern flared brighter at his touch.

"I wasn't sure St. Valentine's Dagger of Love would work when I used it on Elan. I didn't know it worked on Kaira. I wanted to find a way. In ancient Rome, I discovered a way to preserve souls using sacred mathematics. Your own calculations provided the foundation."

Nykronus's eyes held centuries of carefully guarded knowledge. "I used my immortal essence as an anchor, binding your soul through time itself."

The revelation hit Myst like a physical force. "While the others were reincarnated because of Verendana's actions..."

"Yes. I spent centuries maintaining the preservation spell, appearing at crucial moments throughout history to reinforce it. Each generation of the Order unknowingly contributed to the pattern, but the core mathematics required my constant attention."

Nykronus gestured at the glowing designs. "These same principles you developed as St. Michael's apprentice became your protection. You both sacrificed yourself to protect the realms. I created waypoints across time, mathematical anchors where I could strengthen the bonds keeping your soul intact—to save you and bring you back. St. Michael reappeared because he used his divine essence to lessen the burden placed upon you."

"That's why you sought out Grandma Gianna," Myst whispered. "You needed her translations about soul preservation."

"The cost was significant." Nykronus's voice carried the weight of ages. "Parts of my own power, soul, and memories were sacrificed to maintain the spell. But preserving St. Michael's chosen apprentice was worth the price."

Myst felt the truth settle into his bones as he watched Nykronus. This being had dedicated centuries to protecting his soul, ensuring he would return at the right moment. The depth of that commitment staggered him.

"Ancient Maya..." Myst started.

"Could not be preserved the same way. The mathematics would only work for a single soul. So I used the dagger on her after she passed." Sorrow flickered across Nykronus's ageless features. "I had to choose. You were the best choice. You already made a selfless choice to save a future you didn't even know."

The geometric patterns surrounding Myst pulsed erratically, matching the chaos in his mind. His knees buckled as memories crashed through him like tidal waves—ancient mathematical formulas colliding with modern military tactics, two lifetimes of muscle memory fighting for control.

"Make it stop," he gasped, clutching his head. The chamber walls seemed to ripple, stone morphing into marble then back again. One moment, he smelled incense and candle wax; the next, gun oil and electronics.

His hands traced defensive patterns in the air without conscious thought, sacred geometry manifesting in trails of blue light. His tablet sparked and whined, its screen flooding with calculations he hadn't input. Reality bent around him as the timelines bled together.

"Who am I?" The words came out in Latin, then English. He saw his modern family—Maya, Kaira, Elan—but overlaid with faces from centuries past. Combat stances from Elan and Austin's Special Forces training merged with the Order's ritual gestures. Divine mathematics flowed through his mind alongside tactical assessments.

"Both lives are equally real," St. Michael's voice cut through the chaos. "Both experiences have shaped who you are."

Myst's breath came easier as understanding dawned. The geometric patterns steadied, modern and ancient symbols interweaving in harmony. His tablet's readings aligned perfectly with remembered ritual measurements. The two skill sets weren't fighting anymore - they were combining into something new.

His hands moved in practiced motions, military precision enhancing ancient spellwork. Modern tactical thinking provided new applications for divine mathematics. The chamber hummed with power as both aspects of himself found balance.

"I remember everything now," Myst said, watching reality stabilize around him. "Both lives. Both purposes. Memories from when we existed between planes and observing key moments in time." The geometric patterns settled into a new configuration, reflecting his integrated understanding. He wasn't just a modern soldier or an ancient mathematician—he was both, and something more.

St. Michael's armor gleamed in the blue light as he approached Myst. "Your mathematical gift wasn't random. I chose you specifically for your ability to see patterns others couldn't - to understand the divine mathematics at their deepest level."

Nykronus traced one of the geometric lines with his staff. "My task was ensuring you would be reborn at precisely this moment in time. The preservation spell was designed to activate when the three realms began merging."

"The technology," Myst said, understanding dawning. "You knew modern advances would affect the stability between realms."

"Yes." Nykronus gestured, and the air filled with shimmering points of light - a map of sacred sites across time. "I maintained the preservation spell through these anchor points. Each location served as a mathematical checkpoint, allowing me to strengthen the bonds holding your soul intact."

St. Michael's wings shifted, casting strange shadows. "The Three Marias helped maintain balance while Nykronus guided bloodlines to ensure proper reincarnation for you, while your sister unlocked her full potential as a Guardian."

"But why now?" Myst asked, though he could already sense the answer forming.

"You're the only one who understands both worlds," St. Michael explained. "Ancient seals and modern technology. Divine mathematics and digital computation. The Order's defenses must evolve - and you alone can bridge that gap."

Nykronus nodded. "The sanctuaries need redesigning. Lazarus grows stronger, and the old protections won't hold. Your unique perspective makes you essential to preventing the realms from collapsing entirely."

The geometric patterns pulsed as Myst processed this. His rebirth wasn't just about preserving knowledge - it was about adapting ancient protections for a modern world at precisely the right moment in time.

"The preservation wasn't just about keeping your knowledge intact," St. Michael said, his celestial armor gleaming with an other-worldly radiance that cast dancing reflections across the chamber walls. "We needed someone who could understand both worlds - someone who could see the divine patterns in modern technology and translate them into something new."

Nykronus stepped forward, his dark robes absorbing the pulsing light like a void against the brilliance. "The sacred sites I used as anchor points formed a mathematical framework across time itself." He gestured with fluid grace, and points of golden light bloomed in the air, forming a complex web of interconnected locations that spun and shifted like a living constellation. "Each checkpoint allowed me to strengthen the preservation spell, weaving threads of protection through centuries to ensure your soul would reach this precise moment."

"The Three Marias were essential," St. Michael added, his voice resonating with divine authority. "Their ancient power helped maintain balance while Nykronus guided the bloodlines through time. Your sister's path as a Guardian and your rebirth were carefully orchestrated, pieces of a puzzle centuries in the making."

Myst watched the glowing pattern of anchor points, his trained mind recognizing how they aligned perfectly with known sanctuary locations worldwide. The mathematical precision behind it took his breath away - centuries of careful calculations and adjustments, all leading to this singular moment in time.

"The sanctuaries need updating," Nykronus said gravely, his ancient eyes reflecting centuries of wisdom and concern. "Lazarus grows stronger with each passing day, and the old protections won't hold against modern threats. Your understanding of both divine mathematics and current technology makes you uniquely qualified to adapt our defenses for this new age."

Reality rippled around them as the weight of this truth settled in, making the air itself feel heavy with possibility. The chamber walls seemed to flex and waver like liquid mercury, ancient stone blending seamlessly with modern steel. The geometric patterns shifted in response, adjusting and realigning themselves to maintain stability between the merging realms.

"The collapse must be prevented," St. Michael stated, his wings unfurling slightly with tension. "The barriers between worlds grow thinner each day, wearing away like ancient stone. Without properly adapted protections, all three realms risk destruction - and everything we've fought to preserve will be lost."

Myst felt the enormity of the task ahead pressing down on his shoulders like a physical weight. His rebirth hadn't been a random act of chance or mere preservation - it was a carefully planned response to a threat that had been foreseen centuries ago, orchestrated across the very fabric of time itself. The future of the realms themselves depended on successfully merging ancient wisdom with modern innovation, and he alone possessed the unique perspective to bridge that crucial gap.

CHAPTER

ELEVEN

Reagan stifled a yawn as Austin set a steaming cup of coffee on her desk. The command center's dim lighting cast a blue glow across the banks of monitors, displaying supernatural activity on a large map of the world. Ancient runes pulsed steadily along the modernized walls, their soft amber light a stark contrast to the LED screens.

At their stations, Erikson and Zoe fought off sleep, maintaining their vigilance over the night shift operations. Erikson adjusted his headset while Zoe stretched in her chair.

The protective wards flickered - just for a moment.

"Spooky," Zoe said, forcing a laugh. "Like someone walked over my grave."

One of the operators raised his hand. "Ma'am, got an anomaly in sector seven."

Reagan leaned forward, squinting at her security feed as static crackled across the screen. She tapped the side of the monitor with her knuckles.

The protection symbols embedded in the walls pulsed erratically, their usual steady rhythm disrupted.

"We should probably get ready," Zoe muttered, her fingers flying across her keyboard.

Murmurs spread through the command center as more monitors displayed interference. Magical sensors spiked, their readings jumping beyond normal parameters. The ancient ward stones set into the foundation began to hum, their vibrations traveling through the floor.

"System failure in sectors three through six," Erikson called out, his voice tight. "Magic signatures are off the charts."

The central security alarm blared, red warning lights bathing the command center. Protection runes flashed from amber to crimson. Computer screens filled with threat warnings as energy readings surged past safety thresholds.

"This is Night Supervisor. All teams mobilize," Reagan barked into her comm. "This is not a drill."

Security teams grabbed enhanced weapons from the armory while operators initiated emergency protocols. Ancient defenses hummed to full power, modern security measures engaging in sync. First response teams moved into defensive positions as multiple breach points appeared on the main display.

Technology systems began failing in sequence. Magical barriers strained against unseen pressure. Static noise-filled communication channels.

Through the failing security feeds, Reagan caught the first glimpse of dark figures moving with inhuman speed. Both technological and magical defenses collapsed simultaneously, leaving the Order's integrated security compromised.

"Full alert status," Reagan commanded. "All teams to defensive positions. We are under attack."

Reagan's voice crackled through failing comm channels as tactical teams moved with practiced precision through the Order's halls. Ancient ward stones pulsed beneath their feet, their power surging through the facility's foundation.

"Teams Alpha through Delta, secure the perimeter," she ordered, watching dots of blue light move across her tactical display. "Echo and Foxtrot, maintain interior defense lines."

In the armory, Erikson distributed enhanced weapons, his movements swift and economical. "Four to a team. Check your crystals, people."

Sacred symbols etched into rifle barrels began to glow as blessed ammunition slid into place. The sharp clicks of magazines loading echoed through the chamber.

"Comms failing in sector five," Zoe called out, her fingers dancing across multiple keyboards. She grabbed a handful of communication crystals, synchronizing their frequencies. "Backup channels only."

Tech-enhanced armor powered up with a low hum as Order members secured chest plates and gauntlets. Blue energy coursed through the metallic fibers, ancient runes awakening beneath modern alloys.

"Team leads, sound off," Reagan commanded, her voice steady despite the static. The ward stones' vibrations intensified, sending tremors through the command center's floor.

Zoe moved between the assembled teams, performing last-minute equipment checks. "Crystal sync confirmed. Sacred seals at full power." She adjusted frequency modulators on their tactical gear, ensuring the ancient and modern systems worked in harmony.

The defensive lines formed with practiced efficiency - four-person teams taking predetermined positions throughout the facility. Enhanced weapons hummed with building energy as blessed rounds chambered. Protection wards flared to life along walls and doorways, their amber light mixing with the red emergency beacons.

Reagan watched the tactical display as family members took their positions. Maya's marker pulsed at the eastern defensive point - the St. Michael medallion around her neck, casting a brilliant blue glow through the corridor. Through the security feed, Reagan caught a glimpse of her niece's determined expression as Maya checked her enhanced rifle.

"Eastern point secured," Maya's voice crackled through the comm. "Medallion's responding to something big."

Myst appeared at Reagan's side, his tablet displaying real-time troop movements. "Teams Bravo and Charlie are in position. Delta is moving to reinforce the north wing." He shared a quick look with his aunt, years of tactical training evident in his calm demeanor.

Two levels below, Kaira's hands flew across ancient tomes, securing irreplaceable texts in spelled containment units. Sacred seals flared to life as she activated each protection ritual, modern scanning systems confirming successful archival lockdown.

"Archives secured," Kaira reported. "Initiating final containment protocols."

Throughout the facility, extended family members of the Order took their posts. Cousins who had trained together since childhood now stood ready at critical junctions. Uncles and aunts who had passed down combat techniques through generations manned defensive positions.

The facility's hybrid defenses engaged in a precise sequence of events. Ancient ward stones pulsed in harmony with modern shield generators. Spelled barriers shimmered into existence as automated turrets powered up. Security cameras linked to scrying pools, providing both technological and magical surveillance.

Maya caught Myst's eye through a security feed as her medallion flared brighter. He gave her a slight nod - the silent communication perfected through years of twin-bond training. Kaira looked up at a monitor showing Reagan and Myst, allowing herself a brief moment of connection before returning to her tasks.

Layered protection spells cascaded through the facility's architecture. Modern systems completed diagnostic checks as magical barriers reached full power. In the most sacred areas, ancient seals activated automatically, mechanical locks engaging in concert with centuries-old protective enchantments.

The Order's hybrid defenses stood ready - family, technology, and ancient magic united against whatever approached.

Reagan watched the defensive grid power up across her monitors. Blue energy cascaded through the facility's infrastructure as ancient wards merged with modern technology. Each screen showed teams in position, their markers steady despite the growing interference.

The first anomaly appeared on the perimeter sensors—a darkness more profound than the night itself. More shadows materialized, moving with unnatural fluidity. The tech readings made Reagan's breath catch - energy signatures unlike anything in their database.

Through the surveillance feeds, she saw them emerge. Cultists, but changed. Crystal formations protruded from their flesh, pulsating with an inner light that caused the ward stones to resonate in response. Their movements followed precise patterns, testing the defensive lines with calculated precision.

"Multiple breaches detected," Erikson reported, his voice tight. "They're probing for weaknesses."

Static crackled across the comm channels as Maya's team reported increased pressure along the eastern perimeter. The energy readings continued to climb, exceeding known thresholds.

Reagan felt it before the sensors registered - a massive surge of power that made the air itself feel heavy. Reality twisted, folding in on itself as space tore open in the center of their defensive formation.

Through the breach stepped a figure that made the ward stones scream in protest. Lazarus moved with fluid grace, his form both familiar and wrong. Cybernetic enhancements gleamed beneath his skin, merging seamlessly with flesh. Ancient symbols crawled across his modified body, their power disrupting the Order's defensive grid wherever his gaze fell.

With a gesture, he sent cascading failures through their systems. Screens flickered as protection spells wavered. Yet he maintained perfect composure, surveying the assembled Order forces with almost clinical detachment.

Reagan caught Austin's worried glance across the command center. Around the facility, she saw the same concern reflected in the faces of her family members as they realized just how outmatched they might be.

The first explosion rocked the eastern wing, followed instantly by three more detonations that shook the facility's foundations. Reagan steadied herself against the command console as alerts flooded her screens. Through the security feeds, she watched cultists pour through the breach points, their crystalline augmentations casting prismatic light across the corridors.

"Echo Team, hold that junction," she ordered, watching Team Lead Martinez direct suppressing fire. Blessed rounds sparked against energy shields emanating from the cultists' crystal tech. Two cultists dropped as rounds found gaps in their defenses, but more pushed forward.

"North sector compromised," Erikson reported. "Delta Team falling back to secondary positions."

On her tactical display, Reagan tracked the spreading combat. Order teams maintained disciplined fire from reinforced positions, but the cultists' new tech was unlike anything they'd encountered. Energy beams sliced through sacred barriers that had stood for centuries.

A screech of static cut through the comm channels as Team Charlie reported casualties. Reagan's stomach turned as she recognized the voice of her cousin James calling for medical support. Through fragmenting video feeds, she glimpsed Order members dragging wounded to safety while others maintained covering fire.

"Reroute Beta Team to support Charlie's position," Reagan commanded, her fingers flying across the console to update tactical overlays. The ward stones beneath the facility pulsed erratically, ancient defenses struggling to adapt to the hybrid threats.

More alarms blared as security systems failed in sequence. Sacred barriers flickered and died as crystalline energy weapons overloaded their magical matrices. Reagan watched protection spells that had guarded the Order for generations collapse under the sustained assault.

"We're losing long-range comms," Zoe called out, frantically working to maintain their tactical network. "Switching to local channels only."

Through the chaos of battle, Reagan caught glimpses of the cultists' coordinated movements. They weren't just attacking - they were herding the defenders, pushing them toward specific points within the facility. Whatever their objective, this was no simple assault.

Stanley braced against the vault's reinforced doorway as another explosion rocked the facility. Ancient weapons thrummed behind him, their power building in response to the threats outside. His enhanced rifle clicked empty - the blessed rounds barely slowing the crystal-augmented cultists advancing down the corridor.

"They're not just attacking - they're targeting specific artifacts," he growled into his comm, switching to his backup weapon. The sacred shield mounted on the wall near him pulsed with increasing intensity.

Through the smoke and chaos, he watched Order teams attempt standard containment protocols only to have their tactics shattered by hybrid attacks. Energy beams laced with corrupted magic cut through defensive positions. Reality rippled around the cultists as they pressed forward, their movements distorting the very fabric of space itself.

"Standard patterns aren't working," Maya's voice crackled through his earpiece. "Switching to adaptive response protocols."

Order teams began shifting tactics mid-battle, breaking into smaller units that could respond faster to the reality distortions. Traditional firing lines gave way to guerrilla-style strikes as defenders learned to anticipate the cultists' dimensional shifts.

A massive blast of crystalline energy struck the vault's outer defenses. Sacred seals flared as they absorbed the impact, but Stanley saw hairline cracks spreading through the ancient barriers. Behind him, weapons of power began resonating in harmony, responding to the imminent threat.

"Multiple breaches on vault level," he reported, watching Order teams fall back under the cultists' relentless advance. "They're using focused attacks - they know exactly what they're after."

The shield on the wall suddenly blazed with blue fire. Other artifacts in the vault awakened, their combined power making the air thick with potential. Stanley felt the weight of centuries pressing against him as he made split-second decisions about which relics to prioritize if the defenses failed.

Another blast shook the vault's foundations. Sacred weapons hummed louder, their song building toward a crescendo as the hybrid assault intensified. Through gaps in the failing barriers, Stanley caught glimpses of cultists moving with inhuman precision, their crystal tech pulsing in perfect rhythm with their corrupted spellwork.

Reagan's screens flickered and died one by one as system after system failed. The command center plunged into darkness before emergency lighting cast everything in a blood-red glow. Ancient runes etched into the walls flared to life, their amber light providing an eerie backup to the failing modern technology.

"We've lost the main grid," Erikson shouted, yanking off his now-useless headset. "Switching to crystal comms."

Through fragmenting security feeds, Reagan watched Order members engage the cultists in close combat as their enhanced weapons malfunctioned. Maya ducked under a crystalline blade, her training taking over as she struck with practiced precision. Beside her, Myst moved in perfect sync, years of twin-combat drills evident in their coordinated defense.

In the eastern chamber, magical energy crackled as Zoe deflected corrupted spells. Her counter-attacks illuminated the ancient stones, but the cultists pressed forward, their hybrid abilities overwhelming traditional magical defenses.

"Team Charlie, fall back!" Reagan ordered through failing comms. She watched in horror as another squad took heavy casualties, their modern weapons barely slowing the enhanced cultists. Despite their discipline, Order members were being systematically pushed back.

The first line buckled as multiple breach points widened. Crystal-enhanced cultists poured through the gaps, their augmented bodies shrugging off conventional attacks. More Order members fell; their training was insufficient against this overwhelming force.

"All teams, fall back to secondary positions," Reagan commanded, her voice steady despite the situation. "Priority one is preservation of forces."

The strategic retreat began as teams covered each other's withdrawal. Through static-filled feeds, Reagan saw the full scale of their defeat - dozens of cultists advancing methodically. At the same time, Order members limped toward fallback positions, carrying their wounded.

The first defensive line collapsed completely as reality itself seemed to tear apart, allowing more corrupted forces to enter. Reagan's heart sank as she realized their strongest defenses had failed in less than an hour.

"Everyone fall back," she ordered, watching the remaining teams scramble to regroup. "I repeat, all forces to secondary positions."

Kaira stood guard at the archive entrance, ancient texts secured behind layers of spelled barriers. Smoke from the ongoing battle drifted through the corridors, carrying the acrid scent of discharged energy weapons and burned stone. Her hands remained steady on her rifle, enhanced sights scanning the approaching darkness.

A figure emerged from the smoke - tall, graceful, familiar in a way that made Kaira's chest tighten. Verendana moved with fluid precision, crystal formations gleaming beneath her skin. Their eyes met across the distance, recognition sparking between them like lightning.

Power crackled in the air as they faced each other. Verendana's augmentations pulsed with corrupted energy, while protection wards flared around Kaira in response. Neither woman moved, the weight of their shared past hanging heavy between them.

"Still playing guardian, I see." Verendana's voice carried traces of an accent Kaira remembered from centuries ago. "Some things never change."

"And you're still serving the wrong side." Kaira's grip tightened on her weapon. "I remember when you stood with us, before your obsession with St. Valentine twisted everything."

Verendana's laugh held no warmth. "Twisted? He opened my eyes - literally and figuratively. Or have you forgotten how your precious Order left me blind?"

"We tried to help you," Kaira countered, memories of ancient healing chambers surfacing. "Valentine didn't cure you - he corrupted you."

"The Order's version of help was letting me suffer while they debated ethics." Crystal formations rippled beneath Verendana's skin. "Valentine acted while your leaders theorized. He gave me sight, power, purpose."

"At what cost?" Kaira's protective instincts flared. "Look what you've become."

"I've become stronger than the Order ever allowed." Verendana's augmentations pulsed brighter. "Strong enough to take what should have been freely given. *Saint* Valentine was betrayed and chose the right side. He was my savior and was reincarnated as my son. You had no right to imprison my son!"

Kaira's heart pounded as Verendana's crystal augmentations pulsed with increasing intensity. The air crackled with corrupted energy, making the archive's ward stones flare in response. Behind her, ancient texts began to resonate, their pages rustling with building power.

"You really think I'm just here for Dante, don't you?" Verendana's laugh echoed through the chamber. "He was just the beginning." Serpent-like shadows shifted, forming intricate patterns that distorted the space around her. "The Three Marias hold secrets the Order has hidden for centuries. Secrets that could reshape reality itself."

Kaira channeled power through her enhanced weapon, blessed energy merging with traditional spells as she maintained her defensive stance. The archive's protection matrices hummed in harmony with her actions, as centuries of Order training flowed through her muscle memory.

Verendana thrust her hand forward, crystal shards erupting from her skin. They twisted through the air, carrying waves of corrupted magic. Kaira countered with a barrier of pure energy, Order sigils blazing to life around her. The collision sent ripples through reality itself.

"Your family took everything from me," Verendana snarled, her augmentations pulsing faster. "The Order chose who was worthy of power, of healing, of knowledge. The Marias' wisdom belongs to all, not just your precious bloodlines."

Ancient texts began to glow behind Kaira, their pages illuminated with internal light. She felt their power responding to the threat, centuries of accumulated knowledge becoming an active defense. The archive's very walls seemed to pulse with awakening energy.

"This was never about Dante's imprisonment," Kaira realized, watching crystal formations spread across Verendana's skin. "You're after the Marias' original teachings - the power they sealed away."

"Finally seeing clearly?" Verendana's augmentations flared brighter. "Like I did when Valentine showed me the truth? The Order has hoarded the Marias' real legacy long enough. I'm not just after their teachings, I'm here to put an end to the three Marias—once and for all."

Sacred barriers rippled as Verendana unleashed another wave of crystal-enhanced power. Kaira wove traditional spells with modern defenses, feeling the weight of generations of Order knowledge supporting her stance. Behind her, the ancient texts continued to resonate, their power building in response to the escalating conflict.

Kaira's mind raced as she maintained the protective barrier. Behind her, the archive's ancient texts pulsed with increasing urgency, their power resonating through the chamber. Each beat matched her racing heartbeat as she processed the magnitude of Verendana's revelation.

Through the smoke-filled corridors, she heard the sounds of battle - her family and fellow Order members fighting to protect everything they held sacred. Maya's voice crackled through failing comms, calling for support in the eastern wing. Myst's energy signature flared as he engaged multiple cultists.

Verendana pressed forward, her crystal augmentations sending waves of corrupted power against Kaira's defenses. "Choose wisely, old friend. Your children or these dusty books? Time grows short."

The archive's protective matrices strained under the assault. Centuries of accumulated knowledge lay vulnerable behind failing barriers. Kaira felt the weight of responsibility pressing down - generations of Order guardians had died protecting these secrets.

Yet her children fought somewhere in the chaos beyond. Maya and Myst's lives hung in the balance, their young powers still developing. They weren't ready to face this level of threat.

Verendana's next attack shattered the outer barrier. Crystal shards pierced the remaining defenses, their corrupted energy eating through ancient protections. "The Three Marias' power was never meant to be hidden. Their secrets can reshape reality itself."

The archive's texts flared brighter in response to the immediate threat. Their power called to Kaira, offering strength if she stayed to defend them. But another explosion rocked the facility, and Maya's pained cry cut through the failing comm system.

Kaira's hands steadied on her weapon as clarity struck. The Three Marias' secrets were vital, but her children were everything to her. With practiced precision, she activated the archive's final defense protocol—a last-resort measure that would seal the chamber completely.

"You won't reach these texts," Kaira declared, backing toward the exit as ancient mechanisms engaged. "But you've revealed more than you intended. The Three Marias aren't just knowledge to be protected - they're still active in our world."

Verendana's crystal formations pulsed with rage as massive stone barriers began sliding into place. "You have no idea what forces you're truly dealing with."

Kaira watched in horror as crystalline light erupted from Verendana's augmentations, forming intricate patterns in the air. What started as random energy discharge coalesced into precise technical schematics—detailed blueprints of Order sanctuaries worldwide.

"You see it now?" Verendana's augmentations pulsed with each word. "Every sanctuary, every hidden refuge, mapped and analyzed over decades."

The glowing diagrams shifted, revealing layer upon layer of security systems, both magical and technological. Red lines traced paths through defenses, highlighting vulnerabilities that Kaira hadn't known existed. Her stomach dropped as she recognized the implications - this wasn't just about breaking into one facility.

"The crystal tech was phase one." Verendana gestured, and new schematics bloomed in the air. "Hybrid attacks to test responses. Each sanctuary's unique defenses, cataloged and countered."

Networks of corrupted sites appeared, forming a web that spanned continents. Kaira saw patterns emerge - systematic targeting of key Order strongholds, each attack building on data gathered from the last. The technical precision behind it all spoke of years of careful planning.

"You've been compromising our defenses all along," Kaira breathed, watching timeline projections materialize. "Every skirmish, every probe..."

"Testing reactions. Analyzing responses." Verendana's smile held no warmth. "Your precious Order, so confident in ancient protections, never saw the pattern. Tech and magic, merged in ways your scholars claimed impossible."

The floating displays showed hybrid attack sequences—crystal-enhanced cultists using corrupted magic in precisely calculated ways. Each assault had peeled back another layer of Order defenses, feeding data into a master plan that spanned years.

"All those random attacks," Kaira said, pieces falling into place. "They weren't random at all."

"Every engagement mapped another weakness." Verendana's augmentations flared brighter. "Every retreat gave us more data. Your Order's greatest strength - its predictability - became its fatal flaw."

Maya's medallion pulsed against her chest, its rhythm syncing with distant energies she'd never felt before. Through the chaos of battle, patterns emerged - not just in the cultists' movements, but in the very fabric of reality around them. Her fingers traced the ancient metal as understanding dawned.

Across the chamber, Myst's eyes widened as he processed the mathematical sequences of the crystal formations. "These aren't random," he called out, ducking under a corrupted energy blast. "They're following prime number progressions - creating harmonic resonances between realms!"

Order members exchanged knowing looks as sanctuary after sanctuary reported similar attacks. The crystal tech wasn't just enhancing cultists - it was creating precise interference patterns in the barriers between worlds. Each blast weakened dimensional stability in calculated ways.

Reagan's screens filled with alert notifications as more facilities came under assault. The corrupted network spread like a virus, following ley lines and ancient power nodes. Status indicators shifted from green to red as sanctuary defenses failed in synchronized patterns.

"The Three Marias," Kaira breathed, watching energy signatures pulse across global maps. "They're not just guardians - they're anchor points keeping the realms separated. The crystal tech is designed to disrupt their influence."

Maya felt her medallion grow warmer as the truth crystallized. Her family's bloodline wasn't chosen randomly - they were connected to forces far older than the Order itself. The weight of generations pressed down as she recognized their unique position in the coming conflict.

Time itself seemed to shudder as reality barriers weakened. Multiple realms pressed against failing dimensional walls, their energies bleeding through in ways that threatened global stability. What had appeared to be isolated attacks was revealed as a coordinated assault on the very foundations of existence.

The Order's role suddenly became clear - not just guardians of knowledge, but protectors of the boundaries between worlds. As those boundaries dissolved, chaos from countless realms threatened to pour through the growing cracks in reality's fabric.

Maya's medallion pulsed furiously against her chest as she processed Verendana's revealed plans. The systematic attacks, the crystal tech's true purpose - it wasn't just about breaching Order sanctuaries. The cultists aimed to shatter the barriers between realms completely.

As Maya came across the Archive's large screen display, Kaira caught her daughter's eye. Understanding passed between them as Maya's fingers traced the ancient symbols on her medallion. The Three Marias weren't just legendary figures; they were keystones maintaining the stability of reality.

"Mom, the sanctuaries-" Maya's voice cracked. "They're failing in sequence. The crystal formations are creating harmonic disruptions."

Reagan's screens showed more facilities going dark. Order members fought desperately at each location, but the coordinated assault overwhelmed their defenses. The corrupted network spread along ley lines, following paths laid down centuries ago.

"We have to choose," Kaira said, watching barrier integrity readings plummet. "The archives contain knowledge vital to maintaining dimensional stability. But if we stay to defend them..."

"The cultists will trap us here," Myst finished, deflecting another crystal-enhanced attack. "Cut us off from supporting other sanctuaries."

Ancient texts pulsed with power behind failing shields. Generations of accumulated wisdom about the Three Marias, the Order's true purpose, the delicate balance between realms - all of it lay vulnerable. Yet defending this knowledge meant sacrificing their ability to protect other locations.

The family stood at the crossroads. Stay and preserve crucial information about reality's foundations, or evacuate and maintain their ability to fight. Either choice carried devastating consequences.

Crystal formations crept closer, their corrupted energy eating through remaining defenses. Verendana's forces pressed their advantage, knowing the Order's impossible position. Time ran short as reality itself shuddered around them.

Kaira met Reagan's eyes once more. The weight of generations pressed down as they faced their critical decision. The Order's future, and the stability of multiple realms, hung in the balance with their next move.

Maya's medallion flared brighter, resonating with distant powers. The Three Marias' influence rippled through the chaos, offering guidance without words. Whatever choice they made would forever reshape their world.

Stanley crouched behind an ancient Celtic shield, its metal thrumming with awakening power. The artifact vault's protective wards pulsed in rhythm with his heartbeat as he watched cultists pour through the breached entrance. His fingers traced familiar runes along the shield's edge, centuries of muscle memory guiding his movements.

Ancient weapons stirred around him - Saxon blades, Roman spears, Persian bows, all resonating with sacred energy. Each piece seemed to recognize his presence, their dormant powers flickering to life. His knowledge of their histories, gained through lifetimes of wielding them, would prove crucial in the coming minutes.

The first wave of cultists charged forward, crystal augmentations blazing. Stanley raised the Celtic shield, channeling its protective magic. A Roman gladius leapt into his other hand, its blade igniting with blue flame. The weapons responded to his touch, ancient powers merging seamlessly with his combat training.

"Come on then," he muttered, Australian accent thick with tension. His mustache twitched as he assessed the approaching threats. Multiple entry points needed guarding, and precious artifacts lay vulnerable throughout the vault.

Sacred weapons activated around him - spears launching themselves at attackers, shields forming protective barriers, ancient arrows finding marks with impossible accuracy. Each artifact chose its moment, defending itself and its companions with unleashed power.

Stanley moved between display cases, prioritizing which pieces could be saved. His expertise helped identify the most crucial items - those whose loss would devastate the Order's knowledge base. But time grew short as more cultists breached the outer defenses.

The vault's security matrices flared warnings as major breaches formed in multiple sections. Stanley watched as ancient weapons depleted themselves, holding back the tide, their sacred energies burning out in final acts of defense. His heart ached at each loss, centuries of history disappearing in moments of sacrifice.

The Celtic shield vibrated against his arm as the vault defenses began to fail systematically. He had to choose - stay and lose every-thing, or save what he could while retreat remained possible. The weight of responsibility pressed down as he made his decision.

Maya's medallion pulsed with increasing urgency as smoke filled the corridors. Through gaps in the chaos, she caught glimpses of her family scattered across different sectors of the facility. Her mother's silhouette flickered near the archive entrance, while Myst's energy signature flared from somewhere in the tactical center.

"Mom? Myst?" Static crackled through her comm unit. No response. The crystal formations weren't just disrupting magical barriers - they'd knocked out all standard communications too. Maya pressed her hand against the medallion, trying to sense her family's presence through their shared connection.

Reality rippled around her as crystal-enhanced cultists pressed their attack. The eastern wing's defenses buckled under concentrated assault. Maya channeled her Guardian powers, creating a barrier of pure energy that pushed back the immediate threats. But isolation gnawed at her confidence - she'd never faced this level of danger alone.

Through a gap in the smoke, she caught Myst's eye across the central chamber. Her twin brother nodded once, his hands already moving through practiced tactical formations. Even without words, their lifetime of training spoke volumes. They'd find each other again.

Kaira's voice cut through the chaos, more static than words. "-plit up... rendezvous... protocol seven-" The transmission died completely as another reality distortion wave rolled through the facility.

Reagan's tactical displays showed Order teams scattered throughout the complex. Red warning indicators spread across her screens as more sections went dark. She fought to coordinate their withdrawal, but with communications down, she could only trust in their training.

Maya felt tears sting her eyes as smoke obscured her last view of her family. The medallion's pulse strengthened, almost like a heartbeat against her chest. She had to trust their bonds would hold through whatever came next. Their shared training would see them through.

Through the haze, she saw Myst direct his team toward their designated evacuation route. Kaira's energy signature moved purposefully through the archive section, protecting what knowledge she could. Each family member faced their own battles, but their coordinated movements spoke of lifelong preparation for this exact scenario.

Maya felt the building shudder as evacuation protocols activated throughout the sanctuary. Red emergency lights pulsed in sync with blaring alarms while automated systems initiated portal generation sequences. The medallion at her throat thrummed with increasing urgency.

"Eastern wing, move now!" Reagan's voice crackled through failing comms. "Portal network at forty percent power. Two minutes until full activation."

Through smoke-filled corridors, Maya helped a wounded Order member toward the nearest emergency exit point. The woman's arm was severely burned from crystal energy discharge, but she managed to stay upright with Maya's support. Behind them, the sounds of battle grew closer as the last defenders bought precious seconds for others to escape.

Across the central chamber, Myst directed groups of evacuees toward designated exit points, his tactical training evident in every precise movement. His hands flew through practiced signals, coordinating the flow of people toward safety while monitoring enemy advancement.

Stanley emerged from the artifact vault, precious relics secured in an enchanted satchel. His face was grimy with smoke and sweat. Still, his eyes held fierce determination as he covered the retreat of junior Order members.

Through a gap in the chaos, Maya caught a glimpse of Verendana. The cultist leader stood amid shattered archive displays, crystal augmentations pulsing as she downloaded centuries of protected knowledge. Sacred texts and technical data streamed into corrupted storage matrices while ancient protections crumbled.

The portal network hummed to life, reality tearing open in controlled bursts across the facility. Each doorway led to a different sanctuary location, spreading survivors too thin to track. Maya saw her mother's silhouette briefly through the smoke, their eyes meeting in silent promise. They would find each other again. They would discover Elan and the others.

Emergency exit portals flared with increasing intensity as power levels reached their peak. Maya helped the injured woman through the nearest gateway, feeling reality bend around them. Behind her, the sanctuary's defenses failed in cascading waves. Generations of accumulated protections collapsed as the Order's headquarters fell to enemy forces.

But even as defeat loomed, hope remained. Their family bonds would endure. They would regroup, rebuild, and return stronger. Maya stepped through the portal, carrying that determination with her into uncertainty.

CHAPTER

TWELVE

Dawn crept across the temple's weathered marble, casting long shadows through columns carved with sacred geometry. The patterns pulsed with a faint blue luminescence, responding to the first rays of sunlight. Incense smoke drifted upward from bronze braziers, carrying prayers to forgotten gods.

Myst leaned against the balcony's stone railing, his ceremonial robes rippling in the cool morning breeze. Below, Roman legionaries performed equipment checks at their camp, the metallic sounds of armor and weapons carrying across the valley.

The temple complex sprawled beneath him, its architecture a perfect blend of Roman precision and sacred mysticism. Merchants already lined the approaching road, their carts laden with offerings and trade goods. A group of priests crossed the courtyard, sandals scraping against ancient stones as they prepared for morning rituals.

In the training yard below, Maya moved through sword forms with fluid grace. Her blade caught the pre-dawn light, flashing as she executed each strike and parry. Her movements matched the temple's geometric patterns - precise angles and perfect circles drawn in the air.

Myst watched his sister's practice without saying a word. They'd developed this morning routine over centuries, each finding comfort in the other's presence. Maya paused between forms, her eyes meeting his briefly. A slight nod passed between them, volumes spoken in silence.

Temple attendants lit more incense, the smoke creating shifting veils through the courtyard. The scent of myrrh and frankincense mingled with the crisp morning air. Priests began their morning chants, the ancient words echoing off stone walls that had stood since the empire's founding.

Maya sheathed her sword and bowed to the training yard's guardian statue. She moved with the deliberate grace of someone who had performed these actions countless times, each gesture infused with meaning accumulated over centuries.

The familiar weight of routine settled over the temple complex. Prayers were offered, duties were attended to, and life continued as it had for centuries. Yet beneath this tranquil surface, both siblings felt the subtle tension in the air - like the stillness before a storm.

Maya's skin prickled as the morning light dimmed. She paused mid-stride, blade lowered, and looked skyward. Dark clouds boiled up from the horizon, spreading across the clear blue expanse at an impossible speed. The weather shifted from calm to ominous in moments.

A horse whinnied in the stables, followed by another, then another. The animals stamped and kicked at their stalls. Birds took flight from the temple roofs in swirling, chaotic patterns.

"Something's wrong." Maya crossed the training yard, her gaze fixed on the temple's protective wards. The ancient symbols carved into the marble columns flickered like guttering candles, their usual steady blue glow pulsing erratically.

Through the temple's eastern archway, dust clouds rose from the distant roads. The morning sun caught glints of metal - armies on the move. Too many to be routine patrols.

Priests hurried past her, their commonly measured steps quick and urgent. They carried armfuls of scrolls and sacred items, speaking in hushed tones. One dropped a ceremonial bowl, its clang against the stone floor echoing through the corridors. He didn't stop to retrieve it.

The temple dogs huddled in corners, ears flat, tails tucked. Even the mice that usually scurried along the walls had vanished. In the aviary, the messenger birds thrashed against their cages.

Maya felt it in her bones - a weight in the air, a pressure building like the moment before lightning strikes. The sacred flame in the central altar, meant to burn eternally and steadily, danced and sputtered.

"Maya." Myst appeared at her side, his face tense. "The wards in the eastern chamber failed completely. Three more are fading."

A cold wind whipped through the courtyard, carrying the scent of rain and something else - something ancient and wrong. The dark clouds overhead spiraled like ink in water, their patterns too deliberate to be natural.

Temple bells began to ring - not the measured tolls of prayer times, but a frantic, desperate warning.

Myst traced the geometric patterns etched into the marble walls of his study, his fingers following paths worn smooth by centuries of similar gestures. Sacred mathematics filled the scrolls spread across his desk - circles intersecting with triangles, squares transforming into spirals. The calculations spoke to him in ways words never could.

He paused at the window, watching Maya in the courtyard below. Her morning practice hadn't changed in three hundred years. Left foot forward, blade angled just so, each movement precise as a compass point. The familiarity of it settled something in his chest.

The morning light caught the silver threads in her dark hair - earned through centuries rather than age. She moved through her forms with the same grace she'd shown when they first arrived at this temple, though her eyes held more wisdom now.

Numbers danced through his mind as he observed her practice. The angle of her sword matched the sacred ratio. Her footwork traced patterns that echoed the temple's protective wards. Even in combat training, she embodied the mathematical perfection they'd spent lifetimes studying.

He returned to his calculations, appreciation for these quiet moments growing stronger. The scratch of a stylus against parchment, the weight of his ceremonial robes, the scent of ink and ancient stone - each detail etched itself into his memory.

The geometric figures beneath his hands shifted from abstract symbols to profound truth. Lines connected, angles aligned, and the patterns revealed themselves with crystalline clarity. The mathematics he'd puzzled over for centuries finally made sense - not just in his mind, but in his bones.

Like his sister's sword forms below, every element is aligned in perfect harmony. The calculations weren't just numbers anymore, but a map leading to an inevitable conclusion. His fingers traced the final equation, understanding blooming like dawn across still waters.

Maya completed her practice with a bow to the east. The morning sun caught her blade one last time before she sheathed it, the flash of light matching the clarity in Myst's mind. Everything - their studies, their training, their very presence in this time - had led to this moment of understanding.

Maya's sword froze mid-strike as the temple's protective wards pulsed with unusual energy. The blue geometric patterns carved into the marble columns flickered like candlelight in a storm. Her skin prickled with awareness - something fundamental had shifted in the fabric of reality.

In his study above, Myst's calculations began to move. The ink itself crawled across the parchment, sacred ratios twisting into new configurations. He pressed his palm against the scroll, but the numbers continued their dance beneath his fingers. The mathematical constants that had governed their work for centuries were changing.

The air thickened around Maya as she lowered her blade. The training yard's familiar stones rippled like water, though they remained solid beneath her feet. She blinked, but the distortion remained. The very space around her seemed to bend and flex.

Through their twin bond, Maya felt Myst's sharp intake of breath. His surprise mirrored hers as reality itself seemed to hiccup. The temple's usual morning sounds - priests chanting, birds calling, merchants haggling - became muffled, as if heard through water.

Maya's feet carried her toward the temple steps, each movement deliberate against the strange resistance in the air. The sacred geometry etched into the stairs pulsed with increasing frequency, the blue glow intensifying with each flash.

Myst appeared in the doorway above, his expression matching the tension Maya felt building in her chest. The siblings locked eyes across the courtyard, centuries of shared experience allowing them to communicate without words. This wasn't a natural phenomenon - something was interfering with the fundamental laws that governed their world.

The mathematical patterns that protected the temple continued their erratic dance, their usual steady rhythm disrupted by whatever force pressed against the boundaries of reality. Maya felt the change in her bones, an ancient instinct warning of danger. The sacred formulas they'd studied for hundreds of years were being rewritten by an unseen hand.

Myst traced protective sigils in the air as priests filed into the temple's inner sanctum. Their white robes whispered against marble floors, heads bowed in concentration as they took their positions around the central altar. The familiar scent of sacred oils filled the chamber as they anointed the stone with practiced movements.

Through the eastern windows, he watched attendants light the sacred fires in precise order. First the Dawn Flame, then the Warrior's Torch, followed by the Scholar's Light. Blue flames leaped from brazier to brazier, each ignition triggering geometric patterns carved into nearby columns.

The temple's protective mathematics activated in waves. Lines of azure light raced along the walls, forming intricate lattices that pulsed with ancient power. Each intersection sparked as the energy flowed through the sacred geometry, illuminating symbols that had stood guard for centuries.

A horn blast echoed from the distant hills - three short notes followed by a long tone. The Roman signal for movement. More horns answered, their calls bouncing off valley walls. Through the window, Myst saw dust clouds rising from multiple roads leading to the temple complex.

He squared his shoulders, adjusting his ceremonial robes with steady hands. Centuries of study had prepared him for this moment. The calculations were clear, the signs unmistakable. All his mathematical models pointed to this convergence of events.

Priests began their morning chants, their voices rising in harmony with the temple's humming energy. The sacred fires cast dancing shadows on the walls as more geometric patterns awakened. Myst felt the power building, resonating with something deep in his bones.

Military horns sounded again, closer now. The temple's guardian statues stirred, their stone eyes tracking movement only they could see. Morning light streamed through the windows, catching the activated patterns in brilliant arrays of blue and gold.

Myst took his position before the central altar, joining the circle of priests. The time for contemplation was over. As the chants grew stronger and the geometric patterns pulsed with increasing intensity, he centered himself for what was to come.

Maya's sword arm trembled as reality rippled like heat waves across the temple courtyard. The air split open with a sound like tearing silk, revealing glimpses of other places through jagged holes—ancient forests, sprawling cities, vast deserts. Each tear lasted only seconds before sealing, but new ones appeared constantly.

The sacred geometry carved into the temple walls blazed with blue fire. Mathematical patterns that had lain dormant for centuries activated in cascading waves. Circles transformed into spheres, triangles extended into pyramids, and two-dimensional designs gained impossible depth.

Divine energy manifested as visible streams of golden light, pouring from the temple's highest spires. The power coalesced around the tears in reality, attempting to stitch the fabric of existence back together. Maya watched streams of pure creation weave through the air like living threads.

Stone guardians stepped from their pedestals, their marble forms flowing like water as ancient magic awakened them. They took up positions at key points around the temple complex, their weapons raised. The geometric wards between them connected in nets of blue light, forming barriers against the chaos outside.

Maya moved with practiced grace to her assigned position at the temple's eastern gate. Her muscles remembered this dance from lives long past, though her mind couldn't recall when she'd learned it. Each step aligned perfectly with the sacred patterns beneath her feet, adding her own power to the temple's defenses.

The mundane world beyond the temple grounds grew dim and distant. Markets fell silent, birds stopped singing, and even the wind died away. Every day, reality receded like an outgoing tide, leaving the temple complex isolated in a bubble of sacred space. Through the tears in the air, Maya glimpsed impossible geometries and landscapes that had never existed on Earth.

Maya's sword hung heavy at her side as she watched the last rays of normal sunlight fade behind the gathering supernatural storm. The familiar weight of centuries of training settled in her bones. Still, something felt different this morning - final, like the last note of a song.

Through gaps in the temple columns, she caught glimpses of Myst arranging ceremonial items on the altar. His movements were precise, each object placed according to sacred geometry. The silver threads in his dark hair caught the dying light, matching her own.

Incense smoke curled around ancient pillars as priests hurried through their preparations. They laid out sacred oils, arranged candles in perfect circles, and unrolled scrolls covered in mathematical formulas. Their white robes whispered against marble floors, the sound nearly lost beneath the rising hum of power.

Maya traced the protective sigils etched into her sword's hilt. The blade had served her through countless battles, but this felt different. The weight of it spoke of endings rather than victory.

Myst paused in his preparations, looking up from the altar. Their eyes met across the temple chamber, centuries of shared experiences passing between them in that single glance. He nodded once, the gesture containing all the words they didn't need to speak.

The last natural sunbeam pierced through the temple's eastern window, catching the activated wards in brilliant arrays of blue and gold. For a perfect moment, the light transformed the chamber into something transcendent - every line clean, every angle precise, every shadow exactly where it should be.

Then the moment passed. The storm swallowed the sun, plunging the temple into artificial twilight. Only the sacred fires remained, their blue flames casting strange shadows as reality continued to tear around them.

Maya took her position by the eastern gate, feeling the weight of what was to come settle around her shoulders like a familiar cloak. The marble was cool beneath her feet as she centered herself, preparing for the ritual that would change everything.

Myst's fingers traced the worn edges of the cabinet, each drawer labeled with precise geometric symbols. He pulled them open with practiced care, the wood sliding smoothly after centuries of use. The scent of preserved herbs filled the air - sage gathered under full moons, rosemary dried in sacred smoke, lavender bound with golden thread.

He selected each bundle according to the calculations etched in his mind, measuring angles and distances between stems. The dried plants whispered against each other as he laid them on silk cloths, forming the first layer of the ritual array.

The crystal chamber yielded its treasures next. Clear quartz points, each facet reflecting blue flame light. Amethyst clusters carved into perfect geometric shapes. Obsidian spheres ground to exact proportions. He tested their weight in his palm, feeling the resonance between each piece before adding it to his collection.

From the highest shelf, he retrieved the copper instruments—a compass, a protractor, and a ruler—each tool inscribed with formulae that spiraled around their edges. The metal hummed against his skin, responding to the building energy in the temple.

The sacred texts came last, their parchment pages crackling as he selected specific volumes. Mathematical treatises, geometric prophecies, and astronomical charts - each chosen for the precise ratios hidden in their words.

At the altar, Myst began the arrangement. He placed each item according to calculations refined over centuries of study. Crystals formed the foundation, their facets aligning with cardinal points. Herbs created connecting lines between them, their stems following exact angles. The copper tools marked intersection points in the pattern, their metal surfaces beginning to glow with stored power.

The temple's energy shifted as the pattern grew. Blue light pulsed through floor markings that had remained dormant for ages. Ancient symbols carved into the walls brightened in response to each new addition. The air thickened with potential, making it harder to breathe.

Myst felt the power building with each precisely placed component. The mathematical perfection of the arrangement drew energy up from the earth itself, channeling it through the sacred geometry. Static crackled between his fingers as he positioned the final elements, the entire pattern humming with contained force.

Myst's hands moved with practiced efficiency as he traced the sacred circle on the temple floor. White chalk whispered against ancient stone, leaving perfect arcs in its wake. He paused at each cardinal point, double-checking his measurements against the copper instruments laid out beside him.

The geometric patterns grew more complex with each stroke - triangles nested within circles, squares transforming into three-dimensional cubes through careful shading. Blue energy followed his chalk lines, the temple's power recognizing the mathematical precision of his work.

He positioned the crystal formations next, starting with a pure quartz point at true north. Each subsequent placement required careful calculation, the angles between stones matching ratios found in nature. Amethyst clusters formed secondary nodes, their purple depths catching and amplifying the building energy.

Maya brought him bundles of herbs from the temple stores, each wrapped in silk and labeled with geometric symbols. He placed them at precise intervals around the circle's edge - sage at north, rosemary east, lavender south, thyme west. The plants' natural energies blended with the mathematical patterns, creating harmonic resonances that made the air hum.

The sacred texts lay open around him, their pages weighted with polished stones. He cross-referenced the astronomical charts, confirming the positions of celestial bodies. His finger traced down columns of numbers, checking and rechecking the time variables that would affect the ritual.

Ancient formulae filled the margins of the texts, divine mathematics that described the fundamental nature of reality. Myst compared them to his own calculations, ensuring every aspect of the circle matched the requirements laid out by scholars centuries dead.

The power continued gathering as he worked, drawn by the perfect geometry taking shape on the floor. It pooled in the spaces between lines, filled the angles between crystals, and wove through the dried stems of the herbs. Each new element added to the whole, building a complex mathematical structure that existed in more dimensions than the eye could see.

The air in the temple grew thick, like breathing through honey. Myst's movements slowed as he worked, each gesture requiring more effort against the increasing resistance. The sacred geometry etched into the walls pulsed with intensifying light, blue patterns crawling across stone surfaces like living things.

Crystal formations around the ritual circle began to hum, their resonance building from barely perceptible to a clear tone that made Myst's teeth ache. The sound changed pitch as more power flowed through the mathematical array he'd constructed, harmonizing with frequencies beyond human hearing.

Incense smoke coiled in impossible ways, forming geometric shapes that hung suspended in the heavy air. The fragrant clouds twisted into perfect spirals and fractals before dissolving, only to reform in new patterns that defied natural movement.

Reality bent around the edges of Myst's vision. Straight lines curved, right angles became acute, then obtuse, then something else entirely. The mathematical patterns he'd activated began to extend beyond their two-dimensional confines, gaining depth and dimension that shouldn't exist in normal space.

High above in the temple's vaulted ceiling, Michael observed the proceedings in perfect stillness. His presence pressed against the ritual space like a physical weight, divine power interacting with the sacred geometry in cascading waves of energy. His wings, partially unfurled, cast shadows that broke into rainbow fragments where they touched the activated patterns.

The ritual items responded to the archangel's proximity. Crystals brightened, their inner light pulsing in time with the temple's heartbeat. Herbs released their essence without burning, their power drawn out by the divine presence. Sacred texts on the altar fluttered their pages without wind.

Tension built in visible waves, like heat distortion over summer roads. Myst felt it gathering in his bones, in the spaces between thoughts, in the mathematical constants that governed reality itself. The power differential between divine and mortal space created pressure that made his ears pop and his vision blur.

Myst placed the final crystal at the southeastern point of the sacred circle, completing the mathematical array. Power surged through the pattern, making the quartz formations pulse with inner light. The geometric designs traced in chalk blazed with blue fire, each line perfectly measured, each angle precise to the fraction of a degree.

His hands moved with certainty born from centuries of preparation, positioning the last bundle of herbs between the crystal nodes. The plants' natural energy merged seamlessly with the mathematical constructs, creating harmonics that resonated through multiple dimensions.

The completed circle hummed with contained power. Incense smoke twisted through impossible geometries, forming shapes that existed simultaneously in multiple planes of reality. The sacred texts lay open at cardinal points, their formulae glowing with activated potential.

Above, Michael's presence pressed against the ritual space like a physical weight. His wings cast fractured shadows across the temple floor, divine energy interacting with the sacred geometry in visible waves. The pressure between the celestial and mortal planes made the air thick and challenging to breathe.

Myst straightened, surveying his work with critical eyes. Every component sat exactly where calculations demanded - not a crystal out of alignment, not an herb misplaced, not a single chalk line imperfect.

The power built steadily, approaching the critical threshold centuries of mathematics had predicted.

Michael moved forward from his position near the ceiling, his approach causing the sacred patterns to pulse with increasing intensity. The archangel's movement shifted reality around him, bending space in ways that made Myst's vision blur at the edges.

The temple's geometric wards responded to Michael's proximity, their blue light brightening until it rivaled the sacred fires. Each intersection point in the mathematical array blazed like a star, creating a perfect lattice of power that extended beyond normal space.

Myst felt the weight of the moment settle around him like a physical presence. Everything they had worked toward for centuries had led to this precise configuration of space, time, and sacred geometry. The ritual space hummed with readiness, waiting for the final components to be set in motion.

Myst stood at the edge of the glowing circle, acutely aware of Michael's presence beside him. The air between them shimmered with divine energy, making the geometric patterns pulse like a living heartbeat. Each breath felt heavy with power, the sacred mathematics working to hold reality stable around them.

Michael's wings cast prismatic shadows across the ritual space. "The price of what we attempt has always been fixed." The archangel's voice resonated through multiple dimensions, causing the crystal formations to chime in harmony. "Universal constants cannot be violated without consequence."

He gestured, and lines of pure light traced complex equations in the air. "For every action, an equal reaction. For every change, a balancing force." The mathematical formulae twisted into three-dimensional shapes, demonstrating principles too complex for human language.

Myst nodded, recognizing the fundamental laws being illustrated. His centuries of study had prepared him for this moment, enabling him to follow the divine calculations that revealed the cost of their intended manipulation of reality.

Michael traced a perfect circle in the air, then folded it through impossible angles. "Time and space are not separate concerns, but a single fabric." The demonstration rippled outward, causing the temple's sacred geometry to flare in response. "What we seek to alter affects both simultaneously."

The weight of understanding settled over Myst as he watched reality bend according to Michael's will. Each principle was built upon the last, forming a complete picture of what the ritual would require. The mathematical certainty left no room for doubt or hope of another solution.

"The equations must balance," Michael continued, his presence intensifying until the air crackled with contained power. "The universe demands equilibrium." Divine light traced more complex formulae between them, showing exactly how that balance would be maintained.

Myst's fingers traced the mathematical equations hanging in the air, their divine light burning cold against his skin. Each formula revealed another layer of what they sought to accomplish—and what it would cost.

"The soul cannot simply be preserved," Michael explained, his voice resonating through multiple dimensions. "It must be anchored, bound through precise calculations that account for every moment of existence."

The glowing equations shifted, showing the complex web of time and space that held a single soul in place. Myst saw how each decision point created new branches, how memories formed the foundation of identity. The mathematics of consciousness itself unfolded before him in perfect, terrible clarity.

"To save them, portions must be sacrificed," Michael continued. "Like a surgeon removing diseased tissue, we must cut away certain moments, certain memories. The calculations show no other way."

The formula expanded, revealing how tampering with time created ripples that had to be contained. Each change required a corresponding loss to maintain universal balance. The mathematics were as immutable as gravity - for every moment preserved, another must be surrendered.

"Your own memories will fragment," Michael said, his wings casting fractured shadows across the temple floor. "The price of preserving their timeline is the dissolution of your own."

Myst watched the equations dance, showing how his consciousness would scatter across multiple timestreams. The mathematical precision required was staggering - one miscalculation could unravel reality itself.

"Even I must pay a price," Michael added softly. "Divine law bends only so far before breaking. My intervention here will cost me direct influence for centuries to come."

The full implications crystallized in Myst's mind. They weren't just changing the past - they were rewriting the fundamental structure of multiple souls across time and space. The mathematics showed the cost in cold, precise detail: memories sacrificed, timelines altered, consciousness fragmented.

But as each requirement became clear, Myst's determination only grew stronger. The equations might be merciless, but they also showed the path forward. If this was the price to save them, he would pay it gladly.

Myst watched as Michael traced equations in the air, each gesture leaving trails of divine light that hung suspended between them. The mathematics were unlike anything in the mortal texts he'd studied - formulae that existed in more dimensions than his mind could fully grasp.

"These are the fundamental constants," Michael said, causing the glowing symbols to rotate and transform. The temple's sacred geometry pulsed in response, blue patterns crawling across the walls in perfect synchronization.

Reality bent around them as Michael demonstrated each principle. Space folded into impossible angles, time stretched and compressed like taffy, probability collapsed into singular points of certainty. The crystal formations hummed at frequencies that made Myst's bones vibrate.

"The anchor points must be precise." Michael's wings shifted, casting prismatic shadows that fragmented the light. "Each moment we preserve creates ripples that must be contained."

The mathematical array floating between them expanded, showing cascading chains of cause and effect. Myst saw how changing even a single variable could unravel entire timelines. The calculations required accuracy beyond human capability - precision measured in units he had no words for.

"Success depends on perfect alignment." Michael gestured, and new equations bloomed in the air. "Time, space, consciousness - all must balance according to these constants."

Myst's centuries of study let him follow the divine mathematics, seeing how each formula built upon the last. The temple's sacred geometry responded to the lessons, pulsing with increasing intensity as more variables were revealed. Critical points glowed brighter than others, marking moments where precision would be absolutely essential.

The full scope of what they attempted crystallized in his mind. These weren't just theoretical calculations - they were the mathematical framework that would let them rewrite reality itself. Every equation had to be perfect, every variable accounted for, or the entire structure would collapse.

Myst absorbed the divine mathematics hanging in the air between them, each formula burning itself into his consciousness. The full weight of what they attempted pressed against his mind - not just changing time, but fundamentally rewriting the fabric of multiple souls across different eras. The price would be steep: his own memories scattered, Michael's influence diminished, reality itself bent to its breaking point.

The sacred geometry pulsed around them as understanding deepened. Blue light crawled up the temple walls in ever more complex patterns, reflecting the expansion of Myst's comprehension. Each new revelation built upon centuries of study, transforming theoretical knowledge into practical certainty.

Michael's wings shifted, casting rainbow fragments across the ritual circle. Divine energy flowed between them, transferring knowledge that no mortal texts could contain. Myst felt the information settling into his mind, filling gaps he hadn't known existed. The mathematical precision required would strain the very limits of possibility.

"You understand now." Michael's voice resonated through multiple dimensions. "Once begun, there can be no deviation from these calculations."

Myst nodded, his hands steady as he traced a final equation in the air. The temple's power surged in response, crystal formations humming at frequencies that made reality vibrate. Every component of the ritual space thrummed with contained energy, waiting to be unleashed.

"I accept the cost." Myst's voice carried absolute certainty. The mathematics allowed no room for doubt or hesitation. Each variable had been accounted for, each consequence calculated to the tiniest fraction.

The air grew thick with potential as the sacred space reached full charge. Incense smoke twisted through impossible geometries while the ritual circle blazed with inner light. Perfect alignment had been achieved - all that remained was the final catalyst.

Michael's presence intensified, divine power pressing against the mortal plane. "Then we are ready for what comes next."

Reality split with surgical precision, a seam of golden light threading through the temple's sacred space. The tear widened without sound, geometric patterns folding outward like an origami flower blooming in reverse. Power rippled through the chamber as Nykronus stepped through, his form solidifying from threads of temporal energy.

The ritual circle's blue fire surged in response, crystal formations shifting from a steady hum to crystalline chimes. St. Michael's wings snapped fully open, casting kaleidoscope shadows that danced across the temple walls. Ancient Myst's breath caught as the mathematical equations hanging in the air twisted, incorporating new variables.

Nykronus moved with deliberate grace, each step leaving traces of time magic that merged with the temple's existing patterns. The sacred geometry responded, blue lines crawling across stone surfaces to form new configurations. Power levels shifted and realigned, the carefully constructed ritual space adapting to his presence.

Recognition dawned in Ancient Myst's eyes as temporal formulae rewrote themselves, showing possibilities that hadn't existed moments before. The mathematics expanded, revealing solutions that bridged gaps he hadn't known how to cross.

St. Michael inclined his head in acknowledgment, divine energy pulsing in harmony with the time magic Nykronus brought. "Your timing is precise," the archangel's voice resonated through multiple dimensions.

The oppressive weight of inevitability lifted from the chamber. Where before the calculations had shown only sacrifice, new patterns emerged in the sacred geometry. Crystal formations brightened, their resonance shifting to a higher frequency that spoke of potential rather than loss.

Hope infused the temple's atmosphere, altering the quality of light and energy. The ritual space hummed with renewed purpose as three sources of power—divine, temporal, and mathematical—aligned in perfect harmony.

Nykronus traced patterns in the air, his fingers leaving trails of temporal energy that merged with the existing mathematical framework. "The equations assume linear progression," he said, manipulating the glowing formulae. "But time is not a river - it's an ocean."

Ancient Myst watched as the calculations transformed, showing new pathways through probability space. Where, before, mathematics demanded sacrifice, now they revealed loops and bridges between moments. The crystal formations pulsed in response, their resonance shifting to match the temporal frequencies Nykronus demonstrated.

"Instead of cutting away memories, we can fold them." Nykronus gestured, causing the sacred geometry to ripple across the temple walls. "Create pockets of preserved time, anchored by mathematical constants."

The blue fire of the ritual circle flared as new patterns emerged. Ancient Myst saw how the adjustments would work - precise manipulations of space-time that could protect consciousness without destroying it. The calculations expanded, showing preservation techniques he'd never considered possible.

St. Michael's wings shifted, divine light refracting through the temporal equations. "The power requirements remain significant," he observed, but his tone held consideration rather than rejection.

"But distributed differently," Nykronus explained, adjusting variables in the floating formulae. "Rather than overwhelming force, we apply precise pressure at key moments."

Ancient Myst's fingers traced the new calculations, feeling how they balanced. The mathematics sang with elegant simplicity - each adjustment building on existing patterns rather than forcing new ones. The temple's sacred geometry adapted smoothly, incorporating the temporal elements without strain.

The crystal formations chimed in perfect harmony as the complete method became clear. Souls could be preserved through the careful folding of time, rather than the brutal excision of memories. The mathematical precision required was still staggering, but achievable through the combined application of divine power and temporal manipulation.

Where before Ancient Myst had seen only sacrifice, now he glimpsed preservation. Hope manifested in the precise angles of the sacred geometry, in the resonance of the crystals, in the way divine and temporal energy merged without conflict. The path forward finally aligned with mathematical certainty.

The temple's sacred geometry shifted as three distinct powers flowed together. Ancient Myst watched Nykronus weave streams of temporal energy through the mathematical framework. At the same time, St. Michael's divine presence filled the spaces between calculations. The crystal formations sang at frequencies that made his bones vibrate, each note perfect and pure.

Blue fire crawled up the temple walls in response to the power convergence. Ancient Myst's carefully constructed equations twisted into new forms as Nykronus's time magic merged with them, creating patterns that existed in more dimensions than the human mind could grasp. St. Michael's wings cast prismatic shadows that bent reality wherever they fell.

"The guardianship must span precise intervals," Nykronus said, tracing temporal anchor points in the air. The glowing formulae revealed exact moments when protection would be needed, mathematical constants that would maintain reality's stability across centuries.

Ancient Myst nodded as St. Michael added divine variables to the calculations. "These points will serve as foundations," the archangel's voice resonated through multiple dimensions. "Sacred geometry maintaining equilibrium between timestreams."

The temple's power grid pulsed as they refined the protection methods. Ancient Myst saw how his role would work - maintaining the mathematical precision required to keep the temporal anchors stable. Divine energy would reinforce the calculations, while time magic preserved the crucial moments they needed to protect.

Nykronus manipulated the floating equations, revealing a network of time travel coordinates. "These are the critical junctures," he explained, showing how each point connected to the others. "Where intervention will be both possible and necessary."

The crystal formations hummed in harmony as the complete plan took shape. Ancient Myst traced the mathematical paths that would guide their efforts across centuries, seeing how each component supported the others. The temple's sacred geometry reflected the emerging pattern, blue light forming intricate webs between the power sources.

Ancient Myst felt the power convergence settle into perfect equilibrium. The temple's sacred geometry adapted seamlessly as three distinct energies merged - his mathematical precision, Nykronus's time magic, and St. Michael's divine presence. Blue fire traced complex patterns across the walls while crystal formations resonated in perfect harmony.

"I will maintain the temporal anchors," Nykronus said, his form shimmering with contained power. "Watch over the critical moments across centuries until all paths align."

St. Michael's wings shifted, casting rainbow light through the chamber. "My power will reinforce the mathematical constants, though more subtly than before. Divine influence working through natural law rather than direct intervention."

Ancient Myst traced the glowing equations that defined his role. "I'll ensure the calculations remain stable, preserving the bridge points between timestreams." The mathematics sang with crystalline clarity in his mind, showing exactly how each component would function.

The temple's power grid pulsed as their commitment solidified.

Sacred geometry crawled across every surface, adapting to incorporate the merged energies. Time magic stabilized the ritual space while divine power harmonized with the mathematical framework. Perfect balance radiated through the chamber.

Hope bloomed in Ancient Myst's chest as he saw how their adjusted plan would work. The modified ritual would preserve rather than destroy, protect rather than sacrifice. Each role supported the others with mathematical precision - Nykronus watching through time, St. Michael maintaining divine constants, Ancient Myst securing the calculations that bound it all together.

The crystal formations chimed in approval as the final pieces settled into place. Their combined power had transformed what seemed impossible into elegant certainty. Ancient Myst understood his new destiny with perfect clarity - not just guardian of mathematical truth, but preserver of crucial moments across time itself.

Ancient Myst's hands moved with practiced precision as he traced the outer ring of the ritual circle. Blue fire followed his fingertips, burning sacred geometry into the temple floor. Across from him, Nykronus carved temporal runes that pulsed with golden light. At the same time, St. Michael's wing-tips left trails of divine radiance as he completed his section.

The three distinct patterns merged where they met, ancient mathematics adapting to accommodate the hybrid energies. Time runes twisted into impossible angles, flowing seamlessly into divine symbols that burned with celestial fire. Sacred geometry crawled across the temple floor, creating nested layers of protection and power.

Nykronus pressed his palm against key points in the circle, establishing temporal anchors that would stabilize their work across centuries. The crystal formations hummed in response, their resonance shifting to match the frequencies he introduced. Ancient Myst adjusted his calculations on the fly, mathematical formulae morphing to incorporate each new variable.

Time crystals floated into position around the circle's perimeter, suspended by invisible forces. Their faceted surfaces caught and amplified the ritual energies, creating a lattice of power that filled the sacred space. Divine relics - a sword, a chalice, and a weathered tome - arranged themselves at precise intervals, each item pulsing with its own inner light.

The mathematical framework activated as the components settled into place, equations blazing to life in the air above the circle. Three distinct types of power flowed together - temporal, divine, and mathematical - merging into something entirely new. The sacred items responded to the energy convergence, their auras brightening and synchronizing with the rhythm of the ritual.

Ancient Myst felt the patterns stabilizing, power levels evening out as the ritual circle reached a state of equilibrium. Crystal formations chimed in perfect harmony while time magic wove through divine frequencies. His calculator remained steady, maintaining the precise balance required for what would come next.

Ancient Maya stepped into the ritual circle, her presence adding new harmonics to the crystal resonance. Her eyes met her brother's across the sacred space, decades of shared experience flowing between them without words. Ancient Myst's hands stilled on the mathematical framework as he absorbed her silent strength.

Time magic swirled around them as she took her position. The siblings' bond manifested in subtle ways - the synchronized rhythm of their breathing, the matching angles of their stance, the way their energies naturally aligned. Ancient Maya's power flowed into the ritual space, her contribution seamlessly integrating with the existing patterns.

She traced sigils in the air, adding her own calculations to the mathematical framework. Where her brother focused on preservation, her formulae spoke of protection and renewal. Hope was evident in her actions, suggesting possibilities beyond mere survival.

The sacred geometry responded to their combined influence, blue fire crawling across the temple floor in increasingly complex patterns. Divine light from St. Michael's presence merged with Nykronus's golden time magic, creating a prismatic cascade that filled the chamber. Crystal formations pulsed in harmony with the convergence of power.

The ancient Maya's eyes held a complete understanding as she gazed at her twin. No explanations were needed - she knew exactly what her role would be and accepted it without reservation. Her strength flowed into the ritual circle, stabilizing the mathematical constants her brother had established.

The three distinct powers reached perfect alignment. Sacred geometry glowed with inner light while time magic anchored reality around them. Divine energy pulsed through the chamber in waves that bent space itself. Mathematical patterns expanded across multiple dimensions, each calculation precisely accurate.

Ancient Maya and Ancient Myst stood as living anchors, their sibling bond helping to contain the overwhelming energies. Reality rippled around them as the power continued building. The crystal formations sang with increasing intensity as all components synchronized into perfect harmony.

Ancient Myst felt each element slide into its final position with mathematical precision. The time crystals pulsed in perfect synchronization, their faceted surfaces catching and amplifying the ritual's power. Divine relics settled into their prescribed places, forming a sword, a chalice, and a tome that formed an equilateral triangle, anchoring the outer circle.

Nykronus pressed his hands against the temporal anchor points, golden energy flowing from his fingertips to lock each coordinate in place. The crystal formations responded with ascending harmonics as reality stabilized around the fixed points. Ancient Myst watched divine seals activate in sequence, St. Michael's power burning through multiple dimensions as each sigil ignited.

Ancient Myst verified the mathematical constants, his calculations showing perfect alignment across all variables. The three of them - himself, Nykronus, and St. Michael - took their positions at precise intervals around the ritual circle. Power built between them, their distinct energies merging into something that transcended ordinary reality.

The temple walls began to hum with contained force, stone surfaces vibrating at frequencies that made Ancient Myst's bones resonate. Electric tension filled the air as power levels approached critical mass. He felt time rippling around them, reality becoming fluid as the barriers between worlds grew thin.

Sacred geometry blazed across every surface, blue fire tracing impossibly complex patterns that spoke of mathematical truth. Divine light poured from St. Michael's form, refracting through the crystal matrix to fill the chamber with prismatic radiance. The space between dimensions stretched and warped, worlds pressing close enough to touch.

Ancient Myst maintained its focus on the mathematical framework as reality responded to their work. The calculations remained perfect despite the overwhelming energies flowing through the sacred space. Each component performed exactly as designed, power ramping toward the inevitable moment of transformation.

Ancient Myst's fingers traced the final calculations floating in the air, each equation pulsing with perfect mathematical precision. The sacred geometry responded instantly, blue fire crawling across the temple floor in intricate patterns that locked their preparations in place.

Through their twin bond, he sensed Ancient Maya moving to a protected alcove near the temple entrance. Her energy remained connected to the ritual space while maintaining a safe distance from the overwhelming forces about to be unleashed.

Nykronus pressed his palms against the time crystals, golden light flowing from his fingertips to stabilize the temporal anchors. The crystal formations hummed in harmony as reality settled around their fixed points. Ancient Myst watched the mathematical framework adapt, showing perfect alignment across all variables.

St. Michael's divine presence filled the spaces between calculations, his power merging seamlessly with the temporal and mathematical energies. Protection spells blazed to life along the chamber walls, layers of sacred geometry forming an impenetrable barrier around their working space.

The three distinct powers reached a perfect equilibrium: Ancient Myst's mathematical precision, Nykronus's time magic, and St. Michael's divine influence. Reality rippled around them as the energies built toward critical mass. Crystal formations sang with increasing intensity as all components synchronized into perfect harmony.

Ancient Myst felt each element slide into its final position. The ritual circle pulsed with contained power, every sigil and rune glowing at precisely the right frequency. Divine relics—sword, chalice, and tome—formed a perfect triangle that anchored the outer boundaries of their working space.

Hope blazed in his chest as he verified the final calculations. Everything aligned exactly as planned, each component ready to perform its designated function. The temple hummed with barely contained power as they prepared to begin the ritual that would change everything.

Ancient Myst's voice carried through the temple chamber as he spoke the first words of the ritual. "In nomine temporis, in nomine mathematica, in nomine divinus." The sacred geometry blazed beneath his feet, blue fire racing through each line and curve he'd traced.

Golden light pulsed from the time crystals as Nykronus channeled temporal energy into the ritual space. The air shimmered with afterimages - moments from past and future bleeding through as reality's barriers thinned. St. Michael's wings flared with divine radiance, casting prismatic light across the chamber walls.

Ancient Myst stood at the center point of the ritual circle, feeling three distinct powers flow through him. The mathematical framework responded to his presence, equations burning in the air with crystalline clarity. Reality twisted around him as the energies built, stone walls seeming to breathe as space itself became fluid.

Power rolled through the temple in waves, each pulse stronger than the last. Time magic wove through streams of divine light while mathematical patterns shifted to accommodate the hybrid energies. The crystal formations sang in ascending harmonics as the forces merged and amplified.

Temple stones vibrated at frequencies that made Ancient Myst's teeth ache. His calculations blazed to life in complex patterns, mathematical truth manifesting in physical form. Divine seals activated in sequence around the circle's perimeter, each one adding new layers of protection to their working space.

Nykronus pressed his hands against the temporal anchor points, locking each coordinate in place. Golden energy spiraled outward from these fixed points, stabilizing reality around them. The sacred space transformed as power continued to build - air growing thick with potential, light bending in impossible ways, sound taking on a physical form.

The three distinct energies intertwined completely, becoming something entirely new. Ancient Myst felt the mathematical framework adapt to contain this hybrid force, his calculations expanding through multiple dimensions as the ritual truly began.

Ancient Myst felt the divine light pour through him as it merged with Nykronus's time magic. The energies twisted together like strands of DNA, mathematical patterns automatically adjusting to contain their combined force. His essence began to shift as the power transformed him from within, his cells resonating at new frequencies.

Nykronus's hands pressed against key points in the ritual circle, establishing temporal bonds that anchored their work across centuries. Golden light spiraled from his fingertips, reality bending and flexing as each coordinate locked into place. The crystal formations pulsed in harmony with the temporal frequencies.

St. Michael's wings flared with celestial radiance as he channeled divine power into the mathematical framework. Sacred geometry crawled across the temple floor, equations blazing to life in physical form. Reality warped around them, space becoming malleable as the barriers between dimensions grew thin.

Time anchors snapped into position with audible cracks, mathematical seals forming in concentric rings around the ritual space. Divine protection manifested in layers of prismatic light, each one adding new frequencies to their work. The temple stones sang with contained power.

From her protected alcove, Ancient Maya watched her brother's transformation with perfect understanding. His form shifted between states as the energies rebuilt him from the atomic level up. She felt each change through their twin bond, sensing how the power reshaped his essence.

The ritual's force reached unprecedented levels, crystal formations vibrating at frequencies that made reality itself shudder. Future connection points established themselves in the mathematical framework, equations extending through time to anchor specific moments. Ancient Myst's calculations adapted automatically, expanding to accommodate the temporal and divine hybrid energy that filled the sacred space.

Ancient Myst's flesh rippled as the power coursed through him. His bones shifted beneath his skin, temporal energy wrapping around his essence like silk threads. Divine light poured into his spirit, burning away what was mortal and temporary. The mathematical framework adapted instantly, equations flowing through his bloodstream as sacred geometry etched itself into his very atoms.

Blue fire crawled across his skin, forming protective shells of pure calculation. His cells vibrated at impossible frequencies as time magic rewove his basic structure. Reality bent around him, accommodating the changes as his form flickered between states of being. Through it all, the mathematical patterns held steady, guiding the transformation with perfect precision.

The three distinct powers surged toward their peak. Temple stones groaned under the strain, crystal formations vibrating so intensely they became transparent. Time warped visibly around the ritual circle - the future and past bleeding into the present, creating overlapping images that were painful to look at. St. Michael's divine presence filled every molecule of air, making it thick enough to taste.

Ancient Myst's calculations blazed across multiple dimensions as the transformation accelerated. His body absorbed impossible amounts of energy; the mathematical framework automatically adjusted to handle the increased flow. Reality rippled like water around him while divine light poured through his changing form.

The temple's structure buckled under the growing power, stones shifting in ways that defied physics. Time magic swirled in golden torrents, bending space itself as it flowed through the ritual circle.

Divine radiance burned away shadows, filling every corner with celestial fire. Through it all, Ancient Myst's mathematical precision held firm, containing the overwhelming energies within carefully calculated boundaries.

His transformation gained momentum, changes cascading through his system faster than human senses could track. Yet each shift followed exact mathematical principles, every alteration precisely controlled by the framework he'd established.

Ancient Myst's body vibrated at frequencies that threatened to tear him apart. Mathematical patterns crawled beneath his skin, equations burning through his bloodstream as the transformation reached its peak. His cells resonated with temporal energy while divine light reshaped his essence from within.

The time anchors pulsed with golden radiance, each one perfectly aligned to maintain stability across centuries. Reality bent around these fixed points, creating a lattice of temporal coordinates that secured their working through past and future. Crystal formations sang in ascending harmonics as the anchors locked into position.

St. Michael's wings flared with celestial fire, divine protection wrapping around the ritual space in prismatic layers. Each seal activated in sequence, burning away any weakness or instability that might compromise their work. The mathematical framework adapted instantly, sacred geometry flowing through multiple dimensions to contain the hybrid energies.

Ancient Myst felt his essence crystallize as the mathematical seals secured his core identity. His calculations blazed through every atom of his being, preserving what was vital while allowing necessary changes. The framework held steady despite overwhelming power, maintaining perfect precision as reality warped around him.

The path ahead materialized in the mathematical patterns, future coordinates locking into place within the temporal matrix. Each point aligned exactly as planned, creating a stable trajectory through time itself. The crystal formations pulsed in harmony as these coordinates synchronized with the ritual's energy.

Power levels began stabilizing as the transformation reached completion. Time magic settled into predetermined patterns, golden light flowing smoothly through the anchored coordinates. Divine energy maintained a steady presence, neither increasing nor diminishing as it merged with the other forces.

Sacred geometry locked into its final configuration, blue fire tracing permanent lines through multiple dimensions. The mathematical framework demonstrated perfect alignment across all variables, with each calculation remaining steady as the ritual energies balanced.

The temple chamber hummed at a constant frequency as all components synchronized. Reality stabilized around their working space, temporal distortions smoothing out as the power found equilibrium. Ancient Myst felt the change settle into his transformed essence, his calculations confirming successful transition to the ritual's next phase.

Golden light poured from Nykronus's form as time magic drained his essence. His fingers pressed against the ritual circle, centuries of accumulated power flowing out of him in steady streams. Ancient Myst watched the temporal energy weave through mathematical patterns, forming new bonds that would echo through time.

Nykronus's face grew gaunt as the guardian bond took shape. His immortal power transferred into the framework, establishing an eternal watch that would span centuries. Knowledge older than civilization itself passed through the connection - secrets of time and space, mysteries of reality's deepest foundations.

The weight of future responsibility settled across Ancient Myst's shoulders as Nykronus's wisdom poured into him. Calculations expanded to accommodate this vast influx of information, mathematical patterns adapting to store centuries of accumulated knowledge.

Nykronus's physical form began shifting as more power drained from him. Golden light crawled across his skin, time magic leaving permanent marks in its wake. Ancient symbols appeared on his flesh - circles within circles, spirals that spoke of eternal cycles, runes that defied normal space.

The guardian symbols blazed with inner fire as they manifested. Each mark bound another portion of Nykronus's power, storing it for future use. His immortal essence transformed, taking on new patterns that reflected his eternal commitment.

Ancient Myst felt the mathematical framework respond as Nykronus's power settled into its new configuration. The calculations showed centuries of duty stretching ahead - an unbroken chain of responsibility that would echo through time. Golden light continued pouring from Nykronus's form as the transfer deepened, marking the beginning of an endless watch.

St. Michael's radiance flickered as divine memories began slipping from his consciousness. His wings, once blazing with celestial fire, dimmed to a soft pearl sheen. Ancient knowledge - battles fought in heaven's highest spheres, wisdom gained through eternal service - sealed itself away in protected corners of his spirit.

Sacred equations spiraled through the air, mathematical patterns adapting to contain his transforming essence. Each memory locked away produced a subtle shift in the divine light pouring from his form. The mathematical framework adjusted automatically, creating new pathways to preserve what must be protected.

"The seals are forming." Ancient Myst tracked the changes through his calculations, watching as protective barriers established themselves around St. Michael's core being. Divine shields materialized in layers, each one precisely calibrated to preserve specific aspects of celestial power.

St. Michael's wings folded close against his back as more memories faded. The protection spell wove through his essence, carefully storing away knowledge that spanned creation itself. His divine nature responded to the mathematical patterns, allowing itself to be contained without resistance.

Golden light from the time anchors merged with the protection formation, adding temporal stability to the divine shields. Sacred knowledge settled into specially prepared spaces, preserved but sealed away from conscious access. The mathematical framework showed perfect alignment as each component locked into place.

Ancient Myst watched as power levels stabilized with the completion of the protective barriers. Divine essence secured itself behind multiple layers of sacred geometry, each shield calibrated to maintain perfect balance. The ritual space hummed at just the right frequency as St. Michael's transformation continued, future safety assured through precise mathematical control.

Memory seals activated in sequence, storing celestial wisdom in protected spaces that would endure through time. Divine light pulsed in steady waves as the process unfolded, power carefully preserved within the established boundaries. The mathematical framework adapted to each change, maintaining stability as more memories faded into sealed containment.

Ancient Maya watched from her alcove as protective energies wrapped around her like a second skin. Blue mathematical patterns crawled across her arms, forming shields that would preserve her essence through time. Her twin bond with Myst pulsed firmly and steadily, their connection adapting to accommodate the changes flowing through them both.

Time magic settled into her cells, golden light weaving protective layers that would guard her natural cycle of rebirth. She felt each safeguard lock into place, securing her future path through centuries yet to come. The mathematical framework demonstrated perfect alignment as these protections were established.

The three distinct powers—mathematical precision, time magic, and divine influence—found perfect harmony within the ritual space. Temple stones sang at specific frequencies as energy balanced between all components. Sacred geometry flowed through multiple dimensions, distributing power evenly across their work.

Time streams stabilized around their fixed points, reality smoothing out as temporal distortions settled into predetermined patterns. Divine protection wrapped around them in prismatic layers, each one precisely calibrated to maintain eternal balance. The crystal formations pulsed in steady rhythm as all elements synchronized.

Ancient Maya felt hope bloom in her chest as she sensed the perfect equilibrium forming. Her essence resonated with the balanced energies, future safety assured through mathematical precision. The ritual space hummed as power levels stabilized across all variables.

The mathematical framework showed flawless alignment as the three powers merged completely. Sacred geometry locked into its final configuration, equations blazing with crystalline clarity as balance maintained itself through multiple dimensions. Time magic flowed while divine protection settled into permanent patterns.

Ancient Myst watched as Nykronus's form shimmered with acceptance of his eternal duty. Golden threads of time magic wrapped around him, binding him to his role as guardian through the ages. His eyes held ancient wisdom as he nodded to Ancient Myst, a silent acknowledgment of the weight they now shared.

St. Michael's memories sealed themselves away behind layers of divine protection. His celestial knowledge settled into protected spaces, preserved but hidden from immediate access. The mathematical framework adapted perfectly, maintaining the delicate balance required for this transformation.

Sacred geometry stabilized throughout the temple chamber, blue fire tracing permanent lines through multiple dimensions. The calculations showed perfect alignment across all variables as time magic settled into predetermined patterns. Ancient Myst felt his own essence secure within these protective boundaries, mathematical precision ensuring his future safety.

The air shimmered as three distinct presences materialized within the ritual space. Maria Makiling appeared first, her form wrapped in forest shadows and morning mist. Maria Cacao emerged next, bringing the rich scent of earth and growing things. Maria Sinukuan completed their trinity, power radiating from her like summer heat.

The Three Marias moved in perfect synchronization, their combined presence adding new depth to the ritual's protective layers. They wove their ancient magic through the mathematical framework, strengthening bonds that would echo through centuries.

Divine protection wrapped around them all in prismatic layers, each one precisely calibrated to maintain eternal balance. The guardian duty established itself firmly within the mathematical patterns, creating unbreakable bonds that would endure through time.

Ancient Myst felt the final pieces lock into place as all prices were paid in full. Time magic flowed, emitting a nearly invisible aura, as the divine protection settled into permanent patterns. The sacred geometry showed flawless alignment as the three powers merged completely, creating perfect conditions for the transformation ahead.

Ancient Myst's physical form began to fade, his edges growing transparent as sacred geometry wrapped around him in a cocoon of pure light. Mathematical patterns crawled across his dissolving flesh, each equation precisely aligned to guide his transformation. The Three Marias raised their hands in unison, their ancient blessing flowing into the framework of power surrounding him.

Time magic coiled around his essence like golden serpents, restructuring his very being according to the ritual's demands. Divine energy from St. Michael burned through his spirit, purifying every aspect of his existence. Reality bent perfectly around the temple space, following exact calculations that Ancient Myst had laid out.

The crystal formations pulsed as power levels reached perfect harmony. Time anchors blazed with golden fire, each one fully engaged and maintaining stability across centuries. Sacred mathematics completed its complex patterns, blue fire tracing permanent lines through multiple dimensions.

Divine protection surrounded them all in prismatic layers, each one precisely calibrated by the presence of St. Michael. Nykronus pressed his hands against the ritual circle, establishing the eternal watch that would span ages. His immortal power flowed into the framework, marking the beginning of an endless vigil.

The Three Marias moved in perfect synchronization, their combined magic strengthening bonds that would echo through time. Maria Makiling's forest shadows merged with Maria Cacao's earth magic while Maria Sinukuan's power radiated through the mathematical seals.

St. Michael's wings flared with celestial fire as he gave his final blessing, divine light pouring into the transformation matrix. The mathematical framework adapted instantly, sacred geometry flowing through multiple dimensions to contain these hybrid energies.

Ancient Myst felt the power convergence reach its peak as all elements synchronized perfectly. Time magic settled into predetermined patterns while divine protection wrapped around their working in unbreakable layers. The ritual space hummed louder as all components found perfect equilibrium.

Ancient Myst felt his essence crystallize as mathematical patterns locked into place around his core being. The calculations blazed through every atom, preserving what was vital while allowing necessary changes. Time magic flowed like liquid gold through these patterns, creating a perfect stasis field that would maintain his identity through centuries.

Divine light from St. Michael's presence wove through the mathematical framework, adding layers of celestial protection to the preservation matrix. Each shield activated in sequence, burning away any weakness that might compromise the stasis field. The calculations adapted instantly, sacred geometry flowing through multiple dimensions to contain these hybrid energies.

His future path materialized in the mathematical patterns, coordinates locking into place within the temporal matrix. Each point aligned exactly as planned, creating a stable trajectory through time itself. Knowledge accumulated over centuries compressed into protected spaces within his essence, safely stored behind multiple layers of mathematical shields.

Nykronus pressed his hands against the ritual circle, establishing the eternal bond between guardian and ward. Golden threads of time magic wrapped around them both, binding their fates together across centuries yet to come. Sacred duty flowed through this connection - an unbreakable commitment that would echo through the ages.

The guardian bond deepened as more power flowed between them. Protection spells are activated in a precise sequence, each one adding another layer of security to their eternal connection. Time magic sealed these bonds permanently, mathematical patterns adapting to accommodate the growing power.

Ancient Myst felt the watch guarantee itself through multiple dimensions. Future protection was secured upon the completion of the guardian bond. Mathematical precision guided every aspect of this preservation, ensuring perfect stasis that would endure through time.

Ancient Maya watched her brother's form shimmer with ethereal light, her heart aching as his physical presence began to fade. Mathematical patterns wrapped around him like a living cocoon, each equation perfectly aligned to guide his transformation. Their twin bond pulsed despite the changes flowing through him, their connection adapting to bridge the centuries that would soon separate them.

Their eyes met across the ritual space. No words were needed -

their shared gaze carried all the love, trust, and promises that had sustained them through countless lifetimes. She pressed her hand against the mathematical barrier, feeling the warmth of his essence respond even as his physical form grew more transparent. She could not see the faces of the three women who were surrounding her brother, but she did not feel uneasy. She knew her brother was destined for greatness.

The Three Marias moved in perfect synchronization around them, their ancient magic weaving protective layers through the twin bond. These sacred threads would preserve their connection across time itself, maintaining the precious link between their souls.

Time magic flowed like liquid gold through the mathematical framework, creating stable pathways for their future reunion. Each coordinate locked precisely into place, ensuring they would find each other again when the moment was right. The crystal formations pulsed in harmony as these temporal anchors secured themselves.

St. Michael's divine light poured into the transformation matrix, adding celestial protection to the preservation spells. His wings flared with renewed radiance as he blessed the pathways being established. The mathematical patterns adapted instantly, sacred geometry flowing through multiple dimensions to contain these hybrid energies.

The Three Marias raised their hands in unison, their combined power confirming the destiny being woven. Maria Makiling's forest shadows merged with Maria Cacao's earth magic while Maria Sinukuan's strength radiated through the mathematical seals. Their ancient blessing flowed into the framework, strengthening bonds that would echo through centuries.

Time streams stabilized around their fixed points as the transformation neared completion. Reality smoothed out as temporal distortions settled into predetermined patterns. Divine protection wrapped around them in prismatic layers, each one precisely calibrated to maintain eternal balance.

Ancient Myst felt the final transformations take hold as mathematical patterns crystallized around his essence. His consciousness expanded through the framework, settling into perfectly preserved spaces within the ritual matrix. Each calculation blazed with crystalline clarity, securing vital aspects of his being while allowing necessary changes to flow through him.

Nykronus stood firm at the circle's edge, golden threads of time magic wrapping around him as he accepted his role as eternal guardian. His immortal power merged seamlessly with the mathematical framework, establishing unbreakable bonds that would span centuries.

St. Michael's divine memories sealed themselves behind pristine barriers, knowledge of celestial battles, and heavenly wisdom safely stored away. His wings folded close as the protection spells completed their work, each memory finding its proper place in the preserved matrix.

Sacred geometry flowed through multiple dimensions, blue fire tracing permanent lines that would maintain perfect balance. The crystal formations pulsed in steady rhythm as all elements synchronized completely. Time magic settled into smooth, predetermined patterns while divine protection wrapped around their working in unbreakable layers.

Ancient Myst's physical form dissolved into pure light as the transformation reached its peak. Mathematical shields adapted instantly, preserving his core essence while allowing his being to transcend normal space. The calculations showed flawless alignment as his consciousness expanded beyond mortal limitations.

His future path materialized within the temporal matrix, each coordinate precisely placed to guide him through centuries yet to come. Sacred duty flowed through every pattern, establishing permanent bonds between guardian and ward.

Hope radiated through the mathematical framework as Ancient Myst's transformation completed. His essence, now fully preserved within the sacred geometry, pulsed with certainty of purpose. The eternal watch had begun, time magic flowing smooth and steady while divine protection settled into permanent patterns.

PART THREE

"In the evening of life, we will be judged on love alone."
— **St. John of the Cross**

CHAPTER

THIRTEEN

Maya stumbled as another tremor rocked the Order's headquarters. Emergency portals blazed to life around the central chamber, their edges crackling with unstable energy. Members of the Order rushed through them in organized chaos, each group heading to their designated sanctuary points across the globe.

"Eastern sanctuaries compromised!" A knight's voice cut through the noise. Blood trickled down his arm where crystalline shards had pierced his skin. The corruption spread through his veins in geometric patterns, transforming flesh into faceted stone.

"Reroute teams four and seven to the Alpine points." A technician swiped her hand through a holographic display, her fingers leaving trails of light as she recalibrated portal coordinates. The crystal growths on her neck pulsed with each movement.

Maya's tech interface sparked and sputtered. The hybrid systems that usually enhanced her abilities flickered in and out, sending sharp pains through her neural pathways. Around her, other augmented Order members clutched their heads or limbs as their enhancements malfunctioned.

"Portal's destabilizing!" An operator slammed his crystallizing hand against the control panel. "We need to move now!"

Maya grabbed two junior members who had collapsed from tech feedback. She dragged them toward the nearest stable portal, its surface rippling like mercury. The corruption was spreading faster now - she could see it creeping across the chamber walls in fractal patterns.

"Maya, through here!" Reagan waved her toward a different portal. "The others are compromised!"

She changed direction, hauling her unconscious charges across the trembling floor. More crystals burst through the ground with each shake, their edges sharp and hungry. The corruption had reached the ceiling, spreading across ancient stonework like cancer.

Maya heaved the junior members through the portal first, watching their bodies vanish into the silvery surface. She took one last look at the crumbling chamber. Reagan nodded to her, already turning to help another group.

The portal's energy field washed over Maya as she stepped through. It sealed shut behind her with a sound like breaking glass.

Maya stumbled as the portal's energies released her onto the cold stone floor of Edinburgh's sanctuary. Her ears rang from the dimensional shift, and the scent of antiseptic mixed with incense filled her nose. The sanctuary's vaulted ceiling stretched above, its ancient stonework etched with protective runes that pulsed with pale blue light.

She pushed herself up, steadying against a nearby pillar. The sanctuary's main hall buzzed with frantic activity. Healers in white robes rushed between makeshift cots while evacuees from the London attack huddled in small groups, their faces drawn with shock and exhaustion.

"Over here!" A healer waved her toward a cluster of wounded. "We need help with triage."

Maya sprinted to the group, dropping to her knees beside a man clutching his bloodied arm. Crystalline shards glinted within the wound - remnants of a shattered ward stone. She placed her hands over the injury, drawing on her healing knowledge.

"Hold still." She traced the edges of the wound, carefully extracting each shard. The man's face contorted, but he remained silent. "Almost done."

Another portal flared behind her, depositing more evacuees. Their cries echoed off the stone walls as healers rushed to assist. Maya finished binding the man's arm and moved to the next patient, her hands already glowing with healing energy.

"The children?" A woman grabbed Maya's sleeve, her eyes wild with fear. "Did they make it through?"

"The young ones came through first." Maya gestured toward the far corner, where several Order members watched over a group of sanctuary students. "They're safe."

Relief flooded the woman's face before she slumped back onto her cot. Maya checked her vital signs, noting the magical exhaustion that had likely caused her collapse. She pulled a blanket over the woman's shoulders before moving to the following urgent case.

The stream of evacuees continued as more portals activated around the hall. Maya worked methodically, treating the worst injuries first while directing those with minor wounds to the waiting area. Her healing energy flowed steadily despite her growing fatigue.

Maya's hands trembled as she pulled the medallion from beneath her tunic. Its surface glowed with a soft amber light, warming her palm. The critically wounded knight before her gasped for breath, crystal shards protruding from his chest in a spreading pattern.

"Stay with me." She pressed the medallion against his sternum. The metal grew hot, pulsing in sync with his failing heartbeat. Traditional healing spells had barely slowed the crystal's growth. Still, the medallion's ancient power cut through the corruption like a blade through silk.

Asha prowled around them, her black and orange fur bristling. The cat's eyes glowed with an inner fire as she watched Maya work.

"Something's wrong." Maya frowned as the healing energy sputtered and sparked. Where crystal met flesh, her magic scattered like water on hot steel. "The tech is blocking the connection."

She adjusted her grip, channeling power through the medallion instead of her usual methods. The crystal's advance slowed, but didn't stop completely. Sweat beaded on her forehead as she fought against the foreign elements invading the knight's body.

Asha's ears flattened suddenly. The cat leaped onto a nearby table, knocking over a tray of medical supplies. Her tail lashed as she stared at the sanctuary's western wall.

"What is it?" Maya kept one hand on the medallion while reaching for her companion.

Asha hissed, the sound carrying an otherworldly resonance. Through their bond, Maya felt what the cat sensed - corruption spreading through the sanctuary's ancient stone like poison through veins. The protective networks that had stood for centuries were being systematically infected.

A sharp crack split the air. Maya spun toward the sound, keeping the medallion pressed to her patient's chest. Dark energy rippled across the sanctuary's defensive wards, leaving trails of crystalline corruption in its wake.

"They're tracking the networks." Maya's blood ran cold as she recognized the Assembly's signature in the spreading darkness. Their magic had evolved, using the Order's own sanctuary pathways as a roadmap straight to their door.

Maya frowned as her healing energy met resistance in the crystalline wounds. The magic that normally knitted flesh and bone seemed to slide off, like glass water. She increased the power, focusing harder, but the injuries barely responded.

"Something's wrong." She turned to the senior healer beside her. "These crystal wounds aren't healing properly."

Brother Marcus leaned in to examine the patient's arm. "I've noticed the same. Traditional methods aren't working as they should." He pressed his lips into a thin line. "Whatever they used in London, it's not like the crystals we've encountered before."

A commotion near the main doors drew their attention. A messenger burst through, his Order robes singed and torn. He stumbled toward the command table where the sanctuary leaders had gathered.

"Paris has fallen." His voice carried across the hall. "Vienna and

Prague, too. They used the same crystal weapons - our wards shattered like glass."

The room fell silent. Maya's hands stilled over her patient's wounds as the implications sank in. Three major sanctuaries were lost in a single day.

"How many survived?" One of the leaders stepped forward.

"Paris managed to evacuate most of their people. Vienna..." The messenger shook his head. "We lost contact before they could activate their emergency portals. Prague's status is unknown."

Whispers rippled through the gathered evacuees. Maya caught fragments of conversations - mentions of coordinated attacks, of defenses failing simultaneously, of centuries-old protections crumbling in minutes.

"What about Rome?" Another leader demanded.

"Still holding, but under heavy assault. They've activated the ancient wards beneath St. Peter's." The messenger swayed on his feet. "But they don't know how long they'll last against these new weapons."

Maya returned to her patient, seeking another approach to heal the crystal-infected wounds. Nothing in her centuries of experience had prepared her for injuries that rejected healing magic so completely. She tried combining different healing techniques, but the crystalline damage remained stubbornly resistant.

More wounded arrived through the portals, many bearing the same mysterious crystal injuries. The healing ward quickly filled beyond capacity, and Maya could see the growing concern on the faces of her fellow healers as they encountered the same resistance to their magic.

Mount Everest (Chomolungma), Tibet – The Earth's highest peak at 8,848.86 meters (29,031.7 feet)

Beneath a mountain in Tibet, Myst's fingers flew across holographic displays, tracking the remnants of Order forces across a global map dotted with red warning indicators. The command center hummed with quantum processors and ancient magic, crystalline matrices merging technology with spellcraft in ways that would have seemed impossible just months ago.

"We've lost contact with Prague completely." His second-in-command, Sister Chen, swiped away another failing signal node. "Berlin's holding, but their eastern perimeter's showing signs of crystal corruption."

Myst zoomed in on the European theater, where blue infection patterns spread like frost across the continent. Each sanctuary that fell weakened the entire network; their ancient wards, designed to work in concert, now failing one by one.

"Reroute the Dublin contingent to support Berlin." He traced a path through the quantum ether, establishing new defensive algorithms. "And get me a direct line to Cardinal Santos in Manila."

The holographic display flickered, resolving into the weathered face of the Cardinal. "Myst. We're barely holding here. The crystal armies hit our southern walls an hour ago."

"What's your status?"

"Down to skeleton crew. We evacuated most civilians through the emergency portals, but..." The Cardinal's image stuttered with interference. "These weapons they're using - they're not just corrupting bodies anymore. They're infecting our very wards, turning our own defenses against us."

Myst pulled up Manila's defensive grid, watching as centuries-old protection spells twisted and fractured under the crystal assault. The mathematical patterns were familiar - too familiar. They matched theoretical models he'd worked on years ago, before anyone understood the actual dangers of quantum manipulation.

"Hold what you can, Cardinal. I'm sending reinforcements from Seoul." Myst authorized the transfer with a gesture, knowing it might not be enough. Nothing seemed to be enough anymore.

Sister Chen appeared at his shoulder. "Sir, we're detecting massive energy signatures approaching the Himalayan sanctuaries. Pattern matches what we saw before Paris fell."

Myst's hands clenched on the control panel. They'd chosen this location for its natural defenses and isolation, but if the enemy had found them here...

Myst's vision blurred as he stared at the tactical displays, ancient symbols suddenly overlaying the modern holographic readouts. His head throbbed as mathematical formulas he'd never learned surfaced in his mind - complex multidimensional equations that felt both foreign and intimately familiar. The symbols pulsed in time with his heartbeat, their golden light casting strange shadows across the command center's walls.

"Sir?" Sister Chen's voice seemed distant. "Are you alright?"

He blinked, trying to focus as the ancient knowledge pressed against his consciousness. The equations weren't random - they formed patterns, defensive arrays he somehow recognized from a time before the Order existed. His fingers moved across the controls without conscious thought, overlaying the attack data with geometric progressions that spanned centuries.

"Look at this." He highlighted a series of points on the global map. "The Assembly isn't just hitting random targets. There's a mathematical progression to their attacks."

The holographic display shifted as he input the new parameters. Lines of force connected each fallen sanctuary, forming an intricate web that pulsed with dark energy. The pattern was elegant in its brutality - each fallen ward weakening its neighbors in a cascading failure that amplified the spread of the crystal corruption.

"They're not just destroying our defenses," Myst muttered, ancient knowledge flowing through him like a river breaking through a dam. "They're using them. Converting our own protection matrices into weapons."

Sister Chen leaned closer to the display. "But how? These wards were laid down by the founding knights themselves."

"Because they're using principles older than the Order." Myst's hands shook as he traced the attack pattern. "This is pre-Christian mathematics. Egyptian. Babylonian. Maybe older." The knowledge felt like fire in his brain, each revelation bringing fresh waves of pain as memories that weren't his own surfaced and merged with his tactical analysis.

～

London, England

Elan crouched behind a shattered pillar as another wave of crystal-enhanced cultists poured through the sanctuary's broken wards. Their bodies gleamed with an unnatural sheen, limbs transformed into jagged crystalline blades that sparked against the ancient stonework. The air crackled with corrupted magic, leaving an acrid taste in his mouth.

Winterstar hummed in his grip, its celestial steel vibrating in response to the hybrid weapons. He'd seen how regular blades shattered against the crystal armor, but Winterstar's edge cut through like they were made of glass.

"Left flank's collapsing!" Brother Thomas shouted from his position near the altar. Blood streamed from a cut above his eye as he struggled to maintain what remained of the sanctuary's defensive spells.

Elan rolled from cover, Winterstar leading his charge. The sword's cold light intensified as it met the first cultist's crystal blade. The hybrid weapon cracked, then exploded in a shower of fragments. Elan didn't pause, letting muscle memory and the sword's guidance carry him through the next three opponents. Each strike shattered their crystalline additions, leaving them vulnerable to the Order's conventional weapons.

A cultist lunged at him, both arms transformed into serrated crystal spears. Elan parried the first thrust, but the second caught his sleeve, tearing through fabric and skin. The wound burned with unnatural cold. He pivoted, bringing Winterstar down in an overhead arc that split both crystal arms at their junction with flesh.

The cultist screamed - not in pain, but in rage. The crystals began regenerating almost immediately, spreading further across their host's body. Elan reversed his grip and struck again, this time channeling energy through Winterstar's blade. The sword's star-forged metal pulsed with white light, and the crystal corruption retreated, leaving the cultist unconscious but human.

"They're adapting!" Elan shouted to the defending knights. "Use consecrated weapons only - anything else just makes them stronger!"

He pressed forward, Winterstar's light creating a path through the crystalline horde. Each strike required more energy, but the sword responded to his need, its power flowing into him as they fought as one.

Elan spun as a massive form crashed through the sanctuary wall. A Bungisngis towered above them, its single eye gleaming with crystal corruption, its trademark laugh now a discordant shriek that sent more minor cultists scrambling for cover.

"Hold the line!" Elan shouted, but several knights retreated as the giant ripped a marble column from its base.

A shimmer of light materialized beside him—a Diwata manifested in warrior form, her ethereal armor glowing with ancient power. She raised her hands, roots and vines bursting through the sanctuary floor to entangle the Bungisngis' legs.

The giant roared, its crystallized flesh shattering the vegetation, but the delay gave Elan the opening he needed. He charged forward, Winterstar blazing. The sword's light intensified as spectral forms emerged from the shadows - Manes spirits answering the Order's call, their ghostly hands reaching for the corrupted giant.

The Bungisngis swung wildly, but the Manes passed through its defenses, their touch causing the crystal corruption to crack and splinter. Elan leaped, driving Winterstar into the giant's chest. The blade struck true, sending pulses of purifying energy through the crystalline infection.

As the giant fell, a scroll fluttered from its remains. Elan snatched it up, his blood running cold as he recognized Verendana's signature mark. But this wasn't a battle plan or spell formula - it was a detailed dossier on the Durant family, including information that even the Order didn't possess.

Notes about Reagan's daily routine at the police station, where she rejoined after she retired. Maya's preferred healing techniques. Even Myst's classified location. But what chilled him most were the personal details—things only someone who had been watching them for years would know.

At the bottom, in Verendana's flowing script: "The jailer's daughter remembers. Your bloodline ends where mine was forever changed."

The vendetta wasn't just about the Order or Saint Valentine. This was personal - a centuries-old grudge carried by the blind girl whose sight had been restored, now twisted into an obsession with destroying the Durant family specifically.

Elan gestured for the remaining knights to form up around him. Their numbers had dwindled to barely two dozen, but each warrior clutched a consecrated weapon that glowed with divine energy. He needed to find Maya and Myst, but first, they had to secure their position.

"Brother Thomas, status on the wards?"

"Eastern quadrant's completely corrupted." Thomas pressed his palm against a wall covered in fractured runes. "Western holds, barely. But the crystal infection's spreading through the foundation stones."

Elan ran his fingers along Winterstar's frost-covered blade. The sword's light pulsed erratically, responding to something beneath their feet. He dropped to one knee, placing his free hand on the flagstones. A deep vibration thrummed through the stone, like a discordant heartbeat.

"The ley lines." Brother Thomas's face paled. "They're not just attacking the sanctuaries - they're poisoning the earth's power itself."

Elan traced a crack in the floor that sparkled with trapped crystal energy. The pattern matched others he'd seen in fallen sanctuaries across Europe. Not random corruption, but a calculated assault on the planet's magical arteries.

"Each sanctuary they corrupt adds to their network." Elan stood, mapping the pattern in his mind. The Assembly wasn't just destroying their strongholds - they were transforming them into nodes of crystal power, using the Order's own sacred sites to spread their infection through the ancient ley lines that connected them.

A knight rushed in from the western corridor. "Sir! We found traces of recent portal activity in the library. Multiple signatures heading east."

Elan's heart leaped. Maya had been working in the healing ward when the attack began. If she'd managed to evacuate through the library portals...

"Hold this position." He clasped Brother Thomas's shoulder. "Keep the western wards intact as long as you can. I need to find my family before the crystal corruption cuts off all escape routes."

The remaining knights formed a defensive circle around their section of the sanctuary. Elan sprinted toward the library, Winterstar's light illuminating the crystal-corrupted corridors ahead. He had to reach Maya and Myst before the Assembly's poison severed their last connections to safety.

Kaira clutched the leather-bound tome to her chest as she darted between shadows in the narrow Roman alley. Sweat trickled down her neck despite the cool night air. The ancient text's weight reminded her of its significance - one of the last uncorrupted copies of the Order's founding documents.

Footsteps echoed off the stone walls ahead. She pressed herself against a doorway, holding her breath as an Assembly search team passed. Their crystalline augmentations caught the moonlight, casting fractured reflections across the cobblestones. The texts in her bag seemed to pulse with energy, responding to the corrupted magic.

She waited until their steps faded before slipping out. Two more blocks to the next safe house. The route had been carefully planned - each handoff point chosen to avoid the Assembly's detection arrays.

A crystal shard crunched under her boot. Kaira froze. Down the street, one of the search team members turned. The crystalline growths on his face shifted, focusing like camera lenses.

"There!" His voice carried an unnatural resonance.

Kaira bolted down a side street, her feet finding purchase on worn stones. The sacred texts bounced against her back as she ran. Behind her, the crystalline pursuers' footsteps rang like breaking glass.

An unmarked wooden door appeared on her left - the backup entrance to safe house four. She yanked it open, diving inside just as crystal shards embedded themselves in the wall where she'd stood. The door's protective wards flared as she slammed it shut.

Inside, Brother Paolo grabbed her arm, pulling her toward a hidden panel. "Quickly! The wards won't hold long."

They slipped through the panel into a narrow passage as crystal-enhanced fists began pounding on the door. Kaira heard the ancient wood splinter, but by then they were already emerging in a different alley three blocks away.

"The texts?" Brother Paolo held out his hands.

Kaira passed over the bag, her fingers lingering on the leather bindings. "All seven volumes. Uncorrupted."

"Good. The next courier will take them to the mountain sanctuary." He secured the books in a warded case. "You should go. More search teams are converging on this district."

Kaira pressed her palm against the ancient stone wall, channeling her power through the centuries-old masonry. The protective symbols she traced glowed with a soft blue light, weaving into the existing wards. Her abilities had grown stronger since discovering her connection to the Three Marias, and she poured that strength into safeguarding the knowledge within.

"The texts need more than physical protection." She traced another set of symbols, these pulsing with a deeper resonance. "They're not just after the books themselves."

Brother Paolo nodded as he arranged the volumes in a specific pattern. "We've noticed they're targeting our archives systematically. Not destroying them - copying them somehow."

Kaira's fingers brushed across a section of wall that felt wrong. The stone was colder, with hairline cracks spreading in a geometric pattern. She scraped away a layer of grime, revealing crystal growth beneath the surface.

"Paolo, look at this."

He leaned closer, examining the crystalline formation. "These patterns... they match the diagrams in Volume Three."

Kaira pulled out the referenced book, flipping to a chapter on ancient mathematical principles. The crystal's growth followed the same sacred geometry the Order had used to establish their original ward network.

"They're not just copying our knowledge." She traced the crystal's path across the wall. "They're using it to create some kind of... crystalline network. These aren't random growths - they're following the same patterns as our ward system."

Paolo's face paled as he compared the wall patterns to the diagrams in the book. "If they've deciphered these principles, they could use our own protective network against us. Turn every sanctuary into a node in their crystal web."

The implications chilled Kaira. Each archive they corrupted wasn't just a loss of knowledge - it was another piece in the Assembly's larger plan. She reinforced her protective wards, adding layers of complexity that would resist crystal corruption.

In Antarctica's hidden sanctuary, Erikson Ghostcloak's boots crunched across the crystalline floor as he surveyed the tactical displays. The command center's walls pulsed with corrupted ley line energy, transforming the once-pristine ice into geometric patterns of dark crystal.

"All teams report ready." His voice carried through the quantum-enhanced communications network. The faces of his fellow coordinators appeared on floating screens - Reagan in New York, Stanley in Australia, Austin in Ukraine, and Zoe in India.

"Eastern seaboard sanctuaries targeted." Reagan's image flickered as she adjusted something off-screen. "Crystal resonators in position."

"Southeast Asia grid primed." Zoe's fingers danced across unseen controls. "Local ley lines showing preliminary corruption patterns."

"European network compromised." Austin's face was bathed in the sickly glow of crystal formations. "Ukraine sanctuary's defenses have been inverted."

"Pacific rim ready." Stanley's distinctive mustache twitched as he spoke. "Australian node activated."

Erikson placed his hand on the master control crystal, feeling its cold power pulse through his veins. The Assembly had spent years positioning these nodes, carefully corrupting each sanctuary's natural defenses until they formed a global network of crystal power.

"Initiate synchronized attack protocol." His words triggered a cascade of responses across the displays. "Convert all compromised wards... now."

Five simultaneous bursts of energy rippled through the ley line network. On the global display, points of light representing Order sanctuaries began shifting from blue to red as their ancient protections turned inward, transformed by the crystal corruption into weapons against their own defenders.

The once-separate attacks merged into a single coordinated assault, each coordinator managing their region's crystal forces with precision. The Assembly's years of infiltration and preparation culminated in this moment, as the Order's own defensive network became the instrument of its destruction.

Myst's fingers flew across the holographic controls, ancient knowledge burning through his skull as the pattern emerged. "Command, this is Myst. The attacks - they're following pre-Christian mathematical principles. Each fallen sanctuary amplifies the corruption of its neighbors."

The secure channel crackled. Maya's voice cut through, breathless from what sounded like running. Confirming pattern analysis from medical archives. The crystal spread matches healing ward layouts. They're using our own regenerative matrices against us."

"Kaira here." Her transmission carried static from somewhere in Rome. "I'm seeing the same geometric progressions in the founding texts. The Assembly isn't just copying our knowledge - they're converting our entire ward network into crystal nodes."

Elan's voice joined from London, Winterstar's hum audible in the background. "The ley lines are being poisoned systematically. Each sanctuary they corrupt becomes part of their network." A clash of steel punctuated his words. "The crystal formations - they're following the same sacred geometry we used to establish the original wardstones."

The secure channel fell silent as each family member processed the implications. Their separate discoveries, viewed from different angles across the globe, formed a complete picture of the Assembly's master plan.

"They're initiating something." Maya's voice sharpened. "Energy signatures spiking across all compromised locations."

"Five simultaneous power surges." Myst highlighted the pattern on his display. "New York, Ukraine, India, Australia..."

"And Antarctica." Kaira finished. "They're using our own defensive network as a weapon."

Through their secure connection, each family member watched as sanctuary after sanctuary shifted from safety to corruption, their ancient protections twisted by crystal power. The Assembly's years of careful infiltration had led to this moment—a synchronized attack that turned the Order's most significant strengths against itself.

The crystal network pulsed with sickly light as each corrupted sanctuary joined the Assembly's web. Elan watched the tactical display through narrowed eyes as red lines of power stretched between fallen strongholds, forming geometric patterns that seemed to twist reality itself.

A knight stumbled beside him, catching himself against a wall. "Sir, something's wrong with the air."

Elan saw it too. The space around them rippled like heat waves over hot pavement, but carried an otherworldly chill. Where crystal corruption had taken root, the very fabric of existence appeared to fold and bend.

In New York, concrete cracked and reformed into crystalline spires. Trees in Central Park twisted into impossible shapes, their branches becoming geometric fractals that caught and refracted light in ways that hurt the eyes.

The Ukrainian sanctuary's stone walls bled into the surrounding countryside, reality warping until it was impossible to tell where architecture ended and landscape began. Crystal growths spread through the corrupted zones, transforming everything they touched into versions of themselves that followed alien mathematical rules.

Through the tactical feeds, Elan witnessed similar distortions at each central node. In India, ancient temples phased in and out of existence as crystal corruption rewrote their structural properties. Australia's red earth crystallized into vast geometric patterns visible from orbit. And in Antarctica, the ice itself seemed to flow upward, defying gravity as it formed new structures guided by the Assembly's corrupted calculations.

"The crystal tech isn't just creating a network," Brother Thomas said, his voice tight with horror. "It's using our sacred geometries to rewrite local physics. Each corrupted site is becoming a reality anchor point."

Elan pressed his palm against Winterstar's pommel, feeling the sword's celestial steel vibrate in response to the warping space around them. The weapon's pure energy seemed to stabilize reality in its immediate vicinity, pushing back against the crystal corruption's influence. But its effect was limited to a small radius, and the distortions were spreading faster with each new site that fell to the Assembly's control.

Static crackled across the secure channel before three new signatures registered. Elan's heart jumped as Nykronus's deep voice cut through the interference.

"The crystal network is destabilizing more than just physical space. The barriers between dimensions are growing thin."

"We're seeing temporal anomalies here in Benevento," Grandma Mazza added. "Objects shifting between past and present. The church bells rang yesterday's vespers this morning."

Lola Rose's voice carried an edge of urgency. "The old wards are failing. I've got readings that match the 842 A.D. incident - when Kaira first crossed through."

Elan steadied himself against a wall as reality rippled around him. Through Winterstar's connection, he felt the dimensional fabric stretching like an overtaxed rubber band.

"The Assembly isn't just corrupting space," Nykronus continued. "They're using the crystal network to deliberately weaken temporal boundaries. Each sanctuary they convert becomes an anchor point for their calculations."

"The mathematical principles." Maya's voice sparked with recognition. "They're not just copying our ward designs - they're reverse-engineering the time travel mechanics from the 842 event."

Grandma Mazza spoke rapid Italian to someone off-channel before returning. "The original portal site here is showing increased activity. The crystals are somehow resonating with leftover temporal energy from Kaira's crossing."

"Multiple sites reporting similar phenomena," Lola Rose added. "London, Rome, Constantinople - anywhere with significant historical connections to the Order is experiencing temporal bleed-through."

Through the tactical display, Elan watched as more anomaly

reports flooded in. The Assembly's crystal network wasn't just spreading across space, but reaching through time itself, using the Order's own history as connection points for their corruption.

~

Mexico City, Mexico

Verendana's fingers traced the crystalline control panel, its surface cold against her skin. The command center deep beneath Mexico City hummed with power as corruption spread through the global network. Geometric patterns shifted across the walls, each pulse representing another sanctuary falling to their influence.

"Eastern node activated." Her voice carried the weight of centuries. "Begin precision strikes on secondary targets."

The holographic display showed New York's crystal spires piercing the sky. She adjusted a series of controls, directing energy through the corrupted ley lines. The crystals responded instantly, geometric patterns spreading through the city's underground like roots of a poisoned tree.

"Magnificent, isn't it?" She turned to Dante, who stood rigid beside her throne of crystalline shards. "Each sanctuary they built becomes our weapon. Their own sacred geometry turned against them."

A warning flashed across the display - resistance in London. Verendana's lips curled into a smile as she redirected power from the Mexican node. The crystal formations beneath her feet pulsed with renewed energy, sending waves of corruption through the network.

"Target their archive vaults first," she commanded. "Convert the knowledge repositories. Let their own histories fuel our advancement."

The tactical overlay showed clusters of red dots representing strike teams moving through each compromised location. She'd positioned them carefully over the years, waiting for this moment when the Order's defenses would turn inward.

Another alert - temporal anomalies growing stronger around the primary nodes. Verendana adjusted the crystal resonance, fine-tuning the network's frequency. The ancient mathematics flowed through her mind, each calculation precise and purposeful. This wasn't just about destroying the Order's present - she was systematically corrupting their entire timeline.

"The barriers are thinning exactly as calculated." She manipulated the controls, directing the crystal growth with surgical precision. "Soon their precious sanctuaries will become our gateways through time itself."

CHAPTER
FOURTEEN

Numbers blazed through Myst's mind like lightning, ancient equations burning across his consciousness. He stumbled back from the tactical display, his hand clutching the edge of the stone table. The holographic battle plans scattered beneath his fingers, replaced by geometric patterns that sparked and danced in the air.

Sacred forms materialized around him - circles intersecting with precise angles, triangles folding into impossible dimensions. The mathematics of creation itself poured into his thoughts, each formula carrying the weight of centuries. His breath caught as knowledge far older than human civilization crystallized in his mind.

The air shimmered with golden light as more patterns emerged, spinning and transforming into new forms. Platonic solids morphed into complex fractals, each shape carrying layers of meaning that transcended ordinary physics. Through the haze of information flooding his senses, Myst recognized fragments of the Order's ward designs - but these were the original forms, pure and uncorrupted.

Blood trickled from his nose as another wave of equations crashed through his consciousness. The geometric displays surrounding him shifted faster, sacred ratios and divine proportions weaving into structures that defied conventional space. His fingers moved unconsciously, tracing symbols in the air that left trails of light hanging in their wake.

"The original proofs," he gasped, his voice rough. The knowledge burned like fire behind his eyes, each new revelation threatening to overwhelm his mortal mind. "This is how they first shaped reality."

The patterns continued to spiral around him, ancient mathematics made visible through powers he barely understood. Each symbol carried echoes of the first geometers who had discovered these fundamental truths. These original architects had learned to bend the fabric of creation to their will.

The Order's monitoring systems erupted in chaos. Screens flickered with cascading symbols, their usual tactical displays consumed by the mathematical energy pouring from Myst. Ancient ward-stones embedded in the chamber walls pulsed with irregular patterns, their carefully calibrated frequencies disrupted by waves of primordial geometry.

Myst watched through pain-blurred vision as the quantum arrays crashed one by one. The holographic interfaces dissolved into pure mathematical constructs, sacred ratios, and divine proportions, rendering their modern protocols obsolete. Sparks showered from several terminals as their protection wards overloaded.

"The systems can't handle the original formulas," he muttered, recognizing how the ancient mathematics was interfering with the Order's hybrid tech. These were the pure forms that had preceded their current understanding - raw and untamed by centuries of refinement.

A deep vibration shuddered through the chamber's foundation stones. Myst's attention snapped to the preservation spells woven into the walls - spells that had maintained the Order's sanctuary for centuries. The mathematical energy flooding the room was affecting them too, causing ripples in their usually stable matrices.

Hairline cracks appeared in the spelled stone, geometric patterns warping as the ancient equations interfered with their structure. The preservation wards flickered like failing lightbulbs, their protective geometries struggling to maintain coherence against the surge of primal mathematics.

"No, no, no." Myst pressed his palms against the nearest wall, feeling the tremors in the spelled stone. The preservation matrix was destabilizing, its carefully balanced formulas being overwhelmed by the raw power of the original proofs. Centuries of protection spells were unraveling as the pure mathematics exposed flaws in their underlying structure.

A stone block crashed to the floor nearby as its supporting enchantments failed. The sound echoed through the chamber like a gunshot, accompanied by the crackle of failing systems and the deep groan of stressed architecture. More cracks spiderwebbed across the ceiling as the preservation spells continued to destabilize the area.

Blood sprayed across ancient stone as St. Michael's blade found its mark. The attacker crumpled, dark energy dissipating from their body. More cultists poured through the monastery's breached walls, their twisted forms illuminated by burning cars in the courtyard.

Michael pivoted, positioning himself between the attackers and Pope Francis, who knelt in prayer behind him. The Pope's whispered Latin carried through the chapel, invoking divine protection over the sacred ground.

A cultist's energy blast struck Michael's sword, the impact sending a jolt through his arms. The familiar weight of the weapon triggered something - a flash of memory burst through his mind.

Stone walls dissolved into desert sand. The clash of steel became the thunder of charging horses. He saw himself leading Heaven's armies across ancient battlefields, wings spread wide as divine light poured from his sword. The memories crashed over him like waves - countless battles fought across millennia, always standing as the shield between darkness and light.

Michael staggered as present reality reasserted itself. His shoulder blades burned as divine energy coursed through his celestial form. Ghostly wings began to manifest, their translucent outline casting shifting shadows on the chapel walls.

"Stay behind me, Your Holiness." Michael's voice carried the weight of ages as he advanced on the cultists. His partially manifested wings flared wider, holy light rippling along their ethereal feathers.

The cultists hesitated, their dark magic faltering as they faced the emerging divine presence. Michael pressed the advantage, his sword leaving trails of celestial fire as he cut through their ranks. Each strike was backed by the muscle memory of countless battles, his movements fluid and precise.

His wings pulsed with increasing solidity as the combat intensified. Divine energy crackled around him, causing the nearest cultists to stumble back. Their twisted forms withered under the holy radiance pouring from his partially manifested celestial aspect.

"The Archangel!" One of the cultists screamed in recognition. "Fall back! We cannot-"

Michael's blade silenced them mid-sentence. More cultists scrambled through the breach, but their earlier confidence had evaporated in the face of his awakening power.

Michael's sword clashed against the cultist's crystalline blade. The impact sent familiar vibrations through his arms, triggering a cascade of fractured memories. Desert winds howled across ancient battlefields. Armies of corrupted angels advanced with weapons that pulsed with dark energy—technology that bore a haunting similarity to the Assembly's crystal technology.

The names crashed through his consciousness: Samael, Belial, Mastema. Fallen brothers who had wielded similar corruption in ages past. His body moved on instinct, flowing through combat forms he hadn't consciously remembered until this moment.

Divine light rippled across his skin as fragments of celestial armor materialized and faded. The cultist's eyes widened as Michael's form flickered between mortal and divine aspects. His partially manifested wings cast shifting shadows, growing more substantial with each surge of returning memory.

Stone walls dissolved into ancient Rome. He envisioned himself establishing the first sanctuaries, weaving protection spells into geometric patterns that would still guard the Order's strongholds. The mathematical precision of those original wards resonated with the current moment, highlighting how the Assembly's corruption was unraveling their divine foundation.

Although Heavenshard was held firmly in his fists, his visions revealed a humming Winterstar in his grip, its connection to his true nature strengthening as more memories surfaced. The blade recognized its master, responding with increasing power as the seals on his divine essence continued to crack.

A familiar face caught his attention through the chaos - Verendana. Recognition slammed into him like a physical blow. He had encountered her before, centuries ago, when she first discovered the corrupted crystals. The memory left him vulnerable for a crucial moment.

Dark energy sliced across his shoulder as he stumbled. The pain triggered another surge of power, a divine light blazing from his form. The sanctuary's walls groaned as his unleashed power strained against the ancient preservation spells that had been cast upon them. Warning symbols flared across the ward-stones as his divine essence threatened to overwhelm their carefully balanced matrices.

Michael fought to contain the surging power while maintaining his defense against the cultists. Each recovered memory made it harder to maintain control, his sealed knowledge battling against current limitations. The preservation spells flickered dangerously as his divine nature pressed against their boundaries.

Nykronus materialized at the Vatican's eastern anchor point, his hands pressed against ancient stone humming with failing preservation spells. Power flowed from his fingertips into the ward-stones, their crystalline matrices drinking his energy like water in desert sand.

Time magic rippled around him as he channeled power into the preservation network. The spell's drain tore through his defenses, ripping memories from the depths of his consciousness. He saw his father Felix in the courtyard of their Roman villa, teaching him the foundations of chronomancy. The image shifted - Elan appearing through the time portal in the Colosseum, confused but determined.

His body trembled as more memories surfaced. Training sessions with Maya and Myst, their young faces eager to learn the Order's secrets. Michael, standing guard during countless rituals, his divine presence a constant through centuries of service.

Blood trickled from Nykronus's nose as he pulled away from the anchor point. His reflection in polished marble showed deepening lines on his face, strands of gray spreading through his dark hair. The preservation spells were consuming his life force at a faster rate than expected.

He teleported to St. Peter's Basilica, stumbling as he rematerialized. This anchor point pulsed with dangerous instability, Myst's mathematical patterns creating interference in the ancient matrices. The geometric forms twisted through normal space, threatening to tear the fabric of reality.

"Hold together," Nykronus growled, pouring more power into the failing wards. Another memory crashed through his mind - meeting Gianna in 1960s Venice, where he recognized the potential she carried. The preservation spell greedily devoured the energy of that moment, along with countless others.

Warning symbols flared across the ward-stones as Myst's equations grew more chaotic. Nykronus's hands shook as he redirected power from lesser wards, sacrificing peripheral defenses to maintain the Basilica's core protection. Each decision felt like betrayal, but the alternative was total collapse.

Nykronus's vision blurred as the crystal tech's interference rippled through the Vatican's temporal barriers. The scene before him fractured, splitting into multiple overlapping realities. He watched himself standing in a medieval church, head bowed as monks carried two shrouded bodies. The figures resolved into Elan and Kaira, but the timeline felt wrong - he couldn't tell if this was a future yet to come or a past that had been altered.

Sacred geometric patterns warped around him, their perfect symmetry distorting as the Assembly's corrupted crystals pulsed with dark energy. The ancient wards tried to compensate, but their pure mathematics couldn't maintain stability against the hybrid technology's unnatural frequencies.

Through the temporal distortion, he glimpsed two parallel scenes playing out in the same space. Myst knelt in a circle of runes, his form flickering between youth and age as Michael performed a complex ritual. In the overlapping reality, their positions were reversed - Michael submitted to the memory-wiping spell while Myst channeled the power. Both versions felt equally real, equally valid.

"The realms," Myst's voice echoed from multiple points in time. "They're collapsing. We have to forget."

The preservation spells crackled and sparked as waves of hybrid energy washed through the sacred sites. Centuries-old protections began to unravel, their carefully crafted matrices unable to withstand the Assembly's technological interference. The crystal formations hummed at frequencies that set Nykronus's teeth on edge, their vibrations disrupting the natural flow of time.

Blood ran from his nose as he fought to adapt the ancient defenses. His hands traced new patterns in the air, weaving modern shielding techniques into the traditional wards. The hybrid magic felt wrong, but he had no choice - the old ways alone couldn't stand against the Assembly's corrupted technology.

The overlapping timelines continued to shift and blur. Nykronus saw multiple versions of events playing out simultaneously, each equally valid yet somehow contradictory. He no longer knew which path had led to this moment, or what changes had fractured reality so severely.

Nykronus pressed his palm against the vibrating ward-stone, channeling temporal energy to reinforce the weakening seals. Through the magical connection, he sensed Myst's consciousness straining against the barriers - pure mathematical knowledge trying to break free all at once. The preservation spells sparked and sputtered as they fought to contain the surge of information.

Across the Vatican, similar pressure built around Michael's divine essence. Each clash of steel released more of the Archangel's power, as holy light seeped through the cracks in the ancient bindings. Nykronus redirected power from secondary wards, trying to maintain the delicate balance that kept Michael's true nature contained.

Blood dripped onto ancient stone as Nykronus traced new temporal patterns. The seals needed careful adjustment - allowing crucial memories to surface while preventing the devastating flood of complete revelation. He wove strands of chronomancy through the preservation matrix, creating channels for controlled release.

But the Assembly's attacks made precise control nearly impossible. Each battle pushed Michael closer to his divine aspect, while Myst's tactical calculations brushed against more profound mathematical truths. The seals groaned under increasing pressure as both fought to access abilities they didn't fully remember possessing.

Warning symbols flared across the ward stones as the preservation network further destabilized. Nykronus felt the strain in his bones as he poured more power into the failing spells. If the seals broke completely, the shock of complete restoration could shatter minds and tear reality. Yet without access to specific memories, they couldn't hope to defeat the Assembly.

His hands shook as he adjusted the temporal flows, trying to find the razor's edge between necessary knowledge and catastrophic revelation. Too many restrictions would leave them vulnerable, but too much freedom risked total collapse of the preservation spells that maintained their fragile reality.

Myst's fingers flew across the ancient terminal in Tibet's mountain sanctuary, holographic displays showing the scattered Order forces worldwide. Each location pulsed with different warning levels: red for critical, yellow for compromised, and green for stable. Too much red filled his vision.

"Edinburgh's defenses are holding," Maya's voice crackled through the comm system. "But we've lost contact with the outer perimeter teams."

"London's east wall is breached," Elan reported, the sound of combat carrying through his transmission. "Falling back to the inner sanctum."

Status updates continued to pour in. Kaira coordinated evacuation efforts in Benevento while Erikson fortified the Antarctic facility's failing shield matrix. Reagan's voice cut through the chaos from New

York, directing emergency response teams as cultists pressed their attack.

"Australia's wards are at thirty percent," Stanley's distinctive accent carried notes of strain. "Could use some backup down here."

Austin's transmission from Ukraine was fragmented, with interference from Crystal Tech disrupting the communication channels. "...multiple hostiles... requesting immediate..."

"India's sanctuary is compromised," Zoe's voice remained steady despite the dire situation. "Moving survivors to the secondary location."

Myst's hands trembled as he tried to allocate their dwindling resources. Each sanctuary needed reinforcement, but their forces were stretched desperately thin. The Assembly had coordinated their attacks perfectly, striking all major Order strongholds simultaneously.

"Prioritize evacuation protocols," Myst commanded, watching more red warnings bloom across his displays. "Save who you can, preserve what's essential. We can rebuild structures - we can't replace people."

The geometric patterns covering the walls of his chamber pulsed with unstable energy as another wave of crystal tech interference washed through the global network. Ancient equations warped and twisted, their perfect symmetry disrupted by the Assembly's corrupted technology.

Kaira wiped sweat from her brow as she sealed the final archive container. The ancient texts and relics hummed with residual power, their protective spells interacting with the Vatican's failing wards. Her hands shook slightly as she activated the transport sigils etched into the container's surface.

"Last batch secured, Myst." She pressed her hand against the communication crystal mounted on the archive room's wall. "Everything critical is in the sanctuary now."

"Acknowledged." Myst's voice came through distorted, crystal tech interference warping the sound. "Michael's holding the main entrance, but we need you both to fall back. The outer defenses won't last much longer."

A distant explosion rattled the shelves in the archive. Dust and fragments of stone drifted down from the ceiling as the preservation spells struggled to maintain structural integrity. Kaira grabbed her pack and headed for the door, pausing only to check that the containment wards on the empty shelves were sealed correctly.

"Michael?" She touched the comm crystal again. "I'm heading to your position."

"Stay back." His voice carried an edge of divine power that made the crystal resonate. "The Assembly's brought in heavy weapons. I'll meet you at the secondary exit."

Another blast shook the building. Through the archive's narrow windows, Kaira glimpsed flashes of combat - holy light clashing against the sickly glow of corrupted crystal tech. Michael's partially manifested wings cast shifting shadows across the courtyard as he engaged multiple cultists.

"The preservation matrix is critical," Myst warned through the comm. "Get clear before it fails completely. We can't lose either of you."

Kaira hurried through the darkened corridors, her footsteps echoing off ancient stone. The Vatican's power felt wrong, destabilized by the Assembly's attacks and Michael's increasingly uncontained divine essence. Warning symbols flared across the wardstones she passed, their usually pristine geometry twisted into chaotic patterns.

Myst's fingers flew across the holographic controls as reality rippled around him. The sanctuary's walls seemed to breathe, ancient stone flexing like living tissue. Through the command center's windows, he watched clouds flow backward across a sky that shifted between day and night every few seconds.

"Multiple temporal anomalies detected in Paris," Maya's voice crackled through the distorted comms. "Civilians reporting dinosaurs in the Champs-Élysées."

A status alert flashed red - the Assembly's hybrid tech was creating interference patterns in the preservation matrix. Mathematical formulas that had maintained reality's stability for centuries were being corrupted by the crystal resonance. The pure equations couldn't handle the technological pollution.

"London team, be advised," Myst transmitted. "Temporal shielding is failing in your sector. Expect-"

The feed cut out as another reality wave pulsed through the sanctuary. The walls shimmered like heat mirages, momentarily transparent. Through them, Myst glimpsed impossible geometries and creatures that shouldn't exist.

"Multiple breaches reported," Reagan's transmission barely cut through the static. "We've got Revolutionary War soldiers appearing in Times Square. The preservation spells are going haywire."

Myst watched in horror as the holographic displays showed reality fractures spreading across the globe. The Assembly's corrupted crystals were acting like prisms, splitting time and space into conflicting streams. Ancient protection spells designed to maintain the natural order were being twisted into chaos engines.

"Antarctic base, multiple containment failures," Erikson reported. "The crystal corruption is releasing entities from the vault. We need immediate support."

But there was no support to send. Every member of the Order was dealing with their own cascading disasters as reality began to break down around them. The preservation spells that had maintained separation between worlds for millennia were unraveling, allowing things to slip through from other dimensions.

"Tokyo sanctuary compromised," another voice cut through. "Yokai manifesting in the financial district. Preservation matrix critical."

Myst's hands shook as he tried to stabilize the equations, but the crystal corruption had spread too far. Mathematical perfection warped under technological interference, creating unpredictable reactions in the ancient protection spells.

Reality buckled at the Vatican sanctuary as mathematical formulas twisted through the air in glowing streams. Myst stumbled as the floor rippled beneath his feet, ancient stone flowing like liquid. Through fractured vision, he saw multiple versions of the command center overlapping - some pristine, others in ruins, all equally real.

His mind raced with equations that felt both familiar and foreign. Pure mathematics poured through his consciousness, revealing patterns he shouldn't understand yet somehow knew intimately. The preservation spells' geometric forms spoke to him in a language of perfect symmetry and divine proportion.

Across the sanctuary, Michael's partially manifested wings cast shifting shadows as more of his divine essence broke free. Each pulse of celestial power sent ripples through the destabilizing reality matrix. The Archangel's memories crashed against the preservation seals, fragments of ancient knowledge aligning with Myst's mathematical revelations.

"The equations," Myst gasped, recognizing celestial formulas hidden within Michael's wing patterns. "They're the same as the preservation spells."

Divine light blazed from Michael's form as another seal cracked. Memories of crafting the original protection matrices flooded his awareness - perfect mathematical patterns that Myst now instinctively understood. Their knowledge resonated across time and space, twin aspects of the same cosmic truth.

The sanctuary walls groaned as reality continued to distort. Myst watched mathematical formulas spiral through the air, their pure geometry warping under the crystal tech's corruption. But now he saw more than just equations - he glimpsed the divine principles behind their structure, the same patterns Michael had woven into the first wards.

Their partially restored knowledge created feedback loops in the preservation matrix. Each recovered memory amplified the others, divine power and mathematical precision building toward a critical threshold. The sanctuary's reality fabric stretched dangerously thin as their combined understanding threatened to overwhelm the ancient seals.

Nykronus's knees hit the marble floor as another preservation spell shattered. Blood leaked from his ears, the price of channeling too much temporal energy. Around him, the Vatican's reality rippled like a heat mirage, sacred geometries twisting into impossible shapes.

"Hold," he gasped, pressing both palms against the central wardstone. Its surface burned cold against his skin as he poured more of his life force into the failing matrix. The preservation network screamed in his mind, mathematical patterns fracturing under the crystal tech's corruption.

A wave of temporal feedback slammed through his body. Through blurred vision, he watched his hands age and rejuvenate in rapid cycles. The price of maintaining the spells grew steeper with each passing moment.

Three cultists materialized through a breach in the eastern wall, their crystal-powered weapons humming with unnatural frequencies. Nykronus couldn't spare the energy to fight them - every scrap of power was devoted to preventing the total collapse of the preservation matrix.

"The wards are failing," one cultist called out. "Signal the others!"

More Assembly forces poured through reality fractures around the sanctuary. Their corrupted crystals pulsed in sync, creating interference patterns that further destabilized the ancient protections. Each group targeted key wardstones, their attacks precise and coordinated.

Nykronus tasted copper as blood ran from his nose. He redirected power from peripheral systems, sacrificing outer defenses to maintain the core preservation spells. The Assembly forces pressed closer, taking advantage of the weakening barriers.

"The matrix is nearly broken," another cultist shouted. "Push harder!"

The preservation network trembled on the edge of catastrophic failure. Nykronus felt reality straining against its bonds, held together only by his desperate channeling of temporal energy. His vision darkened at the edges as the spells consumed more of his life force.

Blood streamed from Nykronus's nose as another preservation spell shattered. The Vatican's marble floors rippled like water, ancient stone losing cohesion as reality destabilized. Through the command center's windows, he watched clouds flow backward across a sky that shifted between day and night every few seconds.

"Multiple temporal anomalies detected," Maya's voice crackled through the distorted comms. "Revolutionary soldiers in Times Square. Dinosaurs in Paris. The barriers between times are dissolving."

The holographic displays showed reality fractures spreading across the globe. The Assembly's corrupted crystals acted like prisms, splitting time and space into conflicting streams. Ancient protection spells, designed to maintain the natural order, were twisted into chaos engines.

"Antarctic base, containment failures in progress," Erikson reported.

"Crystal corruption is releasing entities from the vault. Tokyo sanctuary reports yokai manifesting in the financial district."

Nykronus's hands trembled as he traced new patterns in the air, trying to stabilize the failing wards. But the crystal tech's interference had spread too far, corrupting the pure mathematical foundations of the preservation matrix. Each attempt to reinforce the spells only accelerated their decay.

"They planned this," Michael's voice carried divine resonance that made the crystals hum. "The Assembly isn't just attacking our strongholds - they're using our own defensive matrix against us. The crystal corruption spreads through the preservation network itself."

The revelation hit Nykronus like a physical blow. Every attempt to strengthen the wards helped distribute the corruption further. The Assembly had turned the Order's greatest protection into a weapon, using their interconnected sanctuaries to spread chaos across reality itself.

Through fractured vision, Nykronus watched mathematical formulas spiral through the air, their pure geometry warping under technological interference. The preservation spells that had maintained separation between worlds for millennia were unraveling, and the Order had unknowingly contributed to making it possible.

Elan's voice cut through the chaos of failing communications. "Everyone, fall back. Rendezvous at the Basilica of Eternal Light. It's our last stronghold with intact wards."

The ancient sanctuary in Belém stood as their final bastion, its divine protections still holding against the Assembly's corruption. Through fractured comm channels, acknowledgments filtered in from scattered Order forces.

"Copy that," Reagan transmitted from New York. "Securing transport now."

"En route from London," Stanley confirmed, his voice breaking through static.

Myst collapsed against a console, his mind burning as equations and memories crashed through weakening mental barriers. Mathematical truths he had not yet comprehended flooded his consciousness.

The sanctuary's geometry seemed to pulse in sync with his racing thoughts, each revelation threatening to overwhelm him.

Across the chamber, Michael dropped to one knee. Golden lightning crackled across his partially manifested wings, each arc causing reality to shudder. The marble floor beneath him cracked and reformed in endless patterns as his divine power leaked through failing seals.

"The memories," Michael gasped, his voice resonating with celestial harmonics. "Too much, too fast."

Ancient knowledge hammered against their minds - battlefield strategies, divine equations, cosmic truths meant to stay hidden until the right moment. Myst saw complex temporal matrices in his mind's eye, understanding their structure even as the knowledge threatened to break him.

Michael's wings flared brighter, golden bolts of energy lashing out to strike the walls. Where they hit, reality rippled and warped. Sacred symbols carved into the stone began to glow, responding to his uncontained divine essence. The very air seemed to vibrate with power as more seals cracked under the strain.

"Hold on," Elan called out to them both. "Just make it to Belém. The Basilica's preservation matrix is stronger - it can help contain this."

Myst gripped the console tighter, trying to anchor himself as another wave of mathematical revelations threatened to overwhelm him. Through the haze of too much knowledge, he heard the others coordinating their retreat to Brazil. They had to move fast, before the memories broke through completely.

CHAPTER
FIFTEEN

Belém, Pará, Brazil
    Elan's fingers flew across the holographic controls in the Basilica's command center. Ancient stone walls thrummed with divine energy as the sanctuary's preservation matrix struggled to maintain stability. Through the reinforced windows, golden light bathed the Amazon rainforest in perpetual twilight.

"Shanghai sanctuary, confirm status." Elan marked another red zone on the global map as static answered his call. "Moscow command, please respond." More silence.

The loss of contact burned in his chest. Good people, friends, all potentially lost to the temporal storms. He pushed the pain aside and focused on the survivors.

"This is Durant. All remaining Order forces converge on Belém. The Basilica's wards are holding." He transmitted new authorization codes across the secure channels. "Regional commanders, establish emergency protocols. Civilian evacuation takes priority."

Acknowledgments filtered in from the scattered remnants. London, Cape Town, and Sydney sanctuaries reported successful evacuations. Mexico City maintained a defensive line against Assembly forces. Tokyo went dark mid-transmission.

The sound of rotor blades cut through his concentration. A black helicopter descended through the golden haze, touching down on the Basilica's indoor landing pad. Elan's heart skipped as he recognized the pilot.

Kaira jumped from the cockpit, her dark hair wild from the flight. She crossed the pad in quick strides, closing the distance between them as the retractable rooftop folded shut. Their embrace carried the desperate strength of survivors.

"The New York sanctuary?" Elan breathed in her familiar scent.

"Gone. Reagan got most of our people out before the temporal cascade hit." Kaira pulled back, her eyes reflecting the golden light. "But we lost more than we should have. They stayed behind to seal the vault."

Elan squeezed her hand. Another friend has fallen victim to the Assembly's madness. But having Kaira here, alive and whole, gave him strength to continue. They had a war to win, and now they had a chance to regroup.

Elan leaned over the command console, his knuckles white against the metal edge. The holographic display flickered as another transmission cut through the static.

"... repeat, this is General Minh Luu. Beijing sanctuary compromised. Assembly forces..." The signal stabilized. "Durant, if you're receiving, we've secured the St. Gabriel's Horn of Proclamation. Request immediate extraction coordinates."

"Copy, General. Transmitting nav-points now." Elan's fingers danced across the interface. "The Basilica's temporal shields are stable. Get your people here."

"Understood. Luu out."

A new signal pierced through. "Vatican command, Cardinal Varvaro reporting." The aged voice carried steel beneath its weariness. "Our defensive line holds, but not for long. Assembly cultists breached the outer walls."

"Cardinal, abandon the position." Elan mapped the shortest route through the temporal corridors. "The sacred texts are more valuable than stone walls. We need your knowledge here."

"Agreed. Initiating Protocol Exodus."

More voices joined the channel. Commander Yeboah from Dubai. Field Director Ragle in Singapore. Each report painted the same picture - Assembly forces striking at Order sanctuaries worldwide, temporal storms erasing centuries of history.

Kaira worked beside him, coordinating evacuation routes through the remaining safe zones. Her presence steadied him as he relayed orders to the scattered teams.

"This is Durant to all Order assets. Fall back to Belém. The Basilica stands as our last fortress." He transmitted authentication codes. "If retreat is impossible, go dark. Survive. We'll find you when the storms pass."

Acknowledgments echoed across the secure channel. Some are clear, while others are broken by interference. Each voice represented another thread of hope in their fraying tapestry.

The holographic map pulsed with movement as surviving teams marked their positions. Green markers converged on Brazil while red zones spread across continents. A symphony of coordination amid chaos.

From his position at the Basilica's command center, Elan tracked the assault on Edinburgh through multiple holographic feeds. Crystal-enhanced cultists smashed against the sanctuary's outer wards, their corrupted energy warping reality around them. Trees twisted into impossible shapes, stone melted like wax, and the sky above the Scottish capital fractured into prismatic shards.

"Edinburgh team, fall back to position theta," Elan directed through the hybrid comms. Winterstar hummed at his side, its celestial energy highlighting weaknesses in the Assembly's formation. "They're concentrating force on your western flank."

Myst's voice cut through the channel from his flight. "Running the numbers now. Crystal resonance patterns suggest they'll breach sector seven in three minutes. Recommend shifting defenders to the chapel's northwest corner."

"Confirmed." Maya's team moved through the chaos with practiced precision. Her medallion pulsed with stabilizing energy, temporary patches in the fractured reality spreading from her position. Beside her,

Asha's fur bristled as she tracked corruption patterns through the sanctuary grounds.

"Sonic disruption ready," Zoe transmitted from her plane over India, her drone hovering above Edinburgh's spires. "Targeting crystal frequencies now."

Stanley's gruff voice joined in. "Enhanced weapons primed. My boat's two hours out from Brazil, but I've got remote targeting locked on Edinburgh's perimeter."

"Almost at the Basilica," Erikson reported, his monitoring feeds showing real-time perimeter data. "Sending updated ward configurations."

Assembly forces surged through the outer defenses, reality warping in their wake. Maya's team executed a fighting retreat, drawing the cultists deeper into the sanctuary grounds. Trap crystals activated along predetermined paths, reinforcing ward boundaries with concentrated bursts of sacred energy.

"Now!" Elan commanded.

Multiple strikes hit simultaneously - Zoe's sonic pulse shattered crystal resonance patterns, Stanley's enhanced weapons struck from calculated angles, and Maya's team closed the trap. The corrupted energy imploded, contained within strengthened ward boundaries.

For the first time, they'd successfully contained a corrupted site.

Elan watched the feeds as Maya's team secured the remaining artifacts at the Edinburgh sanctuary. Her voice came through clear and steady.

"Sanctuary sealed. Ward matrices holding at ninety-three percent. Beginning extraction protocol."

"Copy that." Elan marked Edinburgh green on the global map. "Safe journey, Maya. I love you, kiddo."

Zoe's plane banked over the Indian Ocean, her drone returning to its housing pod. "Heading your way, Durant. Four hours flight time remaining. I've got three sanctuaries' worth of data cores secured."

"Good work." Elan tracked her flight path through relatively stable air corridors. "Stanley, status?"

"Two days out by sea." Stanley's accent carried through the static.

"Got a full hold of enhanced weapons and shield generators. Assembly tried intercepting us off Madagascar. Big mistake."

Myst's calculations streamed across a secondary display. "Running final probability matrices for remaining sanctuary defense patterns. Maya's containment strategy worked - implementing similar protocols for Mexico City and Cape Town."

"Send me those numbers," Erikson cut in. His transport showed steady progress through the Amazon basin. "I can optimize the ward configurations based on the Edinburgh success."

Kaira worked beside Elan, coordinating their convergence. Her fingers traced paths through the temporal distortions, finding stable routes to guide their teams home.

The command center hummed with focused energy as reports continued flowing in. Each team member contributed their expertise as they moved toward their final destination. Their coordinated efforts had turned the tide in Edinburgh—the first real victory against the Assembly's temporal assault.

Maya's transport lifted off from Scottish soil, her course already plotted for Brazil. Asha kept watch through the cockpit window, her fur still bristling from residual energy.

"Airborne and outbound," Maya reported. "ETA six hours assuming stable corridors."

Maya gripped the transport's controls as they passed over another corrupted zone in Northern Spain. The medallion at her throat pulsed with an unfamiliar rhythm, its usual steady warmth replaced by sharp, staccato beats. Asha's ears flattened against her head, orange fur standing on end.

"Something's different." Maya adjusted their altitude, studying the crystalline patterns spreading across the landscape below. The medallion's energy signature shifted, matching the corruption's frequency before inverting it. "You feel that too, girl?"

Asha padded closer, her glowing form reflected in the cockpit glass. The cat's eyes narrowed at the fractured reality beneath them.

A sudden surge of power from the corrupted site sent the transport lurching. Maya's hands tightened on the controls as warning lights flashed across the console. The medallion flared hot against her skin, its energy spreading through her body in waves.

Time seemed to slow. The corruption's crystalline patterns became visible layers in her mind - like blueprints overlapping reality. Her consciousness expanded, allowing her to see the temporal fractures as clear as day. Without thinking, Maya reached out with her newfound awareness and began unweaving the corrupted energy strands.

The medallion amplified her efforts, its power flowing through her with unprecedented clarity. Where before she could only sense the corruption's presence, now she could manipulate its very structure.

"This is new." Maya's fingers moved across the controls, instinctively adjusting their course to avoid the worst temporal distortions. The transport stabilized as she channeled the medallion's energy into a protective barrier around them.

Asha pressed against her leg, purring with increased intensity. The cat's own energy merged with Maya's, strengthening their shared connection to the medallion's power.

Below them, the corrupted zone pulsed with malevolent energy. But now Maya could see the patterns within patterns, the weaknesses in the Assembly's temporal manipulation. Her newfound ability to perceive and interact with these energy structures opened possibilities she'd never imagined.

Maya closed her eyes, letting the medallion's energy flow through her like water. Each pulse matched her heartbeat, but the surges still felt wild, untamed. She steadied her breathing, remembering her father's meditation techniques.

"Focus on one point," she whispered to herself. The transport's autopilot maintained its course while she experimented.

Asha jumped onto her lap, the cat's warmth anchoring her. Maya directed her attention to a small crystal formation visible through the cockpit window. The medallion's energy responded, reaching out toward the corruption below.

Instead of fighting the surge, she let it build naturally. The power rose like a wave, but this time she guided its direction. The crystal's sickly purple glow flickered, then stabilized as she matched its frequency.

Her hands moved through the air, conducting an invisible symphony. Each gesture redirected the medallion's output, like adjusting the flow of a river. The crystal structure below began to unravel.

"Myst, you seeing this?" She activated the video feed to her brother. "I'm sending you the sensor data."

Myst's face appeared on the console screen, his eyes widening as he processed the information. "These energy signatures... they're inverting the corruption patterns. How are you doing that?"

"Watch." Maya demonstrated the technique, letting the medallion's power flow through precise movements. "The crystals have a base frequency. If you match it, then shift to its inverse..."

"The corruption cancels itself out." Myst's fingers flew across his keyboard. "The mathematical models align perfectly. This could change everything."

Maya guided her brother through the process, explaining how she perceived the energy layers. Asha purred louder, her own energy harmonizing with the medallion's output.

"It's like conducting music," Maya explained. "Each crystal formation has its own rhythm. Once you find it, you can rewrite the song."

"Sending these calculations to Dad now." Myst's excitement was palpable. "With this data, we might be able to modify our ward configurations to automatically counter their crystal tech."

Myst's fingers flew across three holographic keyboards, ancient geometrical patterns overlaying modern tactical displays. The sanctuary's preservation matrix hummed around him as he integrated Maya's new data with centuries-old defensive formulas.

"The Order's ward configurations follow sacred geometry," he muttered, sketching equations in the air. "But the Assembly's crystal tech operates on quantum principles."

Numbers danced through his mind - Fibonacci sequences merging with wave functions, golden ratios intersecting probability matrices. He pulled up archived texts from the Vatican library, comparing medieval diagrams to real-time sensor feeds.

The solution crystallized as he overlaid Maya's energy signatures onto traditional ward patterns. Ancient symbols have been transformed into mathematical constants, with their power amplified through modern computation.

"Commander Yeboah, try these modified coordinates." Myst transmitted the hybrid calculations to Dubai. "The wards should auto-adjust to counter crystal resonance."

He watched through satellite feeds as Dubai's defensive line shifted. Sacred geometry merged with quantum fields, creating a dynamic barrier that adapted to Assembly attacks. The corrupted energy dissipated against evolved ward boundaries.

"Containment holding at ninety-seven percent," Yeboah reported. "Whatever you did, it's working."

Myst nodded, already applying the principles to other sanctuary locations. Each site required unique calibration—the sacred mathematics responded differently to local temporal conditions. He mapped corruption patterns across multiple dimensions, letting ancient wisdom inform his modern tactical response.

The hybrid defense strategy took shape: traditional wards powered by quantum calculations, sacred geometry expressed through adaptive algorithms. Past and present merged into an evolving shield against temporal corruption.

Myst's eyes darted between screens as memory fragments clicked into place. Ancient battles replayed in his mind - not from history books, but lived experiences. His past life as a monk provided crucial insights into Assembly tactics.

"They always attack in threes," he murmured, marking potential strike points on the tactical display. "Crystal formations mirror their old ritual patterns."

The Assembly hadn't changed its core strategies in over a millennium. Their crystal tech simply replaced blood rituals, but the underlying geometric principles remained constant. Myst overlaid modern satellite imagery with medieval manuscripts, confirming his theory.

"Dad, check these probability matrices." He transmitted the data to Elan's command console. "Their crystal placement follows the same triangulation they used in the Battle of Antioch."

The sanctuary's quantum processors hummed as they integrated sacred geometry into their calculations. Medieval ward symbols have been transformed into dynamic algorithms, with their protective power amplified through modern technology. Ancient knowledge, enhanced by quantum computing, has given rise to a hybrid defense system unlike anything seen before.

Myst adjusted the sanctuary's shield generators, aligning their output with traditional ward patterns. The resulting energy field pulsed with both sacred and technological power. On his screens, Assembly crystal formations appeared as familiar patterns—echoes of rituals he'd witnessed centuries ago.

"Maya, your new data confirms it." He studied the corrupted zones through multiple spectral layers. "Their crystal tech is just an evolution of their old magic. Same patterns, different medium."

The sanctuary's hybrid defenses responded automatically to Assembly probes, sacred algorithms adapting faster than human reactions. Quantum-enhanced wards shifted like living things, maintaining optimal geometric configurations against temporal assault.

Medieval wisdom merged seamlessly with modern innovation, creating something greater than the sum of its parts. Each system enhanced the other - sacred geometry providing the framework, technology supplying the power and precision.

Mexico City, Mexico

Verendana's hologram flickered above the corrupted crystal matrix, her form distorted by waves of temporal energy. The Assembly leader's eyes gleamed with triumph as she addressed her gathered followers.

"The Order thinks they've won a victory in Edinburgh." Her laugh echoed across the chamber. "They fail to see the bigger picture. Each corrupted site serves as a node in our grand design."

Through the surveillance feed, Elan watched the transmission from the Basilica's command center. His jaw clenched as Verendana gestured to a map showing the spread of crystal formations across the globe.

"The crystals aren't just weapons - they're keys." She traced lines between major areas of corruption. "When they reach critical mass, the temporal barriers between past and present will shatter completely. Reality itself will bend to our will."

Warning signals flashed across Elan's monitors. Energy readings from corrupted sites worldwide began to spike. The crystal formations pulsed in sync, their power building toward some catastrophic threshold.

"The Order built their sanctuaries on sacred ground, thinking to protect them." Verendana's image stabilized, her smile cruel. "But they never understood the true purpose of those locations. The ley lines connecting them form a perfect circuit - one we've spent centuries preparing to activate."

Sensor data streamed across Elan's screens. Crystal resonance patterns shifted into new configurations, each corrupted site amplifying the others. The temporal distortions grew stronger, reality warping more severely around the nodes.

"Our ancestors knew this day would come." Verendana spread her arms wide. "The Valentine Protocol isn't just about resurrection - it's about rewriting history itself. When the crystals reach full power, we'll tear down the walls between epochs. Past, present, and future will become one."

Energy readings continued climbing. The crystals' purple glow intensified across all sites, their corruption spreading faster than the Order's containment efforts could manage. Temporal shockwaves rippled outward, distorting space-time in expanding circles.

"The final phase has begun." Verendana's voice carried absolute conviction. "No force in heaven or earth can stop what's coming."

The hologram shifted as Verendana stepped through a corrupted gateway, her physical form materializing in Mexico City's inner sanctum. Purple crystal formations pulsed around her, their energy synchronizing with sites across the globe. She pressed her palm against the nearest crystal cluster, connecting to the Assembly's network.

"Feel it," she commanded her followers. "The barriers weaken with each pulse."

Reality fractured visibly now, temporal rifts spreading like cracks in glass. The sacred ground beneath their feet trembled as ancient wards failed against the rising corruption. Through their crystal matrix, Verendana sensed similar collapses at other key locations - Edinburgh's recent containment was already unraveling, Dubai's quantum shields were flickering out, and Cape Town's temporal anchors were breaking free.

The network of corrupted sanctuaries hummed with building power. Each site fed energy into the others, amplifying the destruction of reality's natural boundaries. Time itself bent around the crystal formations, past and present bleeding together in waves of distortion.

"Rio's barriers are down," one of her lieutenants reported. "Sydney falling... Tokyo breached."

Verendana closed her eyes, savoring the cascade of failing defenses. The Valentine Protocol's true purpose unfolded exactly as planned - not just corruption of individual sites, but a synchronized assault on the fundamental structure of time itself. Each sanctuary's fall strengthened the others, creating a self-sustaining cycle of temporal destruction.

"The Order built these sanctuaries to contain power." She traced the spreading patterns of corruption with her fingers. "They never realized they were creating the perfect circuit for our purposes. Their own defensive network becomes the instrument of their undoing."

The crystal matrix pulsed again, this time stronger. Reality rippled outward from each corrupted site, the barriers between epochs growing thinner with each surge. Through their network, Verendana felt the power building toward critical mass. The Valentine Protocol's final phase accelerated, feeding on its own momentum.

~

Belém, Pará, Brazil

Elan felt Winterstar pulse against his back, its familiar warmth turning sharp and urgent. The sword's energy signature changed, broadcasting a clear warning through their connected consciousness. Next to him in the Brazil sanctuary's inner chamber, St. Michael's ethereal form tensed.

"Canterbury." Michael's voice carried divine authority. "The Assembly strikes at the heart of ancient power."

The tactical displays confirmed it - massive crystal formations materializing around Canterbury's sacred grounds. Centuries of accumulated divine energy made the site's ley line nexus a prime target for manipulation.

Winterstar's crystalline blade glowed with intense blue-white light, resonating with Michael's own divine weapons. The Horn of Proclamation and Shield hummed in harmony, their combined power filling the chamber.

"We must breach through." Michael raised the Horn. "The corrupted space between here and Canterbury makes normal portals impossible."

Elan drew Winterstar, its familiar weight both comforting and electric. The sword's energy merged with his own as crystal interference patterns splashed across their monitoring screens. Standard transportation methods would scatter them across multiple dimensions.

"Channel your connection through the blade," Michael instructed. "Divine weapons can cut paths where mortal means fail."

The Horn's clear note pierced reality itself, while the Shield's protective field expanded around them. Winterstar's power surged through Elan's arms as he focused on Canterbury's coordinates. Three divine artifacts working in concert, forcing open a passage through corrupted space.

Reality twisted and buckled. Crystal resonance fought against the formation of their portal, threatening to tear it apart. Elan felt Winterstar's determination match his own - they would not be denied.

The portal stabilized for a brief moment, its edges ragged against waves of corruption. Elan and Michael plunged through, divine energy barely containing the chaos around them. Space itself seemed to scream as they forced their way across dimensions.

Canterbury, United Kingdom – Approximately 7,474 km from Belém, Pará, Brazil

They emerged into devastation. Canterbury's ancient grounds lay under siege, crystal formations spreading like cancer through sacred soil. Assembly forces pressed forward while emergency wards flickered and failed. The very air crackled with conflicting energies as centuries of accumulated power began to unravel.

Elan braced against a fallen column as crystal shards exploded around him. Winterstar's blade deflected the deadly fragments while Michael's Horn sang out from the cathedral's western tower. They'd split up to defend Canterbury's key points, but something felt different now.

Winterstar's familiar resonance changed, its energy signature shifting to a new frequency. The sword pulled at Elan's grip, turning his attention eastward across the corrupted grounds. Its crystal blade pulsed with increasing intensity, each wave stronger than the last.

Through their mental connection, Elan sensed Winterstar reaching for something - another divine weapon calling across the distorted space. The sword's power built like a mounting crescendo, harmonizing with a distant twin.

Heavenshard. The name surfaced in Elan's mind as Winterstar's crystal matrix aligned with its counterpart. Both blades sang to each other through reality's fractured barriers, their combined energy cutting through the Assembly's interference.

The pull grew stronger. Winterstar nearly dragged Elan off his feet, its desire to reunite with Heavenshard overwhelming his physical control. The sword's usually cool surface burned hot against his palms while its inner light blazed like captured stars.

Crystal formations between the weapons cracked and shattered as their resonance increased. Winterstar's power surged through Elan's arms, demanding movement, connection, completion. Its sister blade called from somewhere beyond the corruption, their shared divine energy building toward critical mass.

Elan struggled to maintain his defensive position as Winterstar strained against his grip. The sword's single-minded focus on reaching Heavenshard made it nearly impossible to wield. Their usual synchronized movement had become a constant battle for control, as both divine weapons fought to breach the distance between them.

Elan let Winterstar guide his movements, the blade pulling him through Canterbury's corrupted grounds. Crystal formations shattered in his wake as the sword carved a path toward its counterpart. Each step brought stronger resonance, Winterstar's energy signature intensifying as the distance closed.

He rounded the cathedral's eastern corner and saw her - a woman wielding a crystalline blade that mirrored his own. Heavenshard blazed with inner light, its surface rippling with the same stellar patterns as Winterstar. Both weapons strained toward each other, nearly dragging their bearers off balance.

Their eyes met across the battlefield. No words needed - the swords' shared purpose made introductions redundant. They moved in unison, closing the gap between them as Assembly cultists converged from all sides.

Elan's back pressed against hers, Winterstar and Heavenshard crossing in a defensive arc. The blades' combined resonance created a barrier of pure energy, disrupting the cultists' crystal-enhanced attacks. Purple corruption shattered against divine light.

"They're stronger than before," she called over her shoulder, Heavenshard singing through the air as she parried an enhanced cultist's strike.

"The weapons know what to do." Elan let Winterstar guide his movements, matching her rhythm instinctively.

Divine energy flowed between the crossed blades, building with each synchronized strike. The swords moved in perfect harmony, their wielders following their lead. Where Winterstar struck, Heavenshard defended. When she attacked, he covered her flank.

Crystal tech exploded around them as the swords' resonance grew stronger. The cultists' enhanced abilities flickered and failed when they were caught in the harmonics between the blades. Their corruption-fueled strength meant nothing against two divine weapons working as one.

Elan felt Winterstar's satisfaction through their connection. This was right - this was how the swords were meant to be used. Together, they created something greater than either blade alone; their shared power disrupted the very foundations of the Assembly's crystal network.

The air crackled as Winterstar and Heavenshard crossed, their resonance building with each synchronized movement. Elan felt the combined energy of the weapons flow through him, stabilizing the fractured reality around them. Purple corruption retreated from their divine light, temporal distortions smoothing out in expanding circles.

Ancient ward patterns emerged from Canterbury's sacred ground, responding to the harmonics of the swords. The geometric symbols glowed with renewed power, their sacred mathematics amplified by divine resonance. Elan watched as crystalline formations crumbled, centuries-old protections reactivating.

Through his connection with Winterstar, fragments of memory surfaced—images of the blades' creation flickering through time's torn fabric. He glimpsed a celestial forge, divine fire tempering crystal matrices into perfect resonance. Twin weapons born from the same star-metal, designed to work in concert.

St. Michael's ethereal form wavered atop the cathedral tower, the Horn lowering as sealed memories stirred. The archangel's ancient eyes fixed on the paired swords, recognition spreading across his divine features. These were more than just weapons - they were keys to something greater, their true purpose hidden even from heaven's general.

The swords pulsed in response to Michael's awakening awareness. Their combined power reached toward him, divine energies interacting in ways unseen for millennia. Winterstar burned hot in Elan's grip while Heavenshard sang with increasing intensity, both blades calling to their original creator.

Michael's form solidified as forgotten knowledge surfaced. The Horn of Proclamation hummed at a new frequency, harmonizing with the crossed swords. Three divine artifacts resonating together, their sealed powers awakening in Canterbury's sacred air.

Elan moved in perfect sync with the female warrior, their blades creating geometric patterns of light with each strike. Winterstar's familiar weight guided his movements while Heavenshard complemented each motion. The swords communicated, coordinating their wielders' actions without need for words.

Purple crystal formations crumbled as they advanced across Canterbury's grounds. Where their blades crossed, corruption couldn't take hold. Divine energy radiated outward in waves, purifying tainted earth and stabilizing fractured reality.

"Left!" His partner spun without hesitation, Heavenshard intercepting a cultist's crystal-enhanced blade. At the same time, Winterstar swept low, disrupting the corruption feeding their enemy's power. The Assembly fighter stumbled as his enhanced abilities flickered and failed.

Their synchronized defense created expanding zones of stability. Crystal techs sputtered and died within their reach. Each paired strike strengthened the effect, divine resonance building between the blades. Winterstar's cool blue light merged with Heavenshard's radiance, forming patterns that matched the ancient ward geometry of Canterbury.

Elan felt the swords' satisfaction through their mental link. This was their intended purpose: working in concert to counter the spread of corruption. Where one blade's power might falter, the other reinforced it. Their combined energy restored sacred ground to its original state, centuries of accumulated divine power reactivating under their influence.

Assembly cultists fell back as their crystal enhancements failed. The paired swords cut through corrupted space like scissors through paper, their divine resonance unraveling carefully laid temporal distortions. Purple crystalline growths withered and cracked, unable to maintain their hold in the purified zones.

Each synchronized movement expanded its sphere of influence. Winterstar's familiar energy flowed stronger with Heavenshard nearby, both blades feeding off each other's power. Their wielders followed their lead, footwork, and strikes, aligning with practiced ease despite never having fought together before.

Purple light flared as Assembly forces converged on their position. Elan's arms burned from wielding Winterstar, but the sword's energy kept him moving. Beside him, his newfound partner matched his rhythm perfectly, Heavenshard blazing with equal intensity.

"They're targeting us specifically now." She deflected a crystal-enhanced blast while Elan covered her flank.

The Assembly cultists pressed closer, their attacks growing more coordinated. Purple corruption spread through Canterbury's grounds faster than the swords could purify it. Crystal formations erupted from the earth, forcing Elan and his partner to dodge constantly.

Winterstar pulsed a warning through their mental link. Above them, massive crystal structures formed impossible geometric patterns, their resonance building toward something catastrophic. The sanctuary's remaining wards flickered under the assault.

"They're trying to overwhelm the defenses!" Elan shouted as another crystal formation burst from the ground.

The swords' power increased with each synchronized strike, their divine energy reaching levels Elan had never experienced. Winterstar burned like a star in his hands, its connection to Heavenshard growing stronger by the second. Both blades hummed at frequencies that made reality itself vibrate.

Assembly forces formed a ring around them, crystal tech users channeling massive amounts of corruption into the sacred ground. Purple energy coursed through geometric patterns that mirrored the sanctuary's original wards. The very air crackled with conflicting powers.

Through Winterstar's link, Elan sensed something building between the paired blades. Their combined resonance approached a critical threshold, divine energy accumulating faster than they could direct it. The swords pulled at their wielders, trying to complete some long-forgotten purpose.

St. Michael's use of his fellow archangel Gabriel's Horn sang out from the cathedral tower, its note joining the swords' harmonics. Three divine artifacts resonating together, their sealed powers awakening fully for the first time in centuries. The Assembly forces pressed closer, determined to stop whatever was happening.

Purple crystal formations erupted through Canterbury's ancient stones, their corruption spreading like poison through sacred ground. Elan's arms burned from wielding Winterstar, but the sword's divine energy kept him moving. Assembly forces pressed forward in coordinated waves, their enhanced abilities tearing reality apart.

"Eastern perimeter breached!" Commander Yeboah's voice crackled through comms. "Cardinal Varvaro, we need those wards reinforced!"

Temporal rifts split the air above the cathedral, bleeding past and present together. Through them, Elan glimpsed other battles across centuries - Order forces defending this same ground against different threats. The boundaries between times grew thinner with each assault by the Assembly.

St. Michael's Horn sang out from the tower, its divine note stabilizing fractured space. Below, Order strike teams moved with military precision, targeting crystal formations with blessed weapons. General Minh's tactical protocols kept their forces organized despite reality's increasing instability.

Winterstar pulsed in harmony with Heavenshard as Elan and his newfound partner cut through corrupted zones. The paired swords' resonance disrupted crystal tech, creating safe spaces in the chaos. But for every area they purified, two more fell to corruption.

"They're targeting the nexus points!" Field Director Ragle's warning echoed across command channels. "All teams converge on primary ley line junctions!"

The ground buckled as massive crystal structures formed impossible geometric patterns. Purple energy coursed through them, mirroring and corrupting Canterbury's ancient ward designs. Each surge sent ripples through nearby timelines, threatening to tear reality apart completely.

Order forces rallied around key positions, their blessed weapons flaring against the spread of corruption. Centuries of defending sacred ground had prepared them for this moment. However, the Assembly's assault felt different - more coordinated and purposeful. They weren't just attacking the sanctuary; they were systematically unraveling its fundamental nature.

Elan felt Winterstar's urgency through their mental link. The sword recognized something in the Assembly's patterns, some greater design hidden beneath the chaos. Whatever Verendana planned, this battle was only part of it. The real threat still lay in wait to emerge.

The swords' combined resonance peaked, their divine energy filling the sacred air of Canterbury. Above them, St. Michael raised the Horn of Proclamation one final time. The note pierced reality itself, cutting through the Assembly's corruption.

"Now!" Michael's voice carried divine authority. "The swords will guide us!"

Elan felt Winterstar pulse in perfect sync with Heavenshard. Golden light erupted around them as the three divine artifacts resonated together. Reality bent and folded, responding to their combined power.

Through their mental link, Elan understood - the swords could breach the corrupted space between Canterbury and Brazil. This was part of their original purpose: the ability to create paths where none existed.

"Everyone, fall back to my position!" Elan commanded through the tactical net. "Emergency translocation in thirty seconds!"

Order forces converged on their location as the divine light intensified. The swords' power enveloped them all, reality warping as Michael's Horn completed the harmonic sequence.

Space itself seemed to fold. For a timeless moment, they existed everywhere and nowhere. Then reality snapped back into focus.

They stood in the Basilica's main chamber, Brazil's eternal twilight filtering through stained glass windows. The combined power of three divine artifacts had pierced the Assembly's corruption, bringing them safely home.

But there was no time to rest. The real battle was about to begin.

CHAPTER

SIXTEEN

Purple light filtered through the Basilica's stained glass windows, casting otherworldly shadows across marble floors. Elan gripped Winterstar tighter as waves of Assembly corruption battered against the sanctuary's ancient wards. This was their final refuge—humanity's last bastion against forces that threatened to unravel reality itself.

"The outer wards won't hold much longer." Cardinal Varvaro pressed his palm against a stone pillar, feeling the resonance of sacred ground beneath. "We need the artifacts."

Elan nodded to his partner across the chamber. Together, they raised Winterstar and Heavenshard in perfect synchronization. Divine energy flowed between the paired blades, their combined power reinforcing the Basilica's defenses. Above in the bell tower, St. Michael lifted Gabriel's Horn to his lips.

The Horn's pure note rang out, joining the swords' harmonics. Three divine artifacts working in concert, their sealed powers awakening to their true purpose. Golden light rippled through the geometric patterns in the marble floor, pushing back against the purple corruption that seeped through the cracks in reality.

"The resonance is stabilizing." Field Director Ragle studied the readings on her tactical display. "Corruption levels dropping in all sectors."

Order strike teams took up defensive positions throughout the Basilica's vast chamber. They'd lost too much ground already - Canterbury, Rome, Jerusalem. Each sacred site had fallen to the Assembly's relentless assault. This sanctuary, located in the heart of Brazil, was all that remained.

Winterstar pulsed against Elan's palm, its divine energy synchronizing with Heavenshard's answering call. The swords' combined power flowed into ancient ward-stones buried beneath the Basilica's foundations. Above, Gabriel's Horn maintained its pure note, weaving the energies together into an impenetrable barrier.

For now, at least, they were safe. But Elan felt Winterstar's urgency through their mental link. The sword knew this reprieve was temporary. The Assembly would eventually find a way through. Everything depended on what they did next.

Maya's medallion burned against her chest, its crystalline surface pulsing with an inner light she'd never seen before. The sensation crawled across her skin - like static electricity mixed with ice water. Her fingers traced the medallion's edge as reality rippled around them.

"There." Maya pointed toward a spot near the Basilica's eastern wall where the air seemed to fold in on itself. "The fracture's getting wider."

Kaira placed a steadying hand on her daughter's shoulder. "What do you see?"

"It's like... looking through broken glass. Multiple versions of the same space, but they're all wrong somehow." Maya squinted at the distortion. The medallion's power flowed through her, revealing tears in the fabric of reality that normal eyes couldn't perceive. "Some show different times, others show places that never existed."

Asha prowled in figure-eights around Maya's feet, her orange and black fur bristling. The cat's eyes glowed with the same inner light as the medallion.

"Focus on the strongest distortion," Asha said. "The medallion will help you trace it to its source."

Maya closed her eyes, letting the medallion's awareness guide her senses. The fracture's edges felt jagged and raw, like a wound in space-time that refused to heal. She followed its path along the wall, the medallion growing warmer with each step.

"This one's different from the others." Maya pressed her palm against the cool stone. "It's not random damage. Something... or some-one... tore through deliberately."

"The Assembly," Kaira whispered. "They're forcing their way between realities."

The medallion flared brighter in response to the name, confirming their fears. Maya felt its protective power wrap around her like a shield, pushing back against the wrongness seeping through the fracture.

"You're doing well," Asha said, rubbing against Maya's legs. "The medallion chose you for a reason. Trust in its guidance."

Myst knelt before the central altar, his fingers tracing arcane symbols etched into the marble floor. Each line pulsed with fading energy, telling a story of weakening barriers and collapsing timelines. Nykronus stood to his right, while Michael's presence filled the space to his left; their combined auras helped him filter through the over-whelming temporal data.

"The convergence points are accelerating." Myst's voice carried an echo, as if speaking across multiple realities at once. "Each fracture creates new instabilities."

Stanley adjusted his cowboy hat, keeping watch over the eastern approach while Zoe settled cross-legged nearby, her guitar balanced on her knee.

"Need help focusing, mate?" Stanley's Australian accent carried across the chamber.

"The calculations... they're scattered." Myst pressed his palms flat against the floor. "Too many variables."

"Music helps align temporal frequencies." Nykronus nodded to Zoe. "Your gift may provide the clarity he needs."

Zoe strummed a gentle melody, her voice carrying power that seemed to smooth the jagged edges of reality:

"Through shattered time and broken space,
Where memories dance and moments chase,
I'll be your anchor in the storm,
When chaos takes familiar form."
The notes wove through the air, creating patterns that matched the floor's pulsing symbols. Myst's breathing steadied as the musical frequencies helped organize the temporal data flooding his consciousness. Zoe continued:
"Let my song guide you through the haze,
Past forgotten nights and endless days,
Till calculations clear and bright
Reveal the path to set things right."
"There." Myst's eyes snapped open, now seeing the patterns with crystal clarity. "Thirty-seven hours, twelve minutes until complete temporal collapse. The Assembly's corruption will breach the final barriers at multiple points simultaneously."
Michael's wings shifted, casting patterns of light across the altar. "Then we must act swiftly. The timestreams grow more unstable with each passing moment."

Through the Basilica's towering windows, Maya watched darkness gather. The Assembly's forces stretched across the horizon, their numbers beyond counting. Purple corruption twisted the air around them, distorting reality itself.
Verendana stood at the head of her legion, her white dress unstained despite the corruption swirling at her feet. Beside her, Lazarus's presence cast deeper shadows across the gathered horde. His eyes held an emptiness that made Maya's skin crawl.
Aswang prowled the front lines, their misshapen forms shifting between human and beast. Their Tiktik scouts circled overhead, their wing beats creating that distinctive sound that grew softer as they drew closer. Maya's medallion pulsed in warning at their presence.
Behind them, corrupted Babaylan shamans swayed in unison, their chants raising purple mist from the earth. The ground cracked beneath

their feet as Pah serpents writhed up from the depths, their scales gleaming with unnatural light.

Diwata spirits drifted through the Assembly's ranks, their once-beautiful forms twisted by dark magic into something terrible. Their ethereal glow now carried hints of decay and madness.

A Bungisngis towered over the gathered forces, its single eye reflecting the corruption that had claimed it. Its perpetual laughter echoed across the battlefield, a sound that set Maya's teeth on edge.

The Malefic Assembly's cultists filled the spaces between these creatures, their robes adorned with symbols that hurt Maya's eyes to look at. They carried artifacts of their own - corrupted mirrors of the sacred relics the Order protected.

Maya's medallion grew hot against her skin as the horde pressed against the sanctuary's barriers. Through its power, she could see the purple corruption eating away at reality's edges, spreading outward from where Verendana and Lazarus stood.

Purple energy crackled across the Basilica's wards as Verendana raised her hands. Reality fractured around her, creating mirror images that rippled outward like rings in a pond. Through the medallion's power, Maya saw each version of Verendana leading an identical assault from different points in time.

"She's attacking through multiple timestreams," Maya called out. The medallion burned against her chest as corrupted energy battered the sanctuary's defenses.

Nykronus pressed his hands against the nearest ward-stone, his face tight with concentration. "The barriers are holding, but-"

A sound like shattering glass cut through his words. Crystalline corruption sprouted from a hairline crack in the marble floor, its purple tendrils spreading in geometric patterns. The corruption pulsed with each wave of Verendana's assault, growing larger with every beat.

"Eastern ward is compromised," Reagan reported. Her tactical display showed similar breaches forming along the Basilica's outer perimeter. "The corruption's finding weak points in the temporal matrix."

More crystal growths burst through the floor, their jagged edges catching the light from the stained glass windows. Maya watched in horror as they began forming complex lattices, each new crystal adding to the corruption's strength. The purple glow intensified with each temporal assault, consuming the ancient stone beneath their feet.

Elan and his divine partner adjusted their stance, bringing Winterstar and Heavenshard to bear against the spreading corruption. Divine energy flowed from the paired blades, pushing back against the crystal growth. But for every patch they cleared, two more appeared elsewhere in the vast chamber.

Through the windows, Maya saw multiple versions of the Assembly's forces advancing in perfect synchronization. Each timestream showed the same scene from slightly different angles, creating a dizzying kaleidoscope effect. The corrupted Babaylan's chants echoed across realities, their combined power fueling Verendana's assault.

The crystal corruption reached one of the main support pillars, purple energy racing up its length like lightning. Ancient ward-symbols flared in response, but the corruption began seeping through them, leaving trails of crystalline decay in its wake.

Maya stared at the spreading crystal corruption, her medallion's warmth pulsing in time with each new growth. Through its power, she noticed something odd about the purple light - it seemed to flicker at regular intervals, like a heartbeat or... a frequency.

"The crystals." She pressed her hand against the medallion. "They're resonating on a specific wavelength."

Asha's fur sparked with energy as she padded closer. "You can see the patterns?"

"Not just see them." Maya closed her eyes, letting the medallion's awareness flow through her. The crystal corruption's frequency became clearer—a discordant note that scraped against reality itself. But beneath that...

"There's an inverse frequency." Maya's eyes snapped open. "If we could match it, amplify it-"

"It would cancel out the corruption's resonance." Nykronus moved to her side, his presence steadying the chaotic energies swirling around them. "The medallion gives you the sight, but focusing that much power requires precision."

Asha twined between Maya's feet, her form glowing brighter. "Let us help guide you. The medallion knows what to do - trust its instincts."

Maya gripped the medallion tighter, feeling its energy merge with Asha's otherworldly presence. Nykronus placed his hands on her shoulders, anchoring her as the medallion's power surged through her body.

The frequency of crystal corruption became visible as purple waves in her mind's eye. Maya focused on the spaces between those waves, finding the inverse pattern hidden within. The medallion grew hot against her palm as she pushed her awareness into those gaps.

Golden light pulsed outward from the medallion, matching the corruption's frequency but inverted - peaks where the purple energy showed troughs, troughs where it peaked. Where the two frequencies met, they canceled each other out in flashes of pure white light.

The nearest crystal growths began to shatter, their resonance disrupted by the medallion's counterforce. Maya felt Asha's and Nykronus's energy supporting her, helping her maintain the precise frequency needed to break down the corruption's hold on reality.

Myst knelt beside the corrupted ward-stone, his fingers tracing equations in the air. Ancient symbols merged with modern mathematical formulas as he worked to counter the Assembly's hybrid technology. The temporal calculations flowed through his mind, each number carrying weight beyond its mathematical value.

Kaira watched her son work, her heart swelling with pride. The same determined expression he'd worn during countless homework sessions now focused on saving reality itself. She moved closer, recognizing some of the base equations from their evening study sessions.

"The corruption's using a quantum-temporal matrix," Myst muttered, adjusting his calculations. "But if we apply the old ward formulas using modern computational theory..."

"Just like those advanced calculus problems we tackled." Kaira knelt beside him, pointing to a string of symbols. "Remember how we broke them down into smaller parts?"

Myst's eyes lit up. "That's it!" His fingers flew faster, combining ancient ward symbols with differential equations. "The Assembly's using hybrid tech, but they're still bound by mathematical principles. If we treat each corruption point as a variable..."

The symbols began to glow as Myst input the final calculations. Purple crystal growths near the ward-stone flickered, their resonance disrupted by the mathematical counterforce.

"Mom..." Myst looked up from his work, a smile breaking through his concentration. "Remember how I used to complain about doing math during dinner?"

"Every single night." Kaira squeezed his shoulder.

"Thanks for not giving up on me. All those extra practice problems..." He gestured to the equations floating before them. "I never thought I'd be using them to save the world."

"You always had it in you." Kaira watched as his calculations spread through the ward network, mathematical precision turning chaos into order. "I just helped you find your way."

Michael staggered, pressing his palm against the nearest pillar. Images crashed through his mind - memories breaking free from seals he'd placed centuries ago. The marble felt cool against his skin, anchoring him as the flood of remembrance threatened to overwhelm his consciousness.

Rome burned. Soldiers marched. A sword flashed in firelight. Each memory carried weight, power that rippled through the present moment. His wings trembled as he fought to contain the temporal energy radiating from each unlocked remembrance.

The preservation seals had served their purpose, keeping specific memories safely contained until they were needed. But now, with reality straining at its seams, those careful barriers crumbled.

He saw Verendana as she once was - before corruption touched her soul. The jailer's daughter, healed by Valentine's touch. Her smile, pure and grateful, twisted in his mind until it became the snarl she wore now.

Across the chamber, Nykronus's form flickered like a candle in the wind. Sweat beaded on his forehead as he fought to hold multiple timelines in alignment. Purple corruption pressed against his barriers, seeking weak points in reality's fabric.

"The seals-" Nykronus grunted, his fingers weaving complex patterns in the air. "They're breaking too fast."

Reality rippled around them. Through the windows, the Brazilian jungle shifted between different seasons, different eras. Modern buildings phased in and out of existence as timeline boundaries blurred.

"I can't-" Nykronus's voice cracked as another wave of temporal distortion washed through the Basilica. His hands shook with effort, each gesture leaving trails of light in the air as he struggled to maintain stability.

The floor beneath their feet switched between marble, packed earth, and ancient stone. Columns transformed from Brazilian baroque to Roman classical and back again. The very air seemed to shimmer as multiple versions of history vied for the same space.

Michael pushed away from the pillar, forcing his wings to steady. More memories surfaced - battles fought, alliances forged, sacrifices made. Each one carried fragments of power he'd sealed away, waiting for the moment they'd be needed most.

Purple corruption crackled against golden ward-light as Maya felt the rich man's coin burn in her pocket—a relic indicating Lazarus was nearby and a relic from what seemed like a lifetime ago. Around her, reality fractured like breaking glass - each shard showing a different version of the battle unfolding.

The Horn of Proclamation blazed in Michael's grip, its surface etched with symbols that pulsed brighter with each passing moment. Divine energy rolled from it in waves, pushing back against both the Assembly's assault and reality's collapse.

Stanley's armor ignited with celestial fire, ancient runes awakening across its surface. He charged through a cluster of corrupted Aswang, the armor's power turning their shadowy forms to ash. "Been waiting centuries for this!" His voice carried over the chaos.

Moonbow sang in Zoe's hands, each arrow trailing silver light as she picked off Assembly cultists trying to breach the eastern ward. The bow's power grew stronger, resonating with the other artifacts as their true purpose began to stir.

Winterstar and Heavenshard moved in perfect harmony as Elan and his divine partner carved through waves of corrupted Diwata. The paired blades left trails of light and shadow, their combined power creating zones where reality stabilized around them.

Kaira's shield pulsed with energy drawn from Vulcan's ancient forge. She braced against a temporal shockwave, the shield's power creating a bubble of stable space around their group. Purple crystals shattered against its surface, unable to corrupt its divine metal.

The artifacts' power built upon itself, each one growing stronger in the presence of the others. Maya watched golden light race between them like lightning, forming a complex web of divine energy. The rich man's coin vibrated faster, responding to the rising power.

Through the medallion's sight, Maya saw patterns of light connecting each artifact - bonds forged long ago, finally awakening. The Horn's call pierced through dimensions, Moonbow's arrows flew true across realities, while Winterstar and Heavenshard cut through corruption's root.

Reality buckled and warped around them, but the artifacts' combined power created islands of stability in the chaos. The Assembly pressed their attack while time itself unraveled at the edges of Maya's vision.

Purple lightning crackled around Verendana as she raised her arms, her white dress rippling in waves of temporal distortion. The corruption crystals pulsed in response, their glow intensifying until the light hurt Maya's eyes.

"The Valentine Protocol was never about resurrection." Verendana's voice echoed across multiple timelines, each version speaking in perfect sync. "That was merely the catalyst we needed."

The corruption spread faster now, purple energy eating through reality's foundations. Maya watched in horror-struck silence as sections of the Basilica's walls simply ceased to exist, replaced by windows into other times and places.

"Valentine's sacrifice created the first crack." Verendana's form split and merged as she stepped through the deteriorating barriers. "Each attempt to bring him back weakened the walls between worlds. And now..."

She pressed her hand against the nearest reality breach. Purple energy surged through her fingers, widening the tear. Through it, Maya glimpsed impossible geometries and writhing darkness.

"When the barriers fall completely, what lies beyond time will enter our world." Verendana's smile turned cruel, "Valentine's love opened the door. Our corruption will tear it from its hinges."

The rich man's coin burned hotter in Maya's pocket as reality groaned around them. Entire sections of the Basilica collapsed into a temporal void, leaving behind patches of pure nothing that hurt to look at.

Lazarus moved to Verendana's side, his empty eyes reflecting the corruption's purple glow. The barriers between timelines shuddered as he raised his hands, adding his power to hers.

"The Assembly never wanted to restore Valentine." Verendana's laugh echoed across dimensions. "We wanted to finish what his death started. Complete temporal collapse. The end of all barriers. The merging of all possible worlds."

Maya's medallion pulsed frantically as more reality barriers disintegrated. Through her power, she saw the truth of Verendana's words -

the corruption wasn't just destroying their world, but also creating gaps for something else to enter.

The remaining walls between realities buckled under the strain. Purple crystal corruption raced through the widening cracks, each growth bringing reality closer to total collapse.

Maya's medallion burned against her chest as purple corruption spread through the foundations of reality. The ancient metal grew hot enough to sear through her shirt, but she didn't dare remove it. Through its power, she glimpsed layers of time folding in on themselves, reality fracturing along mathematical fault lines.

The medallion's energy surged through her body, no longer content to provide mere sight. Raw power surged through her veins, causing her skin to glow with a golden light. Maya gasped as awareness expanded beyond physical limits - she could feel every timeline, every possibility converging on this moment.

"Let it flow," Asha whispered, pressing against Maya's leg. "The medallion chose you for this."

Maya closed her eyes, surrendering to the artifact's power. Golden energy exploded outward from her core, forming a sphere of pure temporal force. The medallion's heat became unbearable, then transcendent as its full potential awakened through her.

Across the chamber, Myst's fingers flew through complex equations. Numbers and symbols twisted in the air before him, ancient ward formulas merging with quantum mathematics. His mind raced as patterns emerged from the chaos - patterns he'd seen before in his mother's advanced calculus lessons.

"The corruption isn't random," he muttered, adjusting variables. "It's following Fibonacci sequences, but inverted through non-Euclidean space..."

The equations crystallized in his mind. Years of study collapsed into a single moment of perfect understanding. Myst saw how the Assembly's temporal attack utilized mathematical principles he'd practiced countless times - only twisted, corrupted.

"They're using golden ratios to break reality," he called out. "But if we apply the inverse..."

His calculations sparked with blue light as they integrated with the ward network. Where corruption spread in fibonacci spirals, Myst's equations generated counter-spirals, creating zones of mathematical stability in the chaos.

Maya felt Myst's calculations merge with the medallion's power, adding precision to raw force. Golden energy flowed through the mathematical framework, turning theory into reality-altering truth.

Elan moved in perfect sync with Michael, their blades humming with shared purpose. Winterstar's cold light merged with Heavenshard's radiance as they circled a cluster of corruption crystals. Through countless battles together, they'd developed an instinctive rhythm - where one blade fell, the other rose to meet it.

"Just like old times," Elan said, adjusting his grip on Winterstar's frost-touched hilt, thinking back to countless missions he executed in the Marines.

Michael didn't respond, but his wings flared with divine light as he brought Heavenshard around in a precise arc. Elan matched the movement, Winterstar trailing shadows that complemented Heavenshard's brilliance.

The two blades crossed, their energies intertwining. Ice-blue light from Winterstar spiraled around Heavenshard's golden radiance. Where the energies met, reality itself seemed to hold its breath.

They struck as one, blades moving in mirror patterns. Divine power exploded outward, frost and light combining into a wave of pure force that shattered corruption crystals and stabilized fractured timelines.

Michael staggered as the strike triggered another sealed memory. His grip on Heavenshard tightened as images flooded his mind - the forging of the artifacts, their true purpose finally clear.

He saw the weapons laid out in a perfect circle, each one radiating with newly forged power. The Horn of Proclamation, Moonbow, Winterstar, and Heavenshard, the shield from Vulcan's forge - they weren't just divine weapons. They were keys, crafted to work in harmony with one another.

The memory sharpened. He watched his past self arrange the artifacts in specific patterns, encoding their purpose into their very essence. They were meant to stabilize reality in times of crisis, each one representing a different aspect of divine order. Together, they formed a matrix of power that could anchor existence itself.

But there was something else, something crucial about their arrangement. The memory showed him placing a final piece in the center of the circle—a medallion that would one day find its way to Maya.

Austin's voice cut through the chaos. "Now! Execute Pattern Sigma!"

Order forces surged forward in perfect formation. Reagan led the eastern flank, her squad moving with practiced precision through reality's broken fragments. Where corruption crystals blocked their path, concentrated bursts of blessed ammunition shattered the purple growths.

Through the medallion's sight, Maya watched golden threads of power connect the Order's movements. Each squad positioned itself at precise intervals, forming a complex geometric pattern across the Basilica's fractured space. Their coordinated advance created zones of stability, pushing back against the chaos of collapsing timelines.

"Hold the pattern!" Austin commanded. Holy fire erupted from blessed weapons as Order forces engaged corrupted entities attempting to breach their formation. He raised his hand, divine energy cascading from his fingers to reinforce weak points in their defensive grid.

Nykronus stumbled, preservation spells unraveling around him. Centuries of carefully maintained temporal seals stretched to breaking point. He felt each one like a physical wound - memories and power he'd locked away, now straining to break free.

"The seals won't hold." Sweat beaded on his brow as he fought to maintain the spells. "Too much temporal disruption."

Through failing barriers, he glimpsed the truth he'd hidden from himself - why he'd sealed away so much of his power and memory. The preservation spells weren't just containing the past; they were protecting the present from knowledge that could shatter it.

Nykronus made his choice. With trembling fingers, he began unraveling the core structure of the preservation spells. It is better to release the power gradually than to have it explode outward when the seals fail completely. Each thread of magic he dissolved sent ripples through nearby timelines, but he maintained enough control to direct the energy into the Order's defensive pattern.

"The pattern holds!" Reagan called out as her squad secured another section of stable space. Order forces pressed their advantage, their coordinated movements creating an expanding zone of protected reality within the chaos.

Maya felt the medallion's power surge through her as Michael raised the Horn of Proclamation. Its clear note pierced through reality's chaos, crystalline and pure. The sound resonated with something deep within the medallion, making it vibrate against her chest.

Elan and Michael moved in perfect synchronization, their blades leaving trails of light and shadow in their wake. Winterstar's frost-touched edge carved precise angles through space while Heavenshard's radiance filled them with divine power. The two swords traced complex geometric patterns in the air, each movement expanding the zone of stability around them.

The Horn's second note struck a different harmony, and Maya gasped as golden energy exploded from the medallion. The power flowed outward in precise mathematical waves, guided by the framework Winterstar and Heavenshard had carved into reality itself.

Where the three energies met - the Horn's clarion call, the blades' geometric sanctuary, and the medallion's golden force - reality stabilized. Purple corruption crystals crumbled to dust. Fractured timelines snapped back into proper alignment. The chaotic blending of past and present was once again separated into distinct streams.

The medallion burned brighter, drawing power from the other artifacts. It focused their combined energy through its ancient metal, transforming raw divine force into a stabilizing resonance that spread through the Basilica. The Horn's third note locked the effect in place, its sound echoing across dimensions as the artifacts worked in perfect harmony.

Maya watched through the medallion's sight as a dome of pure golden energy expanded outward from their position. Where it touched corrupted space, reality healed itself. The barriers between timelines reinforced themselves, preservation seals rebuilding under the combined power of the artifacts.

Maya watched through the medallion's sight as the golden energy field pressed against corrupted zones. The purple crystals didn't shatter or dissolve - instead, their violent glow dimmed to a dull gray. The formations remained intact but lifeless, like volcanic rock after the lava had cooled.

Myst's calculations sparked through the air, forming new ward boundaries around the inert corruption. Complex mathematical symbols locked into place, creating containment fields that pulsed with steady blue light. Where the wards touched gray crystal, they generated resonant frequencies that kept the corruption dormant.

"The sanctuaries are being quarantined," Myst called out, adjusting variables in his floating equations. "The corruption's still there, but it can't spread anymore."

Through fractured reality, Maya glimpsed multiple versions of the Basilica trying to occupy the same space. But as the artifacts' power continued flowing through the medallion, the temporal overlap began to separate. Past and present untangled themselves, each timeline retreating to its proper place in the flow of history.

The Order's preservation spells surged with renewed strength. Austin directed squads to reinforce key points as reality stabilized around them. Their blessed ammunition no longer shattered corruption crystals; instead, it helped maintain the new containment boundaries.

Rifts in space-time slowly pulled themselves closed like healing wounds. Maya felt each one through the medallion - reality's fabric knitting itself back together under the influence of the artifacts. The chaotic bleeding between past and present slowed, then stopped altogether as temporal barriers reasserted themselves.

The gray crystal formations stood silent within their new prison of mathematical wards and divine energy. Not destroyed, but contained. Not eliminated, but rendered dormant until they could be adequately dealt with.

Maya's legs trembled as the golden energy faded. The medallion's power receded, leaving her drained and aching. Through its dimmed sight, she witnessed the devastating toll of their victory.

Entire sections of the Basilica had simply ceased to exist, leaving behind empty voids where sacred ground once stood. Ancient pillars lay shattered, their blessed stone reduced to rubble. Corruption crystals might be contained, but they'd taken countless sanctuaries with them. Centuries of history and power, gone in moments.

Order members moved through the wreckage, helping wounded comrades. Many limped or clutched injuries from the reality distortions. Others searched desperately for missing squad members who'd been caught in temporal rifts. Maya watched Austin direct rescue efforts, his voice hoarse as he called out names that received no response.

"Three sanctuaries completely lost," Reagan reported, her uniform torn and bloody. "Five more are damaged beyond our ability to repair. The preservation spells..." She shook her head. "Too much was destroyed. We can't restore them."

Nykronus slumped against a broken column, his face gray with exhaustion. The effort of maintaining reality through the crisis had drained him severely. His hands shook as he tried to stand, preservation spells unraveling around him like tattered silk.

"The seals," he whispered, voice barely audible. "Had to release too much. The power..." He closed his eyes, decades of carefully preserved strength spent in those crucial moments.

Maya saw Zoe moving between injured Order members, offering what healing she could. But even divine restoration had limits. Some wounds from the corrupted time-space wouldn't close properly. Others left traces of purple energy that resisted all treatment.

Reagan's voice carried across the ruined sanctuary as he coordinated recovery efforts. "Get the wounded to safe zones. Seal off unstable areas. Someone find Erikson - we need temporal trauma assessment."

The cost settled over them like heavy ash - sanctuaries destroyed, Order members lost or broken, and their strongest ally reduced to a shadow of himself. They'd contained the corruption, but the price of victory weighed on them all.

Maya walked through what remained of the eastern sanctuary, the medallion's dim glow revealing scars that would never heal. Purple crystal formations, though dormant now, had fused with ancient stone at a molecular level. The corruption had become part of the sacred ground itself, leaving permanent marks like frozen lightning across walls and floors.

Through fractured doorways, she glimpsed spaces where reality refused to settle. Time flowed strangely in those pockets - water dripping upward from puddles, dust falling in spiral patterns that defied gravity. The temporal damage had written itself into the fabric of existence. No amount of power could fully restore what was lost.

"The digital archives," Myst's voice cracked as he stared at shattered servers and crushed hard drives. "Everything we scanned, all the knowledge we tried to preserve..." He picked up a fragment of corrupted crystal that had pierced through storage banks. "The temporal disruption didn't just destroy the hardware. It erased the data across all timelines. Those records don't exist anymore - never existed."

Centuries of carefully preserved texts, ritual instructions, and sacred histories - gone in moments. The Order had worked for decades to digitize its most precious documents, believing that technology could protect its legacy. Instead, the corruption had used those same digital pathways to erase knowledge from the very fabric of time itself.

Maya touched a wall where crystal growth had merged with ancient stone. The medallion's power flickered weakly, revealing layers of damage that extended beyond physical space. Some wounds couldn't be healed. Some losses couldn't be undone. The corruption had left permanent scars not just on the sanctuaries, but on reality itself.

Asha pressed against her leg, offering silent comfort as they surveyed the devastation. The cat's fur sparkled with traces of golden energy, but even her mysterious power couldn't restore what time itself had forgotten.

Maya watched her brother's equations dance through the air, understanding dawning as she recognized patterns she'd seen in their mother's architectural designs. The same golden ratios, the same perfect symmetry - but Myst wielded them with an instinctive grace that went beyond mere calculation.

"Mom wasn't just teaching us math," Myst said, his fingers tracing glowing symbols. "She was preparing us. These formulas - they're in our blood."

Through the medallion's sight, Maya saw threads of power linking their family. The same divine energy that flowed through Elan's connection to Winterstar pulsed in her medallion and sparkled in Myst's equations.

Elan flexed his hand around Winterstar's hilt, feeling the sword's cold energy merge with his own strength. The blade no longer felt foreign - it was an extension of himself, as natural as the combat instincts he'd honed through years of service.

"The artifacts choose their wielders," Michael said, memories flickering behind his eyes. "But they also adapt to them. Your military training, your protective instincts - Winterstar resonates with those qualities."

Michael's brow furrowed as another memory surfaced. "The weapons were forged to be wielded together by those with the strength to bear them. Family bonds make that connection stronger." He shook his head. "There's more, but it's still locked away."

Nykronus stepped forward, his preservation spells now barely visible. "I've watched over the artifacts for centuries, guiding them to those who could use them properly. But this..." He gestured to the family's combined power. "This is what they were meant for. Unity. Harmony between different kinds of strength."

Maya felt the truth of it through the medallion. Her power, Myst's calculations, Elan's martial prowess - separate threads weaving into something greater. The artifacts weren't just weapons or tools; they were also symbols of power. They were catalysts, awakening potential that had always existed within them.

～

Unknown Location

Purple mist swirled around Verendana as she pulled Lazarus

through a fracturing timeline. Her fingers dug into his arm, keeping them anchored together as reality bent around them. Through the chaos, she glimpsed the Assembly's forces retreating through similar rifts - not fleeing in panic, but withdrawing with calculated precision.

"The texts," Lazarus gasped, clutching a bundle of papers to his chest. Ancient pages torn from the Order's archives during the battle, their edges stained with corruption. "Dante's location-"

"Safe." Verendana's voice cut through the temporal distortion. "The knowledge is ours now."

Maya watched through the medallion's sight as enemy forces disappeared into temporal rifts. The Assembly wasn't running scared - their movements were too coordinated, too purposeful. They'd gotten what they came for.

Purple energy crackled around the remaining corruption crystals as Assembly forces used them to mask their retreat. The dormant formations pulsed briefly with renewed power, creating interference that blocked the medallion's tracking ability.

"They're not just escaping," Michael said, Heavenshard's glow reflecting in his eyes. "They're covering their tracks across multiple timelines."

Through gaps in reality, Maya caught glimpses of Verendana and Lazarus moving between moments. The Assembly leader's face showed no fear, only cold satisfaction as she guided her forces through the temporal maze. In her wake, reality sealed itself, blocking any attempt at pursuit.

The last thing Maya saw before the rifts closed was Lazarus clutching papers covered in familiar handwriting—Dante's precise script, detailing locations and dates. Knowledge torn from the Order's most sacred records, now in the hands of their enemies.

The Assembly may have retreated, but they'd achieved their goal. They had Dante's trail, and the power to follow it through time itself.

Maya watched Myst adjust holographic displays showing corruption crystal analysis. The purple formations had evolved since their containment, developing new molecular structures that defied conventional physics. Her brother's calculations floated beside modernized scanning equipment, merging ancient mathematical principles with cutting-edge technology.

"The crystals are adapting," Myst said, manipulating 3D models with practiced gestures. "They're incorporating elements from our containment fields into their structure. Learning from what we use against them."

Reagan moved between workstations where Order members combined traditional blessed ammunition with prototype smart rounds. Holy water mixed with programmable nanomaterials. Sacred oils enhanced with adaptive polymers. The old ways have been strengthened by modern innovation.

"We can't rely solely on preservation spells anymore," Reagan said, examining a modified rifle. "The Assembly's using temporal tech we've never seen before. We need countermeasures that can evolve as fast as they do."

Through the medallion's sight, Maya observed the hybrid defense grid taking shape around the remaining sanctuaries. Blessed stone reinforced with carbon fiber composites. Ward boundaries are maintained by quantum field generators. Ancient and modern, working in harmony.

Elan practiced with Winterstar, the sword's frost-touched edge leaving trails through augmented reality targeting projections. Combat data from his military experience led to the creation of new training programs, helping other Order members adapt traditional fighting styles to contemporary threats.

"The artifacts are changing too," Maya said, feeling the medallion's power flow differently than before. It interfaced more smoothly with their new systems, as if it had updated itself to meet current needs. "They're not just relics anymore. They're growing with us."

In their temporary command center, the family gathered around holographic maps showing temporal distortion patterns. Myst's equations merged with tactical overlays as they planned their next moves. The Assembly had Dante's trail, but they also had new weapons and strategies of their own.

~

Maya watched Austin coordinate with Order branches across continents, his voice steady as he directed recovery teams through secure channels. Tablets and phones displayed damage reports from sacred sites worldwide - corruption crystals had emerged far beyond the Basilica's walls.

"Tokyo shrine contained minimal casualties," Austin reported. "London Sanctuary lost its eastern wing but preserved the archives. Still waiting on status from Cairo and São Paulo."

Through the medallion's sight, Maya observed her family gathered in a quiet corner of the command center. Elan cleaned Winterstar's frost-touched blade with practiced care, while Myst sketched new equations in his tablet. The adrenaline had faded, leaving them drained but grateful to be together.

Asha curled in Maya's lap, purring softly as the medallion's power settled into a steady, warm pulse. The artifact felt different now - more integrated with her own energy rather than a separate force. Its golden light dimmed to a subtle glow, ready but resting.

Heavenshard's radiance faded as Michael placed it carefully beside Winterstar. The divine weapons hummed briefly in harmony before falling silent, their power banked like embers waiting to ignite again.

"The containment fields are holding," Myst said, his fingers flying over the tablet's surface. "But the corruption's geometric patterns - they're following rules we've never seen before. Look at these progression sequences..."

He showed Maya his screen, where complex mathematical formulas sprawled across multiple pages. New principles born from the clash of temporal forces, waiting to be understood.

In a secure room deep within the compound, Verendana spread Dante's stolen papers across a steel table. Purple energy flickered around her fingers as she traced lines of text, her cold smile reflected in the polished surface. Behind her, Lazarus examined corruption crystal samples through reinforced glass, their gray surfaces occasionally pulsing with dormant power.

SEVENTEEN

Kaira traced her fingers along the cracked stonework of the Milan sanctuary's eastern wall. Ancient protective runes pulsed weakly beneath layers of carbon-fiber reinforcement. The damage went deeper than physical breaks - temporal energies had disrupted centuries of accumulated blessed power.

"Third ward boundary's completely down," Reagan called from the courtyard. She consulted a tablet displaying overlapping scan results. "Corruption crystals breached the foundation here and here." Red markers highlighted compromised sections on the 3D model.

In the sanctuary's central chamber, Myst and Stanley worked to stabilize the remaining defensive systems. Stanley's hands moved through practiced motions as he renewed traditional ward patterns. At the same time, Myst adjusted quantum field projectors to amplify the ancient protections.

"The old magic still works," Stanley said, his Australian accent softened by concentration. "Just needs proper support now." Sweat beaded on his forehead as he completed another blessing circuit.

Myst nodded, eyes fixed on real-time energy readings. "Quantum harmonics are matching the ward frequencies. We can use the resonance to strengthen both."

Through the sanctuary's broken windows, Kaira watched Order teams moving with practiced efficiency. They'd done this too many times now - cataloging damage, salvaging artifacts, rebuilding defenses. Each site required unique solutions based on its original protections.

"Prague reports similar breaches," Reagan said, accepting a status update from her earpiece. "But Constantinople held. Whatever they did with those modified Tesla coils actually worked."

Kaira moved to where Myst was aligning a new projector array. Her architect's eye caught the geometric patterns in his setup - sacred geometry translated into modern configurations. The same principles she'd studied in ancient texts, adapted for contemporary threats.

"The hybrid systems are holding in Rome," Myst reported, adjusting power levels. "But we need to modify these designs for each location. The old wards all have their own... frequencies, I guess you could say."

Stanley paused his work on the blessing to examine Myst's calculations. His mustache twitched as he traced equations with a calloused finger. "Like tuning different instruments to play the same song. Each sanctuary needs its own arrangement."

Erikson paced the western corridor of the sanctuary, his footsteps echoing off the millennium-old stone. Austin followed, marking key positions on his tactical display.

"We'll need quantum sensors here and here." Erikson traced his fingers along the wall. "The old detection wards are still viable, but they won't catch temporal signatures."

Austin tapped commands into his tablet. "Already requisitioned Mark VII arrays from Vatican storage. They're calibrated for both magical and technological intrusion."

"Good. The Malefic Assembly's getting creative with their breach methods." Erikson paused at an intersection, examining the worn carvings that lined the archway. "They're mixing old blood magic with quantum tunneling."

"Like what they pulled in Dresden?" Austin's fingers flew across the screen as he updated security protocols.

"Exactly. We can't rely on just one defensive layer anymore."

In the makeshift infirmary down the hall, Zoe moved between rows of cots. Her hands glowed with soft healing light as she tended to wounded Order members. The air hummed with her healing songs—ancient melodies woven with modern harmonies.

"Hold still," she murmured to a young acolyte with temporal burns across his arms. The kid had caught the edge of a time-rip during the sanctuary breach. Her power flowed into his wounds, reversing the chronological damage.

Two more healers worked nearby, their traditional herbs and poultices complementing modern medical equipment. One administered blessed nanites through an IV while chanting recovery prayers. Another used a quantum field stabilizer to help a veteran whose timeline had been partially displaced.

"Time wounds are getting worse," Zoe said to the senior healer. "They're targeting personal chronology now, not just physical damage."

The healer nodded grimly as she adjusted the stabilizer's settings. "The Assembly's learning. We need to adapt our treatment protocols."

Zoe moved to the next patient, her blonde hair glowing in the infirmary's blessed light. She began another healing song, this one incorporating frequencies that could anchor displaced timelines. Modern science and ancient magic, working in harmony to counter evolving threats.

In the sanctuary's makeshift command center, Elan watched as his family gathered around worn, folding tables. His mother, Rose, dabbed at the tears in her eyes as she wrapped her arms around Kaira.

"My children rebuilt what was lost." Rose's voice cracked with emotion. "A mother couldn't be prouder."

Jhan clapped his brother's shoulder. "You did it, bro. Actually did it. Remember when we were kids playing knights in the backyard? Now look at you - Knight Prime of an actual order."

Kristinn hugged Elan tight. "Big brother, always protecting everyone. Some things never change."

Across the room, Gianna Mazza's eyes met Nykronus's gaze. A lifetime of memories passed between them in that silent exchange - a romance from centuries past, known only to them. She gave him a subtle, knowing smile before turning back to her granddaughter.

"Kaira, tesoro." Gianna took her hands. "You've honored our family's legacy in ways I never imagined possible."

Through the command center's windows, Field Director Ragle coordinated teams across the sanctuary grounds. His voice carried authority as he directed reconstruction efforts.

"I need those quantum stabilizers operational within the hour," Ragle barked into his comm unit. "Priority on the eastern ward boundary. Get those blessed steel supports in place first."

He turned to a group of technicians. "The temporal anchor points need reinforcement. Double-check all the harmonic frequencies against the original ward patterns. We can't afford any resonance mismatches."

Workers moved with practiced efficiency, mixing modern materials with blessed components. Some carried tablets displaying technical specifications while others consulted ancient texts for proper blessing formulas.

"Director," a young acolyte called out. "Constantinople sent their modified ward schematics. They're ready to implement their reinforcement patterns here."

Ragle nodded sharply. "Good. Get their quantum-harmonic calculations to our engineering team. We'll need to adapt their solutions for Milan's existing ward structure."

Michael stood at the sanctuary's highest point, his form flickering between corporeal and ethereal as memories surfaced in disjointed fragments. Each pulse of the quantum stabilizers below sent ripples through his consciousness, unlocking sealed recollections.

The sword at his hip - he remembered forging it in divine fire. But there were others. Uriel's spear of truth. Gabriel's horn of revelation. Raphael's staff of healing. Ariel's bow of justice. Each artifact carried a piece of their essence, created to protect humanity across the ages.

His hand traced preservation runes carved into the stone beneath his feet. The patterns sparked recognition - spells woven into reality's fabric, designed to maintain sacred places against time's erosion. He had taught these to the first guardians, showing them how to anchor divine power in the mortal realm.

Battles flashed through his mind. Rome's catacombs, corrupted by dark magic. Constantinople's walls, breached by demon hordes. The fields of Britain, where knights fought alongside angels against the forces of chaos. Victory after victory, yet the enemy always returned in new forms.

"The war never ends," he murmured, his voice carrying echoes of countless conflicts. "We push back darkness, but it finds new shadows to hide in."

But significant gaps remained in his memory. Names of fallen companions blurred together. Critical moments stayed shrouded in fog. The full extent of his power, the deeper purposes behind ancient choices - these remained frustratingly out of reach.

He felt the quantum harmonics pulsing below, modern technology attempting to replicate what once came naturally to him. Some part of him recognized the principles behind it, but a complete understanding eluded him, hovering just beyond his grasp.

His form solidified briefly as another memory surfaced - teaching the first Order members how to forge blessed weapons. But the memory fractured before he could grasp its full significance, leaving him with more questions than answers.

Myst's fingers flew across the holographic interface, ancient formulas materializing in his mind faster than he could type them. Numbers and symbols danced before his eyes - not just modern mathematical notation, but older forms of sacred geometry that felt as natural as breathing.

He paused, staring at a particularly complex equation describing temporal ward harmonics. The solution had appeared in his thoughts fully formed, like remembering something long forgotten rather than figuring it out anew.

"That's not possible," he muttered, double-checking his calculations.

However, the math was perfect—a seamless blend of quantum mechanics and eighth-century blessing formulas. Knowledge from a life lived over a millennium ago merged with his modern physics education.

The quantum stabilizer hummed beside him, its readings matching exactly what his hybrid calculations had predicted. Ancient ward patterns pulsed in sync with the device's output, each system strengthening the other.

More formulas surfaced in his mind. Protection circles are expressed as wave functions. Blessing geometries translated into quantum field equations. The underlying mathematics had always been the same - his ancestors had simply used different symbols to express identical principles.

His hands moved almost automatically now, recording calculations that bridged centuries of mathematical evolution. Each formula felt both familiar and new, like meeting an old friend who had grown and changed over time.

The stabilizer's harmonics shifted, automatically adjusting to match his new equations. Modern technology responds to ancient wisdom, finding balance in their synthesis. Myst recognized the elegant simplicity of it - past and present working in concert, neither diminishing the other.

Stanley peered over his shoulder, whistling softly at the complex mathematical dance unfolding on the display. "Your old self was quite the mathematician."

"Still am," Myst replied, fingers never stopping their work. "Just took a while to remember."

Maya sat cross-legged in the sanctuary's meditation chamber, her medallion floating inches above her palm. The metal had transformed, its surface now swirling with iridescent patterns that resembled the flowing waters of Mount Makiling's streams. The once-solid silver now rippled like liquid moonlight, responding to her thoughts.

Power thrummed through her connection to the Three Marias.

Maria Makiling's presence felt like cool mountain mist, while Maria Cacao's energy carried the rich warmth of fertile soil. Maria Sinukuan's essence burned bright and fierce, ready to defend what was sacred.

"Show me," Maya whispered. The medallion pulsed, projecting a dome of protective energy that expanded outward. Unlike before, when her shields had been simple barriers, this one shimmered with layers of interwoven power. Each layer carried the blessing of a different Maria - Makiling's mists obscured what lay within, Cacao's earth-power strengthened the foundation, and Sinukuan's fierce protection burned away hostile energies.

She stretched out her awareness, feeling how the Marias' powers had become permanently intertwined with her own. Their ancient knowledge flowed through her, teaching her ways to weave protection that went beyond physical shields. She could now hide entire locations from sight, anchor protective spells into the land itself, and channel divine fire against those who would do harm.

The medallion responded to these new abilities, its form shifting to better channel each aspect. When she drew on Makiling's power, it rippled like water. For Cacao's earth-blessing, it took on the warm glow of rich soil. And when Sinukuan's protective fury flowed through her, it blazed with inner fire.

Maya opened her eyes, watching the interplay of energies. Her connection to the Marias had evolved beyond simple communication - they were now part of her, their powers and knowledge permanently merged with her own. The medallion had transformed to reflect this change, becoming a living conduit for abilities that bridged the mortal and divine realms.

She let the protective dome fade, but kept the medallion floating above her palm. Its surface continued to shift and flow, adapting to each new facet of her enhanced powers.

Elan watched Maya manipulate the transformed medallion, his chest tight with a mix of pride and concern. The iridescent patterns dancing across its surface reminded him of the first time he'd seen Kaira work with blessed artifacts - that same raw potential. Still, his daughter wielded power that went far beyond anything they'd encountered.

"She's not just channeling the Marias anymore," Kaira whispered beside him, her hand finding his. "They've become part of her."

Through the meditation chamber's doorway, they could see Myst in the adjacent room, his fingers moving across quantum interfaces. At the same time, ancient formulas materialized in glowing displays. The mathematics he produced merged centuries of knowledge in ways that shouldn't have been possible.

"Remember when our biggest worry was them learning to walk?" Elan's voice caught. The memory of tiny hands gripping his fingers felt simultaneously decades ago and just yesterday.

Kaira leaned against him. "Now Maya's weaving divine shields, and Myst is rewriting the laws of reality." She paused, watching Maya layer protections that shimmered with otherworldly power. "This is just the beginning, isn't it?"

"They were born in the ninth century, conceived in our time." Elan shook his head. "Everything they are defies what we thought possible."

Maya's medallion pulsed, sending ripples of blessed energy through the chamber. At the exact moment, Myst's calculations caused the quantum stabilizers to hum in perfect harmony with the ancient wards. Brother and sister, their powers different but complementary, working in ways that bridged centuries.

"We can't protect them from this," Kaira said softly. "All we can do is help them understand who they are."

Elan squeezed her hand, watching their children reshape reality in their own unique ways. "They're already stronger than we ever were."

Myst's fingers traced the quantum interface one last time before powering down the system. The familiar hum of calculations faded, leaving only the soft echo of his sister's protective dome in the adjacent chamber. His recovered memories weighed heavily - centuries of knowledge crammed into a modern mind that still struggled to process it all.

"Maya?" He stepped into the meditation chamber where she sat cross-legged, her medallion floating above her palm. "Got a minute?"

She opened her eyes, the iridescent patterns of her medallion reflecting in them. "What's up?"

Myst settled beside her on the cold stone floor. "Remember that time in ninth-century Rome when we snuck into the kitchens and stole those honey cakes?"

"The ones meant for the bishop's feast?" Maya laughed. "Sister Agatha was furious."

"Yeah." Myst smiled, but it didn't reach his eyes. "These memories, they're becoming too much. Every calculation I make, every formula I write - it's like living two lives at once."

The medallion's glow dimmed as Maya sensed her brother's troubled thoughts. "You're thinking of stepping back."

"I want to enlist. Like Dad did." The words tumbled out. "Join the Navy, serve normally. Maybe find someone, start a family." He glanced at her. "You've got this covered - the Marias, the protection spells. You're stronger than I ever was."

Maya set the medallion down. "You want me to back you up when you tell everyone at dinner."

"Mom and Dad will understand eventually, but..." He shrugged. "The Order might not."

"They'll have to." Maya squeezed his hand. "You deserve your own life, Myst. Not just recovered memories of someone else's."

Reagan stared at the photos on her desk - faces of knights who wouldn't be coming home. Her hands trembled as she traced their names. Jim Snyder, who'd just joined the Order. Andrew, the technician, is three weeks from retirement. Dorene Phillip, whose daughter's graduation is next month.

The weight of command pressed down on her shoulders like a physical burden. Intelligence said the Assembly's forces would be coming, but she underestimated the creatures that joined the cultists. Instead, they'd walked into an ambush of dark magic and corrupted tech.

A gentle knock at her office door made her look up. Austin stood there.

"Hey." His voice was soft as he crossed to her desk. "Got your message."

Reagan's composure cracked. "I sent them in there, Austin. My call. My responsibility."

He pulled up a chair beside her, taking her hands in his. "Reagan, you can't do this to yourself."

"Assembly had creatures from folklore helping them. Turned our bulletproof vests into tissue paper." Her voice caught. "Andrew... he shielded two operators with his own body. Dorene got three members out before..." She couldn't finish.

"How many members were in the command center?"

"Thirty-seven." Reagan wiped her eyes. "We got them all out."

"And how many would be dead if you didn't get them out?"

"Thirty-seven..."

Austin squeezed her hands. "That's thirty-seven people who are alive because you made that call. Thousands of families didn't lose their loved ones across the network because of your coordination."

"But the ones who sacrificed themselves-"

"Would have made the same choice. You know that." He lifted her chin gently. "Andrew and Dorene - they knew the risks. They chose to serve a world that didn't know they needed them. Just like you do every day."

Reagan leaned into his embrace, letting the tears fall. "I see their faces every time I close my eyes."

"That's what makes you a good leader." Austin held her close. "You care. You remember. And you keep going because others are counting on you."

The aroma of Filipino adobo and Italian osso buco filled Grandma Gianna's dining room. Rose ladled sauce over the tender meat while Gianna arranged fresh-baked focaccia in a basket lined with crisp linen.

Elan helped Kaira set the long oak table, their hands brushing as they placed silverware. Around them, conversations flowed in a mix of English, Tagalog, and Italian.

"Pass the pancit, please," Austin reached across to Reagan, who slid the noodle dish his way. Their wedding rings clinked together as their hands met.

Michael materialized in his chair, his form more solid than usual. "The binding of souls through shared meals - an ancient practice that transcends cultures."

"Some things never change," Nykronus agreed, breaking bread with Stanley. "Though the faces at the table may shift through time."

Zoe hummed a melody between bites, an old song about warriors sharing their last meal before battle. The notes hung in the air, stirring memories in those gathered.

"Remember that feast in Constantinople?" Stanley's eyes twinkled at Erikson. "The one where the wine turned to holy water?"

"Different lifetime," Erikson chuckled, "but the company was just as good."

Myst watched Maya pass dishes around, noting how the Marias' presence seemed to bless each portion she touched. The food tasted richer, more nourishing, where her hands had been.

"Eat more, anak," Rose urged, piling more rice onto Elan's plate. Some things about Filipino mothers never changed, even with divine beings at their table.

"Mangia, mangia," Gianna echoed, mirroring Rose's maternal instincts with her own Italian flair. The two grandmothers exchanged knowing looks - their families had grown in unexpected ways, but love flowed freely as the wine.

The clinking of utensils, mixed with laughter and story-sharing, connected each person more than just the meal before them. Ancient powers and modern bonds wove together as naturally as the steam rising from their plates.

Reagan traced her finger across the holographic map, studying the new defense grid layouts. Beside her, Field Director Ragle nodded in approval as she highlighted key fortification points.

"The hybrid barriers are impressive," Ragle said. "Combining

Myst's quantum formulas with Maya's blessed shields - nothing like it in our history."

"We're installing dedicated training facilities in each sanctuary." Reagan pulled up the architectural plans. "The next generation needs to understand both the old ways and new tech."

Through the command center's windows, she watched initiates practicing in the courtyard. Young knights moved through traditional sword forms while wearing armor enhanced by quantum technology. Others studied ancient texts on tablets that translated sacred knowledge into modern terms.

Austin appeared at her side, setting down two cups of coffee. "Just got word from the archivists. They're moving the most sensitive texts to a new vault system. Multiple locations, each protected by different methods."

"Smart." Reagan sipped her coffee. "Harder to compromise what's scattered and hidden differently."

In the adjacent meditation chamber, Elan sat with Kaira, their fingers intertwined as they watched Maya instruct a group of initiates. Her voice carried clearly as she explained how to recognize divine signatures in everyday objects.

"They're adapting faster than we did," Kaira whispered. "This generation doesn't see boundaries between tech and magic, old and new."

Elan squeezed her hand. "They're building something we never imagined possible."

Through another window, Stanley worked with combat teams, teaching them to blend traditional fighting styles with modern tactical approaches. His red hair caught the sunlight as he demonstrated a move that merged centuries-old sword techniques with current close-quarters combat.

Field Director Ragle's tablet pinged with an alert. "Assembly activity detected in three locations. Small groups, testing our new defenses."

"They're probing," Reagan noted. "Learning our changes." She zoomed in on the map, marking the points of incursion. "We'll be ready."

Myst sat at the kitchen counter, watching his mother prepare beef sinigang—the same recipe she'd learned from his Lola Rose. The familiar scent filled the air. His enlistment papers lay folded in his back pocket, still unsigned.

"You're quieter than usual," Rose said, stirring the pot. "Just like your father before he joined the Marines."

"That obvious, huh?" Myst traced patterns on the granite counter-top, complex quantum equations simplified into absent doodles.

Rose wiped her hands on her apron and sat beside him. "A mother knows. Even with all these ancient memories and powers, you're still my son."

Maya appeared in the doorway, drawn by the cooking aromas and the weight of the conversation. She leaned against the frame, her medallion pulsing softly at her throat.

"I want something that's just mine," Myst said. "Not inherited memories or ancient knowledge. Something I chose."

"Like Dad did," Maya added softly.

Rose touched Myst's cheek, her eyes glistening. "You've always been more than just your past lives, anak."

High above the earthly realm, Michael stood at the edge of celestial boundaries. His armor gleamed with divine light, but uncertainty clouded his usually resolute expression. The memories of his time on Earth had begun to fade like morning mist, slipping through his grasp.

Gabriel's horn lay silent. Raphael's healing waters stood still. Uriel's flame flickered dimly. His fellow archangels had retreated from the mortal realm, their presence growing fainter with each passing age.

Michael gripped his sword, its familiar weight offering little comfort. The battle against darkness required more than just his strength now. He needed the others - their combined powers, their ancient wisdom.

With a thought, he dissolved his corporeal form. His consciousness spread across the celestial planes, searching for traces of his brothers. They had hidden themselves well, scattered across time and space, but Michael could still sense echoes of their grace.

He would find them. Help them remember. The world below needed all of them, now more than ever.

Maya sat cross-legged in the meditation chamber, the medallion hovering above her open palm. Its surface rippled like disturbed water, sending waves of energy through her body. The Marias' combined presence flowed through the ancient metal, transforming abstract sensations into clear visions.

Shadows stretched across her mind - not of the past, but of things yet to come. The medallion pulsed with an urgent rhythm, its glow intensifying. She saw fragments: blood-red skies over familiar cities, tears in reality that shouldn't exist, and creatures that defied description slipping through the cracks.

The medallion grew hot against her skin. Its surface shifted from liquid silver to obsidian black, then back again. Each transformation revealed new threats - some immediate, others lurking months or years ahead.

In the adjacent chamber, Nykronus's fingers danced across quantum interfaces, transcribing calculations that bridged modern physics with ancient power. Streams of data flowed through his hands, forming complex patterns that even he didn't fully understand.

"The convergence points are shifting," he muttered, recording another set of coordinates. "The old formulas won't hold much longer."

His screens filled with equations that merged quantum mechanics with sacred geometry. Each calculation represented a potential weakness in reality's fabric, a point where the barriers between worlds grew dangerously thin.

Nykronus paused, studying a particularly complex sequence. The numbers seemed to pulse with their own inner light, hinting at connections that extended beyond the realm of mathematical logic. He added annotations in an ancient script, linking modern variables to mystical constants that predated written history.

The calculations continued to flow, each one more crucial than the last. Some would strengthen existing wards, while others would help predict where new breaches might form. Every formula he recorded could mean the difference between victory and catastrophic failure.

Zoe's fingers danced across the lute strings, weaving ancient melodies with modern rhythms. The gathered Order members sat transfixed as her music filled the great hall. Each note carried memories of battles fought centuries ago, yet spoke to the challenges they faced today. Her green eyes closed as she let the music flow through her, connecting past and present.

Kaira stepped forward, her voice steady as she addressed the assembled knights. "The Assembly isn't just using dark magic anymore. They're evolving, combining ancient rituals with quantum manipulation. Every encounter shows them growing stronger, more adaptable."

Elan stood at the center of the platform, Kaira and Nykronus flanking him. His gaze swept across the faces of every Order member gathered in the vast chamber. "We've faced darkness before, in every age. But this time, we're not just knights with swords. We're warriors who understand both the old ways and new frontiers. Each of you carries the strength of centuries and the innovation of today."

The Order erupted in cheers, their voices echoing off the ancient stones. Weapons raised high - both traditional blades and quantum-enhanced arms - caught the light streaming through stained glass windows. The sound of unified purpose filled the chamber, a thunderous affirmation of their shared commitment.

Nykronus raised his hands, and the quantum displays behind them shifted to show the Paths of Providence - streams of golden light representing the countless decisions and sacrifices that had led them to this moment. The cheering continued as knights recognized their own threads woven into the greater tapestry.

EPILOGUE

Maya traced her fingers along the smooth quantum display integrated into the ancient stone walls of the Basilica. The holographic interface responded to her touch, bringing up schematics of the newly renovated command center. Centuries-old marble columns now housed state-of-the-art surveillance systems, while preserved frescoes concealed tactical displays.

"The energy signatures are stable." She adjusted several parameters on the screen. "The sacred wards actually enhance our quantum field generators."

Below in the training yard, initiates moved through combat forms that blended traditional swordplay with modern tactical movements. Their practice weapons glowed with both blessed silver and plasma energy. A young knight parried an attack with his blade, then smoothly transitioned into accessing a quantum portal with his free hand.

Maya descended the grand staircase, passing display cases where ancient relics shared space with cutting-edge technology. The Sword of Damascus rested beside a quantum-enhanced battle rifle. The Shield of Faith's golden surface reflected the soft blue light of holographic status readouts.

In the heart of the Basilica, the renovated war room hummed with activity. The ceiling-high stained glass windows now doubled as massive data screens, their sacred imagery morphing into tactical displays when needed. Maya had helped design the integration protocols herself, ensuring the old and new systems worked in perfect harmony.

The Divine Artifacts section occupied its own wing, permanently secured behind both traditional blessed barriers and quantum encryption fields. The Spear of Destiny pulsed with otherworldly energy, its presence strengthening the building's defensive systems. The Crown of Thorns sat in a specially designed containment field, its power carefully monitored by both ancient wards and modern sensors.

"The energy matrix is holding." Maya checked another reading on her tablet. The merger of sacred power and quantum technology created something entirely new. This hybrid system drew strength from both ancient wisdom and modern innovation.

Knights moved through the corridors wearing traditional robes modified with tactical gear. Their quantum communicators bore sacred symbols, blessed by the Order's priests and enhanced by their engineers. Every aspect of the headquarters reflected this careful balance between preserving their heritage and embracing the future.

Maya stood before a group of young Guardians in the Basilica's meditation chamber. Crystal formations lined the walls, their surfaces displaying both ancient runes and quantum readouts. She lifted her hand, summoning a sphere of energy that crackled with both mystical and technological power.

"The Three Marias taught us that power flows through all things." The sphere in her hand shifted colors - forest green for Makiling, deep brown for Cacao, and blazing gold for Sinukuan. "Our enhanced abilities aren't just tools - they're extensions of nature itself."

A young initiate raised her hand. "But how do we control both?"

Maya demonstrated this by splitting the sphere into three distinct streams. "Your quantum implants don't replace your connection to the sacred - they amplify it. Watch."

She guided the energy through the chamber's array of crystals. The readings on nearby monitors spiked as ancient wards activated in harmony with the quantum field generators.

In the command center below, Maya's response teams maintained their vigil. Teams Alpha through Delta monitored the rebuilt gateway nodes, especially the one hidden deep in Palawan's jungle, where Maria Makiling's power ran strongest.

"Director Durant." A technician called up a holographic map. "Gateway synchronization at eighty-seven percent. The Palawan node is stabilizing."

Maya touched her medallion, its surface warm against her skin. Images flashed through her mind - the Three Marias standing at their respective mountains, their combined power flowing through the reconstructed network of portals leading to Aethoria.

The visions shifted, showing her response teams moving through these gateways. Each operator carried both blessed weapons and quantum tech, their movements precise and purposeful. The medallion pulsed again, revealing glimpses of dark forces gathering at the edges of reality—threats that would soon test their new capabilities.

"Remember," Maya turned back to her students, the medallion's warmth fading, "with these gifts comes great responsibility. We're not just soldiers or mystics anymore. We're guardians of both worlds."

Myst adjusted his tie as he stepped out of the Stockton recruiting office into the bright California sun. His heart raced with a mix of excitement and nervousness. The glass door clicked shut behind him as his recruiter gathered the final paperwork inside.

Elan and Kaira waited by their car, his father's posture straight as ever despite being retired. His mother's eyes glistened, but her smile remained steady.

"Here." Elan reached into his pocket and pulled out a worn challenge coin. The metal caught the sunlight, revealing the eagle, globe, and anchor emblem of his command sergeant's rank. "Had this through three deployments. Now it's yours."

"Thanks, Dad." Myst turned the coin over in his palm, feeling its weight.

"Have fun out there. Boot camp's gonna suck, but you'll look back and laugh about it someday."

"I picked sonar tech." Myst pocketed the coin carefully. "Figure I'll get to live in San Diego, maybe catch some waves between shifts."

Kaira stepped forward and wrapped her arms around him. "My baby boy."

"Mom..." But Myst hugged her back just as tight.

Elan joined the embrace, his strong arms encircling them both. Myst breathed in his mother's familiar perfume and the faint scent of his father's aftershave.

"Tell Maya I'm proud of her," Myst said into his mother's shoulder. "She's doing amazing things with the Order."

"You're starting your own path now," Elan said, squeezing his shoulder. "Making your own legacy."

The recruiter emerged from the office, car keys jingling. Myst stepped back from his parents, squaring his shoulders.

"This isn't goodbye." He picked up his small backpack. "I'll see you guys later."

Elan watched from the observation deck as Kaira demonstrated a flowing combination of moves to a group of Order initiates. Her movements blended traditional martial arts with modern tactical positioning, each stance optimized for both close combat and quantum manipulation.

"Remember to maintain your center." Kaira adjusted an initiate's posture. "The energy flows better when you're grounded."

The training room below hummed with activity. Ancient symbols carved into the floor pulsed with power, synchronized with the quantum field generators mounted in the ceiling. The entire facility represented what the Order had become—a seamless fusion of old and new.

Elan's chest swelled with pride as he thought of Maya's contributions to this evolution. Her innovative designs had transformed the Order's headquarters into something unprecedented. And now Myst was forging his own path in the Navy, carrying forward their family's tradition of service.

"Your form is improving." Kaira smiled at a young recruit who successfully completed a complex sequence. The pride in her voice reminded Elan of how she'd encouraged their own children's growth.

He descended to the training floor, joining his wife as she began the next phase of instruction. Together, they demonstrated advanced techniques that incorporated both traditional weapon forms and modern tactical movements. Their synchronized motions spoke of years fighting side by side, their bond stronger for all they'd endured.

"The threats we face are evolving," Elan addressed the group. "So must we." He drew his combat knife, a blessed silver blade gleaming alongside embedded quantum technology. "The old ways and the new each have their place."

Kaira caught his eye and smiled. They'd come so far from their first meeting, through time itself and back again. Now they stood as leaders, teaching the next generation to face whatever challenges lay ahead.

The initiates paired off to practice, their movements echoing across the training room. Elan and Kaira moved among them, offering guidance and corrections, and sharing the wisdom they had earned through their experiences.

Michael stood before the Order's assembled council, his form simultaneously corporeal and ethereal. Divine light rippled beneath his skin, though muted compared to his full glory. The partial restoration of his powers felt strange - like viewing the world through frosted glass rather than the crystal clarity he once possessed.

He adjusted the ceremonial armor that now housed both blessed steel and quantum enhancements. The weight felt familiar yet different, like reuniting with an old friend who had changed over the years.

"The recruits show promise." Michael's voice carried through the chamber, maintaining its supernatural resonance despite his diminished state. "Their integration of divine weapons with quantum tech exceeds expectations."

Kaira and Elan sat among the council members, their presence a comfort as Michael adapted to his new role. Working with the Durant family helped anchor him in this modern world, especially since many of his ancient memories were still locked away.

In the training yard below, his special unit practiced with prototype weapons that channeled divine energy through quantum matrices. A young knight activated her blade's blessed core, sending arcs of holy power crackling along quantum-enhanced edges.

"Remember," Michael called down, "the divine responds to faith as much as skill." He demonstrated, summoning a fraction of his former power into a focused beam. The energy flowed differently now, filtered through the Order's new systems, but its essential nature remained pure.

The partnership felt right, even if it wasn't what he'd initially envisioned. His role as guardian had evolved - no longer a solitary warrior but part of something larger. The Order provided structure and support while he offered guidance and access to divine power.

Maya joined them in the yard, her quantum tablets displaying readings of the divine energy signatures. Michael nodded in approval as she adjusted the calibrations, helping bridge the gap between heavenly and earthly power. The Durant family's dedication to preserving both tradition and progress aligned perfectly with his new purpose.

"The balance is key," Michael told his students. "Divine power flows through all things - even your modern tools." He lifted his reformed sword, its surface reflecting both holy light and quantum readouts.

Reagan surveyed the Los Angeles operations center from her elevated platform. Holographic displays showed real-time feeds from Order facilities across the globe. Her team had spent months integrating the new security protocols, merging traditional methods with cutting-edge technology.

"Beta team is online in Sydney." Austin adjusted the settings on his console. His Naval experience proved invaluable in coordinating their maritime operations.

Stanley's Australian accent crackled through the comm system. "Got movement near the Singapore node. Sending tactical now." His MMA background made him perfect for training response teams in close-quarter combat.

"Confirmed." Zoe's fingers danced across her interface, her DJ's sense of rhythm translating surprisingly well to monitoring global patterns. "Energy signatures match expected parameters."

Erikson stood at the tactical table, his ancestral knowledge of both Order and Malefic operations giving their team unique insights. "The hybrid squad structure is working. Traditional warriors alongside tech specialists - it's creating stronger response capabilities."

Reagan touched the memorial wall, where images of fallen Order members were displayed. Fresh flowers adorned the base, their scent mixing with the electronic hum of equipment. Her team paused their work for a moment of silence, honoring those who had lost their lives.

"Tokyo hub is requesting additional support." Austin pulled up their personnel roster. "They're implementing the new protocols ahead of schedule."

"Send Alpha team," Reagan decided. "They've got the most experience with the hybrid approach."

Zoe adjusted her headset. "I've got Interpol on secure channel three. They're ready to expand our cooperation agreement."

"The Order stays in shadow," Erikson reminded them, "but our allies grow stronger."

Stanley's face appeared on the main screen. "Training camp in Brisbane is showing promising results. These recruits understand both worlds."

Reagan nodded, watching her international teams move like well-oiled machines across the global displays. The future would bring new challenges, but they were ready. The Order had evolved, growing stronger through adaptation while honoring their core mission.

Gianna traced her fingers over the ancient scrolls spread across her study table. The parchment crackled beneath her touch as she compared the prophecies to Nykronus's latest findings. Energy readings from the Assembly's crystal network pulsed on nearby screens, their patterns growing more complex each day.

"The temporal signatures are shifting." Nykronus adjusted his instruments, his weathered hands steady despite the concerning data. "These anomalies don't match any previous patterns."

Through the window of Gianna's villa, the Mediterranean sunset painted the sky in deep purples and golds. A notification chimed - another sacred site discovered, this time in the mountains of Peru. The map on her tablet updated, showing a growing constellation of power points across the globe.

"The hybrid signatures worry me most." Gianna pulled up footage from their monitoring stations. Creatures moved through the shadows, neither entirely natural nor completely supernatural. "They're adapting faster than predicted."

Nykronus nodded toward a section of prophecy text. "The ancient words speak of this - when old and new powers merge, creating things never before seen."

Their sensors detected another temporal fluctuation. Through the villa's windows, they watched the air ripple like heat waves rising from summer pavement. The effect lasted only seconds, but their instruments recorded everything.

"The next generation shows promise." Gianna brought up training footage of Maya's newest recruits. Young faces filled with determination as they worked with both blessed relics and quantum tech. "They bridge both worlds naturally."

"As was foretold." Nykronus compared their energy readings to a set of ancient symbols. "The prophecies speak of children born understanding both languages - of heaven and earth, of past and future."

The Assembly's crystal network flared again on their monitors. Each pulse carried more complex patterns, evolving beyond their original design. New formations appeared in the crystalline structures, creating capabilities that even their creators hadn't anticipated.

Maya sat with her family in the Basilica's private garden, watching the sunset paint the ancient stones in warm hues. Elan and Kaira shared a bench nearby, their hands intertwined. The peace of the moment settled over them like a protective blanket.

Asha's tail twitched. The cat's orange and black fur seemed to glow as she fixed her gaze on something beyond the garden walls. Maya felt it too—a subtle shift in the energy fields surrounding the Basilica.

In his study above, Nykronus pored over Myst's latest calculations. The young man's insights into quantum harmonics had revealed patterns that echoed through both time and space. The mathematical sequences suggested possibilities that even Nykronus hadn't considered.

Maya's medallion grew warm against her skin. Across the garden, Winterstar pulsed in its display case, its blade casting fractals of light across the stone floor. The warnings were clear, but Maya felt strangely calm. Their preparations were solid, their teams ready.

"Whatever comes next," Kaira said, squeezing Elan's hand, "we face it together."

The Order had evolved, growing stronger through each challenge. Maya saw that strength reflected in her family's faces.

Elan's phone buzzed. His face darkened as he read the message. "Stanley just texted. It's too late - the Malefic Assembly broke Dante out."

Acknowledgments

First and foremost, I want to thank God. My faith grows stronger every day, and although I've been Catholic my entire life, I feel as though I'm only now beginning to truly understand what it means to follow Him. I strive to place Jesus before my own needs, and I know that everything I have accomplished—and the blessing of my beautiful family—is only because of His grace.

To Violet and J-Mo: thank you. I actually drafted this book a year ago in a small La Quinta hotel room, all of us tucked together after moving from Hawaii to San Diego. Violet, you've helped me grow closer to Jesus and challenged me to become a better man every single day. Through you, I finally feel like I understand the role a man should have in his home. The memories we create together are treasures I hold close.

Somewhere along this journey, I also discovered woodworking, and it quickly became one of my greatest joys. It still amazes me how much my life has changed and evolved—I feel blessed beyond measure.

My role in the Navy has been hectic, and settling into San Diego with my family made time management difficult. I wasn't in the right place to edit this book as quickly as I had hoped. After seeing the number of errors my narrator found in *Between Realms*, I chose not to rush toward the November 2024 release date. This story—and this series—deserved the same care I gave *Echi Eterni*.

I'm grateful I made that choice. I'm much happier with this edition, and I've already outlined Book Four, with a clear roadmap for the rest of **The Mystic Chronicles**. Thank you to everyone who has supported me, believed in these stories, and walked this path with me.

About the Author

Erhrole Navarro is a first-generation Filipino American author, active-duty Master Chief in the U.S. Navy, devoted husband to Violet, and step-father to two daughters. Originally from San Jose, California, he now lives in San Diego, where he strives each day to honor his late son, Ethan.

His debut novel, *Echi Eterni*, began as a story he wrote in seventh grade and later became the foundation of *The Mystic Chronicles* series. When he's not writing or serving his country, Erhrole enjoys attending church, spending time with his family, and, most recently, building handmade furniture. Through both his craft and his life, he embraces resilience, compassion, and the enduring strength of the human spirit.

The Mystic Chronicles
Anchors of Eternity

by Erhrole Navarro

TBD
2032
12

TBD
2031
13

ECHI
ETERNI
2024
11

THE
ECHO
CYCLE

TBD
2030

BETWEEN
REALMS
2024

TWELVE
ELEVEN
TEN
NINE
EIGHT
SEVEN
ONE
TWO
THREE
FOUR
FIVE
SIX

TBD
2030

PATHS
OF
PROVIDENCE
2026

THE
MYSTIC
CHRONICLES

ERHROLE
NAVARRO

TBD
2029

ANCHORS
OF
ETERNITY
2027

TBD
2029

TBD
2028

TBD
2028

ANCHORS
OF
ETERNITY
2027

THE
ANCHOR
CYCLE